Mike Lunnon-Wood was born in Africa and educated in Australia and New Zealand. Based in the Middle East for ten years, he now lives in West Sussex and has a young son.

MIKE LUNNON-WOOD

ANGEL SEVEN

HarperCollinsPublishers

HarperCollins*Publishers*
77−85 Fulham Palace Road,
Hammersmith, London W6 8JB

A Paperback Original 1997
1 3 5 7 9 8 6 4 2

A catalogue record for this book is
available from the British Library

ISBN 0 00 649979 1

Set in Linotype Postscript Meridien by
Rowland Phototypesetting Ltd,
Bury St Edmunds, Suffolk

Printed and bound in Great Britain by
Caledonian International Book Manufacturing Ltd, Glasgow

For Gabriella

Prologue

Camberley, Surrey, May 1996

He never stood a chance, they said. As the ambulance men gently lifted the broken body to place it on the stretcher it sagged in the middle like a rag doll, the light rain softening the horror of the scene for the few bystanders the police were talking to. He had gone up to the shop for a pint of milk and some eggs, the girl later told the police, just a pint of milk and some eggs. The woman with the little boy, still sobbing, said he had left the shop just behind them and she hadn't seen the car at all. Not till it was over.

The salesman, still sitting in the gutter being sick, was in shock. His car, a newish Mondeo, was up on the pavement and wedged against the grey stone wall of the churchyard, shining in the soft drizzly morning.

It was the man in the estate agent's across the road who was able to give police the best description of the death of Erich Stadle.

'I was looking out of the window,' he said. 'I was expecting a client and she was late. I saw them come from the shop. The woman with the kid and a trolley thing . . .' The policeman nodded and the man continued. 'He was behind her. The car came round the bend from Elm Road fast, then he just seemed to lose control. The man dropped the parcel he had,' he stopped and looked out of the window again, at the mess of cracked and broken eggs and the white stain of the milk on the pavement and the soggy paper bag, 'and he dived at the kid. The kid was in front,' he said. The policeman nodded again.

'He dived at the kid and sort of flicked him up and behind, like a halfback with a ball. Then it hit him. The

7

car, it was up on the pavement, at least the two inside wheels were, anyway.' The man swallowed and stopped for a moment. The policeman waited. People were best given time to think about these things.

'It hit him full on and he went under the wheels.' The man stopped again and gathered himself. 'It was the most extraordinary thing I have ever seen.'

The young constable looked out on the street as the ambulance men wheeled the stretcher to their vehicle. Covered in a red blanket, the body beneath seemed small, not at all like a hero should be, he thought.

It was later that they found the West German driving licence with his name. An hour later an old man living in London hobbled to the pay phone in the hall of the bed and breakfast house he was staying in and placed a collect call to a number in Spain.

'There has been an accident. Stadle is dead.'

1

Dickerson Bay, Antigua, three weeks later

The man was lying beneath the boat which lay in a cradle, hull down beside the house. His brown legs protruded from beneath and bare feet the same colour showed he hadn't worn shoes in daylight for some time. He was caulking the hull, smearing the long strips of marine sealant into the cracks in the old clinkerwork.

Up on the veranda an old dog lay in the shade of a huge flowering bougainvillaea in amongst the neat rows of yellow air bottles and crates of beer empties. An outboard was half stripped on a bench by the door and a big chest freezer took most of the remaining space at that end of the veranda. Below the big picture windows a wicker table twisted with the years and sunshine was surrounded by warped chairs also of wicker, but made comfortable by once lovely embroidered cushions. The garden, dry except for the free-flowering hibiscus, fell away with a spectacular view to seaward. Below and nestled to the right was the Halcyon Bay Hotel complex in amongst the trees and lush watered gardens, and on a good day Barbuda lay visible across the sparkling blue waters of the Caribbean.

The man reached from beneath the boat, groped for the tin of sealant and finding it empty swore softly. It was then he heard the car coming up the drive and the dog began to bark. He didn't stop what he was doing, wanting to get the last of the white putty-like substance on to the boat and off his fingers. The car stopped and he flicked a look across at the pair of legs walking towards him. He had an advert in the local paper to sell the Evinrude on the bench, but this pair of legs didn't look like the type that buys outboards. They looked like the type that walked the halls of academia. Hush Puppies, woollen socks and expensive slacks with turn-ups.

'Unless you have a tin of sealant in your hand you can bugger off,' he said from beneath the boat.

There was a pause before the visitor spoke.

'Mr Carson, I would like to talk to you for a few minutes. I may have an offer to make you.'

Carson pulled himself out from beneath the boat, sliding on the flattened cardboard box he was lying on, and looked up.

He was lean and good-looking in an offbeat way, brown hair parted on the right and brushed back over his temples. He had green eyes and a long nose that had been broken once and a strong jawline. The overall effect was softened by crowsfeet round his eyes which deepened as he squinted in the harsh sunlight at the man standing over him.

'What sort of offer?' he asked, his face dropping into a lopsided grin as he looked up at his visitor, but the grin wasn't in his eyes. They were piercing and knowing and seemed to see the dark side. The visitor wiped his brow with a handkerchief.

'Could we go in out of the sun?' he asked.

Carson nodded and indicated the house and the welcoming hum of the air conditioners. They eased into chairs in the sitting room before Carson remembered his manners and offered the man a drink, walking to the kitchen.

'No thank you,' the man called, surveying the room as Carson poured himself a glass of water from a bottle in the fridge. It was a room as functional and masculine as the veranda. Rattan furniture covered in brightly printed fabrics sat in a blaze of colour on the polished sprung wood floor. An ageing stereo system played a tape obviously recorded from an old album: it scratched and hissed, betraying its era. A pile of magazines sat in a neat tower in one corner and on the sideboard an underwater camera lay on its side, its flash unit pointing upwards as if to highlight the blowups on the wall, all of fish, dolphins and coral and in one a large shark evident in the hazy blue of the print. On the other wall was a scale map of the island and pinned beneath it, like an afterthought, a group of pictures of young men in G-suits clutching helmets beside what the visitor recognized as the EFA project fighter aircraft.

Carson came back and sat down again. He looked at his visitor. 'I don't fly drugs,' he said, 'and I don't fly weapons.'

The man looked back quickly. He was nearer old age than middle and sat tightly in the chair, disciplined and ordered. His hair was short and grey and he did have the look of a university man, but one of the old school where they commanded respect for their knowledge. Behind tortoiseshell glasses his eyes were clear and quick, and as he wiped the last trickles of sweat from his forehead he seemed composed and confident.

'What makes you think I want a pilot, Mr Carson?' he said carefully.

'This island is full of divers, they are a dime a dozen, to use one of your American expressions . . . so it had to be the only other skill I have for sale,' Carson replied.

He had correctly picked the man's nationality; many confused it with Canadian.

'Can we run over some details, Mr Carson?' the man said, and without waiting for a reply he continued, 'My name is Donaldson and we know rather a lot about you, my colleagues and I.'

Carson cut in then, speaking softly, and the smile had left his face. 'Just who might you and your colleagues be?' he asked, sipping his water, his eyes never leaving the other face for a second.

Donaldson removed his glasses and rubbed his brow tiredly. It was always a difficult answer to give. How did you explain so much with a name or title? How did you label men's dreams? How could you rediscover the nobility

11

of the most basic concept, perverted by time and rhetoric, with a name.

'I shall leave that to men who understand it all better ... to explain who we are. It is easier to tell you who we are not,' he said.

He leant forward, and replaced his glasses, confident now like the converted zealot he was.

'I represent no government, in or out of power. Let me assure you of that from the start. No government means no agency, no department, not financed by or guided by, however indirectly. We need a pilot, yes. But a pilot of some rare qualities, and we do not want to fly drugs or guns, Mr Carson.' He paused for a moment, stood and walked to the window and looked out at the blue waters below.

'If you aren't a government, then how the hell do you know so much about me?' Carson asked softly. 'There are certainly files on me, but they are classified.'

'The people I am with have some unusual resources. We have a copy of your file. I can tell you how long you spent with Breget, how long you tested the prototype Rafale, how long you spent on the Euro fighter.' He indicated the photos on the wall. 'I can tell you that you are divorced, no dependants, that your deepest dive was a hundred-and-forty-foot rescue in the water off Grand Turk ... that's an enigma. The man should have been dead, no one else was going to do that dive, not after the two you had done already that day. But you went down anyway, and found him ...'

'His buddy panicked,' Carson said offhandedly.

'And you don't dive with a buddy at all?'

'I don't make mistakes.'

'No, you don't spear fish either, you abhor hunting, you test flew fighter aircraft. You have three citations for valour in the air, each because there was risk to other people. You care. That's why we want you, Mr Carson, because you care about these things. You are a decent human

12

being. There are any number of men who can fly fast jets. But there are very few we can trust not to abuse what we have worked so hard to see completed. You have rare qualities. I have a ticket in your name to take you to London on tomorrow's British Airways flight. I want you to go and meet three men and listen to what they have to say. That's all. Listen and make up your mind.'

He turned and faced Carson, who still sat, the glass now empty in his hand, watching him.

'What for? If you aren't recruiting for an air force then I'm not much use to you. I fly fast jets. If you were from one of the builders you would have said so, and none of this cloak and dagger shit, so that makes you someone who wants to know about fighters, and they are usually extremists and I don't like extremists.' He stood. 'Thanks, but no thanks,' he said with some finality.

'But you haven't heard what we have to say. We are not the kind of extremists you imagine, Mr Carson ... if I could prove that to you, will you go to London?' Donaldson asked carefully.

Carson thought for a minute, then nodded.

'We will be in touch,' Donaldson said, and then added smiling, 'and I do hope someone wants to buy your outboard.'

Washington DC

Robert Condale sat in his stuffy office on the fifth floor of the western aspect of the Pentagon. It was small and almost windowless except for the one tired aluminium frame behind him. He always said that no one took analysts seriously, let alone aeronautical analysts. Two floors below a section of thirty-three people did nothing but imagine what submarines the Russians were building. Up here since the MiG-33 project had been abandoned they were the poor whites of this little neighbourhood. There were just seven of them trying to keep track of what the world outside NATO was building in the way of experimental aircraft.

He pushed his wire-framed glasses back up his nose and agreed with himself for the thousandth time that it was a fool's life being a civilian in the Pentagon, then picked up the report that Karl Schoeman had left on his desk the night before and began reading. His eyebrows merged, increasing his owl-like appearance, and he ran a hand through his tight black curly hair; then, pulling a piece of sticky tape from the dispenser, he began to rub it between two fingers as he read.

Across the hall the man who had written the report was ferreting across his untidy desk looking for a sharp pencil. He had given up sharpening them after cutting himself with a razor blade the year before, and his assistant, a fulfilled college graduate with a husband and two lovers, supplied him handfuls of them pre-sharpened every few days.

'Kerry,' he said, 'have we any pencils or has the defence budget finally gone that far?'

She came over from her own desk and, scooping beneath a pile of European newspapers on the edge of the desk, pulled three clear and handed them to him, raising one eyebrow.

'Thanks ... has Mr Condale got my report on the HST theory?'

'Yes, Karl, he has, and no, Karl,' pre-empting his next question with a smile, 'he hasn't asked for you yet.'

Schoeman looked over at her and smiled. He was still wearing an old trilby hat, the brim up all round, and the pockets of his old tweed jacket were misshapen by years of abuse with tobacco tins, his pipe and two huge bunches of keys. Someone once asked him what they were all for and he cheerfully admitted he couldn't remember. His eyes were bright and cheerful and his face was ruddy and creased like that of a sailor who has spent long years at sea. He looked to most people like a retired shopkeeper, but was in fact the best aeronautical design analyst in the West. He could piece together fragments, snippets from the press, his own knowledge, and offer surprising insights as to exactly what the other team were on to now.

It was Schoeman who, a year before confirmation came from inside Russia, told his masters that the Soviets had built a new generation of fast interceptor jet, and he described it in some detail. They scoffed at the time, but within the next twelve months the covers came off the new MiG-31. These days it was all missiles, he thought sadly; no one other than the home side was making anything decent. Then the bits started coming together again on something very new indeed. Very, very fast and very, very big. He didn't know who had built it, but he was pretty sure it wasn't NATO, unless they had something he didn't know about, which was unlikely. He was in his own pedantic way quite excited about this one.

Trouble was, no one was prepared to believe these things until it was too late. He would have a word with Tim Miller later. Perhaps if Condale didn't want to pursue the report Tim could influence him. Tim Miller was the newest attachment to the section and on secondment for the next five months. He was British, a squadron leader in the Royal Air Force, and for reasons no one could fathom had been given to them for one year as an exchange officer. He would have learnt far more and been of far more use in an operational role, maybe at one of the big NATO installations in Germany or Belgium.

A tall, likeable, smiling man, he was the epitome of everything English and when not in uniform wore an Uppingham tie, invariably creased, and a dark blue blazer. The girls in the typing sections loved his accent and his blond good looks and the bright yellow Volkswagen Beetle he had bought at an auction in Boston just after arriving. Schoeman admired him for the chess games they played over bagels at lunchtime and his complete disdain for

Washington's social set. He had also scored brownie points by visiting the Mirimar Fighter Weapons School one week and out-dogfighting an Eagle with a Hawk single-seater after saying in the mess that speed wasn't everything and being asked to prove it. Schoeman loved that and took him down to a small Czechoslovakian restaurant, where he toasted him with a poisonous vodka that they both thought could only have been made in Cuba.

He was away for the week on a public relations exercise with the military attaché from the British embassy, doing what Miller had described as crawling round on his hands and knees in the boardroom at Lockheed looking for the Holy Grail. What Schoeman didn't know was that although Miller was a serving RAF officer and his secondment to the Pentagon was bona fide, he was also serving masters at MI6. He enjoyed his military intelligence role, saw it as a natural extension to front line service, and was as discreet as necessary. Although a few people may have suspected, no one in the Pentagon knew for sure. But what they did know was that he would be debriefed and debriefed regularly, just as they did their people.

Kerry's phone rang. She answered it and looked over at her mentor. 'Rob says bring coffee and your copy of the HST report.'

Schoeman sighed tiredly. The first unbeliever of many. He shuffled across the hall, knocked and entered Condale's smaller but private office. He stepped over the threshold like a tired warrior about to engage in another battle, reluctantly but professionally.

Condale looked up and waved him to a seat, still fiddling with the sticky tape in his fingers, rolling it and unrolling it, enjoying the tactile sensations.

'Looking at your hypersonic report here . . .' he said finally looking up. 'You think someone has built one? Really?'

Schoeman studied the face before him, trying to establish if there was any sarcasm or mockery in the tone.

16

'Yes, I do. But none of the usual players,' he said simply, fidgeting with his papers.

'Why not the Soviets? Who else has the technology? The French don't, the Brits would have told us. The Aussies still buy ours, the South Africans are still playing with helicopters, and the Chinese are still trying to perfect the bicycle. Who else?' He closed the door and walked back to his desk.

'I don't know,' Schoeman replied honestly, 'but I become more and more convinced as the weeks go by.'

'By what, Karl?' Condale asked.

Schoeman opened his file and began sifting pages, some news cuttings, some buff internal memo pages, some the pale blue printouts that NASA produced, collections of jottings from dozens of sources. He held one up and began to read.

'A collation of sightings of a UFO in southern Europe and North Africa over thirty-six hours. All very similar, all descriptions gelling together. We have a craft estimated between one hundred and three hundred feet long, sharp nose, delta wing and – get this – fast! One Spanish air force pilot estimated its speed well over Mach Six. Three of the sightings were air crew and all three said it wasn't a saucer or dish or special effects wonder, it was an aircraft. Several of the top brains in the industry have gone in recent years. Not died, not to the other side, just disappeared from the job market. Where are they now? I'll tell you. Building and perfecting this thing that we have sightings of.'

'Karl, I respect your analysis. You have been right too often. But we both know the resources needed to build an aircraft like this are fantastic. Here in this country only Lockheed, Boeing, McDonnell Douglas – all at development stage only!' He paused, removed his glasses and wiped them with the end of his tie.

They talked for another two hours, Schoeman twice filling his pipe and smoking it in contravention of the no-smoking policy in the building, belching the acrid smoke into the already stuffy office. He tapped and prodded it, re-lit it, often referring to notes as the words flowed back and forth.

Eventually Condale opened the door in an attempt to clear the air in the office and returned to his chair.

'Have copies gone out to the three?' he asked.

'Yes,' Schoeman said. 'The Flat Earth Society have had theirs.'

'Well, maybe they will entertain your theory. I'm afraid I don't. No more time on this one, Karl.'

Schoeman got up, his sheaf of papers now untidy in the pale green manila folder under one arm. As he walked across the hall, not really surprised by Condale's attitude, he wondered what 'the three' thought of his preliminary report. They were the Director of Aviation Research, two floors above, responsible for co-ordinating all civilian programmes, the US Air Force's own analysts and finally the CIA at Langley.

He had scant respect for the forward thinking of any of them. To them all the MiG and the Etendard were the enemy, and the F series was the answer. Star Wars was a faded dream and nothing stood between. He fumbled the folder as he reached his desk and slung it irreverently into a tray before noticing the visitor at his window seat and smiling broadly.

'Greetings, old one, how are things in the fun factory?' Tim Miller smiled back charmingly. He was sitting with one leg crossed over the other, clasping his left ankle. The blazer was open and the tie loosened.

'Hello, Tim,' Schoeman answered, delighted. 'How was the Holy Grail?'

It was a curious relationship, rather like mentor and student, although it might not appear so to just any observer. Tim Miller was one of those lucky people who didn't need to work, being blessed with a private income, and had joined the RAF because he loved flying fast and alone. Now attached to the obscure department in the Pentagon, he would make the best of it and learn from Karl Schoeman what he could. They had spent hours one night going over the build-up to the release when the Soviets had built the MiG-25, and no one believed a word of it. Miller knew he would have believed Schoeman.

'Lots of huge drinks, and back-slapping and nudge, nudge, wink, wink, say no more.' Miller stood and buttoned his jacket. 'Come, I shall buy you lunch.'

They played checkers in the restaurant and Miller, losing again, agreed to join the older man for the family dinner that night.

'My daughter will be home,' Schoeman said. 'It's time you two met each other, you can discuss the merits of your V-TOLs you love so much . . . she's an astrophysicist, you know.'

Miller smiled and nodded. Karl doted on his daughter and spoke of her often and his pride was as obvious as his love for her.

Carson stepped from the shower and, drying himself briefly, pulled on a soft cotton shirt, stepped into a pair of shorts and walked out on to the veranda with a cold bottle of beer to watch the sun go down. The dog opened one eye at him, cocked its head and went back to sleep.

'Don't you ever go home?' Carson asked it. You're like me, old boy, he thought. You know where you want to be and that's where you will go and stuff the world. He settled down into a chair and sipped the drink and thought about the man who had visited him that morning. Then as the wind freshened he walked towards the old Chevy pick-up, draining the last dregs from the bottle before heading down towards the bay and the small restaurant where he usually ate.

He had only been there an hour when a familiar figure walked round the beach entrance side and waddled up to the bar.

'Peter, my friend,' he said, mounting the nearest stool with some care, 'is my dog still at your house?'

'Yes, Duke, he is. He seems to like it there.'

Duke Williams was one of the island's more colourful characters. He owned the house that Carson rented six months of the year, and was one of Carson's older friends. With a wife that seemed to be perpetually pregnant, lay preaching in the local church and his official duties as a senator in the government, he was always on the go. He regularly attended Rotary lunches, was very involved in local business and still found time to sneak away and very occasionally dive with Carson, on the deep seaward side of Cades Reef.

'He's not as stupid as he looks,' Duke admitted and took the proffered drink from the barmaid. There wasn't a bar on the island where they didn't know the senator's drink. They talked for a while about the tide and the Evinrude, and the old boat that Carson was working on.

A big marmalade-coloured cat eased round the low waist-high wall and sat watching some tourists eat their food with the easy confidence of the house's favourite, sure that eventually he would receive a titbit or two. The woman at the table made baby noises at it, and the cat eased itself down to wait. The wind swirled and shifted delicately, then settled and blew steadily, bringing the sounds of a steel band's calypso beat from round the bay. Nearer it rustled the fronds of the palms and collected the voices of a couple as they walked through the frothy swirl at the water's edge only scant yards away, holding hands like lovers the world over. A party of English tourists settled at a table at the rear, but Carson's eyes were on the inflatable coming in from a large yacht moored in the bay. He had been aboard her once and could imagine the skipper's and owner's dismay as yet more landlubbers blocked his toilets, wore shoes below and threw up into wind. Duke ordered again and they began to throw dice to see who would pick up the tab.

As a politician Duke was as honest as they come for one main reason. He wasn't very good at telling lies or hiding things, and he had been fidgeting on the stool for twenty minutes.

'Out with it, Duke,' Carson said.

His friend looked at him silently for a moment, then spoke quietly. 'You had a visitor today, up at the house.' Carson nodded, sipping his beer from the bottle. 'You should at least hear them out.'

Carson looked astonished at his friend, disbelieving what he was hearing.

'You?' he answered softly. 'You are mixed up in this?'

Duke nodded.

'Why, Duke?' Carson asked quietly, looking around the bar. 'And who the fuck are they?'

'They are good people, Peter. The best. They are not . . . We are not extremists, like you think.'

Carson noted the word he had used that morning. The conversation had been repeated verbatim to Duke by Donaldson.

'I'm not sure I believe all this,' he said, almost to himself. 'I'm a pilot, and a good one, but I fly fast jets. Duke, what the hell do you want with me?'

'Peter, if they need you, they need you. I don't question them.'

'You believe in them implicitly?' Carson asked.

'I do.'

'Why? What for? Who are they?'

'Who? They are better at describing it than me. So go to London. Listen. What harm can that do?'

'Why, Duke?' Carson asked. 'I know you, what have they got that you need?'

The other man smiled, his black face beaming with an almost reverent light.

'All this,' he said pointing at the bright ocean in the moonlight. 'They do the Lord's work, Peter.'

*　　*　　*

21

It was just about then that Miller's old Volkswagen rattled up the long leafy driveway at the Schoeman house just outside Washington. It was an old place nestled in a stand of conifers and maple trees, two-storey, with steep angles of roof tiles and white clapboard walls and ivy creeping up the northern side over the garage. Schoeman could never have afforded the house on his salary alone. His wife had been left it by her father, who had once owned much of the surrounding country-side before the urban sprawl had made his dairy herds untenable.

On the porch was a rocker and three folding chairs gathered around a card table. As Miller climbed from his car Edith Schoeman came out with a drinks tray and, calling a welcome, set it on the table. Karl came out minutes later in a misshapen old cardigan, his eyes crinkling a welcome. They sat there for the next hour talking until another car came up the drive, fast and noisy. It was an ageing Corvette driven with some skill and as it came to a halt in a spray of gravel Edith stood and placed her hands on her hips ready for war.

She was a formidable woman, big-bosomed and loud-voiced, and her fast-greying hair was gathered in sensible waves of clipped order.

'And you drove at fifty all the way?' she barked sarcastically at the driver, who clambered clear and ran up on to the porch. She was in her late twenties, tall and long-legged, with waves of thick brown hair. Her face was bright and animated and her smile wide and genuine.

'Hello Ma, have you been picking on Dad again?'

Edith's face softened and she smiled and hugged her daughter in a strong assured manner, neither shy of the emotional display.

Karl got to his feet. 'Sally, we have a guest tonight. Meet Timothy Miller, from the shop,' he said between his own hug and indicating Miller.

'Hello,' he said, standing up. She studied him with eyes

22

so blue and so pale that they didn't look real, and the smile showed a set of even white teeth against her tan.

'You don't look like the sort of person who works at the shop.' Her eyes were appraising and interested all at once.

'Oh, I don't work. I just sort of hang about in the way.' He grinned back at her, thinking that the evening could be more interesting than he had anticipated.

Dinner was a simple affair of passed bowls of vegetables and blobs of butter on everything. The talk was noisy, interspersed with laughter and Miller's English reserve gave way along with the first bottle of wine. The easy family atmosphere was something he had missed, but he only realized it now, sitting in the long warm room, so different from the bright embassy parties or smoky restaurants. He watched Sally eat with pleasure, her appetite large and unfussy, and she laughed often, her blue eyes reflecting every expression.

'Tim, more potato,' Edith commanded, thrusting the bowl at him.

'Edith, he is not a child,' Karl gently admonished.

'No,' she said, 'he is an officer and a gentleman who eats bagels and cheeseburgers with you.'

Miller smiled and took the bowl.

'What do you fly, Tim?' Sally asked. She had heard her father talk of this new attachment, but like all fathers he had been vague about the more important bits. The only RAF officer she had met before had been an administrator and very boring.

'Anything they will let me,' he said, 'but no multi-engines as yet.'

She looked up, more interested now. 'Fighters?'

'Mmmm,' he said, his mouth full of food.

'What mmmm?' she said, becoming exasperated and tossing her head.

He swallowed and looked at her, remembering suddenly her father's constant chat about her and her profession.

'Sorry, I am very wary about boring people. I forgot you are into flying. My last squadron was Tornadoes.'

She studied him quizzically for a second.

'F-3?'

'Yeah.'

'What do you think of them?'

'Not much,' he replied honestly. 'I'd rather we had 16s.'

She smiled. A squadron leader on Tornadoes was one of the elite. After the last wave of redundancies there were not many of those about, which might make him half good at his job, and he was honest with it.

While Sally and her mother were washing the dishes Miller, banished from the kitchen as a guest, sat on the porch with Karl who began to talk about his HST theory.

'Condale blew you out?'

'He did. He has all the time horizon and the imagination of a caterpillar. I think we should look into it further. I included a couple of names in my narrative of people who would know if this thing was airborne. Why don't you talk to him? You might like to offer to follow it up a little.'

Miller agreed that far and was saved by Sally's arrival back with coffee, but as they sat drinking it on the porch he was thinking, his eyes betraying nothing.

Riyadh, Saudi Arabia

Abdullah bin Said al-Humaid sipped at the small cup of sweet tea and watched the computer screen as the previous night's reports began to flash before his eyes.

He was duty intelligence officer of the day and although it was Friday, the day provided by the Prophet Muhammad for the worship of the one God, Allah, he didn't mind working. The huge underground installation was quiet today. Above ground on Airport Road the heat would be shimmering and dry, and the call of the holy men from the minarets would travel far. Down here there was just the quiet hum of the huge Carrier air conditioners and the muffled voices of the few duty staff. The Naval Command HQ was something of a joke here in Riyadh, hundreds of miles from the nearest stretch of water, but it was here that the satellite communications systems were the safest in any hostilities, and it was also from here that the king ruled the country.

Abdullah's particular speciality was the threat from the north – Iraq and Iran. Of all their regional ongoing dilemmas these two were the real problem. Occasional forays north by Yemeni tribesmen, who owed allegiance to none except their own warlords, were a constant niggling headache for the border authorities. Israel, for all her menace in Southern Lebanon, was not interested in the Kingdom of Saudi Arabia. The United Arab Emirates and Qatar, Bahrain and Kuwait were all part of a co-operation council locally that was surprisingly co-operative considering the Arabs' prime pastime of disagreeing with one another and were in awe of Saudi's mighty wealth and her powerful army, air force and naval presence in the Gulf and Red Sea.

Iraq wanted everything, but at least they were understood. Iran was different. The huge sprawling mountainous land to the north was big enough to worry the Saudis. It wasn't the oil they wanted. They had their own. It was Mecca. The old city in the western province that was the holiest of holies for the world's hundred million Muslims. The Iranians were not like the Saudis, or the other Gulf Arabs. For a start they were not Arab, they were Asian. Persian. They in their time had seen Genghis Khan come and go and had constantly over the centuries raided Turkey, Iraq as now, into China, Pakistan and even Russia. While the Shah had held power he had been predictable to an extent, and his sweeping programmes of modernization had been welcomed by observers in and outside Iran. But he had also created an army and air force second to none in the region, trained by the Americans. They would have been a formidable force settled between East and West,

25

but a formidable force commanded by a modern man with western allegiances. And then came the revolution.

Suddenly here was this huge powerful military machine in the hands of a man who had said more than once that he felt the Shi'ite Muslims were the only faith pure enough to safeguard Mecca, in the heart of Sunni Saudi Arabia. Later the age-old hatreds between the Iraqis and the Iranians flared again and Iraq began hostilities, believing that without the elite officer corps which Ayatollah Khomeini had replaced, the army would never be weaker and the time was right to settle old scores.

Now, years later, the war had scarred the lives of people in both lands because by the end both sides were committing boys to the battle, the men all gone. Saudi Arabia had displayed regional solidarity, pouring millions of dollars a day into the war effort, bolstering Iraq's depleted reserves of ready cash for the war chest. There was only limited altruism in the gesture, Abdullah mused to himself. As long as the Iranians were fighting Iraq on the Basra front then neither could afford to attack any of the other states in the region. Surely it was no coincidence that so soon after the end of the Iran–Iraq war, came the Iraqi invasion of Kuwait.

Even with the new Iranian army nothing more than green boys living on slogans and a promise of paradise, their air force was intact. The aircraft were now ageing F-4s but the pilots, the older ones anyway, were American-trained and very good at their jobs. Iran was still a threat, and that was why Abdullah took the morning's data clearance routine seriously. A network of Iranians who cared more for the riyal than for the Ayatollah channelled information back in a variety of ways and the Iran team worked to keep the Saudi High Command and the Palace informed. In turn the information went on to the Americans and NATO, but there was one organization which gained access long before even the king. And they above all would find concern in this latest piece of data that flicked across the screen in digital sequences. Abdullah fingered the screen as if to prove it was there and as he lowered the small glass cup to its saucer, he felt a shiver up his spine. He sat for a moment and then, looking around to make sure he was alone, he crossed to the switch room and deep in a row of six he eased a rack mount bracket sideways. It activated a set of micro switches that in turn began to feed everything on all seventeen screens in the centre, back into a logging computer that sat on the end of a telephone modem line in fashionable Malaz on the other side of the city. There it would be transmitted in milliseconds out of the kingdom, to where he didn't know. All he knew was it was somewhere to the north in the Gulf. He counted to ten, eased the bracket back into its original position and went back to the control room. The data sat on the screen, seven lines of fresh green Arabic script, pretty as a verse by a classical poet, but warning of megadeath. He hoped they would use the information soon, and breathed a quick prayer to Allah as he lifted the phone. His report was about to put the Saudi armed forces on to Stage Yellow.

Antigua

Carson signalled the waitress with a smile and a raised eyebrow and she flicked the cap from an ice cold beer and slid it down the bar, smiling back at him. He was unusually quiet this evening and since the senator had left had said nothing, just looking out over the moonlit water under the scudding dark clouds.

He didn't want to leave Antigua. He had come to love his six-month stint on the island. This was his third year down here, but he knew he would have to get a job sooner or later. He hadn't flown since the year before, and he recognized the constant need to exercise his skills. He had told Dassault he would not be back the next summer and to find someone else for the next series of air tests. Three years with the French was enough; he found them provincial and tiring and endlessly stubborn. But the pay had been good and they weren't afraid to hire outside the pool of French domestic pilots for the skills they wanted. Carson was rated amongst the top six test pilots in the world, and was the only one who spoke French, so he had named his own price. They had accepted with a Gallic shrug, demanding there and then their pound of flesh. And now, he thought as he sipped the beer, the spook offer from Donaldson. No money mentioned, no names, all very secret indeed. And what the hell was Duke doing involved with it all, and what was the Lord's work?

He shrugged, slightly drunk, and watched the small waves swirl their foamy wash up the sand thirty yards away. Although a loner by nature he sometimes missed the camaraderie of the mess. They had taken him, raw and eager, in the Commonwealth programme when he was just eighteen. He had sat the examination in New Zealand and been in England eleven weeks later with a young Canadian and an Australian called Murphy. They were it from the Commonwealth that year, and had arrived at RAF Linton-on-Ouse ready to gulp down the knowledge and the lore, anything to fly the sleek needle-nosed machines that stood on spindly legs on the oily concrete pan. Murphy went when his Harrier malfunctioned for a second during a simulated vertical landing. It had thrown him and his pupil pilot sideways into the trees and they had died in the flames. Legend said that Murphy had opened his radio with the famous last words, 'Cancel two late lunches', but Carson had never known whether to believe the story. Whenever he had a major problem in an aircraft he was too frightened and too busy to think of anything clever. Twice he had ejected from his aircraft. Pure and simple gut-wrenching terror as the canopy blew away, and the monstrous jerk on the shins as the cables pulled knees clear of the dash, and the unimaginable blast of the charge beneath the seat and the blackout as spine compressed and blood left the head, and hoping to Christ that you were clear of the tail section as it sliced through the air at five hundred knots out of control, nose down, controls jammed and windscreen shattered by a bird strike. He sweated in the warm evening as the memory invaded his senses and rubbed the cool bottle across his brow.

The second time was better. He didn't spend seven weeks in traction after that, having his spine stretched back to its original issued length. Murphy, should have banged out, he thought. Murphy, you always were a stupid arse, but how do you bang out when your aircraft is side-on facing the trees. You would be blasted through the tree trunks like an egg through a slicer. He missed Murphy.

Olivia had understood that. She had understood the look in his eyes when they had talked of the risks, as all flyers do with their wives at least once. He had laughed in his boyish way, and said, 'Yeah, but what a way to go, Mach something into the side of a mountain in three million quid's worth of aircraft.'

But that had been the weekend of Murphy's funeral, and his eyes weren't in on the joke. She had understood the mystique, the 'onward and upward' rationale of the fighter pilots, just as she understood the way that seals felt about their pups, and why El Niño changed the way of the seas around South America. That was the way it was. But she wouldn't live on the base, she didn't want to be there in married quarters when the base commander came round with the medical officer in the car behind, to tell her that he was dead. She didn't want the curtains in the other houses moving as others watched her and tried to remember who had been in the back seat of the aircraft that had gone down. She would rather live off-base, and come and go with her funny bearded friends and intense colleagues who all thought that he was a warmonger, but said so quietly amongst themselves in case they were right. He smiled to himself, remembering them all and how they moved lightly about him as you would move around a large predatory shark in the water. They had never understood why Olivia had married him.

Liv, who had marched in adolescent pigtails along the wide streets of London with others from the anti-Vietnam lobby, had met this career fighter pilot, and they were going out. And everybody laughed: no, not Liv. She had told him that when they honeymooned in Cornwall, he with seven days' leave from Wittering. They had locked up the cottage in Stamford and driven to London and been married in Kensington at the family church, and then on down to Cornwall where Liv's guru had a cottage on the wildest piece of coast in Britain. The doddery old man, once the acclaim of Cambridge microbiologists, now lived there, but on a sabbatical to Florida he happily conceded the use of the place to Liv and her new husband. They dived every day, sailed the little GP14 around the bay and drank cider with the locals in the only pub in miles. They were fishermen and sat fascinated as Liv berated anyone brave enough to admit he used a dredge net. She had been a full equal to Carson and yet opposite in every way. He was reckless and precise all at once, where she was methodically patient till the second she exploded over nothing. He was ice and she was fire and he loved her. But then it began to sour. He spent more time alone, pushing the job while she was away. One day they realized they had grown apart. Nothing dramatic. Nothing sordid. It just wasn't there any more. She left. Went saying she wouldn't be back. They had only been married eighteen months.

RAF Wittering had become a place of memories, and he sought to exorcize them in the sky, but each time he landed and went home the village seemed to close in on him. He tried moving back on to the base, into the mess with the few single men on the squadron, but that just served to further isolate the cause of his distress. Its masculine halls and code of conduct only reminded him more of what he had lost. Murphy, his offsider from day one, was now only a plaque on the wall and a face in the already fading squadron photograph to many of the newer members. Eventually he was saved from probable early retirement by a forward-thinking boss who recommended him for his own squadron in Germany. The new Tornadoes were very different from the Harriers, but they were still very, very fast, and the sensation as the afterburners scorched the runway on take-off was everything every fast jet pilot ever needed. He had been approached for the first time by the private sector then. His reputation as a flyer of extraordinary capabilities was out after the first offer, and three more came his way that year.

His departure from the RAF was premature but indicative of his manner. He had taken four green flight lieutenants on a familiarization flight around the Brüggen area. They had only arrived the day before and just completed their conversions to the Tornado, so the first flight would be very basic: just point out the landmarks, and on the way back we'll see who likes what, he had said. It was his way with new men. Fly with them and watch and see what makes them tick. Some like low levels, some don't, some found the punch in the Tornado hard to get used to after a slower Buccaneer or Harrier. So off they went, twenty minutes local, and on the way back the tail end charlie nearly died.

Carson was above and behind them, his hands resting on the throttle, watching them through the hail-scarred canopy, his eyes constantly scanning the sky. Here at three-fifty feet visual flight rules and fast reflexes keep you alive. The watching was instinctive because this height was theirs and theirs alone, but suddenly from the right, hard in his peripheral vision, a flash of silver. Carson barked, 'Blue break low left! Break low left,' from the position he held above and behind the new pilots, and pushed his own stick down hard and fast. Jesus Christ, it's gonna hit him, where's the other fuckers? There's always three, they're too low, and then the mighty jet wash rolled over him and at last he saw the other Tornado level out at fifty feet with

31

him, the trees flashing past as the three ageing Starfighter 'Widowmakers' streaked feet above them.

'Okay, let's go back up to three-fifty,' he had said as calmly as he could. The kid had landed shaken and scared and stood talking with the other three pilots who had been ahead, but heard the barked warning and had also dropped into the trees to avoid the collision. Without waiting to debrief, Carson jumped into his car and drove to the German base ten miles south, walked into the ops room, into their debrief, and punched his counterpart in the face.

'Keep your pilots at their own flight levels or don't fucking fly at all,' he snarled. The West German squadron leader struggled to his feet and demanded an apology.

'Fuck you,' Carson whispered, his voice like ice. The incident was sealed when Carson still wouldn't apologize, even after being ordered to, and he resigned before his stubbornness cost him a disciplinary dismissal. It had already cost him his squadron.

Six weeks later he was with the French builders of Rafale jets. They were making moves to update the trailing edge of the latest series and beef up the load capacity in an effort to increase its range without drop tanks, while still giving the incredible combat manoeuvring that made it so popular. All the minute modifications needed exhausting tests, and the next year Carson spent more time in the cockpit than ever. He still missed Liv and constantly fought the guilt that declared his work the cause of the end of his marriage. His parents, who still lived in New Zealand, had not seen much of him since he had left for the RAF, and as the years went by they saw less and less of their second child. He had ventured home with Liv in tow, the year they had been married, and it was only her instant love for the mountains of his native Otago that held him there for the promised two weeks. He, like so many young people who travelled, had changed so much that he felt he had little in common with his sister, who was married to a local sheep farmer and by then had three healthy little boys. He had felt awkward with their conversation and his mother's gentle hints to bring Liv back to the land. The Torrey place was up for sale, she had said, and when Carson thought of the old house and the bleak winds off the tops, and the stunted conversation of mutton and wool prices, he could think of nothing worse. He smiled and switched the subject, and had never been back.

He sat on the bar stool another hour, till the waitress began noisily washing glasses, hinting to him that she wanted to go. He finished his drink and walked to the pick-up, admitting to himself that he missed the cool clean loneliness of the sky and the punch and adrenalin surge when he pushed an aircraft to the very limits high above in the thin cold air. He didn't miss the deaths. The fuck-ups. The memory forced its way into his head.

It wasn't your fault, they proved that, his brain was saying. But something else said no. They are all dead. You were too fast. Too fast to see them. Your fault. Killer.

The very discreet inquiry, just three men in the French MoD, found that they shouldn't have been on the firing range. Their pilot was closing on the ground target at over Mach 1 and there was no way he could have known they were there. But the inner anger still boiled, his guilt still there and eating away. There had been the usual warnings on the roads. Military vehicles carrying police had sealed roads, the normal firing range in the Alps had been extended by seven miles for the week's tests. The EFA, new and sleek and shark-like, had sat on the apron, her rocket pods loaded. In reality nothing more than a multi-million-dollar weapons platform, but one that would turn faster loaded than any aircraft ever built. Carson took off and flew the distance to the range feeling the aircraft wallow under her load, the canards working, power on, over the speed of sound as he lined up on the range from twelve miles out at low level, testing the airframe and handling characteristics as he seared inward. When he had lined up,

33

with the airframe bucking beneath him, streaking through the mountain valleys, he let the four rockets go. No one had seen the small Citroën on the narrow road below the mountain side until the avalanche was falling towards it. The occupants, four young French kids on a holiday from university, had been pulverized along with their skis and boots and sleeping bags and the Michelin maps that they were peering at and laughing, as they tried to find out where they were. Sweating, he forced the thoughts from his mind and started the engine.

As Carson drove slowly up the hillside Duke Williams, finally home after a night-time prayer meeting, placed a call to New York to a number that he had never written down, never spoken of, and only ever called twice before in the seventeen years he had had the honour of holding it.

2

London

Carson climbed from the taxi into a cheerless morning. Slate-coloured skies gave the Kew street a dullness it didn't deserve and the young trees in full summer leaf looked incongruous. He paid the taxi-driver and began counting the house numbers up to number thirty-eight. A shiny red geranium stood in potted solitude on the windowsill and the beginnings of an ivy crept up from another pot at the foot of the door on a painted white trellis. He rang the bell almost resenting collecting the tickets and instructions, wishing he was back at Cades Reef.

Footsteps hurried up the hall and the door swung open revealing a bright and appealing little face beneath a shock of red curls. One hand removed a pencil from her mouth as with the other she struggled with two bags of books.

'Hi,' she said happily, 'you must be Mr Carson.'

She looked back over her shoulder, gathered breath and shouted, 'Pop, he's here!' before turning back and pushing past him. 'Sorry. I'm late for lectures, see you later.'

And with that she jogged the five steps to the road, put the pencil back in her mouth and began to scrabble in her bag for the keys to an ancient Morris Minor parked against the kerb.

Carson smiled to himself then looked back into the house and stepped in as a figure appeared at the end of the passage. He was old, but moved with a measured grace that did much to disguise the effects of arthritis and calcified joints. His hair was thin and, although stooped, he was still taller than Carson. As he approached, his eyes smiled a greeting from beneath thick grey eyebrows. His right hand clutched a walking stick that vanity wouldn't allow full use of and he offered his left hand, palm down, to shake.

'Mr Carson, thank you for coming. My name is Meran.' The accent was American.

'You had a forceful advocate in Duke Williams,' Carson answered, carefully taking the proffered hand.

'Never met him myself. We have lots like him, rest assured. Come sit down.' He waved the stick into the drawing room, and ushering the younger man in he followed and lowered himself slowly into a worn leather chair, carefully as old people do. Finally settled, he looked up and smiled again.

Out on the street the Morris backfired as the girl started it up, pencil still in her mouth. As she drove away the sound diminished in the quiet room.

'A fine child that,' Meran said. 'Reading chemistry at London,' as though they were sitting somewhere else.

'Your granddaughter?' Carson asked.

'Haa!' Meran barked. 'You flatter me, boy . . . granddaughter? Heavens, no! Great-granddaughter: I will be ninety-three next month. But we are not sitting here to discuss the state of my senile decay.'

All right, thought Carson, you've set the tone, let's be having you then. 'Nor mine . . . let's get on with it, shall we?' he replied.

Meran's eyes twinkled and he rose from the chair, stick clasped in both his hands.

'The rain has stopped, so they will be playing cricket down on the green; let's walk down and watch. One of the English games I have grown to like. We can talk on the way.'

Carson just looked.

'Come on, boy, the playing fields of England and all that!'

Carson stood and, smiling to himself, followed the stooped, plodding figure to go and watch cricket. As they reached the edge of the field the batsman was dismissed and polite clapping greeted his arrival in the pavilion as his replacement walked out, swinging his bat like an umbrella, his pads flapping against his knees.

Meran looked at Carson. 'What do the names Hiroshima and Nagasaki mean to you?' he asked.

'The same as to the rest of the civilized world, I suppose, the first and last use of nuclear weapons in an armed conflict . . .' Carson answered.

'The first, yes, but the last, no. Only the most recent, young man. Only the most recent.' There he paused before continuing, 'I helped to build those bombs. It was called the Manhattan Project, and I have never been more ashamed of anything in my life. Me, Hans Bethe, Edward Teller, Oppenheimer and Fermi, others, with Groves wielding the whip as we worked and tested. Finally we did it. We made it work . . . and I have devoted the rest of my life to making sure it never works again.'

He stopped, extracted a handkerchief and wiped the corner of his mouth before continuing.

'The question is, young man, do you want to help us achieve that aim? Mmmm?'

'Who is us?' Carson asked, 'and what are you asking me to do?'

He settled back into the bench and crossed his legs, instinctively knowing it was time to listen, because this man would talk. He was obviously authorized to do so as Duke Williams and Donaldson hadn't been. Meran half-smiled before speaking.

'We never gave ourselves a name. It seemed unimportant . . . but we are now known as "of Oslo". It was the city we met in over fifty years ago. A handful of men who were appalled at what we had done. There was a poet, an Englishman whose name was as famous then as it is now, another American by the name of Steerman, who is also dead. An Italian scientist, who still lives and is even older than me, and a Pole.

'Scagallini and Balorki are both too old now, and have given the struggle to younger men. Only I remain on my feet, of the original five. Their legacy is an organization that has over three hundred thousand members world-wide, and active members, Mr Carson. Movers and shakers, as the young term them. No empty rhetoric or armchair subversion. Oslo has members in the American Senate, your Houses of Parliament in New Zealand, in government the world over, in the military, commerce, in industry and finance. We have at our disposal vast sums of money and information. Five British Prime Ministers since the war have known of our existence, advised when we considered the timing right. We have a sister organization in the Russian Republics, we believe even more active than us when you consider the risks they once took. We are strong, Mr Carson, but no hot-headed revolutionaries. We simply have one aim, one thing in common. We like the planet we live on. We like being alive and seeing a future for our children and our grandchildren and even, if you get as old as me, our great-grandchildren. We do not want a world that can be destroyed by our own technology seventeen times over on the whim of two men. Does it not frighten you, Mr Carson, that someone half the world away could turn you into superheated irradiated carbon, you and all you love and hold dear?'

He paused, again wiping his mouth, his eyes shining in fervour.

'All the trees, the plants, the animals, the insects, the birds, the life that was created over millions of years, wiped out in seconds. Oslo is now in a position to influence these things, and we owe it to our children's children that we do just that when the time comes. We have done something remarkable in the last few years or so, we of Oslo.' Meran stopped there before saying, 'Let's have tea, shall we?'

Carson, in deference to age, went to the pavilion and bought the tea, wondering what he was getting into. It wasn't just that he was sceptical, he was also very tired of vocal do-gooders, however well motivated by the sins of their past. As he walked back to the bench where Meran sat, balancing the cups of tea and trying to make sure the little finger sandwiches didn't fall on to the still wet grass, he thought, you are preaching to the converted, sport, but let's hear you out.

The few weekday spectators began to clap politely at something that had happened on the wicket, and as Carson turned his head tea slopped from a cup into its saucer. He swore softly to himself and slowed his pace for the last few yards. Meran sat jaw thrust out, defiant, daring the sky to cloud over again. He turned as Carson approached.

'One of the perks of membership. Tea at the cricket!' He took the cup in a surprisingly steady hand. 'Damned watercress again,' he muttered, peering at the sandwiches. 'This little waterweed harbours more bacteria than the human mouth,' he paused there and turned to look at Carson. 'We have built an aeroplane, Mr Carson, and we want you to fly her.'

'Why me? Lots of jocks around.' He spoke casually, sipping his tea.

The batsman swung carefully under a medium pace ball and lifted it high and far over the field. It would be a six, and people began to clap even before it landed. Carson could see the chap visibly preening himself, and to his left Meran slapped one hand against his thigh, watching his teacup carefully as he did so.

'Because you are the best of what is available on the market, and also present, we believe, the correct attitudinal balance for what we have in mind. We don't need a warmonger, Mr Carson. We need a man who is sick at the thought of all that, a man we can trust with technology beyond that ever given to one individual in the history of this planet.'

The batsman swung again, the crack of the willow on the leather clear across the field. Carson watched the man

39

run, his partner slower off the mark. He's going to get stumped, he thought. The wicket-keeper, an opportunist, stood hovering in silent anticipation as a fielder scrabbled for the ball and returned it with haste. The man's thick gloves scooped it from its trajectory and in one sweep the bails flew into the air. Muffled cries of 'Howzat?' and Carson turned to look at Meran. The bushy eyebrows creased downward like a pair of hairy caterpillars meeting on a twig, the eyes glowered at him.

'Well?' he said. 'Speak up.'

Carson swallowed and apologized for his silence, before qualifying his sentiments, like a schoolboy trying to explain himself. 'Mr Meran, what kind of technology have you got that isn't part of the arms race that frightens you so much?'

The brows reassumed station above the old man's eyes and he smiled.

'It's ahead of that, thank goodness. It will be fitting that we scientists who began the whole thing will finish it. Do you know what radiation does to the cells of animal organisms?'

'Mr Meran, I understand the way you people dislike or even abhor the use of nuclear physics in weaponry, but it has a place in the scheme. It provides power for millions of homes in this country alone. It's not the tool. It's the men surely?' Carson argued.

'Yes, it's the men,' Meran answered, 'but the tool is dangerous and the men haven't the skill or the humanity to possess it safely. Look at Chernobyl. A power station that irradiated fish, milk, reindeer, mutton, over half of Europe ... there are other ways now, clean and safe, no by-products other than heat. But we are still working on those. Have been for fifty years now ...' He faded out as the memories surged through his mind, the memories of men and labs and the lifetime's work on the pursuit of the answer.

'It was fool's gold, young man. Fool's gold, and now it

40

has returned to haunt us. So will you help us?' He looked at Carson. 'Well?'

The pilot looked back at him. 'What is it you want me to do?'

'Come to Majorca with me. Meet my colleague. Hear what we have to offer and decide if you want to help. This much I promise you. It will be the culmination of your career as a pilot, as a flyer. You will fly into history, young man, in more ways than one, either as the successful spearhead of a valiant effort, or as the failed dream of millions.'

Bollocks, Carson thought.

Deia

High in the hills above the cliffs on Majorca's north coast lies the village of Deia. It is composed of clusters of stone buildings separated by narrow cobbled streets and laced with grapevines and olive trees and stone walls. Palms, arches and wide courtyards remain as evidence of Moorish and Arab occupations hundreds of years ago, with the later occupiers more subtle, but equally influential. They were the writers, poets and artists who had found something in the village, something in the ancient timelessness of the thick cool walls and shuttered windows that overlooked mountains washed by the warm wind from the Mediterranean.

The La Residencia Hotel was a converted Majorcan manor house standing on terraced levels in almost medieval splendour. Bought by a freewheeling travel and music entrepreneur, its conversion had been carried out with taste and appealed to those who wanted relaxed elegance. The suites and rooms were simple, the walls hung with paintings and drawings from various modern schools, and in the foyer a glass cabinet contained mementoes and a photograph of the poet Robert Graves, who had spent his last years in the village.

Carson stood reading the poem displayed there, while

41

Meran chatted in Spanish to the receptionist, a tall, striking girl with flame-red hair. Eventually he completed his business and came over to Carson. 'I'm down the road with young Haidermann. They will take your bags up and I have booked a table in the restaurant for nine. We will see you there then, mmmm?' The eyebrows twitched above the blue eyes as he awaited his answer.

'Fine,' Carson replied, thinking, who the hell is young Haidermann?

Langley, Virginia

The headquarters of the Central Intelligence Agency lies off the road on a 700-acre site surrounded by a chain-link fence. No attempt is made to hide the fact that this is the home of America's international intelligence organization. As you pass the guards with their state of the art identification systems, the road winds through the trees half a mile to the main block, a long seven-storey building with a smaller block attached to each corner. The north-west 'facility', as they call it, houses what the staffers call the sieve. Here over two hundred people slowly sift through the thousands of reports that enter Langley from some three thousand sources, including government agencies, embassies, American companies operating abroad, newspapers, wire services, magazines, the United Nations, the World Bank and USAid. The sifters process the reports, throwing out what is duplicated or of no interest, and then pass on the remainder to one of the seventeen intelligence sections. They in turn pass the compiled data on to operations, complete with cross-referenced sources and a specialist's report.

Karl Schoeman's preliminary report on his theory arrived in a standard intra-government envelope and was opened by a twenty-seven-year-old sifter with matrimonial problems. His wife was messing around, he believed, and he had been drinking heavily lately, unable to confront her because he was afraid of the truth, afraid of losing her. As he opened the envelope his mind was on her laughter down the phone the day before, the laughter of a woman talking to her lover. He had stood in the bathroom, his guts twisting, listening to her infidelity as obvious as it was careless.

He quickly leafed through the report, saw who it was from and shrugged; instead of reading it and checking against the ongoing log, he signed the base and entered his number and threw the report into the central tray that would be cross-checked and filed on microfiche. They had a lot of UFO material coming through and periodically the material was scanned by an agency in Washington. The next scan would not be for four months. He pulled the next envelope towards him and split the cover; it was number sixty for the morning and none had received proper care and attention, not with his wife's laughter ringing in his ears.

Two floors up a grade nine messenger was carrying another report into a closed-door meeting. It had arrived from Saudi Arabia the day before and was as yet unsubstantiated, but had already caused considerable interest and Pentagon and navy personnel had been arriving since the morning for the briefing. He pushed his access card into the slot beside the door and punched in his key code number. The door latch clicked on the other side and he entered the darkened room. Around the long table were seated eleven figures, some in uniform and some in civilian dress. One of the navy men leant forward and jabbed a finger at the screen illuminated with an image from a slide projector.

Admiral Tip Saddler was CINC of the American Task Force operating in the northern Indian Ocean and his patch took his people into the Arabian Gulf. A short, wiry man, with salt and pepper hair and weathered features, what he lacked in height he made up for in presence. His men called him 'the bronc' and amongst the ribbons on his chest were both the Navy Cross and the Congressional Medal of Honor, won as a very junior lieutenant in the Gulf of Tonkin.

'Cut the blather,' he snarled. 'Will that thermo head fit the Silkworm? A yes or no will do, or have you cloak and dagger bastards forgotten how to tell the truth?'

Saddler's executive officer, a full captain, smothered a smile. Go for it, Bronc, he thought, give 'em hell. He looked down from the screen as the agency man began speaking in apologetic tones.

'Admiral, we don't know. The report suggests so, but we have to validate it. We will keep you advised.'

'Do that, sonny, because they might just blow the whole friggin' site off the planet. I'm not putting my people into a potential nuclear situation without due reason,' Saddler answered.

'Sir, don't do anything to compromise our situation.'

'Compromise what? My command stands off with those fanatical bastards once a week, and now you tell me you think they have a fucking nuclear warhead! Be advised, I want to know the second you have further data.' Saddler rose to his feet and glowered at the room. 'I'm returning to my command. Captain Jessop here will finish up today's briefing.'

With that he stalked out. The agency staff all looked around at each other, stunned. Jessop smiled across at the senior analyst. 'Right, gentlemen, what do you need to know to be sure?'

One of the CIA men sat up indignantly. 'We are just trying to keep you people informed. We don't need all this.'

Jessop looked back at him. 'Admiral Saddler has seven thousand men and nine ships and he loves every one of 'em, so let's get on with keeping them in one piece.'

The analyst nodded, ignoring the outburst from his colleague, understanding Saddler's feelings.

'Captain Jessop, sir, our reports come from Saudi Arabia.

We have no real network in Iran and they do, so proving this kind of thing is difficult, as I am sure you can imagine.'

'What do you need to prove it?' Jessop repeated.

'I don't know . . . short of someone who has seen the inside of a Silkworm, I just don't know.'

Jessop stood and squared away his cap. 'Thank you, gentlemen. Keep in touch, and if we get hold of a Silkworm we will let you know.'

The two Fleet Intelligence Officers rose with him and together they left the room. They were tired and wanted a shower and some sleep, but knew they would have to wait for that until they rejoined their ships in the Gulf.

The Silkworms were a constant threat they lived with. Chinese-built ship-to-ship missiles, they had ended up in Iran on shore batteries overlooking the narrow Straits of Hormuz. Fitted with high-explosive warheads they were lethal enough, but if the Iranians had built a tactical nuclear warhead that could be delivered by the Silkworm they could have a real problem on their hands. Three of the rockets had been fired at Kuwait across the narrow top end of the Gulf back before the Iraqis had invaded. Although two had fallen short into the sea, the third had hit the shoreline. Intelligence suggested that those launchings were testing the guidance systems for better targets to follow.

They had been caught with their pants down once before. In the eighties during the first Gulf war the USS *Stark* had taken an Exocet missile from an Iraqi fighter pilot who, miles off course and terrified of everything, had pressed his weapons systems into action without thinking, or so the Iraqis claimed. Some said that Saddam had ordered the strike as a live firing trial. There had been thirty-seven dead on the *Stark*. But a nuke, he thought, that would be a thousand at least, and then the secondary deaths as the fallout blew southwards, because they would wait for a southerly wind to do it. They wouldn't risk it blowing on to their own coastline. Not even the Revolutionary Guard would put up with that and the old Ayatollah of the Rock and Rolla would be out of a job, right about the time that the Bronc's rules of engagement allowed him to retaliate once and for all. Then Christ knows what will happen, he thought.

Deia

Charles Haidermann looked every inch the international financier he was. He stood ramrod straight in a white tropical dinner jacket, his hands clasped behind his back, his gaze piercing and direct as Carson ambled towards his table. His once black hair was now iron grey and added a hint of respectability to his otherwise almost too youthful appearance for a man of seventy-five.

He offered his hand as Carson approached and his smile was genuine. 'Is it too soon to welcome you to Oslo, Mr Carson?'

Carson wasn't expecting the direct question and answered carefully. 'I have a feeling that tonight will tell. You must be Haidermann.'

They sat with Meran at a table outside, the night warm and still, and ordered by the light of a candle. Carson took a moment to look around at the other diners, all seated at discreet distances from each other. A lot of money, he thought. They were served their starters before Haidermann began talking, carefully phrasing his words as he sipped at his wine.

'My venerable colleague has told you a little of our group. Let me cover the rest, shall I?'

Carson nodded carefully, still chewing, and said nothing.

'We have in our ranks no fewer than sixteen Nobel Prize-winning scientists, three of whom have helped us on a little project we have put together. I say that with what the British call an understatement.' He smiled for a moment and continued, 'We have also gathered the finest

46

brains in the aeronautical design industry, people from Boeing, Rockwell, NASA, Lockheed, McDonnell Douglas, and we gave them a brief and we gave them money. Lots of money, Mr Carson. We asked them to design and build an aircraft capable of intercepting intercontinental ballistic missiles and shooting them down. We have tried words, pressure groups, media, lobbying. This was Plan B. Direct action. We want to be in a position to intercede in a global conflict.'

Carson burst out laughing. 'You what? One aircraft? Come off it.'

'Perhaps I should start at the beginning,' Meran suggested.

Haidermann nodded.

'It was in Oslo. 1947.' As he began, the memories flooded back.

Alexander Meran sat back in his chair, crossing one long bony leg across the other, and watched Scagallini talk, the watery warmth of the Norwegian sun filtering through the window. He had had the nightmare again last night, the same awful image of the huge swirling superhot mushroom cloud, the face of the child melting over the charred bodies on the black earth, and had woken sweating and frightened, like a hundred other nights in the last year.

He was the youngest of the five men at the table and still honoured to be in their presence. Running one long-fingered hand through his unfashionable collar-length hair, he sat listening and remembered when they had first sat together at this table almost six months before, seventeen months after the *Enola Gay* had lifted her shiny nose over Hiroshima in 1945. The five men had met by chance here in Oslo.

To Meran, himself a respected scientist who had worked on the Manhattan Project, they were distinguished men.

James Steerman had been in the State Department at the time the decisions had been made in the Oval Office to use the atom bomb, and had been deeply disturbed by the issue – not only the horror of the new weapons, but that one man might make a decision that affected so many.

The third man was the Polish Nobel Prize-winning chemist, Andre Balorki, the fourth, the Englishman Noel Chambers, had been appointed Poet Laureate that year. The fifth was the catalyst, an Italian scholar who had spent the war years in prison for his anti-fascist sentiments and had become the guiding light of a pacifist movement. The State Department man, Steerman, had worked hard throughout the war to try and secure the release of the strong-willed little Venetian, who never once ceased fighting for peace from within the walls of his cell. Chambers had met Vittorio Scagallini when he had visited London after Italy fell to the Allies. Meran, a physicist, had worked with Balorki before the war at the Sorbonne in Paris, and found the Pole brilliant. The two had been walking along a quiet street in Oslo when Steerman had hailed Meran from a taxi. Later that day the five men sat and talked for the first time.

They had seen much of each other that summer, and all agreed on one thing: that man's technology was about to return like a vengeful nemesis upon its creator. They feared what the Manhattan Project had created and what it held for the future of the planet.

'So,' Scagallini finished, 'we are agreed then. If we don't stop this madness it will be the end of us.'

'We are five here,' Chambers said, lifting his cup to his lips. 'Hardly an army.'

'Then we must find others who think like we do,' the Italian replied simply.

'The right people only,' cautioned Steerman. 'No hotheads, no known troublemakers. We need people of influence, people who have money or power.'

'People who can keep their word and their silence. That will be important. They will stop us if they can,' Scagallini warned.

'What? Form some sort of underground group?' Chambers asked incredulously.

'It's not that new a concept,' Scagallini replied. 'There have been many down the centuries. Groups of people who had something in common and feared ridicule or persecution for that ideal, creed or knowledge. The Boxers in China, the Calvinists in France, the Catholics in Elizabeth I's England, the Mafiosi, the Freemasons, even some barely known and spoken of in whispers like the Illuminati, all secret societies in modern times . . . but we must be more elusive than any, for in that will lie our survival.'

'We'll never manage to keep it secret,' Chambers said.

Such was the modesty of the group that they never chose a name or aspired to an identity. Their aims spoke for themselves and from that time on they were simply known as the men of Oslo. The men who had dreamed of a time where man would not fear his own stupidity or lack of vision.

They knew that what they desired was in direct conflict with the aims of the powerful governments who were moving headlong into a race to develop the nuclear capability. Finding men who believed enough to assist was done carefully. They were recruited one by one, from all lands and all creeds, from all professions and all ages, and all knew only too well the risks they were undertaking. In time they were going to take on the might of the United States, and soon Russia and whoever else entered the field. Meran was sure that Britain would be involved and the rest of the Allies in turn, and to protect themselves from a sure assault on their credibility, their professional morals, their patriotism and eventually their physical safety, they decided to keep their association known only to themselves and to work through others. A new secret society had been born, one that set out to change the world.

In the next forty years 'Oslo' would become the single most powerful organization ever, that didn't fly a flag or control a national territory. In fact they would be considerably more powerful than most third world countries, and enjoy an annual funding larger than that of Brazil or Australia. By 1948 the original group of five men had swelled to over a hundred, all powerful or influential people who feared what the great powers of Russia and America were capable of.

The Cold War was at its height and the tension was real. In the spring of 1951 James Steerman, now a senator, by chance overheard a heated conversation in a restaurant in New York. He knew both the men at the adjoining table by reputation, one the head of a large downtown brokerage firm and the other his rising star, a tall, much younger man, blessed with a commanding presence if no family money. His name was Charles Haidermann.

He sat and listened carefully. The conversation was fast and angry, with Haidermann allowing his true emotions to rise to the surface as he named the new fears that threatened the world. Klein, his senior partner, mocked his passion and left, expecting Haidermann to follow in his own time. He didn't, and Steerman crossed the few feet to his table.

'May I join you?' he asked.

The young investment banker, recognizing the speaker, nodded.

'I couldn't help overhearing that conversation. Heated words for lunch . . . not good for the digestion,' Steerman probed.

'That man's a fool, Senator,' Haidermann answered acidly.

'Not nice to speak like that about your boss.'

'He's my boss no longer. I just quit.'

'Because he laughed at you?'

'No, because he is a parasite. A vulture getting fat on something evil.'

'Morality on the trading floor!' Steerman said sarcastically.

'No, I have none of that. I just won't invest in atomic weapons research. I don't care how much is to be made. All right? If you don't like it then take a hike, Senator!' Haidermann rose, hands on hips, openly aggressive.

Steerman smiled and in the next four hours recruited the finest investment mind on a soaring Wall Street.

At the same time Scagallini had found the second man in the scheme that was to provide a source of funds for the men from Oslo. He was a Swedish economist who had recently accepted an appointment to the newly created United Nations. In the next three years he put aside his religious convictions and his petty fears and embezzled many millions of dollars from the coffers of his employers. Placed in the hands of Charles Haidermann they multiplied swiftly. As fast as the post-war boom doubled investment, Halvorsen embezzled more and in 1956 Haidermann began to dedicate all his time to Oslo. Halvorsen was not the only source of funds. In the last few years other men had joined the group – bankers and financiers who, normally stimulated by the thought of war, knew that the next major conflict would be the end, threw their muscle into Oslo. Haidermann and his new team were handling investment portfolios across the globe that totalled billions of dollars. They were in on the oil boom, providing much of the development capital for the new age of technology. All this time, the recruiting had been swelling the ranks of the group. Its tentacles had reached into industry, the armed forces in a dozen countries, commerce, government, the arts, through all the strata of society.

Around all the members was a staggering security shield – staggering purely for its simplicity. Few men knew who else was involved, no one spoke of the group, and they never raised their heads in public profile. All manoeuvres were conducted covertly through other organizations and few who contributed to the society knew its true size or scope.

Haidermann, now on the executive committee, was

finally told he could begin releasing funds to specific projects, the first of which was a rolling series of donations to several ecological pressure groups and peace movements. It was also the time that Oslo began to discard sectors of their portfolio and put the money into outright purchases of the media. All this time no Oslo money was spent that would not be recouped in some form or other. Haidermann, himself now a millionaire by his investment skill, had set up a brokerage and investment house just off Wall Street that to all appearances was just another money business. Few people knew they handled just one client, not even the many who worked there.

The executive committee was still the original five men and Haidermann and, other than the tall New Yorker, none was a professional manager. Even Steerman with all his years in politics was honest enough to admit that he didn't have the skills to manage the organization, now so large it had an overall income the size of New Zealand's. Haidermann made a proposal that year, 1963, that would set the pattern for the next two decades of Oslo's slumber. His proposal was to allow the management of the hundreds of companies to be handled by professional managers reporting to their shareholders as usual. The Wall Street offices would be the final tenable front, and then only through miles of covering haze. Haidermann and Steerman had recruited a team of young lawyers who would begin the smoke-screening, ostensibly for a couple of major but shy holding companies. One of them suggested investment in the new computer age and that suggestion, acted upon a few years later, made Oslo the single largest entity in Silicon Valley.

In 1971 contact was made with others across the Iron Curtain. A carefully planned meeting in a conference anteroom between a Soviet agronomist and a French biologist put the two groups in touch, and over the next three years they both probed and tested each other's strengths and weaknesses. Meran and Steerman were both shocked at how powerful the Soviet dissidents were: they already had links in the most sensitive areas of Russia's defence and military machine. They even had members in the KGB and one, they claimed, in the Politburo. They called themselves the Gulag, a macabre joke on where they would all end up if ever discovered. Steerman returned to America and, after long talks with Meran and Scagallini and the by now ailing Chambers, agreed to begin recruiting an intelligence division.

It was Scagallini who, reviewing the portfolio in '89, saw the group's potential. Chambers the poet had died three years before, a venerable, shambling old man who spent his last years in a cottage near Henley. Just before his death he had told Scagallini that they were now powerful and it was time to stop talking and to act. He had wanted a defence system to be developed.

'We can't physically destroy the missiles in their silos, so let's find a way to take them from the sky. Let's take our dove of peace, and give her a wing to cover the innocent.'

Now, before Scagallini lay the answer and he called an extraordinary meeting of the committee. That meeting was held in the spring of 1989 in Portugal. There in the rambling home of one of their benefactors, the men from Oslo created the Omega Project. It was also the time when they all realized that they were getting old and this climax to forty-five years of effort would need younger people in its front line decision-making.

Haidermann, his passionate beliefs about to become reality, was sent back to New York and asked to report in six weeks exactly what development capital Oslo could provide. Steerman returned to begin scouting for talent, as did Meran, and Scagallini, now in his eighty-second year, went to Paris to the Sorbonne where so much of it had all begun, to recruit the man they all agreed should be their project director.

Leo Sagan was a scientist and, rare for that breed, also

an outstanding administrator. He had spent seven years with NASA and had held a physics chair at both the Sorbonne and Cambridge. He was now, Scagallini knew, bored with the muted rhetoric of the campus and ready for a more challenging role. He was also a man of Oslo and had been for sixteen years – one of the many who gave their hearts trustingly, without asking questions. It was a testament to the security of Oslo that until that time Sagan never knew that Scagallini and Meran, both of whom had been his mentors during his student days, were the nuclei of Oslo.

He immediately agreed to manage the project, and asked for two others to join him: Paul Scott, an astrophysicist who was with McDonnell Douglas, and James McReadie, who was about to finish his contract with the Rockwell Corporation. Both were designers who were frustrated with the limitations of their working allowances, and both were involved with advanced aviation science, astrophysics. Rockwell built the space shuttle and McDonnell Douglas high-speed interceptors. Omega was something in between and Sagan knew both men would relish the chance of designing a one-off hybrid with no cost restraints.

'We want,' Scagallini had said to Sagan, 'an aeroplane that will chase and shoot down missiles.'

Project Omega had begun.

Haidermann reported that sufficient funds were now being channelled into current operating accounts for day-to-day spending and McReadie and Scott had been placed on huge retainers.

Both were resident Americans and both would have to be enticed to the base that Sagan had decided upon, like all the other people that the project would eventually employ. That base was to be at Edinburgh in Scotland, a venerable city with its share of academics and visitors to disguise the arrivals and far enough from the myriad companies that would have all the subcontracts for the actual production of component parts not to allow coincidence a chance to put the pieces together.

The first meeting of all three men was in Monterey in California, where Sagan had outlined the requirements.

'We want to build an aircraft that can stop a missile before it gets to ground zero and detonates. That is the end requirement. Give me the fastest weapons platform that was ever devised, and I will find a man who can build a laser system to complement it.'

Sagan was a tall, scholarly man with deep-etched wrinkles in his face that only served to give it character. He was tanned and wore his hair long, too long for the bifocal spectacles he wore. His large hands moved in expressive gestures as he spoke and often stroked the goatee beard he affected. He was one of those rare speakers who could captivate listeners with pauses.

'I am giving you two men the chances of a lifetime ... A no-budget ... one-off design ... that will be the culmination of your careers. To design the first true hypersonic aircraft, thirty years ahead of its time!' He paused again. 'Possible?'

'Yes. It's possible. But the cost! Shit! It will cost plenty,' McReadie responded.

'We have plenty. Can you do it?'

'The technology is there,' Scott replied carefully, thinking, this is too good to be true – to be allowed to build something hypersonic.

It was McReadie who answered with the first positive feel, thinking aloud. 'Conventional power systems won't be enough, in fact conventional power systems won't even be enough to get her up to anything like hypersonic speed.' He leaned forward as he spoke. 'She will need more. She will need ...'

'Scram jets,' Sagan said with a smile. 'That's why we employed you.'

Scott was already sketching on a paper napkin an airframe that could incorporate the technology.

'She will need a funnel effect,' he said to McReadie, 'for the airflow.'

They were hooked.

McReadie also recruited a Swiss woman who had been instrumental in the design of a new plastic heat-shielding system that NASA had seen fit to discount from the Rockwell designs, and Japan was to provide a large number of active members for Oslo and a disproportionate number of the actual construction team who built the sleek, black, needle-nosed interceptor. It was those men who, when given the drawings by McReadie, laboured for hours hand-machining complex metals to customize the huge power plants that could each provide 90,000 pounds of thrust. When combined with the oxygen-enlarged feeder system from Aerojet Liquid Rocket Company, the re-heat facility on the take-off plant would give staggering performance. Much of the equipment would be ordered under false names, or funnelled from university projects or to publicity-shy Arab sheikhs. Many of the suppliers of advanced avionics would understand that secrecy, but many also had to meet their own governmental security watch on forwarding orders, so standard units were ordered and then reworked and tuned. On all purchases there was the one delightful factor. No limits to the budget to constrict them, and no commercial concern for durability. Sagan had summed it up at the first meeting of the team.

'Don't design for a long operational life. She will never need a Certificate of Airworthiness or a major refit. Test flights and then hopefully one mission. So don't let's get bogged down with testing for fatigue after ten thousand hours or anything like that. Just give me the fastest laser weapons platform ever conceived.'

It was like sweet music to engineers frustrated by years of constraint, and a team of 116 people finally assembled in a purpose-built factory in Scotland. They would co-ordinate the subcontracting of work. The factory was on the end of an old MoD runway and the sign outside proclaimed it to be the plant of the Experimental Alloys Company. Assembly would be completed elsewhere at a point yet to be decided and Sagan and Meran delightedly reported to the committee that the project was on time. It wasn't easy. They knew they could keep designing this aircraft for ever, so they used the Lockheed 'skunkworks' methods of small groups empowered to get on with it. The working pace wasn't without its price. One man became an alcoholic, a woman designer in Paris had a heart attack at her desk and a man working in the fuels group took his own life, his marriage having failed with the pressure of work.

It was at this time that an electronic access division was established. All members provided information, but this group would have as their brief radar, satellite and communications access. They looked to cover the most obvious threat and placed their people and gadgets in the USA, Britain and France, the only countries outside the Soviet bloc that could pose problems for Oslo.

At the Omega project Randolph Jennings was the NASA man that McReadie insisted he needed for the scram jets. He was a difficult, cantankerous American who took some time to decide to join the team, constantly bickering with Sagan's motives and beliefs. Eventually he agreed, lured by the promise of a new dream with men who didn't care for sceptics or maybes. Here there was no finance committee or appropriations appeal. The money was there and so was the need.

'Inevitably the project ran over on both time and cost, but it was finally completed in 1995,' Meran said, 'and here we are. We are ready.'

'Take the knives off the kids,' Haidermann said, 'and leave them only with their fists, if you like. That way they both get to go home afterwards. We can't stop war, but we can stop them destroying this planet. Now then, I am not some dithering intellectual.'

Meran smiled into his glass and looked across at Haidermann who looked back. 'No offence meant, Alex,' Haidermann said.

'None taken, dear boy,' Meran replied, mockingly raising his glass again. Haidermann looked back at Carson. 'I am a businessman and very good at getting things done. One of the things we did was to take Oslo from a group of academics full of rhetoric to a power structure second to none. We turn over more than General Motors and Ford put together every year in the US alone. Of the Fortune Five Hundred we control sixty-three companies absolutely and a further hundred and thirty with proxy voting shares. I tell you this because it is important for you to understand exactly who we are. We are concerned people who have the power at last to influence the way things will turn out. Now then, we have built an aeroplane, Mr Carson, and we need a pilot. She flies, she has been tested, but that's all I can tell you. I'm not technical, but these facts I can allow you at this stage without compromising ourselves. She is the biggest, fastest interceptor ever conceived outside of science fiction and she is equipped with state of the art avionics, data systems and, I am told, a weapons system that is fifty years ahead of its time.'

He stopped and sipped his wine and looked across at Carson in the soft light. The tension was electric as he lowered his glass to the white tablecloth and straightened his cuffs.

'Will you fly her for us?' he asked.

'Isn't this all a bit over the top? The Cold War is over. There hasn't been that kind of tension for years,' Carson replied.

'The threat is as real as ever, maybe more so. We now have independent states in what was the USSR that have nuclear arsenals and they are vulnerable to extremists. There are developing countries almost there with nuclear capability. Imagine if Saddam Hussein managed to get a nuclear device? Bought one for hard petrodollars from some impoverished Russian state with more missiles than wheat. It gets worse. The Russians now have their ICBMs ready to be launched by what the media have called Doomsday. In the event that the Russian leadership is wiped out, a rocket will launch and broadcast a signal to a computer that will in turn launch their ICBMs. This is them saying to the West, "Even if your superior technology kills us first, you will go too." Mutual assured destruction to a new level. Ironically that might make the Omega's job easier. Just one rocket to take out rather than dozens of missiles. So. Will you fly her for us?'

Carson looked at them. Hypersonic! Jesus! They must be mad! But I want to see this. He was torn. He had always pushed it. Gone faster, turned faster, always tested the newest stuff. This was irresistible. It would be fast, very fast. He hadn't flown fast, not pushed the envelope since the weapons test of the EFA and then there were dead kids and a crushed Citroën. Never again. No more fuck-ups. His hand began to sweat and he pushed it down on the table-cloth so they wouldn't see it shake. Just see it. Maybe fly it once. Jesus. What am I doing? And before he could stop himself he spoke.

'Maybe.'

Novosibirsk, Russia

The two men in overalls and lightweight jackets slowly climbed the iron steps of the radio tower, the heavy tool-cases on leather straps over their shoulders. The younger of the two, a heavy-set man of Asian features, led the way from the fourth level, his powerful stride testament to the fact that he walked the steps regularly. He looked down only once, waving to the guard at the gates of the transmitter station. He was a maintenance engineer employed by the State Radio Network, one of seven in Novosibirsk responsible for the towers, satellite links and relays in the area. He stole a look back at his older companion. Even though he was nearing sixty years of age he still seemed strong, and amongst his circle of friends he was more respected than the President all those miles away in Moscow.

Ilya Slaveganovich Borkin was an economist at the Ministry of Foreign Affairs, one who studied trends in the western markets and predicted wheat prices and commodity trading levels. He was also the head of Gulag. When they stopped on the sixth level and looked to the east, there below them was the complex containing the Central Data Facility for the Russian Army's northern area of operations and, more importantly, a link for the computer that would, after a signal from a rocket, launch the ICBMs without any human touch or decision.

'There, *tovarich*, is your pimple on the backside of humanity,' the Asian said. Borkin smiled at the analogy. Khan didn't think much of the Russian armed forces, he mused.

'The vents . . . they are to put air into the facility?'

'*Da* . . . fifteen of them, powered by the plant to the left. It is said that there are several levels below ground. The computers are on some lower level with standby generators, so in theory they never go down . . . bombproof?'

Borkin nodded. He had seen the drawings, he had people on the inside. Khan continued, 'It is considered a good posting as they go, warm in winter, a long way from any action, and boredom the only real enemy. The soldiers are good types, but we don't see much of the technical people in the town.' No, thought Borkin, they will never be very far from the lower level. Never very far from their computers.

'You won't be able to get in there,' Khan said with some certainty.

The older man hesitated for a minute before he spoke. 'I just wanted to see it . . . get a feel for what we have to do.'

But it won't be me that does it. I am too old, he thought.

It is time to hand over if they will let me. This will need more than I have to give. It is time for Stravinsky's way.

Minsk

Pyotr Rabanov was a Russian Jew, but unlike most he was Russian first and Jewish second. He had no great desire to be in Israel. To visit, yes, but to live? No. He loved the wide open majesty of the steppe where he was born. He was also a respected engineer in his field, one of the few who had mastered the complexities of computer design. Without the stimulus of a competitive environment he knew his work wasn't the best in the world, but he was considered amongst the top three in Russia and had had several trips to the West to work alongside men from IBM and Cray. For that reason he was always the first to be allowed into the boards, logic systems, conductors, and everything jammed on to the minute chips and the hard disks that made up modern western machines. Unlike most hardware men he was equally at home with software, but the piece spread before him on the bench in his office was one of the new flexible circuits from Xyratex, a British business bought out of IBM by its management. He swiftly made calculations on its applicable feasibility. He looked down at his watch, another western item that he had been given at a conference in Stockholm three years before by a charming Swiss engineer who had worked for Hewlett Packard.

It was eight-thirty; time to leave the office and go home, but he allowed himself the pleasure of slicing through the cable for a first look at its fine flexible silicon matrix. He smiled at the ingenuity, his small brown eyes creasing with pleasure beneath a clear high forehead. He pushed the glasses further up his small nose and brushed a hank of hair clear before holding the cross-section under the magnifying glass and humming a waltz to himself.

My God, he thought, we could never build this in a million years. A bunch of clod-footed factory workers with their obese garlicky wives, supplied with white hats and told they are technology workers, given outdated tools and asked to copy the best. Ha! He sat back and tiredly rubbed his eyes, then finally stood and reached for his jacket. His home in suburban Minsk was a good fifty minutes in his dilapidated old car. His wife, a physics graduate, would arrive home at roughly the same time and usually they would sit and read the few classics that Pyotr had collected over the years, or the odd western technical manual that the Institute subscribed to. But tonight was different. Tonight they were expecting a call from a man who would be awaiting a reply that, once given, could place Pyotr and Natalia Rabanov firmly amongst the ranks of the dissidents. Not the Zionists or the new right wing. These people described themselves as International Disarmamentalists. He thought they might have made the word up, but he liked their sentiments and their name held a perverse warning. They called themselves Gulag.

His wife was already home, her lightweight summer boots in the hall where she had stepped out of them, her coat on the hall stand, and her clear voice echoing from the kitchen as she sang to herself. Pyotr smiled. It was always good to come home.

She had found some fresh cream that day and was folding it into beaten egg whites as they spoke. She was small, dark and extremely volatile with fast, almost Italian gestures supporting her conversation.

'What will they want you to do?' she asked, licking her fingers.

'I don't know, but if they want to disarm the nutcases in the Kremlin they can't be bad,' Pyotr answered, reaching forward to dip his finger into the thickening mix. She slapped his hand with the whisk and splashed the raw mousse everywhere.

'Disarm you, more like it!' she replied warningly.

'Anyway,' he continued, licking the back of his hand, 'I've decided to help if I can. Are you in?'

'What can I offer?' she replied. 'And what will they ask you to do?'

'I told you I . . .'

'Don't give me that. You know what you have to offer!' She looked angrily at him.

He said nothing and eventually she stopped stirring and looked at him, her eyes widening in realization and fear. 'You are going to corrupt Igor, aren't you?' she said softly. 'My God, you can get right into it. You are going to corrupt the software.'

He put his finger into the bowl trying to show a calmness he didn't feel and scooped some of the mixture clear, relishing the taste. In the new Russia fresh eggs and cream were often hard to find in the cities without hard currency.

'Or something,' he replied savouring the taste, but the fear in his stomach was real and twisting.

Igor he thought, Igor running one of those American games rather than the Defence Module G 67-BB. Food for thought. With the entire defence software for the Siberian and Chinese borders corrupted, and the nearest copies in Moscow six hours away, the Doomsday programme would be useless, the ICBMs would be grounded and half the tactical sections of the Red Air Force on visual flight or whatever they called it. He had warned them at the time of the dangers of piling so much on the one system. But they, tight with the foreign exchange and therefore the ability to buy the huge Data General Systems, decided to ignore him. Short of spares and boards, it was already breaking down all too often, and overloaded as it was they would never know that someone had sabotaged it till it was too late. Another twist in his stomach at the thought. My God, Natalia, you are quick off the mark, it only occurred to me on the way home. This is sabotage and treason on a grand scale. People's enemy number one.

*　　*　　*

Four miles away from the Rabanovs' apartment behind the Station Hotel in the old city of Minsk was a fifties concrete four-storey building. The portico on the ground floor had been renovated with smoked glass, but otherwise the original structure remained. The top three floors were the provincial administrative headquarters of what used to be the Committee for State Security, otherwise the KGB. Renamed the Federal Security Service, the FSB, it performed much the same function. The lights on the top floor were still on at midnight as they were most nights. The man in the end office reached for his coffee cup on the end of the plain steel desk and wished that the major would call it a night and go home like normal people; then he could, too. He sipped the sour, lukewarm fluid, then hurriedly put the cup down, did up the buttons on the serge tunic in the regulation way and stood as the door opened. No one except an officer would enter unannounced, and an officer it was.

He was tall, dressed in the uniform of a full colonel with the gold staff emblem on his collar. The deep-set, piercing blue eyes were offset by a ruddy complexion and a strong jaw. His face was cold and his look seemed to cut. As he walked into the room he lightly slapped his gloves against his thigh. The uniform was perfectly pressed and his boots shone like crystal. He stopped and gazed at the sergeant, still adjusting his lower buttons.

'Do you always have to dress in the office?' His voice was like a rasp.

'No, colonel, sir!' The sergeant snapped to attention.

'What is your name?'

'Suvlov, colonel, Rudi Suvlov!'

'Stand easy, Suvlov, and undo that bottom button before your gut breaks through it.'

'Sir!' Suvlov undid the button with relief, knowing this one was not so bad after all.

'My name is Rordino. I have the misfortune to be your new commanding officer. If you are to survive my tenure

64

then learn two things: I like obedience and I like good coffee.'

'Sir!'

'Get me some coffee and tell me where I can find Major Rochenko.'

'Second door up, sir, on the left . . . welcome to Minsk, sir!'

The colonel seemed to smile for a moment and then spoke. 'Still screwing married women, Rudi?'

'Yes, colonel, whenever possible,' the sergeant said, breaking into a smile. 'It's good to see you again, sir.'

'*Da* . . . five years now. You have put on weight, Suvlov. We shall have to get you fit again won't we . . . ? What's Rochenko like?'

'Pardon me, sir . . . but he's a cunt, sir!' he said, snapping to attention.

'Then I'm surprised you haven't fucked him!'

'Pardon, sir?'

'An old lag like you, Rudi? No problem.'

Rordino had read Rochenko's record and knew what to expect. Too long between moves, too long between promotions in someone who was aggressive and bright, usually made for bitterness. This one was too much for even an old lag like Suvlov. Dangerous.

'Well, sir . . .'

'Good judgement, sergeant. This one's a real shit isn't he?'

Suvlov said nothing, staring into space over Rordino's shoulder.

'Well so am I. Get me all the files on the local problems. I will be with Rochenko.'

'Sir!' Suvlov snapped and turned for the door, watched by Rordino.

He waited till he was well up the passage before allowing himself to smile openly. Christ on a crutch! Rordino! He had last seen the officer in Moscow five years ago and then he was just a captain. Captain to full colonel in five years was fast even in the new Security Service. He remembered the young firebrand's handling of the Khazak thing which got him the Moscow move: the story was now a classic. Rordino had tracked down a new group who had been making a deal with the mujahedin in Afghanistan and had blown it wide open in seventeen days. The Uzbeks and Khazaks had made contact and they were going to deal arms. The arms would have been western, channelled through the mujahedin who would have taken their percentage in missiles and land mines. Light arms in and a nuclear warhead out. Rordino had crossed boundaries, entered another service area and trapped both parties in the act of agreeing the methods. The subsequent round-up had netted sixty-odd Uzbeks, Khazaks and other dissidents, the local Security Service senior officer an early retirement, and for Rordino a move to Moscow with his own section. People began to notice the youthful Estonian and now he was a colonel and in charge of the Minsk area.

He knew he wouldn't be home tonight. Rordino worked all the hours of day and always seemed fresh. For five months in Moscow when Rudi had been his orderly room sergeant, the captain had ordered double shifts just to allow his people to keep up. The sergeant thought about what he knew about him. There were stories. He had spent time in the Ukraine, and oddly would sometimes be found visiting children from the Chernobyl area in hospital. The rumour was that one of them was his, illegitimate, but his. He had requested and been given a transfer to St Petersburg and had found it frustrating watching the city slide further into its cycle of corruption, bribes, extortion and crime. Two of his best people had left his team to become bodyguards to the foreign businessmen who had been flooding in to do business in the city, but worse was the impotence. Rordino knew that with the FSB machine and some old-fashioned attitudes he could have cleaned up the organized crime in weeks. But the FSB had no mandate over civil crime. Not their patch. Civil crime was for police and militia. He's a fucking machine, Rudi thought, but he's all right, straight with the men and a demon with anyone unfortunate enough to attract the interest of the service. Now things would start to happen.

He picked up the two cups and carried them down the hall to Major Rochenko's office, knocked and entered.

Husavik, Iceland

The northern end of Iceland is a series of stubbly low hills interspersed with steeper sharp volcanic ridges and criss-crossed by streams of icy water, even in summer. In the winter it is an unforgiving place, swept by harsh winds from the polar ice-cap, freezing the grass and streams and bringing the snow and ice that gave the land its name. Huge areas lie uninhabited between the tiny fishing and farming settlements and it looked bleak and lonely to Carson as the helicopter flew up the valley fast and low. He was pleased to be moving again. He had been stuck in a hotel for three days while they did something but they had collected him that morning. The landscape below was low hills sparsely strewn with snow, grass and rock, and Carson could see the coastline coming up again. The pilot indicated ahead and switched his throat mike on.

'The Arctic Circle is a couple of minutes out from the shore.'

Carson nodded his understanding and the man continued his commentary.

'We are going in there,' he indicated below and ahead where a scattering of old Nissen huts stood inside the perimeter of an old and apparently disused airfield.

'Looks like it could use a lick of paint,' Carson said with typical New Zealand practicality, thinking, shit, look at it! Hasn't been used since the war probably. At least the runway's clear of holes.

'It's supposed to look like that. The real stuff is mostly below ground, set into that hillside,' the pilot said, his gloved thumb indicating a low tussocky shoulder that ran parallel to the north–south runway. Carson looked and smiled to himself. This is more like it, he thought. His fighter pilot's eyes had picked out the lines of radar and satellite dishes, camouflaged in the rocky slopes.

The helicopter began to lose height rapidly and the man spoke again.

'Out quick. I'm not flight-planned to land, and this area is prohibited to traffic. There will be someone to meet you in the hut there.' Carson nodded.

As the craft banked steeply, bled off speed and settled gently on the grassy old concrete pan, Carson unbuckled, jumped clear and ran from the wash as the rotors beat at the air above his head, the helicopter lifting and scuttling upwards and northwards. The whup, whupping faded into the distance and the place seemed very quiet except for the steady hum of a ventilator. He hefted his bag over his shoulder and walked towards the nearest hut, its peeling walls sad and dilapidated, like an old whore under a bright streetlight. When he was a few feet from the door it swung open and a man stepped clear followed by a second armed with a short-barrelled automatic weapon.

'Mr Carson, I presume? My name is Leo Sagan. I am the Omega Project Director. This is Mr Pauli Van Waveren. He is in charge of security, so please bear with us while he asks a few questions, mmmm?'

'If I'm not Carson then you have a problem, someone getting so close,' he said as he lowered his bag to the ground and raised his hands for the body search he thought would be inevitable.

'That won't be necessary, we scanned you from the inside,' Van Waveren said pleasantly.

'What did you have for your main course the night you met Mr Haidermann?'

Carson lowered his hands slowly, somewhat puzzled.

'Something with pâté de foie gras. There was lots of it on the menu . . . liver, I think, it was raw.'

'That was your first course,' Van Waveren said, extending his hand. 'Sorry about this, but we had a couple of people looking around a few months ago. Can't be too sure, ever.'

Carson shook hands and looked at Sagan who smiled broadly, fishing in his pockets and finally producing a packet of cigarettes. Lighting one he said, 'Shouldn't, I know, but one must have some vices especially out here . . . come, let's go down and you can meet your colleagues.'

He pointed towards the end wall of the hut, where an old pin-up still stood vertical and voluptuous beneath the dust over a shelf of used oil tins.

'There is a tunnel below the shelf, part of the warren as we call it. Pauli will lead the way.'

They climbed the steep steps through the gap and dropped into a wide tunnel, brightly lit with neon strip lighting, where Carson was offered a seat on a canary yellow golf cart. He threw his bag on to a wire basket arrangement on the rear, Van Waveren eased the lever forward and they set off.

'There are fifty-three of us underground here at the base,' Sagan began, 'but you will only meet a few this morning. You will want to meet your baby too, no doubt. We never got round to naming her. There have been lots of attempts. Everything from Widow Maker to Little Dove,' he stopped to take a deep drag on the cigarette, 'but nothing seemed appropriate and everyone who built her always seemed to argue about it. Digby calls her Lucy, something about an old Beatles song, I believe.'

'In the sky with diamonds,' Carson said smiling.

'Oh yes, I see,' replied Sagan unconvincingly.

They drove on for a few minutes more, Sagan chatting and Van Waveren silent beneath the seemingly endless neon lighting, before the tunnel widened rapidly into an underground garage of sorts with five or six other golf carts parked in bays. A steel door with a card access system stood smooth in one rock face, and to the right three other tunnels ran away like spokes from a hub.

'Here we are!' Sagan said cheerfully.

3

'Come up to the operations room, the department heads are waiting to meet you,' Sagan said, walking through the steel doors. 'They have been taking bets on the likelihood of your agreeing to fly for us.'

'Who won?' Carson asked dryly.

'It matters not,' Sagan replied, smiling over his shoulder. 'If you are here, that is all that matters.'

He pushed open a swing door and Carson followed him into a large room with several Formica-topped desks laid out like a classroom. A large video screen dominated one end and on a second wall a blackboard still contained formulae that Carson recognized as advanced physics. A rubbish bin full of workings on paper stood overflowing in one corner alongside a coffee machine. Seated on chairs and tables around the room various people talked and smoked and argued amongst themselves. Gradually the talk died away as they realized that Sagan was back with the new pilot.

A tall, elegant English-looking man stepped forward, his creased tie askew like his smile. His eyes were brown and welcoming and as he extended a long, bony hand Carson caught the smell of whisky.

'Digby Allison, at your service, you must be Icarus . . . ha ha! Sorry, old chap, a little bit pissed, am most of the time that I'm not working.' He grinned widely, an appealing, open expression.

Sagan raised an eyebrow. 'Digby does lasers: he designed and built your systems. This is Tavis.'

A large bear-like man with closely cropped red hair

shambled forward, a cigar clamped between his teeth, and nodded formally.

'Tavis is chief engineer. He has a team of seventeen specialists that will keep you airborne.'

'Air force?' Carson asked.

'Originally. Then British Aerospace,' he replied, his accent thick Welsh. 'Don't you worry, boyo, I've worked on every panel and part of her and . . .' his voice took on a menacing tone '. . . if you crash or bend her I will break every bone in your body.'

Carson smiled, pleased with the image. Weak crew chiefs were a hazard.

'Dr Neilson is the medical man here, does sick call and specialized in aviation medicine with NASA,' Sagan continued.

Neilson offered his hand. 'Welcome to the crazy club.'

'Those other three are, left to right, Sileski who does engines, Yamashita who is finishing the computer programming, and Folley who is into radar tracking.' Carson nodded at the three.

'So that leaves last, but certainly not least, Gail Samuels.'

She stepped forward from behind the men, her dark eyes quizzical and moist all at once. Her hair was tied up in a bun with a ribbon and gave her high cheekbones lift and elegance. She was tall, taller than Carson by an inch, and filled out the pale blue jumpsuit in places it was never designed for. She wore no make-up, but her lips were still full and red against creamy skin.

'Welcome to Omega Base, Mr Carson, I am your flight controller.'

The voice was firm, the accent American and her eyes challenged him openly. She had seen hotshot pilots before and very few liked to be controlled from the ground, having to accept that modern technology had taken the freedom from them. They also invariably made a pass, which she found unprofessional in the extreme.

'I shall be a good boy, I promise,' he replied, reading her

perfectly, his voice slightly mocking. 'Let me guess, tactical fighter control on a forward base in Germany or somewhere?'

'How did you know?' she asked, smiling pleasantly but guardedly.

'From your attitude. It's the worst flying I have ever seen from Americans, *ergo*, any controller with your opinion has probably tried to work with those pilots.'

She studied him quizzically for a moment, the others in the room silent. 'All I need is another smart-arse,' she said, a twinkle in her look.

'Come,' said Digby, 'I'll give you the grand tour and introduce you to Lucy.'

He seemed to have sobered up already; perhaps, mused Carson, it was the thought of seeing the aircraft.

'That might be appropriate,' Sagan said. 'I'll see you both up in the control room.'

Aircraft hangars all smell the same – a mixture of oil, metal and aeroplane. Some smell dusty, others of canvas and leather and wood glue that seem to persist from the glorious days of early aviation. Sometimes there is an exotic hint of cordite or hydraulic fluid as a little extra from a fighter, but all have the same basic smell, which was what confused Carson as he and Allison walked the long, sloping access tunnel. This hangar didn't have the smell, it something else. Carson could hear the powerful ventilators humming as Allison pulled the fireproof door back on its oiled runners. The hangar was in darkness and he could feel the rush of cool air swirl around him. Come on then, let's have a look at you. In his mind he had pictured a stretch version of an F-15 or maybe a hybrid of the Blackbird, SR-71. He had seen the Blackbird once at an American base in England and she had looked a big, fast, wicked bitch. So what do we have here? He thought maybe a Blackbird with new power sources. He heard Allison cross behind him as he moved forward into the dark, his nose seeking the smell of hydraulics and oil and kerosene – the smell of home for him. Allison found the light switches somewhere behind him and five banks of quartz halogen studio lights burst into brilliance fifty feet above Carson's head.

There in the centre of the hollowed-out mountainside he stood absolutely silent for half a minute. Allison, who understood it all, eventually walked forward and stood beside him.

'Holy Mother of Christ,' Carson whispered in awe. He walked nearer and looked upward at the needle nose sixteen feet above his head, with the reverence of a young artist gazing at the roof of the Sistine Chapel.

'She's big, she's so big!' he said softly, still staring upward.

'Three feet longer than Concorde,' Allison replied, 'but beamier, much beamier. Up there,' he pointed at the nose, 'and at the leading edges it's all plastic heat tiles. The rest of the skin is a superlight carbon-fibre-reinforced polymer. The engines, of which you have six, include scram jets. They, with the new trailing edges and the airflow channels under her belly, will give you speeds never dreamt of anywhere under two hundred thousand feet. She has an alternative oxygen source for the high altitude burn.' He walked down the shadowed concrete beneath the sleek fuselage. 'The panels are all treated with a Danish compound that's a little better than the stealth stuff on the F-19. She has no radar signature whatsoever, but we are still working on the infrared problem.'

'How fast?' Carson asked like a father asking the sex of his new baby.

'We don't really know . . . not yet. Erich Stadle eased her over Mach Ten seventy thousand feet over Antarctica, but that was only two-thirds power.'

'Holy Mother of Christ,' he said again. 'Buffeting? any shudder?' His mind raced at the thought of controlling a machine doing seven or eight thousand miles an hour. 'The canards will help but . . .'

74

'It's all done with computers,' Allison said with a mirthless chuckle. 'Whatever you instruct, the computers action after considering all factors. The machine is very complex and is self-programming as the aircraft pushes new levels, so the computer works the factors. There is a manual override, but at that speed you are better with the machine.'

Carson nodded quickly, it was the same principle as the Rafale he had flown in France. 'What about weapons systems?'

'Ah, that's my department,' Allison replied. 'Lasers, my dear chap.'

'What the fuck are you talking about?' Carson laughed.

'Concentrated beams of light. You have seen the documentaries about their use in surgery? Well this is the end of the line. The x-ray laser is way ahead of its time and is the culmination of ten years' work by some very bright people and me!'

'You are serious.'

'I am indeed. Star Wars and all that, don't you know?'

The pilot slowly walked the length of the aircraft, running his hand across the smooth carbon-reinforced titanium of the main bogey pylon as he passed it. High above him the gentle fluted underbelly transformed itself into a series of deep channels that would force the airflow into the huge engine intakes, each big enough for a man to stand up inside. In effect the whole underside of the fuselage and wing formed the channels, with trailing edges notched for hypersonic airflow. He turned and walked back past Allison towards the steps that were hooked into an open hatch twelve feet back from the cockpit windows, and began to climb.

Once at the top he didn't enter the hatch, but leaned back and looked down the length of the smooth black body. The upper wing surfaces were also ridged with fine straight strips just proud of the surface. Five-sixths of the way out on each wing there was a vertical stabilizing fin at eighty degrees to the main surface. Below him and within reach was the starboard canard wing, with the obligatory red-stencilled NO STEP instruction. He looked forward and, regretting his civilian gear, made do with just looking. He was far too professional to enter the aircraft without the ultra clean flight suit that would prevent any foreign object damage. More than one aircraft had crashed after a coin or paperclip had fallen into working parts from the cockpit.

'How much fuel does she lift off with?' he shouted down.

'Just over a hundred thousand pounds,' Allison called back.

Jesus! he thought, over seventy-five tons of fuel. He had never flown a multi-engine before, and this was one big aeroplane. He climbed down slowly.

'We have a simulator: your predecessor thought it was very good. We built two cockpits right at the start, because every time Lucy goes up we risk being noticed,' Allison advised.

Carson looked up again from the ground and then back at his guide. 'What happened to him?'

Allison barked a mirthless laugh. 'Believe it or not, he was knocked down by a car on a quiet Camberley street. Never liked Camberley. Erich was good, I liked him very much . . .'

'Did he do notes?' Carson asked.

'Sorry?' The question had shaken Allison from his memories.

'Notes. Test pilots make notes. All the time. Handling characteristics, operational procedures.'

'Yes, yes he did. There are some on tape as well. He sat down after every flight and transcribed from a voice tape.'

'I want to see them as soon as possible,' Carson said, 'and I want to see the simulator. I want to talk to everyone who has anything to do with this aircraft.' His voice was crisp and authoritative.

Allison grinned, straightened his tie and did up the buttons on his blazer with a flourish.

'Step this way, and allow me to take you to our venerable Mr Sagan, who has thirty-six typed pages – single spaced, I might add – of programme for you to complete. I do have some bad news for you, however.'

Carson looked at him. 'What?'

'Lucy is a twin-seater. I am your systems operator.' His tone was serious.

Carson raised an eyebrow. 'Have you been up in her?'

'No, not as yet. All flights till now have been tests only. I did, however, design the laser system and helped write the software that runs it. I am essentially an engineer.'

Carson said nothing, but began walking back towards the doors and then turned back to look at the aircraft. 'How fast does a missile go . . . how fast do we have to go to catch one and shoot it down?' he asked.

'They go up into low earth orbit in a parabolic arc. We don't have to catch them. We can't do that but we can get them as they go over. We designed this aircraft to look for Mach Twenty at least. Double what she has done in tests so far; who knows?'

Carson just stood and looked in silent awe at the huge black shape and finally a smile appeared.

'You said she has a stealth capacity?' he said to Allison. The other nodded.

'I've got a new name for her,' Carson said. 'The radar signal hits and sticks, right? Nothing bouncing back?'

Allison nodded again. 'Yes.'

'She's black as pitch, and whatever hits sticks like shit to a blanket. She's the "Tarbaby".'

Allison laughed out loud, a clear, infectious sound. 'My God, an erudite New Zealander. Uncle Remus, no less!'

'We don't just shear sheep,' Carson answered smiling.

'Tarbaby, I like that . . . come, I'll show you up to Gail's Star Trek set-up.'

From the hangar it was three flights of steel stairs and another neon-lit passage to the control room where another steel door hissed back to admit the pair. Once

77

again Carson stood and looked without saying anything for a moment. Before him, high on the end wall, stood a huge high-resolution video screen. Either side were banks of monitors rather like in a television studio. Twenty feet to the front of the screen was a central control desk set three feet off the floor on a raised dais. Built into the desk were three radar screens, the centre larger than the two outside screens. A series of switches, dials and rack-mounted electronic gear set into the surface of the desk lay silent beneath an overhead light, dimmed and soft. Either side and just behind the main desk stood similar consoles and behind those stood banks of computer hardware. Along each side wall rows of walking booths gave access to miles of circuitry, wiring and systems. To the left of the main console behind a glass wall Carson could also see a second computer and a row of fax machines, computer printers, professional reel-to-reel tape-decks and other hardware, obviously communications equipment. He whistled softly. 'Jesus. It's like something out of a Bond movie.'

'Most of the facility existed,' Allison said. 'Some whacky mining project of many years ago. They dug the tunnels and the caves and it was then taken over by the Icelandic government. We simply did a few alterations and brought the gear in. It takes three of Tavis's people just to keep this set-up running. Ah, here's Gail.'

Carson turned as a door behind them opened and the tall brunette smiled a greeting at them. 'Hi! You're just in time. We are going to fire up the systems and run some access checks.' She stopped by Carson, a clipboard held defensively across her chest. 'What did you think of her?'

'Looks good,' Carson answered carefully.

'She is good. Erich said she was the best,' Gail flashed back.

'We will see.'

'Erich said . . .'

'Look,' he interrupted gently, 'I'm a test pilot. I will make my own judgements. She looks good, that's all I'll say till I've flown her.' Shit, what am I saying, he thought. Fly it? Jesus. I fucked up at Mach 1.5. Mach 20? He felt a ripple of something, unease, guilt, something.

'Why are you so defensive?' she retorted.

'All this hardware doesn't matter a shit if that aircraft isn't right and I'm the bastard that has to fly it, so allow me my little anxieties.' He finished the statement with a smile that took her off guard. She softened and moved a hand up to push a wisp of hair behind her ear in a very feminine gesture.

'Sorry,' she said. 'We've been working very hard down here, and we're all a bit tired . . . come and sit down, and I'll run you through the systems as we warm them up.'

Two men Carson hadn't met entered a moment later and with Gail Samuels they began the start-up routines working from a checklist on the clipboard she held. Within ten minutes the rows of racked equipment had come alive, power indicator lights blinked on and cathode ray tubes brightened in the still dim light.

'The main screen has as its first function the data coming in from our satellite. We put a surveillance satellite into geosync orbit last year. It sits over the North Pole, which is where we expect to begin your intercept run. The data is fed in by a graphics computer which gives us very friendly images.' She flicked a switch on the desk as Carson walked forward, and the main display came alive with a geopolitical map of the top of the world in various shades of blue. He could pick out the Alaskan coastline, Newfoundland, the top end of Russia and the huge mass of Greenland. The centre of the screen, obviously the polar ice-cap, was a different shade of blue, the satellite being able to differentiate the surface mass. So that's where it will happen, he thought. Christ, it will be cold up there, death at seventy degrees below if you had to bang out into that lot. He wondered if the Tarbaby had ejector seats and how did you eject at Mach 10 anyway. He could see small bright blue dots moving slowly across the lower edge of the screen.

'The machine establishes speed and works its identification from that. These blips are commercial aircraft on the polar route. We can then select any of the screens in the room and project the image up on to the main display or one of the peripheral monitors. My console has output from your onboard scanners. Fore and aft for six hundred miles. The rest of the pictures come in from the satellite or from other sources.' She paused and Carson took the opportunity to speak.

'What other sources?'

'We have access to five American satellites, three Russian, one French and two British. In addition, we have data coming into the comms room from everything from the phone to radio transmissions and facsimile.'

'Jesus! How did you get into a Russian satellite?'

She smiled. 'Once data is transmitted it is easy to get at, and we have some very clever people who look after our interests. Back to my console. It also has the sat pix and a few other bits and pieces. The other two,' she turned and walked back a few paces, 'are more specific in their application. The one on the left handles all Russian Air Force movements and the other Eastern European traffic. The operator is ex-Red Air Force. The other side watches US traffic including the carriers. The idea is I watch the missiles and they do risk assessment on the other stuff.'

'Hold on, how can one desk track all US Fleet movements? The bloody carriers are all over the world,' he asked sceptically.

'The data for that desk comes direct from the US military, only they don't know,' she said, and Carson laughed at the sheer audacity of it all.

'The other two screens can give me their images at my console as necessary. We also have a complete systems analysis facility for the aircraft, a bit like they use at NASA.

Often we will know when something is amiss as soon as you will.'

'It all seems a bit like overkill, if all you are doing is guiding me in on my targets,' Carson commented.

'It seems that way, but don't forget lots of this is comms gear, and lots of it is duplicated. Once the action starts, God forbid, it's the girls backing me, and you. The rest are here to advise on their specialities and issue policy.'

Carson looked up at the big screen again and tried to picture a wave of fast dots that would herald the end.

'How much warning will we get to scramble?' he asked softly.

She smiled at the expression before answering. 'We think that we will get as much as two days on some type of standby, and then as little as thirty minutes to get you on your way to your loiter point.'

He stood looking up at the blue-imaged map trying to imagine the chase, one interceptor, maybe three or four hundred missiles, head-on, closing speed, twenty thousand miles per hour, no, it would be a chase or, worse, an intercept from below, have them fly into his gunsights, fucking lasers no less, hope no one has any kryptonite or this superman might just want to stay at home and hide under the bed while the superpowers blast each other into hell. Jesus, this is like some sci-fi plot. Warp speed and Jedi knights. Won't ever happen. She cut into his thoughts with a short remark.

'They will be red.'

'Sorry?'

'They will be red. The computer sorts and identifies by airspeed. Those blue contacts are commercial traffic, all subsonic. Anything supersonic is upgraded to a yellow. Hypersonic or ballistic speed goes to red.'

He nodded his understanding and then asked the obvious. 'What am I?'

'Flashing white, it stands out the best against the blue,' she explained. 'Also your trace is not purely radar because of the stealth kit. You have a transmitter on board that emits ultra high frequency clutter a bit like an aurora. Our hardware sorts it and plots you. To anyone else it would just be atmospherics, so I'm told.'

'How good are you and your girls? On the level!' His voice was almost inaudible. 'This is no standard scenario.'

Gail's reply was equally serious.

'Polly Smith is my relief. She has nerves like steel and is the best controller I have ever seen. Christine Walker is the operator on the West desk. She has never been beaten playing computer games and used to be an analyst with *Jane's*,' naming the world authority on aircraft. 'She can take a mass of data on three screens and two VDUs, explain it and knit all at once. Andrea King is from the same mould and sits alongside Natalia Korov who was, until recently, a controller with the Red Air Force. Natalia can watch a squadron take off and tell you who is the boss by what formation they adopt at what time. And then there's me . . . I am better than Polly because I hate to lose. I can guide you in on a falling pinhead and have it cross your line of fire. It's the best ground support team that has ever been put together. We have one chance, one aircraft. So, Mr Carson, how good are you?' She held him in a direct gaze, her eyes clear and strong, her jaw set firm.

He shrugged. 'Me? I'd rather be diving than getting involved with this madhouse, but if you have to have a pilot, then it might as well be me.' Ain't going to happen, so why not, he thought. 'I'm as good as you will get, because I don't like losing either. I have six thousand hours on fast jets and I can fly anything that has wings. But up there?' He paused, the nonchalance gone, deadly serious, 'That's when you see the difference, where the air is cold and thin and lonely and you live by your reaction speed, that's when you know if your controller is any good. You put me on the target clean, and providing my systems work, I'll deliver. Deal?'

Just fly it once or twice. Push the envelope. Go higher,

faster than anyone outside a space programme had ever gone before.

'Deal,' she replied.

'Lunch?' said Allison. 'All this verbal jousting gives me an appetite.'

The meal was served in a large cafeteria a short walk along one of the passages that led into the accommodation area. The whole place reminded Carson of diagrams he had seen illustrating nuclear shelters, with their huge extractor fans and air scrubbers, generators and power units, completely self-contained below ground. The atmosphere in the café was noisy, with lots of good-natured laughter. Carson followed Digby Allison and Gail into a short queue at the servery where they were joined by Sagan. Other introductions followed. It being a Sunday, various members of the team were going above ground for some of the watery northern sun and relaxation.

'Are you coming up for some vitamin D?' Allison asked jovially.

'I'd like Erich Stadle's notes,' Carson replied.

'I'll bring them up,' Allison said, taking Carson's bag. 'Now let's take you to your quarters via the rest of the warren.'

There was a library with hundreds of tatty paperbacks and a respectable selection of reference volumes stacked up around four very comfortable club chairs. There was a games room with a card table and several writing desks. 'The ping-pong table got ditched,' Allison explained. 'No one used it.' There was a small gymnasium with a running machine and a Nautilus machine that sat gathering dust.

'We will be using this,' Carson said with a wry smile at Allison's expression of horror; he was quickly moved on to the video room where new movies came in each week. A large living room with satellite television dominated the end of that passage level and they dropped one level to the suites.

Carson's had a large sitting area with a desk and a

sensible queen-sized bed pushed against one wall, a bathroom off to the left. Three or four books sat on the shelf over the bed alongside a picture of a pretty girl in a thick, brightly-coloured sweater. A pair of chamois gloves lay discarded on the desk alongside an old Zippo lighter and a Swiss Army knife. Carson had taken rooms like that before and knew whose property it had been before Allison moved forward apologetically.

'Terribly sorry, old chap, these should have been removed. Erich's. I don't suppose anyone knew what to do with them.'

'Leave them,' Carson said softly, and Allison stood back and seemed to understand as Carson picked up the picture of the girl in the sweater and began to wipe the dust away carefully with his cuff. She looked a lot like Olivia. He always felt like an intruder when moving into a dead man's quarters and somehow accepting bits of the previous life eased the feeling.

'I'll see you up there, shall I?' he said, and as Allison left he settled back on the bed and gazed up at the ceiling deep in thought, still holding the picture, the memories of Olivia vivid. The way her hair waved and shimmered in the sun, her strong, clear, ringing laugh, soft eyes. He wondered briefly where she was now, and who with. It didn't hurt any more, that pain was over, but he did miss her sometimes. Missed what it could have been.

By two o'clock he had found his way up the stairs to the deep quadrangle between four of the Nissan huts that formed a sun trap where half a dozen Omega staff lay in deck chairs in various states of undress. A tape deck played Dire Straits and the only fully-dressed person was the security man who sat on the roof of one hut with a radio to his ear to warn of any visitors. Carson found a chair and quietly pulled the thick notebook and ring binder from the bag that Allison had given him. In the bottom of the bag he also found five audio tapes, one of the executive-type dictation recorders and a playback unit. He began with the notebook. Its dog-eared pencil-scrawled pages of jottings and remarks in diary form would provide the best informal briefing that Carson could expect from the only man who had flown the huge black hypersonic interceptor that waited deep inside the rock face for all the world like one of the missiles it was designed to hunt and kill.

The first few pages were observations of start-up procedures as the engines were run up for the first time in the airframe: warm-up time, thrust at idle and a dozen other observations, including instrument defects in the cockpit.

He was disturbed by a cheerful 'Hi!' and he looked up. A stocky, chunky girl with short blonde hair, bright blue eyes and a tanned freckly face looked at him.

'I'm Chris Walker,' she said and smiled widely. 'I'm on the . . .'

'Russian or Western desk?' he replied.

'Western . . . you the new saviour of the world?'

Carson laughed softly and closed the notebook, pleased with the relief and dropped it into the bag.

'The right honourable forgot to introduce me this morning,' she said, dropping into a chair beside him.

'Who?'

'Sir Digby. He's a baronet, you know,' she produced a pair of large pink sunglasses and placed them on the end of her nose. 'Terribly bright,' she added, mimicking his Cambridge accent. Her own was mid-Atlantic, originally American but now softened by exposure to Europe.

'Bright enough to know that if he introduced me to everyone I would never have remembered their names . . . now, however, I will remember you for ever,' Carson said gallantly. She smiled her thanks and began to point out others he hadn't met, prone forms in deck chairs and on loungers. Presently the conversation came back to the project and the notes in the bag at Carson's feet.

'What was he like?' Carson asked. 'You've seen a few pilots in your time – what did you think?'

She took the glasses off for a moment and became serious, running a small hand through her hair before answering.

'Erich was good. Technically very good, almost too much so, if you know what I mean. I have always believed that engineers and pilots are a different kind of animal. Erich was more engineer than pilot . . . don't get me wrong, he was very clever, but he didn't have that certain thing that I had come to expect in fast jet types. He didn't have that arrogance about him. He was a lovely man, soft, kind, but not competitive enough for me.' She looked at Carson to see if he understood. He seemed to because he nodded at her silently.

'How much credence should I give his notes . . . should I start from the word go myself?'

'Shit, no. They will be deadly accurate. Don't you alter anything yet.'

'Are they that good?' he asked, pleased.

'They will be good, and better than anything you would do,' she answered honestly, her eyes crinkling with her smile. 'Because this time they got the right kind of pilot and your notes would be messy, illegible. You're a fighter pilot, not an academic.' She smiled again, hoping to ease the offence he was bound to take.

Instead he laughed softly. 'You're right,' he said. His first ever commander had once likened him to a street fighter amongst the Queensberry Rules set. 'You think it will ever happen?'

She looked at him. 'Honestly? No I don't. But the potential is there. The ability is there. So someone must make sure they can't actually make it happen.' She paused and lit a cigarette, blowing the smoke out with some satisfaction. 'Seems incredible, but we can. Those of us here, all those who helped. We can make sure it never happens. Personally I wonder how long we can sit waiting for them to try? It's simply not practical to think it might be indefinite. I think we should take the fight to them. Force them to disarm the nukes. Then we can all go home and sleep in our own bloody beds. Anyway. We are glad you are here. Once you are up to speed we can stand down.'

'Stand down?'

'Yeah. The old boys reckon we will get notice. A few days at least. Increased tensions over some incident or other, I suppose. Anyway. Long enough for us to be recalled. A few people will stay on the base and the Icelandic military move much closer in and provide the security.'

Digby Allison arrived then, bare-chested, a towel around his neck and teardrop glasses on his long nose. His hair was brushed back in the style of the fifties and it seemed to suit the baggy trousers he wore.

'Hello chaps . . . jolly good. See you've met, then.' He dropped back into a chair with an audible groan that had several others peering at him away from their books.

'Just chatted to Karl. You have a medical this evening and start playing with the simulator tomorrow.' He began to slap suntan lotion on his white skin with vigorous smacking noises.

'What,' Carson asked, 'is a guy like you doing out here?'

'Ah! Yes. I wonder about that myself sometimes. Toffee-nosed bastard with family money and a brace of Purdeys out here with the great unwashed?' He sat up, draping his long bony arms over his knees, and thought for a minute before answering.

'I thought once it was some guilt at my privileged back-ground. That was for about five seconds. My sentiments lie with the others here, obviously, but it was more than that. I went to Winchester and then Cambridge, but found even that had its limitations. Ended up pursuing the really clever applied physics people into MIT. Suddenly I had discovered something that I liked and I was good at, and it didn't really matter where you came from or what your background was.

'I was being judged on my merits rather than my background and it was a delightful change after England. My sister, bless her, has married a chap I was up at Cambridge with. He's now in the right kind of regiment, with the right kind of future. Maybe it's something you can only say from a position of strength, but I found that all immeasurably boring. So I tootled off to the colonies and began working with a very clever German girl. A couple of years later and we had it cracked. It's funny but we both knew it was too important to talk about. Sigrid was my one true love and turned out to be a lesbian,' he said wistfully. 'Magnificent woman, mind like Einstein and legs that went on for ever. But I digress.' He sat back and lowered his head with a sigh.

'Where is she now? Your Sigrid?' Carson asked.

'Last heard of she had taken to drink in Bangkok. She ran off with some chap's wife who subsequently ran off with a bar girl. Why is it that the really brilliant people seem unable to muster one iota of common sense?'

'Darling, if you had any it would hardly be common,' Chris said, imitating his accent.

'Touché,' Allison chuckled.

Carson's medical was a full two hours of prodding, cardiac tests, pacing on the machine in the clinic, responses, reaction tests and eye charts under varying light. He eventually drew the line when Neilson pulled on a rubber glove and was reaching for the lubricant jar. Carson shook his head firmly and started getting dressed.

'You can forget that for starters, and you shouldn't have a problem with anything else.'

'If you are going to spend hours in a cockpit I want to know you don't have haemorrhoids.'

'I don't. What do you know about the physiology of the body at high speeds?' Carson asked.

Neilson smiled to himself as he removed the glove and raised an eyebrow as he turned to face the pilot. 'As much as anyone, we did some work at NASA on it, but I'm the first to admit we know very little. Cockpit ergonomics have you sitting virtually upright for high acceleration sequences and lowering again for aerial manoeuvres. That's as far as we have got with thermo-pressure G-suits and conventional thinking on the subject. I'm afraid it's going to be suck it and see. We are going into speeds never experienced in level flight ... oh sure, the NASA people have all gone hypersonic, but that's straight up, no manoeuvring and no punch other than the initial burn sequence. All we can do is try it bit by bit, and have you as fit as possible.'

Carson tucked in his shirt and looked at him.

'That's what I thought,' he said.

He woke Digby Allison at five the following morning and stood in the Englishman's doorway dressed in tracksuit and trainers.

'What are you doing?' Allison asked groggily, hung over from his habitual evening's intake of Highland malt.

'Going for a run, and so are you. On your feet,' Carson answered pleasantly. Allison groaned out loud.

'Come on, move it.' Carson pulled the blankets back.

'Christ, Peter, let me sleep,' he pleaded.

'On your feet, Digby, you want to be my wizzo, now you run, you push weights, you lay off the bottle, you get fit ... on your feet.' He pulled Digby to a sitting position. 'I'll see you at the rat hole in five minutes.'

'I haven't run since I was at university,' Allison said, rubbing his face, 'and I don't even know what a wizzo is, so let me die peacefully.' He fell back on the mattress with a groan.

'Then I'll bloody tell you, you drunken arsehole,' Carson snapped. 'A wizzo is a weapons systems operator. You have to be as fit as the jock, because you have the same pressures on your cardio-vascular system and you black out and you red out just like us. If you can't operate my systems then you are fuckall good to me. Now, on your feet. We run every morning, every evening till we are both fit. You lay off the piss, and I mean any consumption that leaves your faculties impaired.'

Allison looked up at him, realizing he was serious, then struggled naked and swaying to his feet. 'Point me to my wardrobe, I think I'm going to be sick.'

They ran in the pre-dawn darkness along the airstrip, a guard watching from the Nissen huts. By the end of the first five hundred yards Digby stood, his chest heaving, trying to catch his breath as Carson jogged into the dark away from him. An hour later they had showered and changed and were eating breakfast in the deserted cafeteria.

'You don't rate us very highly do you?' Digby asked around a mouthful of toast.

'No,' Carson answered.

'Care to explain, old chap? We thought we were doing quite well.'

Carson shrugged sardonically and sipped his coffee before answering.

'Your gear looks good, like an enlarged carrier's ops room. The Tarbaby? She looks good, too, but I'll say more when I have pushed her a bit.' He was holding back and Allison knew it.

'What else?' he asked casually.

'The problem lies in the personnel. Technically you all seem competent, but this base has the wrong feel about it. It doesn't have the buzz a reaction unit should have. The rooms are dusty, it doesn't feel like it should. I have money to bet that the tech crew have never trained to turn round the Tarbaby, rearm and refuel. You are academics,' he used Chris Walker's term. 'This base should be run by operators – that's why designs are taken away from designers, because they keep working on the item and never operate it. You people are still working on this, and unless you begin operating we will never get on to target in time.'

Allison nodded and bit into his toast. 'I think that's because we are hoping we never have to,' he replied, his jaws working around the words.

'Then it's money wasted,' Carson said.

'Not entirely, we are not without influence. We shall lead off for change and the others will follow. You shall have your turn-around drills commence at once,' he said. Carson looked up; Digby was serious. 'That's all?'

'All what?'

'All that's wrong?'

Carson looked at him. How do you explain the relationship between the P1 and the back seat guy?

You don't have to like each other, but you must respect them, trust their judgement, know they can do their jobs. You have to have faith in them. He hadn't warmed to Digby, but that was superficial and personal. What was more important was that he trust him. That was earned in many hours of training over weeks and weeks. In the air force when you got a new back seat man you at least knew that he had been through the system, what he knew, what he was trained for. Digby was a civilian. A pointy head. He had no more right to a place in the other seat on a sortie than anyone else in the building.

'For the time being.'

At eight that same morning Carson began his simulator training. The facility was the size of a shipping container mounted on hydraulic legs that moved in sync with the controls inside to simulate the movements of an aircraft. If the simulator looked basic from the outside, from the inside it was exactly the opposite. As Carson stepped off the access ledge into the narrow hatch the technology was overpowering; banks and rows of switches, lights, indicators, light-emitting diodes, small cathode tubes, glass flight instruments set into a black plastic fascia. There were two seats, side by side, wrap-around and each with a series of control knobs for rake and angle ensuring operator comfort. Carson swept his eyes across the layout, absorbing

91

what was standard in modern jets and lingering on what was new.

The seats were set low, and as Carson ran his hand round the hard Kevlar wrap-around frame towards the front he felt the new composite fireproof fabrics that he knew covered the latest in body heating systems. He lowered himself into the left-hand seat and ran it forward with the electric controls tight under the panel mounting all the primary flight instruments, his feet settling on the rudder controls naturally, finding the angle steep. He lowered the seat a couple of inches and felt more comfortable as he heard the operator enter the hatch behind him. He ran his hand lightly over the bank of throttles set into the port side fire-wall, as his right hand found the short, pistol-grip-type control column that lined up perfectly with the natural position his arm found as it lay along the armrest. Ergonomics are good, he thought, very good. He had never liked the left-handed grip that had found its way on to commercial aircraft in recent years, but computerized fly-by-wire had forced that on pilots. Airbus crews had grown to love it, he had heard.

'How does it feel?' a voice said, the operator.

'Good, I was expecting something out of *Star Trek*,' Carson answered.

'My name is Jorgensen,' the other said with a flat midwestern accent. 'I'm here to run you through the first hours. The layout is as conventional as we could make it. Pilots in our experience don't like surprises.' He smiled across as he slid into the right-hand seat.

'Roger that,' Carson chuckled back. 'Where did Oslo find you?'

'Under the dust in a McDonnell Douglas development lab. I did the layout in the F-15 and promptly got forgotten,' he said casually.

'You fly?' Carson asked.

'Scares the shit out of me,' Jorgensen replied honestly, 'but in this I'm top gun! Okay, left to right across your vision . . .' and the initial briefing began. It was an hour before Carson was allowed to commence the start-up sequence; then, with Erich Stadle's notes clear in his mind, he went through his procedures, raised a thumb at an imaginary crew and pressed into the sequence.

From then on he spent five hours a day on the simulator, as Jorgensen pressed more and more complicated problems on to his panels from the control desk. Gradually, as Carson's experience grew, he became faster at reacting to the simulated situations, and his hands found the answers automatically. On the ninth day, Jorgensen switched off the lights in the cockpit, blacked-out half the systems and raised alarms on the remainder. All he got from Carson was a muttered curse as the simulator found straight level flight from its dive on what could only have been complete confidence from the operator. Jorgensen looked up from his controls at Leo Sagan and nodded just the once. Carson was the best pilot he had ever seen, by a long way.

For Carson the work was long and hard, and by no means as simple as it looked. The technology available from the boffins was a quantum leap, even from the new EFAs he had flown, and the radar simulator indicated the same advances. This system looked far better than even the Foxhunter the RAF had been developing for the Tornado. Many of the systems were completely new. The throttles he had run his hands over the first morning were a manual back-up only. The primary automatic system was a bank of touch-sensitive buttons that took the engines up or down by per cent of power, with a computer controlling the sequence back to the mighty scram jets. Take-off was on two conventional power units, the same used by the American B1 bomber, but with a complete upgraded re-heat facility. At just below Mach 1 the scrams ignited, giving the aircraft a performance that Carson found hard to believe. Supported only by Stadle's notes, from a re-heated take-off to thirty thousand feet in sixty seconds, and from thirty up to two hundred in an astonishing six and a half minutes. The take-off power setting was a laughable thirteen per cent of available thrust, and Carson hoped that the canards on the Tarbaby would help settle any instability. If not, at the speeds she was designed to fly at she would tear herself apart in milliseconds.

The further into the training Carson went, and the more familiar he became with her, the more his admiration grew for her builders, the men given the unlimited budget to build the aircraft of their dreams. Without actually flying her he grudgingly agreed to himself that if she was anything like the simulator, she was the ultimate machine for atmospheric flight, never to be re-created, because she could never be economically produced. She was a hawk in amongst the sparrows.

4

Washington DC, August

Karl Schoeman stood beneath a large birch tree, a straw hat on his head and a small pruning saw in his hand, and surveyed the extent of the problem while he puffed on his pipe. Edith had been complaining all year about the tree shading her kitchen and now in the fall as the days became cooler he would do something about it. All over the garden the deciduous varieties were tawny brown and dropping their leaves, the ground crunchy and rustly underfoot. He looked up at the offending branch twenty feet above his head and wondered how to get at it. The base of the tree was devoid of branches for the first twelve feet. What I need is to be twenty years younger and own a chainsaw, he thought.

He was still standing there when the car came up the drive. He recognized the familiar air-cooled note of Miller's ancient Volkswagen and waved a greeting as it pulled to a halt in front of the porch. The two of them then decided to mull the problem over with a case of beers and a stick of spicy salami that Schoeman cut with an old penknife. Edith was shopping in town and the pair indulged beyond what she would normally have allowed; when the beer was finished they began on a bottle of Jamiesons.

'I think,' Miller said between sips of the burnished Irish whiskey, 'that a ground strike is what you need. Come in low and slow, three hundred knots and give the branch a burst. Or even better, a shade denial weapon! A new branch of aerial weaponry. No pun intended.' He chuckled softly as Schoeman raised an eyebrow at him.

'If it's not down when Edith gets home, it will be dinner denial.'

Miller stood and glared at the branch from the porch among the mass of empty beer tins. 'Can't have that, old chap; give me the saw. I shall into the breach!' He balanced precariously on a chair on a table and, eventually reaching the bottom branch, climbed into the lower limbs. A Tarzan-like cry split the afternoon as Schoeman heard the saw rasp.

'Make sure you cut the right branch,' he called from his seat.

It was inevitable that Miller's trip downward after the branch had been cut clear would be more rapid than his ascent, and he landed in an intoxicated heap, his tie askew, his jacket covered in bits of bark from the tree.

'There you are then,' he beamed at his older friend.

'Here, take on some fuel,' Schoeman offered the bottle from the safety of his seat, happily puffing his pipe.

'Actually, I came over to ask you something, Karl,' Miller said as he walked over, brushing at his clothing with unsteady sweeps of his hand.

'Speak then, boy, speak!' He was clearly pleased with the sight of the branch on the ground and the last rays of sun streaming into Edith's kitchen window for the first time in three years. He knew what was coming. He had been aware that Tim and his daughter Sally had been seeing each other recently. A game of American football one afternoon had led to other things, and although the matter had not been discussed in the open, Schoeman knew they had seen a lot of each other. His daughter was normally very close-mouthed about her social life anyway, but complaints about the upkeep of her small flat in Washington that she only used at weekends were a hint.

'You know I have some leave coming up next week?' Schoeman nodded. 'Well, Sally has agreed to join me in Europe, take in some culture . . . when we get back she is going to move her things into my place,' he finished.

Schoeman said nothing, just looked away into the distance.

Miller spoke again. 'Wanted you to know before we did it. I don't expect your blessing, but if you have a problem with the arrangement I'd rather you addressed it with me, not Sally, who has been in a quandary over the whole thing anyway.' It was a new tone of voice, not his usual foppish manner of the archetypal upper-class Englishman, but stronger and more assured.

'She knows what she wants, that girl, always has done. Edith was the same. I appreciate your coming out in the open and telling me like you have, and no, I don't have a problem. You are a fine young man, Tim, and I know she's more than just warming your sheets. That's about as much as a parent can expect these days, anyway, what with drugs, AIDS, crime and what have you . . .' He passed the bottle across and the younger man took it.

In the office two days later Schoeman again pulled his HST theory file from the drawer and opened it out on the desk. It had been haunting him lately. Never had he been so sure of one of his hunches. He began to lay out the cuttings and notes across the desk and eventually stood over the array and pursed his lips in thought. It's not us. The Russians? Unlikely, although they had technical branches of their aerospace industries that were superb. No money for this sort of thing any more. It's not the Brits, they would have told us. Or would they? It's not the French: America had excellent intelligence in the Fourth Republic. But the technology exists and someone has built one. Who? he thought. Who has the resources? He sat down and began to apply all his years of knowledge on to a yellow notepad in a firm scholarly hand. It was a list of men in the business whom he would begin to contact, all specialists in their fields who would know the others in their specialization. There were seven names under the NASA grouping, four with Boeing, five with McDonnell Douglas. There were other names on the list, staff at Sperry, Racal, Rockwell, General Dynamics, Grumman, General Electric, Northrop and, finally, the name of a man who had once headed up the Lockheed skunk works in Burbank, California, a man that Schoeman knew was still working on their experimental fighter programme. If these men couldn't answer some questions, then night would not fall, he thought.

He picked up the telephone for the first of many calls he would make that day. It was the fifth call, to the development lab at General Electric, that first offered hope. Schoeman asked for their senior designer, a man by the name of Leadbetter, whom he had met at a conference two months before. After pleasantries the analyst got down to the question.

'Am I correct in assuming that a very fast aircraft on the drawing boards would have a new engine type?' he asked.

'Could be,' the other replied. 'We've just about exhausted the possible modifications for engines under production.'

'What would the new one involve, basically?' Schoeman asked. He knew the answer, but he didn't want to put words in the other's mouth.

'Scram jets, obviously, that's common knowledge. The problem is getting by the subsonic problem. It only really operates well over Mach One.'

'Got anyone working on it?'

'Sure, everyone has . . .'

'Anyone good, any real bright sparks?' Schoeman pressed.

'No, just guys moved on to that project. Had one, but he left a few years ago. Got head-hunted by some Italian outfit. No loss . . . he was a real prima donna.'

'Which outfit? I need to talk to someone about scrams. I'd like to talk to this man,' Schoeman said excitedly.

'Can't tell you, Karl, we don't know. Got some mail for him a few months ago, forwarded it to a PO box somewhere in Switzerland. That's all I know.'

'I thought you said Italian.'

'I did . . . but the mail went to Switzerland.'

'Can you give me the number of the box?' Schoeman asked.

Two hours later Schoeman, frustrated with the brick walls he was hitting, telephoned a man he knew who worked at Langley. They chatted for a while about their daughters, who were of an age, and finally the analyst broached the topic of the report he had written two months before.

'Don't know what you are talking about, Karl, haven't heard of any follow-ups to anything from your chow-line,' the Company man replied. 'Hypersonic, you say?'

'Yes. Do me a favour and ask about. It may have slipped through, but in my opinion, and recognizing that I'm not using the correct channels, it needs some follow-up.'

'Your people spiked it?'

'They did, but they have been known to get it wrong before.'

'Even so, Karl, you've done your bit. I wouldn't worry about it . . .'

'But I do. I have been in this business the better part of thirty years and in my opinion this is potentially the most exciting development since the F-19. If I'm right then someone has built an aircraft that makes everything else flying look like something the Wright brothers built. We are talking low earth orbit, New York to Sydney in two hours, and I'm damned if I'm going to be ignored by fools!' Schoeman paused for a moment. 'I'm sorry. I am due to retire next year. It seems my whole life has been building up to this and . . .'

'I understand.' The man at Langley wrote it on a pad of ongoing things to do. He, being efficient in his fashion, passed it on to his secretary to have the file pulled. There was none, and three days later she completed the regulation request and it was carried into the vast depths of the central filing facility, where it was dealt with in turn.

There was no priority code attached so it took a further four days to surface above ground in the requester's tray along with an American Express card bill, a batch of correspondence and a memo about the basketball club's events for the next month. After reading the memo, and pondering the American Express account, which she slipped unopened into her handbag, she finally held the microfiche outer in her hand, waving it like a fan in the hot still air. It was the next day before her boss sat at the reader unit and scanned the words and diagrams for twenty minutes before telephoning a colleague two floors below. The man joined them a few minutes later, looked at the reader's screen and uttered a low oath.

'Who is the writer?' he asked.

'Old Karl Schoeman at the Pentagon. Knows his stuff, so I'm told. Anyway, he called and asked why nothing had been done about this. Said I knew nothing but would follow up.'

'Which one of our arseholes down in sifting missed this? I'll have his balls in the wringer for this.'

'So you want it, then?'

'Yeah, it's probably nothing but it should have been at least followed up. That's why we have sifters.'

Edwin Raden was one of four operational division heads at Langley. He was a career intelligence officer, and had been head of station in no fewer than four overseas countries in his career, a career that had been faultless to date. He had maintained the correct apolitical stance, working happily for every administration because he was a firm believer in democracy. The eldest of his three children was now in university, and he and his wife attended their local church when his work permitted a Sunday at home. Two years before he had taken over the 'S' division. Its role was to monitor scientific developments world-wide and make sure that the USA was kept abreast of anything that could be either useful or threatening. It was Raden's people

100

who had watched with interest the progression of the digital audio tape, because ultimately it could cost American industry billions; they had watched the development of clone computers from Taiwan, the modifications to the Harrier in England, and the Zircon spy satellite which they were sure they still didn't have all the details on, however co-operative the Brits had been. They also watched the Russian submarine detection systems, optical fibre research, and had got hold of an Exocet missile guidance system that had malfunctioned, for the experts to establish why. The French didn't know, which didn't surprise him. His people now did know, but they hadn't told the French. His division was also responsible for the protection of information, like the Copperhead missile system, laser guided bombs and night-sights for the same, as well as commercially vital data.

He sat brooding in his office that Sunday morning, having just seen Karl Schoeman's theory on the microfiche reader and now held the developed negatives in photographic form on his desk. He brooded because with all their systems and their expertise, something potentially this big could slip through unnoticed. He was somewhat relieved to see that Schoeman didn't believe the Russians had built a hypersonic. His own information confirmed that, but they had been wrong before. All too often. He knew the USA hadn't built one, but it looked as if someone had, somewhere right under their noses. He didn't like not having the answers. All that was needed was some scare and if he didn't have answers to offer the politicians he would look stupid. Dot the i's and cross the t's. The secret of a successful career in intelligence. He pressed his intercom and asked his secretary to pull all the files on HST development in the domestic and international fields. 'Match up the names, who isn't round the trough, who hasn't been seen in the market for a while, get the Room 56 people on to that. Find out when Paul Hart is back in town . . . no, recall him. I want him on this HST thing.'

'Yes, Mr Raden,' she replied, her hand moving fast in shorthand flicks across the page.

Iranian Air Force Station, Bandar Abbas

Manu Shazahan was a careful man, his survival since the revolution proof of that. He was one of those men who thought clearly about things, formed his own opinions, but kept his own counsel until some chain of events drove him into the open and commitment. As he entered the darkened office of the base commander he was quite calm about what he had to do. Three days before a series of sealed orders had arrived from Tehran. He moved to the large grey filing cabinet, a legacy of the Shah's days of American purchasing, pulled open the third drawer and began to search for the cheap brown paper envelope he knew contained the orders. A bright high moon gave shafts of soft silver light to the task and it wasn't till he had sat at the desk with the folders that he switched on the cheap torch he had taken with him, and began to read.

As adjutant on the base he had access to almost everything and used the access to keep himself abreast of the madness. He hadn't been overly concerned with the war with Iraq – after all, he was an Iranian and they had started it. When it had all ground to a halt in a stalemate he had been relieved like everyone. What did concern him was the ongoing occurrence of acts of stupidity in the Gulf. They had no problem with the Saudis, or the Kuwaitis, or even the Bahrainis for that matter, but there were still others out there, others who didn't belong. American and British navies were patrolling the waters, protecting their ships from fast-boat attacks and mines laid by the Iranian Revolutionary Guard.

Manu Shazahan regarded the old Ayatollah, now dead, as a certifiable lunatic who, armed with the hysterical mobs of Shi'ites and the Guard, had been capable of dragging

Iran into a conflict they could never win, a conflict that would be their last. The new man was more moderate, but there were still factions of extreme zealots, men who worked to their own warped agenda, and now he knew from the rumour and the talk that they had a warhead, a nuclear warhead, bought in from the old Russia. He needed to confirm it one way or another and then to decide what had to be done. He held up one sheaf under the yellow torchlight and began to study the diagrams that lay stapled and innocent, his eyes narrowing with his increasing comprehension.

He had three sons and a daughter who lived with his wife in their small family home near Tabriz. The house next to his had been the family home for three generations and his grandparents had lived there until their deaths before the Revolution. Now his parents lived there, and the year before last he had knocked a hole in the wall and put a gate between the houses. He liked living there. He liked the weekends with his family and the warm feeling as three generations of the Shazahans sat round a fire on a winter's evening, talking and laughing. Anything that put that at risk became a priority for him and although he didn't fully understand the drawings he was studying, he knew that they were important. This was not something that could be passed on by word, as he had done before, but he would advise his father as he normally did. He would do what he could do, the elder Shazahan, teacher, scholar and of late philosopher by the fireside.

Manu stood and walked to the window and imagined the warm water lapping at the barren beach that overlooked the Straits of Hormuz. Across the Straits lay the Sultanate of Oman, and between the shores the tankers and cargo vessels plied their routes up into the head of the Gulf, bringing manufactured goods in and taking oil out. There were also the warships of half a dozen nations making sure the waterway remained open and the merchantmen allowed to pass unhindered as best they could.

103

He replaced the file exactly where he had taken it from and silently left the commander's office.

Minsk

Federal Security Service Colonel Rordino sat back at his desk, his feet up on the surface and listened to the tape that played back on the old reel-to-reel tape-deck perched on a scarred wooden table against the wall. He was wearing civilian clothing, elegant Italian trousers, a soft pure cotton shirt he had bought in England and Church's brogue shoes. He touched his steepled fingers to pursed lips and looked into the middle distance as the tape played.

'Again, Rudi,' he said to the sergeant, 'that bit there.'

They had recently uncovered a new source, an *istochnik*, at Minsk University. Most of their sources were tired and obvious but this new one was subtle and very, very fresh. The message left on the machine was one of many that day, most of which said nothing significant.

'Okay, transcribe it all, and let me have a copy of that one,' he said to the sergeant. The other nodded and was almost out of the door when Rordino looked up again.

'Oh Rudi, bring me whatever we hold on one Rabanov, first name Pyotr. He is a computer type.'

Suvlov nodded and closed the door behind him. Rordino's fingers found their way into their steeple again. *What have you been up to lately Pyotr, hmmm? You have been bowing before your fears for too long, you will be forced to your feet by your conscience and your intellect. You have come to the notice of our Major Rochenko and that was foolish, very foolish. You should have stuck to your world of pure logic systems, and not fallen into the mire of emotion and pride. You are about to do something to appease your guilt.*

He stood, stretched and, collecting his coat, walked down the stairs to where his car was parked on the street. He had a date later, a pretty shop girl from the town. She was married, but her husband was currently serving his fatherland on the Finnish border with a motorized infantry regiment. Rordino liked her long legs in the high stiletto-heeled shoes he had brought her from Moscow, and she was insatiable when most girls were asking him to stop. It was a good relationship. When her good-looking but rather bland husband was home he would help her with money so they could journey to Kiev, and he had promised her the use of a Black Sea apartment for the future. Always dangle a carrot. He wondered if Rochenko had a bit some-where. Probably married to some dreary frump, or hung around the ballet dressing-rooms hoping for a nibble at what the big fish left. He didn't like the dancers, they had thighs like steel traps and disfigured feet from the pointe shoes. He liked soft women and was looking forward to the evening.

Minsk wasn't so bad and it was where he needed to be. After the Khazaks. It had been kept quiet. His determi-nation to catch the deal going down wasn't just for arms. In the shipment there had been something far more valu-able, far more deadly. He didn't care about the assault rifles, or even the surface-to-air missiles. It was the other weapon hidden in a rubbish skip he was after. Beneath the plywood and fibreglass casing the shiny polished sur-face was the size of a five-gallon drum and heavy, very heavy. It was the inner sections of an SS-20 warhead, a thermo-nuclear device big enough to level a major city, irradiate a hundred square kilometres. There was still one missing.

At that moment Pyotr Rabanov was still at his desk in the development lab at the Ministry of Sciences, writing a report on a new piece of hardware from Japan. He had stayed late so as to leave after the late team had come on, two floors above. He had a colleague on the writing team that was responsible for updating the operator software on most of the large state-run computers. The team alternately worked on everything from the Red Army payroll through to the updates to the defence systems, and towards the beginning of each month, when all new programs were loaded, the teams worked split and double shifts to complete the workload.

Rabanov's friend was a bespectacled, hirsute, smiling chap whose clothes perpetually seemed to need ironing, and who cared about nothing except his craft. Suki, as he was called, was without doubt the most talented software writer in the Soviet Union, and was only held back from greater things by his complete disdain for politics and any kind of authority. Natalia mothered him without ceasing, something that fascinated Rabanov, because she wasn't the mothering kind. Once Suki had finished his work, the two of them would walk down into the old town and drink in a restaurant, one of the few that had not been influenced by the new government line on drunkenness. This place still served rough fiery vodka, so cold it was almost frozen, as long as anyone wanted when the normal restaurants would all be closed.

By three the following morning they were sitting wedged in the tight smoky atmosphere with the others of their ilk – night workers, some administrative types, and a couple of soldiers going on leave. The talk was loud and friendly and they were on to their second bottle when Pyotr leaned forward, his voice barely audible above the hubbub.

'Have you ever wanted to do something completely mad, Suki? Just once?'

'What's this we are doing, Petya? I'm to be at work again at seven,' he answered dryly.

'No, I mean really crazy. A blow for your beliefs, Suki.'

'Like what?'

'Like giving me access to the operator updates for Igor?'

'Why not just shoot myself and save them the trouble?' Suki replied without expression. While his voice was level, his eyes were not. They had widened like a pool of oil behind the lenses of his glasses. He sipped his vodka rapidly, gasped loudly as the fire entered his throat and looked over the table at Rabanov. 'I thought that was a very stupid thing to say, in case you missed the point.'

Rabanov wasn't smiling back. 'I'm serious, Suki.'

Suki Yalta didn't have very many friends, not like Rabanov and his wife. They had taken him in three years before when he had been posted from Moscow to join the new facility in Minsk. He had been unhappy and Natalia had fed him, introduced him to some of the single girls she worked with. He had played chess in the park with Rabanov more times than he could remember, and when his father had died it had been Rabanov who had been there. Friends like that you didn't make every day. He was a decent man in a world full of deception, an honest man in a world full of corruption.

'Why?'

Rabanov talked softly, careful to speak obliquely when others paid attention, and told his friend what he wanted to do and why. He told him of the group without naming them, stated their aims and what he knew. Finally his voice faded and he looked across.

'You want to corrupt the system . . . for how long?' Suki asked.

'I don't know. As long as I can, I suppose. Long enough for things to be done in the confusion,' Rabanov replied.

'It will need to be in the user program, unless you get in before the fact with the operator program and access by code or time-bomb.'

Suki was thinking aloud and Rabanov allowed himself to smile. He now had the best mind in Russia working on the problem, simply because it was there.

'You can't do it,' Suki eventually asserted.

'Why not?' Rabanov questioned.

'Because the access codes are very complex. Only eight of us can get in there, well, seven of them, and me. Only they think it's only them! It's very, very complicated, not a wet evening's hacking, anyway.'

'I want to try.'

'You can't do it, I'm telling you.'

Rabanov's face was crestfallen, and the disappointment washed over him in waves. He had expected trouble with it, but not a genius like Suki calling it impossible. Suki leant across and touched his hand kindly.

'Petya, I said you can't . . . I didn't say I couldn't.' He gave a cheeky smile through his tatty beard. 'Now, more vodka. What we will need is a logic loop, that will run the machine back and forth, looking for an exit instruction that isn't there . . . yes?'

The next day a tired but elated Rabanov telephoned the number he had been given. The voice sounded the same and as he spoke his introduction piece he heard a second telephone coming on to the line. Borkin, the head of Gulag, known to Rabanov as Borodino, spoke.

'My colleague is now listening. Go on.'

'It can be done,' Rabanov said simply.

'How soon, *tovarich*?' Borodino asked.

'It will be done over the next two weeks.'

'Good. From now on take your lead from one called Stravinsky. He will be in touch.' Borkin seemed to sense the uncertainty in the other and added, 'Don't worry, he is very good. I am old now, and will take a back seat, but I will be here if you want to confirm anything.'

'Stravinsky?' Rabanov confirmed more to himself than Borodino.

'Yes.'

The main North Eastern Defence System computer, Igor, had operator program changes every month. Operational updates were installed, new refinements included, and the latest alert codes loaded. The program was then dumped on to tape and transferred to the facility in Novosibirsk for reloading on to Igor's hard disks. The complex housing the main computer was impregnable, but for what Rabanov and Suki planned it would be as open as the steppes themselves. They were about to change the basic program so that on command from any keyboard in the line-up a code could set the main central processing unit on to a logic loop that would be inescapable. Each new decision from the alternatives on offer would revert into the loop again and be given a primary function code; no other work could be done till that process was complete. It took priority over everything, including its defence programs, radar image assessment, and missile activation sequences.

There was a keyboard and a modem line in Minsk by which, given a bit of subterfuge, the pair could access Igor and issue the codes to activate the primary workload, the logic loop, that would place Igor out of action until the new master operator programs could arrive from Moscow. That would be a minimum of seven hours, more like fifteen, if the usual things went wrong. Suki would also inject a couple of red herrings in the program, that were mere light relief to him, but would drive the duty technicians crazy trying to track the fault. Once into the task Suki thoroughly enjoyed it and finished with a little nursery rhyme popular, he was told, in the West, but with a local touch of black humour.

Tabriz, Iran

The room was large and spacious, its rough walls hung with fine silk carpets and small prayer rugs, some of immense value. A central fireplace with suspended chimney dominated the room, its huge stone hearth cool as no fire had burned since the last days of spring. Other rugs lay scattered about the floor, and in one corner of the room a western lounge suite offered real comfort. It was early evening and Manu Shazahan sat there with his father as they usually did before the rest of the family joined them for the evening meal. This was the time when they talked of things that would be unseemly to discuss in front of the other members of the family, like Manu's job and his concern about their future. They spoke in Farsi, a language as ancient as Central Asia itself, Persian, which Europeans had first heard two thousand years before Christ.

'What is it you thought you saw, my son?'

'I'm not an engineer, father, but it looked like a rack or cradle of some kind. Lots of electrical wiring specifications, too.'

'It is of concern because you don't understand it?' his father asked.

'No, because of the manner of its arrival. Anything that arrives marked top secret like that means no good, not for us, not for Iran and not for Allah,' Manu replied.

'Then we had better see what it is that troubles you. Bring a copy out if you can.'

Manu nodded. They had an ageing Ricoh copier in the office that would be ample for the job. He had done it before, copied papers for his father who handed them on to others not so impotent.

The following weekend, Ali Shazahan sat with the papers in a coffee shop in Tabriz, a small cup of Turkish coffee before him. His rendezvous was with a man who was a legend in the area, although few had met him. Half-Kurd, half-Turk, a smuggler, a trader, a guide through the mountains, Subotai Orkhan was the Oslo conduit out of Iran for anything that could not be transmitted by radio signal. He was a flamboyant, egocentric, moon-faced man of indeterminate years, who wore sheepskin jackets and claimed to have screwed half the women in eastern Turkey. He had one overriding passion in life, the mountains of Zagros, and he moved through them with complete disregard for national boundaries, be they Iranian, Turkish or Iraqi. This would be the fifth message this year that he had moved for Shazahan, and he was paid well by the Turkish textile manufacturer who received them in Istanbul.

It took him four days to make the crossing, dodging border guards of both countries before he got to his ageing bright yellow Chevrolet in Erzurum where he took money from the wheel bay and, smiling at the NATO troops like a village idiot, took a bus to the airport and caught the next flight to Istanbul. That evening in an Italian restaurant not far from the city centre he walked past the young, beautiful people of the moneyed middle class that most Turks claim doesn't exist, and found his contact at one of the tables. The man had his secretary with him, a pretty girl with large black eyes, who looked at Subotai as though he was an escaped criminal when he sat down with them. He leered at her and she vanished to the ladies' room wondering what on earth her boss had to do with a man like that.

Subotai passed the buff envelope across the table wrapped in a magazine and received in return a gift-wrapped parcel, the size of a packet of cigarettes. He stood, nodded once as the girl returned from powdering her nose and left the room. It was the last time the businessman ever saw Subotai Orkhan. He was finally intercepted crossing the mountains back into Iran, as all who knew him knew must happen eventually, and in the ensuing mêlée he was shot in the leg. He escaped into the high country and the troops decided not to follow for it was late and would soon be dark. It took the wiry, proud, little mountain man three days to die of septicaemia in a cold lonely cave, high above the snowline. The day after he died the original of the plans he had carried were spread on the large drawing table in the central engineering workshops at the Bandar Abbas Air Base, and a selected team of men from the staff began working on the fabrication of the designs.

Langley, Virginia

Paul Hart, the operative that Raden was waiting for, arrived back in Washington two days later and reported at Langley on the Monday morning. The weekend had been strained; his wife, frustrated by her inability to use her education in a meaningful role, had recently begun taking it out on him. He had warned her when she was halfway through her classical history degree that it was useless outside the schoolyard, but she knew better and had tossed her head like a filly taking a saddle for the first time. Three years on, her obstinacy, which he had originally found attractive, had become a barb in his side. Pregnant, she was cranky, uncomfortable and mercurial in her moods, not the warm blossoming image he had previously held of motherhood. The weekend had been a round of sharp clashes which he felt that he should have lost in deference to her condition, and in so doing, angered her even more. For him it was a no-win situation.

Three miles short of the main turnoff into Langley he lit his fourth cigarette of the day and inhaled deeply. He wasn't the normal type of employee of the agency, not in his mannerisms or appearance. He only owned one suit, and wore his blond hair longer than was strictly necessary or allowed by the Company. He had been in the army. For some reason he had joined up, done West Point after UCLA in the beginnings of the 'I'm proud to be an American' era that followed the first few years out of Vietnam. He had watched, appalled and enthralled, as Nixon was impeached, half-proud that he lived in a country where they could impeach a President, and half-ashamed of the need. His army career had been short. He had moved from Rangers across to Intelligence and then, jaded by it all, had resigned his commission, grown his hair and dropped out. But his skills had not gone unnoticed and he was soon recruited by the CIA. He had never cut his hair short or changed his style and now, years later, he was still regarded as a 'fucking hippie' by many of his colleagues and at times by his boss, who found out that Hart was quite capable of outright insubordination; if he believed an instruction was wrong he quite simply wouldn't carry it out. He was a man with morals and talent and a huge share of common sense, something that even the CIA needed sometimes, and Raden had said more than once that, given the right case, Hart was the best operative he had ever seen. He was a bloodhound, persistent, tenacious, methodical, and he was outstanding with technology. He was at home with the computers, the Internet and the technology of the nineties, disliked guns, and could do Rubik's Cube in twenty seconds.

Because he disliked guns, if necessary he was given two other agency men to work with, men who did like guns and the rough stuff, but Raden had made it plain from the start that he was the ranking officer to whom the two goons, as he described them, reported. They varied but more often than not he was given Leroy Chubb and Avery Oxenburger. Leroy was a tall, rangy black from the wrong side of Detroit, a man quick on the uptake who followed orders. He was the perfect foil for the dry-humoured Hart and very different from Oxenburger, who was no more than a lout in his eyes. The big midwesterner seemed to dislike everything that wasn't from Dakota, and was a complete bigot. He had a derogatory name for every nationality he could think of, and somewhere deep in his file in personnel there was a cruelty incident flagged in blue. Interrogation of a man in Bangkok had gone badly wrong, and the huge, frustrated CIA man had used his fists instead of his head. The subject had died in the squalid room, damp and smelling rancid like the waterway below. The second agency man had later confessed to their section leader that Avery Oxenburger had seemed to enjoy the power in his arms and the sickening thud as each blow split the small Thai's face further; the look of a psychopath, he had said.

Once, Oxenburger had tried it on with Hart, and Chubb, his street manners saying what was fair, stood back to watch. The contest that had seemed so one-sided, between the hulking brute and the tall hippie-like thinker was over very quickly. Amongst other things that Hart had studied in some depth was Tai Kwan Do, and his flashing foot had found the other man's testicles and adam's apple in that order in under two seconds. He had then lifted Oxenburger to his feet and explained that never again was he to lay a hand on anyone while he was in control, or his sex life, so often bragged about, would only be a memory. Leroy Chubb had smiled to himself and immediately dropped any reservations he had harboured concerning Hart.

He was waiting when the Californian pulled into the huge car park and watched his loose-limbed frame amble across the five-acre lot to report for his meeting with Raden.

'What's on, boss?' Chubb asked.

'Dunno. Wait in the canteen and I'll come down when I have the job. Where's Avery?'

'Down on the range. He has a new piece,' the black answered laconically.

'Penis envy,' Hart replied, and strode past him into the main block. Chubb watched him and wondered if he had had a bad weekend with the lovely, long-legged homecoming queen he had only seen photos of.

Hart walked into Raden's outer office with a half-smile for his secretary and went straight past her into the inner sanctum. She scurried out from behind her computer screen to intercept him, but too late; she had to make do with glaring daggers at the back of his Hawaiian shirt and Calvin Klein jeans, as he dropped into the visitor's seat at Raden's desk.

'Morning, Edwin,' he said cheerfully.

Raden looked up. 'How can you come in to work in a goddamn holiday shirt, unshaven, and wander, unannounced, into my office? Jesus, Paul, you really piss me off.'

'What have you got for me?' Hart ignored the outburst, and reached over for Raden's coffee which was steaming attractively. Raden beat him to it, snatching it clear.

'Get your own. Ever heard of hypersonic aircraft?'

'Yeah, sort of. One of the . . . Singapore Airlines it was.

114

Advertised them as the way of the future. London to Singapore in fifty minutes or something.' Hart turned to look out at the secretary and mimed a request for coffee with a charming smile. She glared back, snorted and flounced away.

'Well, an old boy at the Pentagon thinks someone has beaten them to it.' He pushed the file across. 'Now I have spoken to his boss who thinks it's bullshit and spiked it, but I want some comfort. The details here are scant, so fill in the gaps.'

'If the Pentagon thinks it's bullshit, and you seem to, then . . .'

'Just follow through. Okay? You're back from leave and I have got nothing else for you. Either prove or disprove the theory or you can find a desk down in commercial and I'll get someone else on this.'

'Naa. I'll do it.'

'Get what you need from personnel and advances. Anything else?'

Hart looked up from the open file.

'Yes, take Oxenburger off my hands, he's a liability. I'll take Leroy Chubb. He's enough if the cavalry want to charge or something.'

'No way. You keep them both. I haven't got a replacement for Avery.'

'I don't need a replacement. Just give him something else to do.'

'I said no. Three-man teams is standard.'

'Are standard,' Hart corrected.

'Just take him and get on with it,' Raden said tiredly.

The secretary arrived back and thumped a half-full cup on the desk.

'Sorry, no time for this, why don't you have it?' he said, standing to leave and smiling sweetly.

He told Oxenburger to take a couple of days off and requested an 'off-facility location', the CIA term for a house or apartment somewhere other than Langley. He was given a four-room office on the Arlington side of the Potomac. It was a dreary place with filthy windows above a shoe shop, but it had seven telephone lines, a fax machine, and a pizza take-away joint a block away. He moved in with Leroy Chubb the next day and they were moving desks around under the meagre lighting trying to maximize the effect of a faulty air conditioner when the telephone team arrived. The five individuals were moved from one task to another wherever telephone investigating would be the prime medium. Briefed and given the initiative, they could cover incredible ground. Three of the team were women, all ex-journalists, who could ferret out information faster than Hart could request it. The other two were trainee operatives who in the next few months would go into the field, this their final stop before the extended training session back at the covert ops school that qualified them.

Hart had worked with the women before and within an hour the phones were in full use. The task was split, one taking American aerospace companies, one the universities, one the air force and another NASA. The final member began listing international agencies that they would need to source to list the French, Italian, British and West German hi-tech manufacturers. Hart himself took Russia, leaving Leroy Chubb the other ex-Soviet bloc possibilities.

By five that afternoon a pattern had developed, and with pizza trays littering the floor and Styrofoam coffee cups overflowing the rubbish-bin, they spread out the day's results on the island of tables pushed together.

'Okay, what have we got? Mrs Collins first, please.' Hart sat back, lit a cigarette and closed his eyes to listen. She leant forward over the table.

'From seven aircraft manufacturers, over sixteen of their top brains dropped out of sight in the last ten years. I picked ten, because that's what we think it would take to get a thing like this together; anyway, of those sixteen, we have found six here in the USA. Two have retired, one's a drunk in a home in Manhattan, one now just plays golf

116

and one bought into a fishing boat in Miami. The last one died last year, we found him in a cemetery in Boise.' She sat down and peered over her glasses at Hart.

'Okay, check on the one with the boat. Is it the sort of thing he could afford on his earnings or have we a bonus of some kind here?'

She nodded and Hart turned to the next. Ten to go he thought.

The searching rolled into day two, and by the second evening they were fairly sure they had seven Americans, technically includable in any project to build a hypersonic, that really had dropped from sight for significant periods of time. Two had resurfaced back in the industry with money in their pockets. All the major manufacturers and agencies agreed that it was possible; no one had as yet designed an economically feasible hypersonic, but yes, there had been talk in the rarefied fields of advance design that suggested someone had begun looking at it, and not just with wind-tunnel tests. There was talk of very advanced work on hybrid alloys and exotic fuels, but no one seemed to know more than that.

Hart had set up a flip chart and begun writing what they knew on the big pages, and a girl had arrived with a computer terminal that they had hooked into a modem line back at Langley.

The people working on the international side had similar dead-ends. British Aerospace, Machi, Dassault, Saab, Aerospatiale had all made similar noises to the inquiries that were coming from magazines, newspapers and scientific and flying journals. By the third day they had begun on hi-tech affiliates, the avionics manufacturers – Racal, Marconi, Sperry, Rockwell, Decca and their ilk – and then moved into the ultra hi-tech world of aviation and aerospace computers.

The list of names grew, the ten became fifteen, and a second column was added, people from the industry in Europe who had also dropped out of sight. By the end of the week they had sixty names, all possibles to follow up. Hart was puzzled: there seemed to be no common denominator, no language, no flag, no age group. In the second week the team began tracing contracts issued for specific items to specialized manufacturers, but the task was now huge. Hart now had the bit between his teeth but he needed more resources. That meant giving Raden a reason and he knew Raden. At his grade promotion was on merit only. No time-served bullshit there. You needed to have a clean sheet and chalk up major brownie points on a regular basis. Raden hadn't had any for a year or two now.

'More people? No way. This is a standard technical follow-through. You already have more than any other job running. More? No.'

'Listen. We have loads of people who have gone to ground. Just disappeared and then reappeared. Americans, Brits, French, Italians. Some of the best brains in the world. The people it would take to pull off something like this. You wanted a follow-through. You got one. Tell you what I think. I think that the old bloke at the Pentagon might be right. Maybe someone is working on this. We need to know who.'

'Security implication?'

'Fucking huge until we know who,' Hart said, playing his cards slowly.

'Russia?'

'It's possible, but unlikely. They couldn't attract these people. More likely that it's the Brits or the French.'

'What if these people didn't know it was Russia who was the end-user? Like the Iraq supergun?'

Hart smothered his smile. Raden was hooked. 'This could be major,' he said. 'If it's out there we need to find it.'

He got his resources. He was given extra people and a second office just up the road over a launderette. He also pulled some favours and was lent a designer from Lockheed who sat with them and made a list of specialized areas of purchase where any group building anything new would have to go. Three agents were then put into the field to follow up and because they were all in the USA, each man had to be accompanied by someone from the FBI, who disliked the CIA working their home ground.

By mid-August they found themselves in a tangle of complex criss-crossing trails that all led nowhere. 'Christ!' Hart said, 'we have companies all over the world who have built things that could go into a brand new aircraft, and not one can tell us where it is now . . .'

Supposed end-users in Colombia, Panama, Holland, Belgium, New Zealand and a dozen other countries simply didn't exist, post boxes had closed, and office addresses were in streets that had been torn down years before. Many of the items had been collected upon completion, and others went to bona fide purchasers who did have addresses and a 'legitimate' reason to buy the components. They had records of purchases, but seemed unable to say who had ordered them, or paid for them, or where they were now. Hart's own resources applied to conventional intelligence records showed nothing taking place behind the Iron Curtain.

There were by now thirty sheets of paper stuck to walls around the original office. Lists of names, companies, countries, that all wove themselves together into a morass of conflicting data. Oslo, well aware that questions would be asked, had produced a complex series of alibis for their people who had re-entered their professions after time abroad, adding further to the problems experienced by Hart's team.

In the end, he reverted to the names of the specialists scattered the world over who they believed would have been involved, or would have known of any efforts.

Leroy Chubb, frustrated by the hours in the office day after day, finally requested and was granted permission to attend a refresher course back at Langley, leaving Hart to continue alone with the telephone team. He alone seemed tireless, a constant factor with his loud shirts and Gauloise cigarettes.

He recalled Oxenburger and sent him into Europe to chase up the first of the names on the list, two in West Germany and one in Italy, armed with a simple list of questions to ask and a warning not to be over-zealous.

5

Miller gently slipped from the warm rumpled sheets and crossed the parquet floor to the window. The shutters were closed and the afternoon light stole through in bright shafts along with the sound of the boat hooters and the occasional cry of a gondolier. Below, on the wide corniche, tourists moved in gaggles with guides, licking ice creams and fidgeting with cameras. The Hotel Gabrieli overlooked the waterway, its high ceilings and marble a part of a bygone age when Venice was part of the Grand Tour of Europe. Now she was just a proud old duchess sinking into the sea with footsore visitors trampling on her dignity.

Sally Schoeman sat up in the bed, a half-smile across her lips and pulled the sheet up over her breasts. 'Afternoon delight', as he called it, had become their ritual, and she loved to retire with him light-headed on wine and feel his weight on her. She ran a hand through her hair in that most feminine of gestures and watched his lean frame in the bright shafts of light at the window. His body shone with sweat and seeing it she realized that she was also hot. August in Venice, she thought and threw back the damp sheet and stretched cat-like on the mattress.

'Come here,' she said, in a low sexy tone, pouting and running a hand provocatively over her left breast, the nipple hardening under the caress. He turned and grinned at her.

'Stop behaving like a tart and get showered. We are going out.'

'I am a tart,' she said languidly, loving the Englishness of the word. 'Now come here and hump my brains out.'

'Said like that, how can I refuse?'

They made love till the sun dropped over the canal and cast its pink hues across the water, her long legs over his and her hair across the pillows. Finally, their bodies slippery with perspiration, a shuddering climax leaving them in deliciously peaceful closeness, she ran her hand through his hair and could feel his pulse in his chest as he slept.

They ate in a small restaurant in one of the alleys behind St Mark's Square, sharing lobster and grilled fish and another bottle of very dry local white wine, and walked in the moonlight to the hotel holding hands, Sally wishing the day would never end.

That night before bed as Miller stood under the shower singing to himself, Sally placed a call home feeling guilty at having left it four days before the first contact. By the time Miller was out of the shower and had re-entered the bedroom, a towel round his waist, Sally was beckoning him to the phone. Saying good-bye to her mother Edith, she held the telephone out to him.

'Dad.'

Karl Schoeman had never displayed openly the disappointment that Miller knew he felt when his daughter had moved in with him and luckily it hadn't affected their working relationship, so he took the phone with some pleasure.

'Karl, how's the seat of democracy?' he began.

They exchanged small talk for a few minutes before Schoeman came to the point.

'Would you mind doing something for me while you are in Venice? Seems a shame when you are there . . .'

'Delighted, dear chap,' Miller interjected.

'See an old friend of mine, he lives there. He is a fuel man, very clever with exotic mixes. He worked on the stuff they were using when the SR-71 cracked through the hundred thousand foot mark. He may know something about my hypersonic.'

Miller took the name and address and gave the phone

back to Sally, promising a visit the following day. He had a little smile on his face.

That same afternoon the stolen plans that had travelled all the way from Bandar Abbas arrived in Frankfurt on the Lufthansa flight from Istanbul, and were taken from a burgeoning pile and opened by an Oslo analyst who lived above a brothel in a new apartment complex. Within minutes he was down knocking on the door, which was answered by a friendly blonde from Munich.

'You are early, darling, but come in,' she said, a whore's smile across her wide open face.

'I need the phone, Gelda . . . it's important.'

Ten minutes later he was connected through four sets of relays to the house in Deia where Haidermann answered and listened without interrupting, watching the logging recorders turn, his face a mask of stone.

Miller rose early the next morning and went for a run along the wide concrete corniche, the newspaper sellers and restaurant staff shaking their heads at his madness as they opened shutters and laid out chairs under awnings. By eight, they were again walking the bustling alleys heading by dead reckoning towards where Miller thought Karl's friend lived. By nine they were lost, and Sally raised the brim of her soft straw hat and looked at him pityingly.

'Some navigator you are. Without a satnav you couldn't find the washroom.' She grabbed the tourist map he was holding and set off bravely, but she too became confused with the alleys and bridges, and finally, eating ice cream, they travelled by gondola arriving only a few feet away from the door they wanted minutes later. The old door was surrounded by flowers in pots and a creeper climbed up the crumbling damp wall. Miller rang the bell and moments later an old voice called in Italian from the courtyard, presumably, he thought, saying wait, I am coming.

She was a wizened old woman of indeterminate years,

her face lined and creased and her back bent. 'Signor Cassalto, please?' Miller requested. She rattled back at him until he held up his hand.

'*Non capisce.*'

'*Deutsch?*' she asked with some disdain, her old head cocked to one side.

'*Inglese?*' he replied hopefully.

'*Si* . . . to wait please.' She turned and walked back into the high-walled courtyard and was back a minute later with a scrap of paper. It had an address written on it.

'Melcesine,' she said thrusting it at him. 'American?' to Sally.

'It's a village on Lake Garda,' Sally said to Miller. '*Si*, American!' to the old woman.

She cackled, pleased with herself and then jabbed a finger at the tatty piece of paper.

'Cassalto, Melcesine . . . ?'

Miller nodded smiling.

'Your friend go yesterday . . . American, yes?'

Sally nodded vigorously. '*Grazie, grazie . . .*'

'*Prego,*' she cackled.

'It's a bit off the track,' he said over dinner that night.

'We have time, and besides Melcesine is supposedly beautiful . . . come on, let's get a car and drive up there. It can't be more than a couple of hours from here,' Sally countered, twirling her fork in spaghetti and holding her hair clear of the plate. He looked across at her as she lifted her head and gazed back, her eyes alive and sparkling and full of mischief as she sucked in the mouthful of spaghetti, one rogue piece flicking sideways against her cheek leaving a smear of bolognaise sauce at the apex of her smile. She wiped it clear with one finger, which she licked clean in a very appealing childlike gesture.

They drove up the next day, Miller grudgingly agreeing to the diversion, but looking every inch the touring gentleman in the drop top Mercedes they had hired.

Melcesine was a small village of narrow streets, cobbled and shady, tucked between the shore of Lake Garda and the massif of Monte Baldo. At one end of the town an old castle dominated a promontory over the lake, with the clutter of buildings moving southwards along the shore to the old harbour where launches took tourists on to the lake amongst the hundreds of windsurfers. They found a hotel above the water, the tenth they had tried, that at last could offer them a room, and the receptionist was able to direct them to the address scrawled on the piece of paper. It was on the shore within walking distance, and after lunch they walked the steep steps down to the lakeside path and counted the numbers down to that given.

It was a grand villa of some bygone age, complete with turrets and steeply pitched roof, bright in the summer sun with white walls and coloured shutters. The gate, cast iron topped with heraldic beasts, swung rustily back and Miller led the way up the path.

'This is a bit upmarket,' he muttered, revelling in the classically styled gardens. Small statues of cupids and nymphs sprayed water from an ornamental fountain and there was a smell of cut grass in the air. A small figure knelt by the base of the southern bay window weeding the rose beds, a broad straw hat balanced precariously on his head.

'Pardon . . . Signor Cassalto?'

The figure sat back and looked, small bright eyes peering from beneath large bushy eyebrows.

'The patron?' Miller tried. 'He is here?' He felt very ill at ease trying out his rusty Italian, especially with a gardener who might only speak dialect. The man stood, lifted the hat and brushed sweat from his brow with his sleeve.

'I am Cassalto,' he said.

'So, my friend Karl thinks someone has built a hypersonic capable flying machine?' Cassalto poured coffee into little cups on the silver tray, careful not to spill any. They were

125

in a sitting room and Miller could see into the study, a desk piled high with papers and a modern computer on one side.

'Yes,' Miller said. 'Sorry to trouble you, but he seems obsessed with it. Thought you may be able to shed some light.'

The old man looked across at Sally, tilting his head back to look through the bifocal spectacles he had produced from a pocket.

'And you are his daughter?' Sally nodded. 'Sorry,' his tone hardened, 'but you will have to leave. The Karl Schoeman I knew had no children.' His eyes had become resolute and his jaw set solid. Sally looked shocked for a moment and then her cheeks reddened and she stood up, looking very much like her mother, Miller thought.

'I am Karl Schoeman's daughter, and I have been for almost thirty years. I have taken time from my summer vacation to do something for him and it's now becoming boring. If you know anything about his god-damned aeroplane, which I doubt by the look of you . . . he can come and talk to you himself.' She looked at Miller. 'Come on, Tim.'

Cassalto sat back in his chair and nodded to himself, waving a hand at her.

'You are Edith's daughter, sit down, sit down. One can't be too careful these days. I had a visit only yesterday by another American, only he had your Central Intelligence Agency written all over him and I stopped doing classified work five years ago.'

Sally, somewhat mollified, sat down again, but only on the edge of the chair in case another insult emerged, her eyes still blazing. Miller acknowledged the comment about the CIA without expression.

'Sit, girl! I knew your parents years ago when you were climbing trees and refusing to wear a dress . . . now then what is it you want?'

Miller sat forward, keen to get on with it now the entertainment was over. 'Karl believes that if anyone in Europe could specify fuel systems and mixes for a hypersonic it would be you, or someone you taught in the last few years. He is very keen to verify what he knows in his heart exists.'

'And you, young man, what do you think?'

'Men have gone to the moon. The technology is possible,' Miller answered carefully.

'Cautious, but noncommittal.' The old man sipped his coffee. 'Do you fly?' Miller nodded. 'Then I will tell you what to tell Karl. To the best of my knowledge, none of my students have been involved in anything like that. Two are bright enough, but lack the vision . . .' he faded away for a moment '. . . sorry I could not be more helpful. But now, how is he?'

They talked for an hour before making their way back to the hotel. Sally, pleased they could now continue the holiday, asked at reception for a map of the lakes. Now they were there they might as well slip over to Como, a place she had never seen but had heard enough about to want to visit. They took the cable car up to the top of Monte Baldo as the sun began to drop, and watched the breathtaking views across the Alps all the way to Austria, the peaks soft in the evening light. Later they walked the narrow streets till they found a restaurant with not too many German windsurfers wanting bratwurst and Löwenbräu, and shared a pizza before walking the lakefront back to their hotel.

Just before three the following morning someone was banging on their door. Miller woke instantly and looked at his watch, its luminous dial clear in the darkness, then, wrapping a towel round his waist, went to the door. He heard Sally stir in the bed as he called out, 'Who is it?' He had been in America long enough to know not to just open the door to anyone, even when in Europe.

'Carabinieri.'

Miller opened the door, his hair dishevelled and eyes bleary.

'What is it, then?' he asked yawning. There were two men at the door, a small, rotund man in grey and a taller, younger man in a dark suit. Both showed him ID. He went into the corridor and shut the door behind him.

'You visit Signor Cassalto today?' The English was stilted and the accent heavy, but he spoke slowly and Miller had no problem understanding him.

'Yes.'

'Why? The reason for your visit.'

Miller was awake now. Alert. 'Aaah. He is an old friend of my companion's father. We promised we would visit him.' This was getting heavy. He had seemed fine when they left. Happy enough with Karl's question. Why call the police in? 'Ask him. He will tell you.'

'He will tell us?'

'Yes. Why not? We had coffee, talked.'

'What time?'

'Three o'clock, maybe half past three. Why are you asking?'

'You are sure about the time?'

'Near enough. It was mid-afternoon.'

'After that you did what?'

Miller stiffened slightly. 'I am not answering any more questions till you tell me what this is about. You can ask him to confirm the time. Or his housekeeper. She was there somewhere.'

The policeman shrugged. 'It was his housekeeper who confirmed that you were there. Cassalto was killed tonight.'

'Oh my God. Oh . . .' Miller was stunned for a second or two. 'I apologize for my behaviour. Of course I will answer any questions you like.'

Half an hour later they were gone, but Miller couldn't sleep and he lay in bed thinking. Finally he looked at his watch. It would soon be dawn. He got up, put on a tracksuit and trainers and slipped out for his habitual run. He took the steep path to the shoreline and began to jog round the

128

lake's edge, weighing up his chances of success as he went. The police hadn't said where the old man had been murdered. If it was at his house then it would be a crime scene and presumably guarded by the local police until they had completed their examination. If it was elsewhere then he had a chance. He got to the gate they had walked through the previous afternoon and carefully peered through. There were no signs of activity and the path was deserted. He slipped through the gate and up to the house, moving very carefully. It was quiet. With all the dramas it was quite possible that the place had not been locked up as securely as it might normally be and when he found an open window in the kitchen he looked up at the dark sky. Thanks, God. He climbed through the window and moving slowly and carefully made his way to the study that he had seen that morning from the sitting room.

The room was lined with books on three walls, the fourth dominated by a bay window and a monk's bench below the sill. The desk was in the centre of the room and he went straight for the computer, hoping that the old man had not bothered with passwords. He fired it up, delighted to see that Cassalto's security was like most home users', non-existent. Thanks, old fella. Finding a box of disks he began downloading files from the C drive. The machine was quite new and he hoped the five disks he had found would be enough. It took twenty minutes and, as he worked, he deleted the files he was copying. He wanted the only copies. He flicked a look at the windows. Dawn was creeping in from the east and he hurried. As he was clearing up he saw the old man's address book and slipped it into his pocket. When he climbed back out of the kitchen window, the floppies in his pocket, he wiped the frames for prints and made his way back to the path, the soft dawn inching its way over the bulk of Monte Baldo. Ten minutes later he was back at the hotel, Sally still sleeping in the bed where he had left her.

Later, over breakfast, he told her about the night's visit

from the police. 'What did he say to you . . . what did they want, I mean why kill him, he's just an old man,' she began. A tear rolled down her cheek. Miller knew it was no more than shock on her part, shock and sympathy.

'They were after information,' he said.

'What?' she said without looking up, wiping a hand across her eyes.

'I'm not sure, but I would say it's the fuel mix ratios for a hypersonic aircraft, Karl's HST. It seems we aren't the only ones interested. Remember he said he had had a visit. I told the police that.'

She raised her head this time.

'But he said that . . .'

'He said his students hadn't. He didn't say he hadn't,' Miller corrected her gently.

'Someone murdered him for that?' she said incredulously.

'Looks like it.'

'What now?'

'Paris, I think,' he said softly. 'There's someone in Paris I want to see.'

She thought for a minute.

'Tim, if whoever did this killed him for that calculation, or whatever it is, I don't know if I want to get involved.'

'We are involved,' Miller replied, smiling sardonically. 'I'll fly you home if you like, but I am going to Paris.' He hoped she would agree to go back to Washington.

The police came back later that morning and an hour's further questioning had Miller getting exasperated.

'Finally, what do you know of the other visitor, the day before yesterday. He was also American?'

'I am not American, I'm British,' Miller replied testily. The officer shrugged as if finding no difference. 'And I don't know who he was. We didn't meet.'

He could hear Sally getting the same questions and she was beginning to lose her temper. Her answers were becoming brusque and she was pushing her hair back

130

angrily with every answer. Eventually they were allowed to leave after Miller had agreed to return at the expense of the Italian government to answer further questions if necessary. As they drove out of Italy, the disks in his bag, he was hoping that he had something to go on. The fuel mix formula for something hypersonic, perhaps. While Tornadoes didn't use exotic mixes, he knew that high altitude flights all used weird and wonderful combinations of kerosene, high octane aviation fuel, oxygen and other additives. He also knew that a successful mix was the secret to performance at those heights. If someone had built a hypersonic, then it couldn't fly on plain old kerosene he thought, not at multi-Mach speeds over seventy thousand. That was something worth killing for in the competitive world of military aviation. Suddenly Karl's obsession with the HST had come home to roost and he was now in the thick of it. But who else had been in on the files? He tried to remember the standard distribution list. There were the Pentagon people, the Air Force themselves, sometimes the CIA . . .

'The Flat Earth Society,' he said bitterly in the dark. Sally started at his sudden outburst.

'Jesus, don't scare me like that . . . the who?'

'The Flat Earth Society. It's what your dad calls the CIA. Remember what Cassalto said yesterday: the visitor had it written all over him. It would be just like them to bungle a thing like this.'

'What do you mean? Just kill him?' she said incredulously. 'Don't be dramatic.'

'Just belay the national pride for a minute. It's possible. I think you'd better go home. I'll go on to Paris and join you there later.'

'No, I'm coming with you,' she said.

'I think not. This is getting rough. It now involves murder and big stakes. This is the first fifteen playing,' he said firmly.

'I'm coming, I'm involved already,' she countered.

131

He thought for a moment and then left it hanging there. He couldn't force her out without making her suspicious or hurting her and he would do neither. Just because you reported to military intelligence didn't mean you had to behave like a bastard.

Minsk

Major Rochenko spread the files before him on the desk. They had arrived that morning from centres all over the country after his requests of the previous week. Now he would begin the job of matching details with the printouts from the computer at Moscow Centre. There was much a computer printout never said, it couldn't convey the tension in a hand-written note of decades before, it couldn't see the importance of a simple question mark in a margin, or a simple soft pencil circle left by a man who had considered something, then discounted it as unimportant, which now could become relevant.

Unlike in popular fiction, the Security Service, spawned by the old KGB, wasn't all green-uniformed machine-gun-toting guards or Mata Hari ladies trying to poison elegant British agents as some post-coital reaction to orders from Smersh. Like any intelligence service, it spent thousands of hours sifting information, leads and tips, building pictures like jigsaw puzzles. Sometimes when the pieces fitted, the rewards were huge. Major Rochenko was an ambitious man, frustrated by fate, and all his career he had been waiting for his jigsaw to arrive. Not just fitting a piece of someone else's, but beginning one himself. This one had begun months before, the first hazy image, and now he knew that somewhere on his desk the answers lay, the image clear.

Now he took his rimless spectacles from their case with precise, efficient movements and placed them across his thin red nose, confident that this was his chance for a colonel's gold tab. The thought of colonels irked him.

Rordino was ten years his junior and a full colonel and had requested Minsk command. Requested! Rochenko hated Minsk, and hated the young colonel who was everything he wasn't, and had achieved everything he hadn't. Now this was his chance.

He had the pieces of a puzzle that would prove the existence of a huge underground organization of dissidents and he wasn't going to hand it over to anyone. Rordino had asked for the Rabanov file a few days before and he was convinced that Rabanov was a piece of his puzzle. Who requests Minsk? He began on the files, his hands working in short sharp jerks as he began to pencil a list of dates, names and reference points. It was time to make some arrests and expand the working parameters a little. This would be a real feather in his cap. Colonel Rochenko, the man who broke it all open. He could see it all before him and, his mean lips set, he worked methodically into the night.

Rabanov sat in the darkened window overlooking the street and the building's main entrance. Inside the room, under the light of a desk lamp, was Suki Yalta, working his way through the ninth series of access codes into the heart of the new user's program. The same program that in less than a week would be installed into Igor. This was the fifth evening they had spent in the building, Rabanov impotent with the software and watching and keeping guard for the staggering genius of the other man as he worked his way through the green screens of complicated hieroglyphics. He heard Yalta laugh softly.

'What?' he whispered.

'We are into Igor's big, sweaty crotch, and we now have his balls!'

'Be precise, for God's sake,' Rabanov said urgently.

'Section nine stroke fifteen . . . the sexy part.'

'Just get on with it, you crazy little bastard,' Rabanov pleaded.

Another laugh, and Rabanov could hear the keys working fast with pauses as Yalta checked his notes. An hour later he was finished and called to Rabanov.

'Let's add the end and go.'

'What end? What are you talking about?'

The keys tapped lightly for a few seconds and Rabanov walked over and looked over his friend's shoulder. Tense and frightened as he was, a smile spread across his face as he read the screen.

'When will that come up?' he asked.

'Just when they think they have it fixed, then back into the loop with the new time-bomb,' Yalta answered as he returned from the depths back up through the system, covering his tracks as he went. You wonderful little man, Rabanov thought, you are a master of your craft and your most talented work will never be seen by your peers – how frustrating that must be.

'Come, I will give you dinner at my place. Natalia has been complaining that we don't see enough of you.'

Tomorrow he would call this Stravinsky character on the new number and give him the news. It was done.

6

Carson and Allison were on their third fast mile that morning, and although it was barely five o'clock, the sun was up and the sky a pale blue above them. Allison was now as fit as he had ever been and the runs were just the beginning of the daily regime. A cooked breakfast followed, then they began four hours of simulator training, which by now included Allison in the cockpit running through his systems. There was no way that Carson could simulate the adrenalin surge, or the real rumble of engines or the G forces. All he could do was get his wizzo as fit and as familiar with the systems as possible. Their relationship was still strained, Carson's scant respect for the other's right to be in the right-hand seat obvious at times.

Much had changed in the last weeks. The New Zealander had got used to the idea of flying the interceptor and now wanted to. Wanted to desperately. If it was half as good as the simulator then it would be the culmination of his career, but it went deeper than that. When he arrived he had regarded them as soft lefties, conservationists in a world of the hunter and the hunted. But slowly and almost by osmosis he began to respect their views, their decency, their beliefs. As that change occurred he realized that if it went off they were ill-equipped indeed and he began to force other issues, operational issues. The ground crew had begun turn-around drills at Carson's request. It had taken more than Digby Allison's pressure to achieve it, however: in the end it had to come from Leo Sagan, the Project Director.

'Look, Leo, if you people think it's all as simple as your

scenario you are wrong. One flight is never enough, even with the duration figures the designers claim. Once something starts, every second the Tarbaby is on the ground she is at risk. She must be refuelled and rearmed as soon as possible . . .' then, remembering the lasers, 'Well, refuelled anyway.'

Sagan looked at him, mulling the thing over, and Carson continued.

'While she's up she's safe, and so are you all. Once she's down from her first sortie they will be all over this place like a bloody rash. She must be turned around as if this were a combat base, which it is, and the sooner you people accept that the better.'

'If you think that is necessary, then I accept your experience in these things,' Sagan said. 'I'll ask Tavis to begin at once.'

'Don't ask him, tell him. And there are other things.' Carson had momentum and kept it moving.

'Like?' Sagan asked dryly.

'Like how long do you think you can maintain an intercept ready status here, how long do you think all these people can be kept on the edges of their seats?'

'I don't understand what you are getting at,' Sagan said.

'You have people who have been here over eighteen months – they're stale and tired. Stand them down. You claim to have an intelligence machine second to none, then you must know when the Tarbaby is likely to fly. You can call any back at that time.'

'It has always been our intention that once we are ready and everything is in place, then we can stand down. We will always have enough warning to get people back here. Global nuclear war doesn't begin overnight! But you are right. That's why we have never pushed them, because they are tired.'

'That's why you will lose.' Carson looked him in the eye. 'They are slack, every man jack of 'em. Give 'em a break, in turn, a couple of weeks in the UK or somewhere,

136

get 'em back and push them like they should be pushed. Drill 'em, train 'em to stand-to every day until they can react as fast as I can. I'm fuck-all good in the Tarbaby if I can't get support, right when I need it, like get refuelled when I need it.'

Sagan's pride was dented and he reacted as Carson expected him to.

'You are presumptuous in the extreme,' he seethed.

'I am what you recruited. A squadron leader trained to run a team to take to combat on three hours' notice. Trained by the best air force in the world, and that's what you will be up against. Do you think it will be just missiles? No. You will have every fighter in the line-up hunting you, or should I say me? I'll be just another trace on some bastard's target infrared screen and they won't be shooting Sidewinders at me. They will be anti-missile missiles. Get with it, Leo! You have the nucleus of a crack team here, but they are tired, slow, and altogether too theoretical. Start operating or I am on my bike, because however much I believe in what we are all doing here, it's all a huge waste of money unless we perform to the very best of our abilities. Now do you understand what I am saying?'

Sagan said nothing, just looked away into the middle distance.

'There is no second place, Leo, there are no medals for a good try. We get this right the first time or we fail, and right now my professional judgement of Omega's ability to react sufficiently quickly gets us a "two out of ten, see me later".'

Sagan smiled at the analogy and nodded his head slowly. 'What do we need to do to get ten out of ten and a gold star?' he asked.

All department heads were given new standards and time to get into shape and the new feel gave urgency to their quest. The gym once used by Carson and Allison alone was now booked solid and Yamashita, the computer programmer, came out of hiding with his boken and trained on the floor of the canteen. The first groups were as excited as kids when they were awaiting the transport that would take them into Reykjavik and out for their rest and recreation trips. The sitting room, once rather like a university common room, became more like an officers' mess, with less reading and more drinking and singing. As they worked harder, so they played harder, and the night the ground crew broke the turn-around record to under fifteen minutes, Digby Allison nearly slipped a disc demonstrating what he called 'real rock and roll' with Chris Walker. It was Sagan who noticed the difference in the simplest way. When Carson asked Tavis how they were doing, Tavis answered, 'Fine, sir', and had almost been at attention when he had said it. While Sagan didn't want a military command structure, he had to admit that if they fell into one simply by behaving like trained personnel, then it wasn't a bad thing. The whole base had a crisp feel about it and it felt good.

Carson completed 120 hours on the simulator and Jorgensen could no longer find fault with anything. That was why he wasn't surprised when Carson went to Sagan and said he was ready to fly his Tarbaby, the Omega. They scheduled his first test flight for the following Tuesday, to give time to organize a fault in the radar at the American airbase outside Reykjavik. While the Tarbaby had a full stealth facility, up that close operators would see a black spot and they wanted to avoid that at all costs.

'We have people on the base,' Sagan said casually to Carson.

'What about the Icelanders?' he asked.

'Oh,' Sagan answered, 'they know we are here, they just pretend we aren't and nobody else notices. On maps this is a no-go area, all inquiries to the Defence Department. They are a proud and independent people who are tired of sitting between the Bear and the Eagle, knowing that they are strategically important and will be the first place to be grabbed by whoever starts it.'

'Fair enough,' said Carson. He hadn't got to know any Icelanders yet, but they sounded like nice, sensible people.

The morning of the flight Carson was up and awake well before dawn and ran alone along the runway, his lithe form in a dark blue tracksuit almost invisible to his ever present watchers, even with their starlight intensifiers. He had given Digby the morning off because he would make this flight alone, like most since he had first flown solo. He wasn't sure how it would be with a civilian alongside him. Flying fast jets was to him something personal that you did alone. Jammed into flight suits and G-suit, sweating or freezing, wedged into the cockpit that was built for a midget, the surge as it shivered and bucked and buffeted its way towards clean flight, the punch of the afterburners and then gear up and the smell of rubber and kerosene. His own Valhalla of adrenalin and fear and split-second reactions in the majesty and pure loneliness of the deep azure sky. It was for him a pilgrimage of the faithful.

He was sitting in the canteen while the early shift cook scrambled eggs for him and chatted about his boyfriend, when Yamashita walked in, softly, on slippered feet, his boken in his hand. Without comment he began his training, lightning sweeps and parries part of the ancient ritual. The wooden sword swished and moaned against the hiss of his feet as they slid across the floor, the movements poetry, the motive a pure derivative of a hideous reality, and Carson felt a curious kinship. He was forty minutes into the session and when he finished he bowed to his imaginary opponent and, wiping his brow clear of the fine sheen of sweat, he came and sat with Carson.

'You fly this morning?' he asked accepting a small cup of black tea from the steward who had appeared from the kitchen. Carson nodded, his green eyes saying, leave me with my space, I left you with yours, but smiling for courtesy's sake.

139

'I wish I was with you. My family home was on an island called Kyushu. Mogi. Not far from Nagasaki.'

Carson studied him with some interest.

'I am an interesting social phenomenon. I have a doctorate in computer science, but my soul belongs in the fifth century. I am a frustrated warrior who longs for combat, and yet I give myself to this cause that is to deny the world the ultimate conflict.' He sipped his tea, his unlined face giving no hint of his age, almond-shaped eyes completely at peace with his self-confessed dilemma.

'We are the same, you and I, Carson San,' he said.

'How's that? Bushido or bust?' Carson chuckled, a little embarrassed.

Yamashita laughed out loud before replying, 'Exactly, America and Russia, France and Britain, honourable opponents for us don't you think?'

The small room was beginning to fill with people and down the hall Carson could hear comings and goings. He smiled, inwardly pleased with the feel, the expectation in the air. Tavis's ground crew would be making checks that had been done a hundred times in the last two weeks, Gail's people warming screens and checking their systems, met reports from Alaska, Greenland's Thule airbase, Reykjavik and the temporary Russian bases north of the Arctic Circle from Aleko to Vorkuta. They would also have been monitoring military deployments over the last few days, and when Carson had been in the control room the night before the traffic status screens were slowly filling. He had stood against the back door, his arms folded over his chest and watched as Gail's team plotted and identified every blip on their screens. There were commercial flights on the great polar route and the military ferry trips. He had watched Gail smile as she listened in on the brief conversation between the pilot of an F-111, one of three tiny blips tucked together over Greenland, and the female voice of an EC-135 tanker skipper; the fighter pilot's sexual innuendo was subtle but there as he nosed his refuelling probe into her trailing hose nozzle. Each aircraft identified went on to the progress screen, split by mission, the civilian jets one side, the military the other. Three hours after they commenced she stood them down, confident that nothing unusual was taking place and the morning's flight could go ahead as planned.

He felt that Gail's attitude to him had changed in recent weeks. She seemed to have lost the initial hostility and was now allowing herself to relax around him, no longer trying to keep the professional image up twenty-four hours a day. A few nights before in the mess, as it was now called, she had pulled the rubber band from her hair, shaken her head to loosen the thick dark wavy mass and accepted a third drink, tapping her finger to the music from Chris's sound system. The gay cook, his turn behind the bar that evening, had blown her a kiss and called her a bitch for having such beautiful hair and she had laughed, delighted, her eyes sparkling and cheeks full of the flush of three brandies. Even Sagan had joined in that night, his blond-grey hair and goatee beard incongruous in the raucous company. Carson, more than a little inebriated, had taken a small, heart-shaped, helium-filled balloon from behind the bar. He broke the seal and inhaled the gas and walked across to Gail, a silly grin on his face and she burst into laughter as he talked in the high-pitched Donald Duck tones helium induces. With the laugh her eyes softened and she smiled. It wasn't the tight, wary smile of their first meeting, where she had sought to sum him up, but open, guileless, honest and softly feminine. He returned it, winked and eased his way back to where Digby was listing to starboard and about to juggle with six oranges while standing on one leg.

Later they had danced to a slow 'old but gold' song from Andrea's collection of tapes and she had rested her head against his shoulder just for a second at the end of the track before formally thanking him for the dance and calling it a night. She was afraid of something, he thought, him, or

141

involvement perhaps. God knows he wasn't wanting that. He still missed Olivia, but if there was a woman who could follow her it would be one like this.

Now the other girls had collected their things and were leaving. Gail was still at her console; he walked around the front and looked over the banks of hardware at her. She was wearing a pair of high quality Polaroid sunglasses and the green screen's glow reflected in their lenses like lime pupils in eyes of black.

'Stops getting bug-eyed,' she said by way of explanation, 'cuts down the flicker and the glare. These tubes can induce epileptic fits in some people.'

He smiled, 'See you later, Bright Eyes,' and walked away towards the door. He didn't see her turn and slip her headset off slowly and watch him, and he didn't see the softness return to her face as the memories of another time and another pilot flooded back.

He showered, shaved twice, and rubbing his hair dry briskly went back into his room where he had laid out his kit on the bed. His flight suits and G-suit had arrived from Holland, tailored specifically for him. He rubbed talc on his lower back and pulled on the soft wool underwear. He then ignored the new pale blue flight overalls and from the wardrobe pulled out his old green RAF issue. It was soft with wear and baggy around the knees and the black and silver wings badge was faded like the squadron leader's stripes on the lapels. He looked wistfully at them and pulled them clear, throwing them on the table. He picked up the heavy silver pressure suit, with the built-in gravity clamps, the chamois gloves and the hard plastic container with his custom-made helmet safely inside, and began the long walk down to the hangar, his mind on just one thing, the huge black hypersonic interceptor. No targets. No firing. No mistakes.

Below in the hangar Tavis's team had finished the routine pre-flight procedures, complicated not only because of the scram jets, but because the engines hadn't been run

142

up over three per cent since her last flight months before. He personally climbed on to the tractor to tow her on to the open pan outside the main doors where beneath the camouflaged tubular steel canopy they would commence the start-up sequence. Slowly she was eased through the doors, her long needle-nose over Tavis's head and the rest of the crew walking proudly beside her main bogeys, out into the cool shadow beneath the canopy. Tavis climbed clear, and unhooking the tractor cleared it and parked off to one side. He then walked back and climbed the light-weight inspection ladder for one last look into the gleaming engine intakes, the crew holding their breaths in case he found something not quite to his liking, but knowing he wouldn't. They were too good for that and they knew it. Behind, in the gloom of the hangar, others had gathered. Yamashita, Sagan, Walker and Dr Neilson stood together, while off to one side Digby Allison stood with Gail Samuels, neither talking and both nervous. Van Waveren's security team were all deployed that morning, with all three watches manning the listening posts and surveillance. To be caught out in the open would be stupid beyond belief.

'Mr Sagan, Mr Carson on the phone.' A security man gave him a cordless instrument. Sagan took it, spoke and nodded.

'Two minutes, Mr Tavis,' he said.

The big Welshman nodded to two of his team and they pulled a grating back, lifted compressed air hoses up from recesses and hooked them into the two main conventional engines for turbine turn.

As Gail turned to head up into the control room where Natalia and Andrea had been all night, Carson walked into the daylight, the baggy, heavy, silver thermosuit and helmet under his arm making him look more like an astro-naut than a pilot. He smiled at her, but she knew his eyes were on the Tarbaby. Three of the ground crew quickly hooked a ladder up against the hatch, but he ignored them and did a complete walk-around pre-flight check of his own, as he had done since a student pilot. Simple things like obvious external damage, tyres and beacons. Sagan looked at Tavis, expecting some disdain at the idea that his team would have overlooked anything, but instead found the opposite. The big man seemed pleased that Carson hadn't forgotten. The check complete, Carson finally climbed the ladder awkwardly, the helmet still under his arm, and disappeared into the cockpit. Only then did he acknowledge their presence with a raised thumb in the window.

Gail strode into the control room, her eyes immediately flicking to the big screen on the wall.

'How are we doing?' she asked dropping into her seat, and reaching for her headset and glasses.

'Four commercials on track two, the west, some military over Thule, but otherwise very quiet,' Andrea answered. Gail nodded as her own eyes absorbed the data.

'No change to the flight plan. North over the Pole, swing east down over Sweden, turn around and come back. Then, down to the Cape Verde Islands and back, total flight duration, give or take two hours, depending on how much he manages to get done this flight, okay?'

The three others nodded, and Gail looked over at the technicians manning the communications panels. They would not be needed this morning other than to monitor the ultra-high frequencies that Carson would use if necessary. Otherwise the whole test would be done under radio silence, once airborne.

Down on the pan in the Tarbaby, Carson settled himself into the Kevlar plastic thermo seat and ran it forward under the wraparound instrument panel. The seat was important, it would determine his comfort, its rake adjustable from upright down to full bed stretch, so the pilot could catnap during the long loiter periods she was capable of. Its heating elements would also keep him warm, even inside the thermosuit; if anything happened to the craft's heating system he would freeze to death in minutes. With the

144

heating system elements in the seat plugged into the suit it maintained a constant comfortable temperature. There was a control on the panel to alter that manually if necessary. He ran one gloved hand over the panel and began to activate systems, and one by one, cathode ray displays of conventional instruments lit up: turn and bank, airspeed, altimeters, artificial horizons, compasses, radios, and the massive bank of electronic counter-measures gear that lay between the two seats. He worked his way along the panel left to right, then reached up to the overhead circuits, his fingers activating back-up systems, reciting the procedure from memory and checking against the list on his knee pads. Finally he rested his left hand against the throttles and took the control column in his right, and raising a thumb in the meldox crystal windscreen, he commenced his start-up sequence. Feeling the compressed air spinning the turbines in the conventional engines, he pressed the ignition relay and the huge upgraded B1 engines rumbled into life, the Tarbaby shivering and rocking on her spindly legs. He watched the temperature gauges and pressures build up, and finally, with a glance at the Honeywell Primus weather radar and the laser inertial navigation system, he pressed the radio button at his throat to live, leaving his little finger to activate the mike on the lower edge of the pistol grip column.

'Tarbaby, ready to roll,' he said, ran the engines up to six per cent power and eased the parking brakes off. He felt the aircraft begin to move beneath him and he applied more power to enter the runway with the minimum delay.

'Roger, you are clear, no traffic north of you, six knots of breeze on the nose, take care now,' Gail's voice came back.

He looked quickly both sides and saw the crew clear holding hands up to ear pads, Tavis risking deafness to raise a thumb with a grin from ear to ear. Carson waved back, increased power, turned on to the runway and, without halting for further checks, hit the green touch-sensitive panel that would have the computers run up thirty per cent power. He would activate the burners himself. He felt her lurch beneath him like a thoroughbred and was pushed back into the seat as she leapt down the runway, his hands light on the column, feeling for the nose to lift as Erich's notes had recorded. The ground flashed past him and the lightness came and he hit the re-heat buttons, the huge afterburners roared as the gases were re-burnt, he counted to three and eased back on the column. The great black needle-nose lifted, the canards working their magic, and, as he eased the power setting up to sixty per cent, then eighty, she pointed her nose towards the heavens. Gear up, then at 7000 feet, prepare for scram jets, the nose still pointing upwards at forty-five degrees accelerating so fast that Carson hit the pressure feed on the air system to force air into his lungs under pressure to fight the Gs.

She blasted her way towards Mach 2 and he pressed the ignition switches for the scram jets and levelled off at 19,000 feet; as the four engines under the huge delta-winged belly condensed the air enough to begin to burn the mixture they crackled, rumbled, and thundered into life. The Tarbaby seemed to shiver like a dog set loose, and Carson raised her nose, shut down the take-off engines, his adrenalin racing as she shook clear of conventional flight and soared upwards, pushing him back into the seat so it was an effort to move his arms forward, and bursting through 137,000 feet before he levelled her off and eased the nose down for the long gentle turn for Sweden.

Jesus Christ! he thought, oh my God! you are fast, my lovely girl, you are so fast you scare me. He looked at the Mach meter hovering at Mach 7 and grinned nervously. She had now lost any awkwardness that she felt at slow speeds, the computers in the fly-by-wire system interpreting his inept touch into pure grace. He looked up, the sky no longer a friendly blue but the deep navy blue of space, it seemed only inches away. A light flashed on in the fuel panel and he looked instantly. Oxygen feed commenced by computer – he was too high for sustained flight and eased the nose lower to cross back down to her comfortable altitude of 110,000 feet. He reached forward, confident now to increase the power settings on the orange scram jet panel. They sat at twenty-six per cent and he eased it up to thirty-five, pushed back in his seat by the huge thrust, a beatific smile spreading across his face, sweating freely in the suit and loving every second of it. Twenty seconds later he began his tests.

He flicked a rocker switch and the head-up display flashed on to the screen clear and concise, speed lower left corner, altitude lower right, missile tracking screen dead centre, the small green light flashing to indicate it would swich to a target screen as he selected a contact. He looked across at the weapons operator's position, its banks of electronics live and deadly, but comforting all the same. Five screens, each five inches across, dominated the display, two the radar screens, and the other three the weapons system screens, one of which was square like a television rather than round. That was the computer display, the pre-programmed system that could operate fully automatically when Carson selected to engage in that mode. The Cray system was also pre-programmed with the locations of every missile silo in the Midwest, or more accurately its command digital switching system. In its combat mode, air-to-air, it could also command the laser to engage in turn up to sixty targets in sequence, topping up the facility as long as contacts kept coming. Head-to-head, in stern chase, or from a flank, the Tarbaby was the most sophisticated interceptor ever built.

Carson dropped the nose and began descending turns, the tiny high-speed control surfaces moving millimetres determined by the digital computers.

'Status please, Gail,' Sagan asked softly from behind her. The atmosphere was charged and tense, as always when the aircraft was up. One mistake and they were compromised.

'Mach Nine, one twelve thousand feet and climbing again, overhead Narvik this time, one per cent oxygen on the first intercept climb, otherwise all systems Grade A,' she replied, never taking her eyes from the blue wall-sized display. Sagan walked across to the duplicated flight instruments, and nervously lit a cigarette, rubbing his chin. He turned as a figure approached; it was Allison.

'Greetings, oh great one,' he murmured disrespectfully.

'Digby,' Sagan replied.

They stood watching the flickering lights and figures for a moment before Allison spoke again.

'Do you ever wonder, Leo, how we will be if it ever happens?'

Sagan looked at him, the hum of the air conditioning in the background against the murmurs of Gail and her team, the subdued lights giving the screens maximum effect to the watchers.

'I mean, I'm nervous now, and this is just a test flight . . .'

'So am I, Digby, so am I,' Sagan answered.

A bank of lights changed from one tone of orange to the next before them and counters whirled before their eyes. Sagan turned and walked back to Gail's console. She sat with one hand to her headset and one on the resolution knob watching her displays, talking softly into her microphone. Andrea had three new contacts on her screens and had just switched them to Gail's primary screen, so that she, as senior controller, could have a look.

'Okay, I have them, no problem, we have increased power, Mach Nine-five. Mach Nine-nine . . . Mach Ten . . . Jesus Christ! Mach Ten-five . . . Mach Eleven, we now have a new record, girls, we are on Mach Eleven-five and stable.'

There was muted hand-clapping from a few of the people around the room.

'Coming round to two-sixty degrees.'

McReadie appeared in the background and stood watching the white symbol move across the blue wall screen as it began its long gentle turn south-west towards the Atlantic and the Cape Verde Islands.

One hundred and thirty-two thousand feet above the Azores and back on oxygen supplement for the fuel mix, Carson eased back the power settings to let speed bleed off for the turn over the Cape Verde Islands. He wanted this turn to be tight, as tight as the computer could handle it, and that meant slow. A maximum rate turn at Mach 11 would be a long, graceful manoeuvre taking several minutes and covering half a continent. Anything more dramatic and the wings would be ripped off the fuselage like crepe paper. He now wanted to see how she behaved at slower speeds and just how quickly she could lose speed without applying air brakes, an extremely hazardous operation even below hypersonic speeds. Then he wanted to see just how fast she would safely accelerate up, should a stern chase by conventional interceptors make it necessary. From what he had seen, she would easily outrun any rockets or air-to-air missiles once at speed, but if ever caught napping at slow speeds, his own pilot reaction and her inherent design limitations would then be the factors. He watched the speed falling surprisingly quickly once he had throttled back the scrams, and as she foundered at Mach 1, the point where he would normally engage the conventional units, he tipped the port wing and pulled the column back hard, his fingers wedged against the power grid to increase power as the turn pulled the nose down. The Gs poured on, and he felt the constricting effects of the suit around his legs. Here we go, he thought, knowing he was already pulling five, going on six. He increased the setting gently, raised the nose a fraction, eight then nine Gs, his jaw dropping, counting the safety margin of thirty seconds aloud to himself, the pale blue sky spiralling gently above his right field of vision. He straightened out for ten seconds, then piled it on again, this time letting the nose drop into the classic fighter aircraft's roll on to a target below – that's nice, not too heavy, he thought, nose up, trim out again, power on, the almost silent whirring of the gyros in the stabilizer unit.

He was dripping with sweat and breathing hard after the heavy turn and as the sun broke through the canopy he pulled the visor down and caught his breath for a few seconds. He knew that the aircraft, her airframe at maximum operating temperature, would have expanded to almost a foot longer than when in subsonic flight. He scanned the radar screens for a full minute, not fully trusting the audible alarms, and then, confident that nothing was in her path, he altered the rake of the seat to straight up from the lowered position of the turn sequence, tightened his straps even more, and went to engage the intercept computer. It was built into the firewall on his left above the throttles, with a course set and optimum altitude desired fed in. When he pressed the red panel above the setting keyboard the computer would feed data into the inertial navigation systems, the engine controls and flight control systems, and deliver him to the intercept point in the fastest possible time, given the conditions. Erich had never tried the system, and Carson set the maximum speed at Mach 15 for an intercept overhead forty degrees latitude. He stooged for a moment or two longer, clipped his visor down, increased the oxygen feed and cooling into his suit, and pressed the red panel into life.

Several things began to happen at once. The canards lifted the nose steeply, the huge scram jets burst into life, and Carson just hoped to Christ that everything was working as the Tarbaby, on eighty per cent power build-up scrambled up to the heavens. He watched the instruments as carefully as he could, his finger hovering over the abort button in case something felt wrong with the aircraft. He was being subjected to gravity forces quite unlike any he had ever felt before, pushed back into his seat, breathing with difficulty, even raising a hand was an enormous effort, his heart pounding in his chest. Six minutes later and having almost blacked out twice, the aircraft burst through 140,000 feet, the oxygen feed pouring the gas into the system that would otherwise be starving even given the exotic mix fuel. He immediately felt the engines ease and on the display his vector point countdown display began flashing. He caught his first full breath for all those minutes, the adrenalin and excitement bursting within him.

In the control room at Omega Base the teams sat mesmerized as Gail read off the figures, even her professionalism faltering. No one had tried the full intercept mode, ever, and as the Mach counter flicked over like an atomic clock through Mach 14 into Mach 15, she seemed to fade out of her commentary in awe. All was silent in the control room, no one sure what to say, the tension thick, all eyes on the screens and displays as the Tarbaby levelled off at 140,000 feet, Mach 15, the huge engines spitting flame two thousand yards out behind her, giving the infrared image a ghostly trail across the screen. Carson broke radio silence, clicked his mike on, and gave a full-throated exhilarating banshee yell to anyone who cared to listen, the high-spirited battle cry blasting through the speakers in the control room, the rush of the engines and cockpit noise apparent in the transmission. The relief was like a dam wall breaking and people all over the room began laughing nervously and shaking their heads at one another. Gail, half-angry with the recklessness of the procedure but admitting it needed to be done sooner or later, was prepared to forgive the break in silence. She leant forward and spoke crisply into her mike.

'Tarbaby, this is Omega.'

He came back instantly.

'Bright Eyes, this is Tarbaby, go ahead.' She could hear the laughter in his voice and could feel his delight.

151

'Tarbaby, Omega ... Congratulations. What is your ETA?'

'Bright Eyes, will be down in forty minutes.'

When Carson landed he sat in the cockpit while the Tarbaby was towed swiftly underground away from prying eyes. He was dripping sweat, exhausted but elated. Finally he climbed down the ladder, careful not to touch any exterior panels which were still hot enough to burn and walked away, stiff-legged, muscles tight after so long sitting. At the hangar door he looked back at her, the ground crew swarming around, the smell of her exhausts rank, even with the blowers on full sucking the stale fumes out of the facility, and he studied her clean lines with a new emotion. It had taken three years longer than planned and a billion dollars over budget to build her, but she was everything she was designed to be. He nodded almost to himself, but more to the Tarbaby as if they had a secret they were going to share, as if he had found at last what he was looking for.

He sat on the floor of his room that evening, still wet from a shower and went through a light series of sit-ups to ease the tired muscles. The desk lamp was on, its light soft about the room, and his clothing lay scattered on the floor where he had dropped it. The de-brief had been long and for him boring. Tavis had wanted everything sixteen times, and Yamashita and the other programmers had still been replaying the intercept mode tapes when he had left, delighted with the software and shouting excitedly at each other. Gail had been there, silent and as professional as ever, only smiling briefly when the 'bright eyes' call sign was used.

He counted to thirty and lay back on the rug, relaxing completely. He expected to feel different somehow, now that he was the fastest man on earth. He had pushed the envelope up to Mach 15, but he didn't feel like he always imagined the likes of Chuck Yeager to feel after blowing out another record. He ran his hand through his hair. The triumph seemed hollow because only he would ever know the sensation, the ultimate communion. But he was pleased all the same. The Omega was everything she was supposed to be, even better than the simulator had promised, and the whole underground facility had a new feel. The crews were cutting turnaround times every day and his initial faith in Tavis hadn't been misplaced. He was confident now – a couple more tests and a few minor bugs to iron out and he knew he would be ready to chase missiles throughout the deep blue of inner earth orbit and succeed.

There was a soft knock at the door and, expecting the steward to take away his flight suits for cleaning, he stayed where he was and called out, 'Come in.' The door opened cautiously.

'Oh . . . are you okay?' It was Gail, with a book and a ring binder under her arm. He sat up, adjusting the towel around his waist.

'Yes, just sort of stretching some muscles,' he replied lamely.

'You left your notes upstairs . . .'

'Ah . . . yes, thank you.' He stood holding on to the towel, revealing a long livid scar under his arm as he reached for the file. She studied his lean tight frame, his bent nose and crooked smile and flecked green eyes, and she smiled.

'What?' he said.

'You . . . you don't look like a fighter pilot,' she replied, shrugging and smiling.

'What do I look like?'

'Like a wet little boy,' she replied honestly, 'except for the scar.'

The scar was the legacy of a moment's inattention to a large barracuda on a reef off Grand Turk, while he was engrossed in trying to get close to a family of dolphins.

'I should have known better,' he said, looking at it with half a smile. He pointed to the coffee-maker.

'Would you like a cup?'

She looked at him, trying to decide if he was trying something on, but in a towel, holding the file, he looked anything but threatening.

'Yes please.'

They sat and talked for a while, Carson having pulled on a shirt and trousers and run a brush through his hair. The conversation was still a little forced, but as time wore on she seemed to relax and the talk eventually wandered off work and the project, and on to more personal things. Gail sipped at her second cup of coffee, holding it up and blowing on it, her long fingers wrapped around the cup as if to draw warmth.

'My folks live in Pensacola. It's a navy town, as you probably know. I used to watch the jets taking off and wish I was a pilot. My dad used to tell me not be sassy. He was one of those old-fashioned types who thought girls should have babies and varicose veins and go to church in that order. He was nice, though. Utterly predictable in every situation, like the rest of middle-class America. Didn't like it when I joined the air force.'

She sipped again and looked across at Carson who lay on the bed. 'What's the book?' he asked.

'Oh, nothing . . . just something I found in the library,' she said, all too casually.

'Let me see,' he said, standing up, knowing he had found something, smiling widely.

'No, it's nothing, just a . . .'

'Come on. Chicken!' He took it from her and laughed delightedly.

'*The Wind in the Willows.*'

She shrugged, smiling.

'I knew it,' he said, flipping a page. 'You're a big kid at heart.'

'Well, yes and no. It's probably been read by more

adults,' she replied. 'It's an English classic of its type, so Digby tells me. My mother once read it to me.'

'Its about a frog and some ferrets or something,' he said, winding her up.

'Not ferrets! Weasels. And he's a toad . . . just like you. And there's a badger and . . .'

'. . . a mole and a riverbank where they all live.' He smiled at her. 'My mother read it, too.'

She smiled. 'Sagan reminds me of Badger.'

She put her head on his shoulder for the second time without the hesitancy of the first occasion and sighed deeply, and Carson, aware that something special was happening, gently stroked the thick dark hair, his strong hands falling to massage the back of her neck beneath the waves, feeling her heartbeat beneath his fingertips. An hour later he pulled the thick eiderdown over them both and closed his eyes, tired after the day. She lay there with him, frightened about what was going to happen sooner or later, but not wanting to leave, not now, not ever, trying to shut out the memories.

She had only ever been in love once. He was a short, stocky, youthful major flying F-15s at Edwards Air Force Base, and when she had married him she had been the most junior controller on the tactical fighter wing. She had had him chasing false contacts most of the mission, his wingman complaining loudly over the air that the new controller was chickenshit. Major Tom Bowden had ignored the outbursts and on arrival back had sent a large goose, oven-ready, to the control room for her with a note that said, 'Let's eat this wild goose for dinner. I have been chasing it all day.' She couldn't refuse and the powerful, dynamic, humorous man had wrapped her around his heart in days. They lived on a quiet street near the base, his two sons by an earlier marriage images of their father, but respectful and polite to their elders, something Tom Bowden wasn't. She had loved him completely and utterly, and with the trust of youth believed he would be there for ever. Two years later his engines flamed out over the Rocky Mountains and although he ejected clear of the airframe bad weather held up the searching helicopters. He died in the snow unable to walk out, his legs broken and his spine compressed by the ejector seat. Three days later the former wife arrived to take the boys back, and Gail Samuels was left stunned, grieving and angry at the world, swearing never again to love anything she couldn't possess completely.

Now she lay in the darkened room, her head against another pilot's shoulder, another fast jet pilot, a risk-taker, something she couldn't possess, couldn't hold. Angry again at herself and her weakness she rubbed away a tear and sat up. Carson stirred and pulled her back down, swept one arm over her, holding her tight against his warm body. She struggled briefly with herself and then relaxed against him, breathing in the smell of his hair and skin and an hour later they made love, she fast and angry and he moving with her as her hips bucked beneath him, feeling the pain as she bit his neck, hating him and loving him all at once, loving his weight on her, the rippling muscles in his back and bunched tight hard loins and the softness in his look.

Two evenings later he was sitting in the mess, still quiet at that hour, reading a textbook on the application of lasers. Digby Allison, delighted that he had found someone as interested as Carson was, began to really introduce him to the basics and they talked for the next two hours about the applied theory.

'What we have isn't so much a flashy new laser – infra-red lasers have been around a while. Okay, the x-ray is new, but what we have is two things. The pulse system means we can vary the application. Rapid high-power pulses from this unit could destroy concrete blocks, single short bursts would simply shatter small areas. The other thing that is unique is the power source. That has always been the drawback, you see.' He sipped a cold drink and then taking the lemon, bit into it, his face puckering at the taste. 'Up till now it's needed huge amounts of power to create a laser beam capable of weapons application. We've got round that problem. We can power this system off the engines through a step-up cadmium coil linked by some fairly advanced physics through super conductors.'

'How powerful is it? I mean, it will take out a missile, but what else?'

'If you pointed it at the ground?' Digby asked

'Yeah?'

'Cut through steel like paper. The beam is focused as if through a magnifying glass. Creates unbelievable heat. Superheat. It's invisible, but it will cut through anything.'

Miller drove the car, Sally curled up asleep in the passenger
seat, the Austrian road beneath the tyres wide and fast
and good. They had decided to drive northwards from Lake
Garda rather than backtrack to Venice or push down to
Milan. They would have been the obvious routes out of
the Lakes, especially in a hired car, except that Miller had
taken the precaution of organizing insurance for the
vehicle to cross borders in case they ventured north. It
wasn't security he had in mind when he had made the
arrangements, but after some thought that morning he
had decided to use the option. It had occurred to him as
they sat eating breakfast, Sally still shocked and not really
believing what had happened the night before to Cassalto.

'I think we shall drive north, through Austria, into Germany and into France that way.' He buttered a roll, wishing the Italians would serve toast with breakfast and
mulling over the reasons he had just said what he did.

'Why? It's the longest route, it will take days,' Sally
countered.

'I thought it would be nice, a drive through the Tyrol
and Bavaria.' He bit into the roll, scattering crumbs across
the tablecloth. 'Very pretty in the summer.' He leaned back
and brushed the crumbs away with his hand.

Sally looked at him, her eyes narrowed. She was wearing
a bright flowery shirt and blue jeans, but her expression
was anything but bright and flowery. It matched her jeans
more.

'I'm sure it is, but that isn't your reason, is it?' she said
carefully.

He sipped his coffee without looking up at her, swallowed and spoke.

'I thought it would be nice . . .'

'Bullshit, Tim. You like driving long distances like I like having teeth pulled! Is it because of what happened last night?'

He looked up, straightened the cuffs on his Jermyn Street shirt and smiled a half-smile. He usually did this manoeuvre when he was about to tell a lie and Sally knew it.

'You have just adjusted your cuffs again,' she said dryly, the anger gone but the tension there. He relented to honesty.

'Might be a good idea. We were there at the house. Whoever did it may be interested enough to follow up. Let's play safe and vacate this runway nice and quietly.'

She considered it for a moment and seemed to slump in her chair.

'You're not telling me the truth,' she said softly.

'I don't want to discuss it.'

She knew better than to challenge him. She was not going to question Tim, not when he spoke in that tone of voice.

Now, just short of the German border, he was driving the car hard. He always treated long-distance car journeys as a chore to be finished as soon as possible. Although he felt safe taking this route to Paris, he did watch his rear view mirror constantly, not sure what to look for other than the same vehicle reappearing more than once. He needed somewhere quiet. Somewhere he could get to a personal computer. Somewhere he could talk on a secure telephone.

Virginia

Paul Hart was sitting alone in the Arlington office hacking his way through the computer data banks, trying to find something new, something they had missed. It was midnight and the others had all gone home. One wall was now painted matt black and turned into a huge chalk board. A complex flow chart had developed of names, dates, specialities, origin countries of design specialities and delivered orders that didn't exist. Somewhere in the computer there lay the answer, somewhere the pieces fitted together.

He stopped tapping at the keys and stood and looked up at the black wall. Incredible, he thought, absolutely incredible. Some outfit has created a maze of diversions, so complex it's impossible to untangle. Every turn is a dead end and we have got nowhere. The best team in the business and we have got nowhere. An organization exists, and it must be vast and powerful and influential and wealthy, yet we know nothing about it or what it stands for or what it wants, and it has built a new kind of aeroplane that can only be trouble for those who don't have the right password. Jesus Christ!

No. Come on. Keep it cool. The answer must be here in front of me. The door swung open and, his train of thought broken, he turned. Leroy Chubb strode through and Hart knew by his face the day wasn't over yet.

'Trouble, boss,' he said.

'What?' Hart asked tiredly.

'Oxenburger. The station chief in Rome has been on the channel to Langley. Seems he checked in as usual, took a couple of names of local talent available for hire and went north. The guy you sent him to talk to wasn't in Venice. Avery found him in some place called Melcesine on Lake Garda. Anyway, the little chat didn't reveal much, so Avery decided to go back that night with the locally hired man. Followed him somewhere. Something went wrong, the old boy struggled, a round was fired and he is now dead ... Station chief is mighty pissed, and the local guy is claiming Avery is a head case and talking about spilling to the carabinieri.'

'I fucking knew it. That man is a goddamn idiot,' Hart snarled.

'Raden is smoothing the Rome people and wants Oxenburger recalled as soon as we can find him,' Chubb continued.

'What do you mean, find him?' Hart said, disbelieving. 'Isn't he at the Rome house?'

Chubb shook his head. 'It gets worse. Oxenburger hasn't been seen since we got the story from the safe guy. Apparently the old man had visitors the morning of that day. Oxenburger saw them from the trees in the garden. He seems to have taken off after them. The local guy, one Luigi Moro, says that he and Avery went up to the hotel these people were staying early the following morning and spread some money around, got the car number and some details. That's when Luigi took off – he thought that Avery was gonna fuck up again . . .' Chubb trailed off, awaiting instructions from the tired-eyed man before him.

'What do they know?' Hart asked quickly.

Chubb shrugged.

'Okay, see if we can ID them. Let's see whose side they are on. If it's the Russians we have got a real problem on our hands. I'd rather not have any shooting, especially if it's them.'

'I'll get on to that. Rome have sent someone up to get the registration cards from the hotel. I'll get them to talk to the local police as well.'

'Do that, then let's get on to it. Close up here, get the team to move this stuff back to Langley. Then join me in Rome. Something is breaking at last.'

Miller sat so that he could see out of the fogged windows of the cheerless German motorway café. Sally sat opposite, trying to finish a beer and a sandwich in some good humour, enjoying the odd mixture of travellers, truck drivers, salesmen and families milling around at the vending machines for packaged sandwiches and coffee in Styrofoam cups that tasted like soup, or soup that tasted like coffee.

Miller sipped at his without taking his eyes from the windows, trying to listen to Sally and remain attentive all at once.

He had chosen this café because all the parking was to the front and he wanted the car visible from the road. He had first picked out the beige Fiat that morning and had seen it on the road several times since. He had slowed at one stage to see if it would pass him on the wide eight-lane autobahn, but it had remained distant. Now, only sixty miles from the French border, it was still there, and he wondered how many beige-coloured Fiats there were. He had never done the mandatory security course for military attachés because, with his casually operated programme, he was not officially attached to the embassy. All he knew about being followed was what he had seen on the movies, and his own common sense. The Fiat had stopped in the car park two minutes before and Miller hoped the driver would not be able to resist the temptation to use the toilet and get something to eat. Then he could see who it was.

'You aren't listening, are you?' Sally said with exasperation.

'Sorry, darling.' He smiled disarmingly, but his eyes were hard and watching the door. A figure had just stepped from the Fiat and was moving towards the café entrance. He was large, wearing a light overcoat and walked straight to the men's room without looking around, something Miller thought very unnatural.

'What's wrong?' she asked quickly.

'Bogey,' he said quietly.

'What?'

'We've been followed. He's here. Listen carefully and do exactly as I say.'

She listened for a minute, then rose and walked towards the door to the toilets, a single entrance leading to two inner doors. Fifteen seconds later she crashed back through the door and, looking very distressed, ran back to Miller

162

at the table. He talked quickly in fluent French, his voice rising in anger, and gesturing he sent her out of the door. Feigning a limp, and hoping no one would notice that he hadn't had one when he had arrived, he moved awkwardly towards the cash register and a group of French truck drivers laughing into their hamburgers.

'Foreign pigs,' he muttered, still speaking perfect French. One of the drivers looked up menacingly, and Miller smiled apologetically. 'Not you, my friend. My wife went to the ladies room and some big bastard in a coat asked her for sex, she refused and he called her a fucking French bitch . . . I hate them. Foreigners. If I had good legs I would . . .' he gestured helplessly.

One stood up.

'I saw her, *mon ami*, leave this to us.' Two others rose with him, wiping huge greasy hands on jeans.

'*Merci, merci*,' Miller whined. They gestured for him to consider it done and as they moved towards the toilets Miller slid out of the door and ran for the car where Sally waited.

The ambulance arrived twenty minutes later and a large man was wheeled out on a stretcher and loaded into the back. Two others needed first aid but refused hospital and drove away in trucks before the police arrived at the scene. The man in the ambulance, an American by his passport, was later released from hospital with cracked ribs, his left wrist broken and concussion. The duty intern, who had worked in the Arab quarter in Paris, recognized brass knuckle injuries when he saw them and called the police to the hospital. There was also the matter of the gun that he had found in a small concealed holster against the man's spine. The American claimed that the attack was entirely unprovoked, but no one believed him and it was only after several calls to the American embassy in Bonn that the local police reluctantly allowed him to leave, minus the weapon, which they said was not permitted in Germany.

Miller and Sally crossed the border at Strasbourg and

spent the night in a small pension outside Nancy. Over dinner Sally looked at Miller with new respect.

'Where did you learn that kind of thing?' she asked.

'What kind of thing?' His mouth full of pâté, showered and in clean clothes, he was once again the master of his own fate.

'The acting, the deviousness, everything.'

'It's a matter of knowing when to enlist help. He was big and of unknown skill. I would have been mad to take him on by myself. Not my sort of thing . . .' he grinned charmingly at her '. . . and we needed a head start. They will have kept him busy for a while.'

She smiled back at him, suddenly very confident in his ability to keep them clear of trouble till Paris.

Minsk

Major Rochenko was pleased with his progress. The investigation was proceeding well and he had brought in two junior captains and a team of three analysts to begin collating the mountains of information that had been coming in from all over the Russian Federation on request from his office. He stayed each evening to review what the day had unfolded. While the progress was there it was slow because he was not willing to brief the two captains fully on what they were looking for, but simply gave them specific tasks to be completed. Like a crossword he fitted them together each evening, locking the link file away at the end of each session. This group was large, he was sure of that, they were widespread and they were very, very clever. No real trace had surfaced, only snippets from informers and a name. Gulag. That wasn't surprising: students and poets and reactionary elements had been using the name in jest for years, but this time it was more than talk around skating rinks and chess games, more than empty threats in underground newspapers. He was getting near something definitive, he felt.

He was glad that Rordino hadn't pressed the issue at all, just signed the authority for more staff, cocky and confident in his immaculately tailored uniform. The service allowed their officers to choose whether to wear uniform and Rochenko had always preferred the anonymity of civilian clothes, rarely reverting to his tired number one greens. Now he sat in his office, the traffic sparse on the street below and a crisp autumn evening closing in, and he imagined stepping into a new set of greens for the trip to Moscow to receive his commendation for breaking open the group called Gulag, the culmination of many months' work. Smiling thinly he set to work again, the sweet taste of success in his mouth. He wrote four names down on the sheet before him and thought about who to bring in. Just the thought of arrest was still enough to instil fear in any Russian. The service was responsible for the domestic security of the state and had widespread powers that were formidable anywhere outside the Politburo itself. Sleep deprivation and drugs would break down the hardest suspect and provide the link between much of the seemingly unrelated data that lay before him on the desk.

He worked a while longer and wrote a further seven names on the list, all known activists. Then he compiled a list of Jews, all of whom he considered suspect merely for not exercising the right to emigrate to Israel. That list was substantial and he referred to a computer printout to cross-check and begin eliminating the young, the old and the low-paid. To Rochenko dissidence was a middle-class pastime, and to the working man the Gulags were not the subject of jokes. He would then begin eliminating until he had a manageable list for the interrogators on the second floor. As he reached across for his coffee the phone rang and, scooping it from its cradle, he hooked it against his neck, still reading the list before him.

'*Da.*' He listened for several seconds and replaced the handset, smiled and reached for his coat. His latest informant had come in with the goods at last. Till now it had been phone messages, cryptic and sporadic. Now here was the meeting he had been looking for. He took his pistol and holster harness from the steel cabinet and slipped it on before pulling on his coat. He often didn't bother with a gun because his driver was armed, and on any job where the possibility of real violence existed he took other armed men. But this informant had said come alone, which was not unusual.

Elated, Rochenko ran down the stairs to street level and called for his driver who was in the guardroom playing cards. The meeting was in an apartment on the western side and as the driver negotiated the light evening traffic he checked his tape recorder in the back seat, thinking, I've got it, I've got it at last. Now that smartarse little puppy Rordino can shove his shitty little provincial office up his arse because it's Moscow Centre for me and, with luck, overseas postings. I'll show that upstart with his petty little border uprising. He tapped the file reassuringly against his knee, smiling to himself and humming a popular tune, till the car stopped at the back of the tall concrete block he was looking for.

He took the steps two at a time and avoiding the babushka in the foyer, the ubiquitous old woman caretaker that old buildings seemed to breed, he rounded the stairwell. On the third floor a man, a tall man in a shabby coat and heavy boots, stepped from a door, pulled a gun clear from his jacket and fired twice.

Rochenko was dead before he hit the floor with two bullets lodged firmly in his skull, the lightweight.22 calibre wadcutter rounds having destroyed everything in their path through to the central cortex. The last thing he ever saw was a bright shiny signet ring on the little finger of the gun hand.

He was found an hour later by his driver, who covered the body then woke up a night shift worker and sent him for the militia and to call the service's provincial headquarters from the phone on the ground floor. Colonel Ror-

dino was at the office when the call came through. With
controlled fury he cancelled the militia involvement,
claiming matters of state security, and drove straight to the
scene, his own team of investigators following. The area
was immediately sealed off with tapes and residents were
pulled from their doorways to see what had happened in
their building, Rordino claiming that it was impossible that
no one had heard anything. By eleven that night he had
accepted the possibility that a silenced weapon was
involved, which meant a professional assassination of a
senior security service officer. At dawn the next morning
he was stripping Rochenko's office with the captains in
the detail, looking for the dead man's current file. It was
nowhere to be found.

'Stupidity!' he bellowed. 'Rank stupidity! You never take
a file from the building. What was the arsehole thinking
of? First he allows himself to get bloody shot, and then
his file ripped off. What was he working on?'

'We don't know, colonel. It was a specific duty,' one
captain replied, snapping to attention.

'Task specific' was used to define ultra-sensitive material
where no one investigator was fully in the picture of all
facets of the investigation.

'Task specific. BULLSHIT! It was a routine bloody follow-
up. He was so frigging dramatic he saw devils in everything.' Rordino calmed himself enough to ask again.

'Captain, my second in command is dead, murdered;
now I want to see everything you have on whatever he was
currently working on. Your friend can pull his other files
and let's see who has a grudge against our man. I didn't like
him any more than you, but he was working for me, and I
want to know why he was shot. Do you understand?'

'YES, COLONEL,' the man answered at full parade
ground volume.

'Get on with it then,' and he walked away to telephone
Moscow Centre.

The death didn't seem to bother Rordino's off-duty

emotions, as he left the office and drove back to his apartment where he got back into bed with the long-legged shop assistant who was about to show him a new trick with a silk scarf he had obtained from one of the expensive black market sources.

Strasbourg, France

Avery Oxenburger sat in some pain and even more embarrassment in the small hotel room in Strasbourg. Hart and Chubb had arrived from Rome that evening, Hart white with anger after the roasting he had received from the head of station in Rome. He was venting it on Oxenburger in no uncertain terms.

'Not only did you precipitate an incident in Italy in which an innocent man died, but you managed to get yourself beaten up in a German freeway toilet. Tell me, Avery, what little diplomatic remark did you make to incite that?'

'Nothing,' he mumbled back, 'not a thing. Bastards just started punching.'

For some reason Hart was beginning to believe him, his mind working the angles.

'If you are lying to me you are finished,' he said.

'No lies, boss, they came in looking for me. I had my flies undone and let me tell ya, you're vulnerable then . . . no lies, boss. It was a set-up.'

'Were you spotted on the road?' Hart asked.

Oxenburger nodded sadly and carefully, mumbling his reply. 'Must have been.'

'So why? Obviously they are scared after the villa fuck-up and they don't want to be followed. So we must assume they know something and the old man did after all. He must have passed something on to them and they've picked up the ball and run with it.'

'Russkies?' Avery asked, mumbling indistinctly and massaging his ribs with his good hand.

'No, thank Christ. You got taken down by a couple of

amateurs. A Brit air force officer on attachment from them to the Pentagon and his American girlfriend, Karl Schoeman's daughter, no less,' Hart replied sardonically.

'What? Goddamn American?'

'Yes, but not quite on our side by the look of it. Seems they are independent until we can call them in. If they don't co-operate then we rescind passports in her case and get some pressure applied through the Pentagon on his people. Shit! they probably thought you were a Soviet or something,' Hart finished frustratedly.

'What now, boss?' Chubb asked.

'Get on to Langley, get our stuff pulled. Whoever they are seeing is in France, I'll put money on it. We are going to visit them all and what's more, the French are going to help. They are not NATO, but by Christ they better help on this one.'

'This is it,' Miller said. 'Rue de la Fontaine.'

It was a wide street that once upon a time had sported a fountain, but now was massed with residential buildings each side and a scattering of shops and cafés. A sad-looking elm tree, stunted by fumes and Dutch elm disease, stood forlornly at the entrance to a building that looked right for numbers.

'Pull over here,' Sally said, re-folding the map. 'This looks like it, could be the one.' She smiled across at him nervously, unsure of what lay ahead and unsure of the commitment they were making to something they didn't fully understand. The traffic surged angrily around them, the Parisian drivers shaking their fists at the foreign plates and impatient in the drizzly morning.

Miller had found a PC in a hotel business centre and scanned through the document files on two of the disks. One name had come up three times and each missive had talked of accelerants and the chemistry of advanced fuels. The address was in the address book. It had been that simple.

A few minutes later they stood at the door to the apartment and spoke into the chained door crack to a pretty, well-scrubbed blonde girl. She told them Dubois wasn't home, that he had left for the Institute already and he could return any time after five that afternoon. They thanked her and spent the day idly driving the streets and walking the pavements, hand in hand, like lovers seeing the sights, but Miller was preoccupied. Late in the afternoon as they strolled past the shops on the Right Bank he decided it was time.

'Come, let's go. I'll drop you at the hotel and shoot over and see Monsieur Dubois.'

'No. I'll come.' She nodded to him and walked alongside holding his arm, long strides matching his as they threaded their way through the streets towards the car.

'Do you really want to follow this through?' he eventually asked, stopping and looking at her.

'Yes,' she replied firmly, 'we have a week or so before I'm due back. I want to see this thing if it exists. What do we do, it could be anywhere. It could be in Russia, East Germany or . . .'

'No, not if Cassalto worked on the SR-71 project. His security grade would be very high and if he was working for the other team he would be there on their side of the pitch. No, this is a European thing, or private enterprise. Neither you or I have heard anything about a hypersonic and that's unusual in itself. With your background it would be unlikely you had not even heard a whisper of something this new, and if it had been in service, then I would have seen a briefing at some stage, particularly if it was Russian front-line kit.'

She nodded.

'In fact it's probably a new shuttle or something the frogs have been hushing up,' he said cheerfully.

This time the door was answered by a tall, bearded man with wavy blond hair and deep-set eyes beneath a wide, intelligent forehead.

'Monsieur Dubois?' Miller asked.

The man's eyes narrowed suspiciously and he nodded slowly.

'My name is Miller, this is Sally Schoeman, can we come in?' Miller said brightly, smiling all the while. The man's eyes widened briefly then narrowed again, as he began to close the door.

'Melcesine,' Miller said softly at the narrowing crack. 'I come from Melcesine.' The door stopped its movement and edged back and Dubois looked out again thinking, before opening it fully and waving them in.

The apartment was small, with bright Mexican prints on the walls and woven rugs on the floors. Pottery of all shapes contained plants, hanging from macramé strips, and an old overstuffed chair backed by bookcases dominated one corner. Something was baking in the oven and the smell permeated the room. Miller could hear someone moving round in the kitchen.

'What is it you want?' Dubois asked. His voice had a deep, resonant quality that implied a slowness of intellect, but looking at the books on the shelves Miller guessed that was misleading.

'I spent some time with Sally here, visiting a Mr Cassalto a few days ago. You know Mr Cassalto of Venice? He has a place in Melcesine.'

'Yes, I know the professor. I have attended seminars of his.' Dubois was very casual.

'Is that all? I don't think I'll bother, then,' Miller said rising to his feet, playing Dubois' innocence against himself.

'Suit yourself,' Dubois said in English. 'I'll be phoning him tonight, anyway.'

'No you won't,' Miller said. 'He's dead,' and taking Sally's hand he pulled her to her feet and turned for the door.

'What did you say?' Dubois asked, shocked, his face a mask of disbelief, rising to his feet also.

171

'I said you won't be phoning him tonight because he is dead,' Miller said harshly, 'so stop playing games with me. If you knew him well at all you would have known that.'

Dubois seemed to crumple, his huge shoulders sagged and tears welled in his eyes. 'No, not possible, I only left him a week ago . . .'

'It happened three nights ago,' Miller said looking at him, realizing that they had been close and regretting his harsh words. Dubois sank slowly into the chair, his grief evident in his eyes. Miller leant down and touched the man's shoulder.

'I'm sorry I spoke like that. Monsieur Dubois, what do you do?'

Dubois looked up with the guileless look of a child wondering at the relevance of the question. 'Why?'

'Just tell me.'

'I am a chemist,' he answered.

'What? Selling aspirins and things?' Miller asked.

'No, no, no . . . I am a research fellow,' he corrected quickly. 'Fuel laboratory in Dharan, Saudi Arabia. I am home on leave.' Miller looked uncertain still and he went on, 'University of Petroleum and Minerals.'

Sally nodded quickly. 'I've heard of it,' she said to Miller.

'What happened to him?' Dubois asked.

Miller looked down at the figure in the chair. 'He was murdered,' he said softly.

Dubois shook his head, staring at the floor.

'What a waste,' he said, 'what a waste. He was brilliant, you know. He was the finest fuels physicist of his generation.' He looked up at Miller. 'You were there?'

'We saw him that day, had coffee. Sally's father and he had known each other many years before. He had something he wanted to give me.'

Miller stopped there and let it sink in. Sally looked at him quickly.

'He trusted me enough to give me something, to bring to you.'

Dubois looked up quickly again, his eyes widening, then he dropped his head. 'I don't know what you are talking about,' he said thickly.

The blonde girl who had answered the door that morning entered from the kitchen, a baby in a papoose arrangement on her front, wiping her hands on a tea towel. She noticed her husband's expression immediately and crossed to him, looking questioningly at Miller and Sally. He brushed her away, almost embarrassed at his emotional state, then told her about Cassalto. She raised her hand to her mouth and covered the baby protectively with the other as if to shield the infant from the thought of death. He spoke quickly in French and she gathered herself and went back to the kitchen to leave her husband alone with the visitors. Miller looked back at Dubois.

'It's a shame you know nothing. Not much point my giving you Cassalto's work on the fuel ratios is there?' he said. Dubois said nothing, stubbornly sitting in the chair, and Sally kept looking at Miller, her confusion complete.

Miller took out a pen and wrote a number on a scrap of paper from his pocket.

'We are at this hotel; you have a day or two to think about it. I will give you the data, but I want to see the aircraft. I'm a pilot, you see, I just want to see it. Cassalto trusted me.'

Pyotr Rabanov sat cross-legged on the floor of their apartment, opposite Natalia his wife, his pipe in his mouth, a chessboard between them, trying to figure a fast demise for her. She was a wily player, defeating his classical moves with a logic that defied belief, taking extraordinary risks and, knowing him so well, anticipating what he would take.

'But you have just put your knight in danger,' he said incredulously, not believing her move.

'So, Marshal of the Red Army, take it!' she said cheekily, her eyes laughing at him. He knew better, there was a trick up her elegant sleeve and he studied the board again.

173

To her it was a game to be played when the snow was deep on the ground or the rain kept one indoors. She rated those who took it seriously as she rated those morons who used to stand in lines for consumer goods without knowing what they were lining up for. All the same she usually won, a fact that irked Pyotr intensely.

She checkmated him four moves later and further damaged his pride by squirting a mouthful of wine at him across the board. He counter-attacked with vodka and they were laughing and rolling on the floor when there was a knock at the door. They stopped their game and looked at each other; they were expecting no callers. Pyotr rose and, tugging his shirt down and straightening his hair, went to the door.

Suki Yalta stood in the hall and Pyotr beckoned him in, smiling and calling to Natalia to heat up the leftovers.

'Suki, welcome, come in and eat something . . . vodka? It's as icy as a Silesian whore's heart,' he gestured to the bottle on the table.

'Thank you, yes, vodka will chill the sleep from me,' he replied.

'Sleep? You always arise from your bed to go visiting?' Pyotr asked, pouring a drink into a small thick-rimmed glass.

'No, I don't, but then I don't get messages to come late at night either.'

Pyotr looked at him in the bright light, looking for a joke. There was none in Suki's eyes.

'Suki, I sent no message,' he said.

Natalia came back in smiling at the visitor, the smile dying on her face as she felt the tension between them.

'Yes you did. I got a message . . .'

'I sent no message, my friend,' Pyotr interrupted

Suki looked back at him, his heart pounding in his chest, Pyotr still holding the glass and bottle, frozen in motion, both men's minds racing, trying to figure who had called this bizarre meeting.

The telephone rang in the tiny hallway, splitting the room with its shrill sound, and Pyotr Rabanov walked towards it, his heart in his mouth, the fear deep in his guts.

'*Da*,' he said, hoping his voice sounded normal.

'Rabanov?' The voice was as cold as a January morning.

'Yes, this is Rabanov . . . who, who is this?' he asked.

'This is the man who ordered the death of a security service officer two nights ago to prevent your arrest and the arrest of others like you, dissidents and fools,' the voice slashed at him.

'I don't understand. I know nothing of this dissident nonsense,' he replied, feigning anger he didn't feel and trying to hide the fear which he did.

'Never again do I want to risk one of my people to keep you from the cells, you and your talented little friend Suki Yalta. He is there with you, I hope?'

Rabanov said nothing, realizing this was the man who had left the message for Suki. The frosty voice rasped again.

'We have come too far, Rabanov, things happen very quickly now. Is your work finished on the Borodino task?'

'I don't know what you are talking about, comrade. You sound like a madman to me,' Rabanov answered firmly. Borodino, he thought, Borodino of Gulag, Christ on a cross, who is this who knows about Borodino?

There was a dry laugh down the line and for a moment he sounded almost human. 'Good, good, Rabanov,' he mocked, then the arctic chill was back. 'This is Stravinsky. Finish it. Listen carefully, this line is clear but it will not always be. I want you to make the following extra changes to the user system, you and Suki . . .' he finished with a warning and hung up.

Rabanov turned to his wife and friend, took the glass from the table where he had put it and swallowed the vodka down in one gulp.

'Was it him?' Suki asked. 'Did he make the call to my building?'

Rabanov nodded. 'Yes, it was.'

'Well, who was it?' he asked impatiently and still frightened.

'Stravinsky . . . he is the new Gulag man. He . . . he had a security officer put to death to keep you and me from arrest.'

The three stood and wondered exactly what kind of organization they had joined that could shoot FSB men, order files corrupted and remain only a name to its members. Gulag.

Bandar Abbas Airbase, Iran

The air conditioning in the specialist workshops behind the maintenance hangar could barely cope with the heat that August morning. The wind had been from the southwest for two days, barely enough to move the air, and what it moved had begun in the Sahara, crossed the huge hot vastness of the Arabian Peninsula, rolled over the tepid waters of the Gulf and risen, monstrously hot and humid, over the coast just six miles south of the base.

The duty administration corporal entered the workshops by the back door wiping the sweat from his face, his shirt dripping, and praying to Allah that this might be his last walk across today. His commanding officer, Captain Shazahan, had been waiting for the last of the pay projections for the visitors and their list of requirements to apply for more cash from the purchasing fund. It was that time of the week again when they closed off the expenses and Captain Shazahan, a stickler for procedure at the best of times, would be reviewing the work this week; he had wanted the extra disbursements from the fund and all casual pay made up at the base.

The corporal nodded to a friend, took some water from the plastic jerrycan and drank deeply before walking to the clipboard outside the high security cage and removing the last of the necessary paperwork. He was pleased; now maybe the arseholes with the pencils and steel desks and calculators would leave him long enough to get some tea in the orderly room. Every one a general, he thought, and their only qualification was that they could read and write. He, Shivaz, could not, he was only nineteen, but at least this was better than war, he was terrified of that. Most of his older brother's friends had gone and half were now dead, and he hoped that Paradise was as good as The Book said it was for their sakes. Not a very devout man as Shi'ites went, he had harboured a natural scepticism of anything that sounded too good.

At least Captain Shazahan wasn't one of the revolutionary types. He was one of the old air force, trained by the Americans, the Great Satans as they were now termed, and had been kept, he suspected, because he was probably the only officer who could keep the base running with any shape. Half the aircraft were sitting broken, unable to fly for lack of spares, and half the other functions of the installation, the radar-tracking of Gulf air traffic and shipping and the training of new pilots, only took place when the badly maintained gear worked and anyone had the interest to check it was being done. They were a long way from Tehran, but to be fair he thought things had taken a new turn of late, with lots of visitors and closed-door meetings. Perhaps the unit would be moving west soon. Nearer home. He hoped so.

Later that afternoon Manu Shazahan received the end of week reports with a raised eyebrow and told the messenger to shut the door behind him. Once alone he pulled the papers clear and began to read with considerable interest the estimates of works completion as they related to expenses. He made some calculations from the figures and looked down at the total. It looked as if the work would be complete and the specialists leaving in a week or so. His father had called three nights before and said in his poetic, wonderfully convoluted fashion that the cradle being built in the high security cage was indeed important, more important than anything either of them had ever dreamed of. He needed to know as soon as possible just when the work would be finished, and then, more importantly, when it would fly loaded. Manu had lain awake at night in the close confines of his room in the officers' quarters wondering how he was going to establish that.

His offices were a good way from the ops room, and the main gate, although visible from his offices, was only one of three that a crew could arrive through. He already knew that it wouldn't be a Bandar Abbas-based pilot. One of the senior operational people had said something over a meal the day before about having to move his trainees from the induction facility to make way for a crew coming in soon. He was complaining loudly, but not too loudly because there were two or three political types around and the worst of the lot, the bearded, illiterate, fanatically devout Revolutionary Council representative, was nearby. That meant the crew coming in were not Iranian Air Force regulars, but Revolutionary Guard or even one of the new ultra extreme units. Popular opinion believed they were limited to the mass demonstrations in Tehran and, a few years ago, the odd suicide unit on the Basra front, but they were everywhere, Manu knew. Paid fantastic salaries to perform on command for the Council, they would do anything, absolutely anything they were ordered to. Wearing full beards or a three-day growth, they were easily identifiable. People who were moderate wore only a moustache or remained clean-shaven, and that in reality was most of the population, sick of war and empty promises, sick of the international isolation, sick of their lives being disrupted by religious fervour, sick of being told what to wear, when to pray and who to hate. They were tired of their hard-won fight against the Shah being played like a puppet by the mullahs with the massed marches and demonstrations carefully orchestrated by the Guard. The swaggering, cocky, power-drunk louts who before the revolution were nothing more than children fed on midnight stories of the return of the Imam, the Ayatollah, the closest man to God on Earth.

It hadn't improved much after the old man's death. He had watched television fascinated and appalled as the Ayatollah's body was carried away by the followers, people in their grief reaching to touch the shrouded corpse and ending up pulling it away from the bearers, the body toppling to the ground. My God, what will they think of us in the West, when we can't even manage a funeral properly, he had thought.

Manu picked up his telephone and placed a call to the family home in Tabriz. It was two hours coming through the tired exchange system and Manu carefully phrased his words to his father, knowing that the call would be monitored, speaking in plain Farsi but in an agreed code, leaving nothing to draw attention at this stage. That same hour his father carefully recorded a high quality digital tape and then on the lightweight transcoder in the bottom drawer of his cupboard, beneath the socks, condensed the whole message thirty-five times till it was no more than a high-pitched signal lasting a second and a half. He then took a taxi to the house of his friend and they sat in the high, cool study at the top of the house and waited for the pre-arranged time for transmission.

The friend was an old man, who in years gone by had traded carpets, caviar and icons across the border with the Russians. As time passed his business had moved into the twentieth century with a healthy line of imports and money invested all over the region, and at last he had handed the whole venture over to his sons who, considering him virtually senile, told him nothing. One daughter-in-law, however, was far brighter than any of the boys, and she knew where the real power lay, keeping the old man informed of day-to-day developments, her veil, compulsory by law, in a heap by the door, pacing the house and smoking, showing an eye for profit that, regrettably, none of his sons displayed. Confident in her below the

179

line management of his business, he gave all his time and influence to keeping the information flow to Oslo as regular and precise as possible. Many years before he had been recruited by a youthful Charles Haidermann while talking investments in New York, and much of his family's current wealth was due to the American with an instinct for a rising market.

Now seventy years old, he sat with Shazahan waiting and talking over a very illegal fine French brandy which had lain in the cellar for fifteen years, the transmitter loaded and set to transmit at a precise time. Finally at 1800 hours GMT the small flickering READY light on the transmitter glowed a constant red, and with an audible alarm seconds later they knew the message had gone out via the switching station in Turkey and down the Mediterranean, quite where they didn't know. A second back-up signal would be received in Saudi Arabia on the gear at the naval headquarters in Riyadh for despatch from the Malaz house.

Five minutes later the first signal arrived in typed form, delivered by a man on a motorbike who was a technician in a small Milan radio station where, in amongst the mass of aerials and gear on the roof of the building, he had built a receiver for the incoming material from the Middle East. The man he delivered it to phoned a Barcelona number and in turn was connected straight through to the house at Deia, where Charles Haidermann awaited the call. An hour later he called an extraordinary meeting of the Oslo committee, something that hadn't been done since the Cuban missile crisis. Then they had been powerless, but now it was different. Now they could do something.

That same evening Haidermann took a call from a senior Oslo man in France who quickly outlined the visit to André Dubois by Miller and Sally Schoeman and Miller's problematic request.

'He said he just wanted to see it and that he is a pilot . . .' the Frenchman finished. Haidermann thought for a full minute. It was inevitable that eventually someone would come across the project and put two and two together.

'All right, what do we know about him – or is it the girl who is the driving force here?' he asked.

'A bit now, we put out a request for data this morning first thing. She is the daughter of an analyst at the Pentagon, her father works with Miller. He is a career Royal Air Force officer on attachment to Washington, but I think there's more to it. We are checking. There is an official investigation going on in the States, by the CIA at present, but these two seem to be unrelated. In fact they may have done a bit of fast thinking just short of the border a few days ago because they managed to shake the CIA man who had been following them. We think it was him who shot Cassalto.'

'Yes, I saw that hypothesis,' Haidermann said, thinking fast. 'He says he won't give us the calculations unless they see the project?'

'Yes.'

'So naive, the English,' Haidermann said, almost to himself. 'He could have talked his way into his death if it was anyone but us . . .'

'*Oui*, but he seems to realize we mean no harm: he has seen two of our people, Cassalto and Dubois, and neither would harm a fly. If they were indicative . . . besides, he is not that naive. He wasn't in the hotel he gave Dubois, he was across the road, with a room booked there just to take messages and he was phoning in for them. He doesn't know we have found him. Well, what do you think?' the Frenchman came back.

'We can't afford any inquiries at present, but we can't afford them hanging around either. We don't need the calculations any more – that stage of the work is complete – but these people are a nuisance. Things are happening quickly that may mean an Omega flight very soon, very soon.' He paused, not for effect but to think again, and the Frenchman spoke.

'I know the situation. Allow me to make a suggestion?'

'Please do, Pierre,' Haidermann replied.

'Bring them in, but keep them there till we have flown or this thing has died down a bit. That way we get the formulae and keep him away from anyone who can harm us till we have had more time to think.'

Haidermann thought about it.

'Okay, go ahead, pick him up. I'll talk to Sagan. I will be there in two days myself with the others.'

'Take care, Charles. The Iranian extremists. Most of them lived in France for years, we know them well. If there are any who are capable of this, it is them.' The Frenchman's voice was sincere.

'Thank you, Pierre, I will take care. *Au revoir.*'

An extremely elegant young French bachelor took a call in his Montmartre rooms a few minutes later, listened and put the phone down. He put his coat on, wrapped a fine white silk scarf around his neck and climbed into a big 1950 Fifteen Citroën, its immaculate paintwork gleaming under the streetlights. The car was a pure indulgence for him; his more serious motoring was done in a turbo-charged Bentley currently in the basement garage. This old masterpiece he used for evening drives through the city, its magnificent profile a common sight outside the gambling clubs and theatres in the summer. Tonight he drove quickly through the streets and twenty minutes later parked at the rear of the hotel where Miller and Sally Schoeman were staying, opposite the one they had said they would be in. He walked in through the service entrance, smiled charmingly at the chefs in the kitchens as if he owned the hotel (which he did not, although he did own seven other units in the city), walked up the stairs to the second floor and knocked on the door of number 16.

'Manager,' he called in English.

Miller opened the door, a towel around his waist still wet from the shower.

'Mr Miller, good evening, my name is Jacques. I believe you saw a friend of mine last night.' He paused. 'May I come in?'

'No,' Miller said, 'you can't.'

'Come now, may I call you Tim? You displayed an interest in seeing something that my friend Mr Dubois is involved with.'

Miller looked warily, caught out in a hotel he thought he was safe in, and vulnerable in the towel. He looked out down the hall and seeing the visitor was alone acquiesced.

'How did you find me?' he said, opening the door.

Jacques laughed out loud for a second. 'You didn't stay where you said you would, but you didn't go very far. In fact, the two hotels are both run by the same manager and reception team – it was pathetically easy. But to the point.'

At that moment Sally came out of the bathroom, also wrapped in a towel, her long hair wet and up under a smaller towel. She looked clean and fresh and very attractive and Jacques smiled at her as he took her hand and kissed it.

'*Enchanté,*' he murmured. 'You must be Miss Schoeman.' He turned again and looked at Miller. 'I admire your taste in women, monsieur. Please pack your things, we will leave in five minutes.' He bowed imperceptibly to Sally who stood looking very confused, and walked to the door.

'Just a minute,' Miller said. 'Leave where?'

Jacques shrugged.

'You wanted to see something we have built?' He paused and then the languid blue eyes narrowed. 'Just keep your half of the bargain, Mr Miller.'

'Where is it?'

'Pack your things, we have a few formalities to complete, a few postcards to write, some calls to make. You may be a few days, how shall we say, out of touch?'

'Where is it?' Miller repeated, tucking his towel in again.

183

'Five minutes: I shall be in the lobby. Hurry, please, I have a seat at a baccarat table with a very lovely girl and she is very impatient when I am late.' He smiled again at Sally, his look frankly appraising and closed the door behind him.

Miller turned to Sally. 'Christ! We're on!'

'I'm scared, Tim,' she said.

'I was,' he answered honestly, 'but not any more. If they were going to try something they would have done it by now.' He looked at her and walked across and held her for a moment.

'If you want to back out you still have time. I want to go, I want to see this thing, but you can go home. You'll be okay as long as I have the calculations.'

She shook her head against his chest.

'No, I'm coming – you go, I go,' she said into his surrounding arms.

'Let's get packed, then,' he said. 'The man has a date.'

They flew from Charles de Gaulle to Stavanger that night, were met by Oslo people and transferred the following morning to the SAS flight to Reykjavik.

'It's in Iceland?' Sally said. 'Brilliant, who would look for anything experimental up there?'

At Reykjavik they were met by Pauli Van Waveren who drove them to a local hotel for what was the first of six two-hour interviews. He studied them both with his hard brown eyes, his hands clasped behind his back like a policeman, and when he spoke, his voice was clipped and staccato.

'So, here you are in Iceland! How lucky you both are, lucky because you chose to make a demand on a group who care about life, enough to bring you here rather than just dump you in a canal somewhere. Just who the hell do you think you are?'

'I'm the guy with Cassalto's work,' Miller said, realizing the Dutchman was correct: they could be dead by now, both of them. 'And I know I could have been worked over for them, but that was a calculated risk and one I gave a sixty per cent chance of happening. I gave twenty per cent to being ignored and the other twenty per cent to our being granted our request.'

'Why did you want to come here?' Van Waveren began.

'I am a fast jets pilot on attachment to the Pentagon from the RAF, Sally is an astrophysicist, we both have a professional interest. We are not here to spy . . .' Miller said, sounding lame and knowing it.

'Bullshit. You work for MI6.'

'I am a serving officer . . .'

'. . . who also reports to MI6,' Van Waveren finished for him.

Sally turned and looked at him. He didn't deny it. The room was silent. She wasn't surprised, not really. Things began to fall into place.

'You would never have got near us unless that was what we wanted, make no mistake. It just so happens that it's easier to keep an eye on you here. The ways things are going it won't matter anyway. The world will know.'

'What things?' Sally asked.

'Not my place to tell you. If it turns out to be all right and things quieten down, then we have another way to keep you silent. Breathe a word and you will find life becoming difficult. You will be unable to get mortgage finance, borrow money anywhere, you will find yourself without a flying licence, without a job, possibly even committed to a hospital for the insane. We can do it. Every time you turn around we will be there. Make no mistake, Mr Miller, we are powerful, and we will use our power to protect what we have and do anything short of killing you. I would personally do just that, and in the past we have done, but I don't dictate policy in this organization – it's run by men who are essentially pacifists. I wouldn't have let you within a thousand miles of our project, but as it turns out, it might just be the best place for you both.' Van Waveren was seething with anger, all his instincts telling

185

him not to proceed, but his respect for Sagan and Haidermann overpowered the more personal reaction.

'Now, again, why did you go to Dubois? Isn't it a little coincidental that you were in Melcesine the day Cassalto was killed? And when you answer, remember this; I spent six years running the anti-terrorism squad in the Hague police. I can smell lies before they are uttered!'

Miller tiredly began to answer, knowing that they would get no further unless he told the truth and told it convincingly.

8

Carson looked across at Digby Allison in the other seat in the simulator and flashed a grin.

'Okay, here we go, target in twenty seconds counting. Now. One, two, you take it.' Allison nodded and began calling instructions to his pilot as any weapons systems operator would.

'Range six hundred miles, dead ahead, round a bit, sorry, left, that's it, on the nose, count down nine seconds, lasers operational, secondary target bearing . . .'

Carson cut in then. 'Cut the bearing shit . . . this isn't a ship, tell me where it is, left, right, behind the other one, six o'clock, nine o'clock, where?'

'Sorry, two o'clock, another behind it, we are tracking three ready to fire, ready to fire, ready . . .'

Carson pressed the fire control button on the column and watched the computer instantly select the next target, pressed again.

'Splash one, splash two . . .' He looked up at the head-up display where the third target should have been – there! He fired again, the contact fading from the screen instantly.

They sat in silence for a few seconds, then Digby spoke over the hum of the gear in the simulator.

'I don't know why we are doing manual tracking-firing when we have a perfectly good computer to do everything.'

'Because, my little pommy mate, Murphy's Law says the kit will break down when you need it most. Let's do it again, we're getting this cracked.'

Carson was pleased with the progress they were making. Soon he would give Digby his first flight in the Tarbaby: that will blow his mind, he thought. They had run through the computer systems over and over, the machine tracking and destroying multiple blips again and again, and Carson, once happy with that, immediately commenced manual systems training.

With luck they would never need the multiple capability with the Russians. Not since they had developed their doomsday system. If the Russian leaders were all killed, a computer would launch a rocket that would broadcast a code to launch the nuclear missiles. Get that rocket and its back-ups and the missiles would never leave their silos. But they trained anyway, because the Russians weren't the only people with multiple launchers.

They were still running every morning and now, on occasions, Yamashita joined them, running tirelessly beside them with his boken in his hand, chatting in a most un-samurai-like manner about girls, cars, and test rugby. He was a fervent supporter of the English team and hated the All Blacks with a vengeance; he described Jonah Lomu as a running tree. The evenings were as varied as Carson could make them, sometimes walking with Gail up on the surface in the soft chilly moonlight, or playing cards or Trivial Pursuit in the mess, reading early and carousing in the bar as the evening livened up, or sometimes just sitting with Gail in her room, a softer, frillier version of his with a large fluffy continental quilt on the bed that he relegated to the floor as they made love. Gail, when alone with Carson, was now quite different from the super-efficient controller whose presence dominated the operators so strongly.

That evening, while he laboured through a technical manual on applied laser technology, she sat naked, cross-legged on her bed brushing her still wet hair, wincing as she eased out the snags and watching him, his eyebrows creased, as he tried to absorb the physics, content simply to be alone with him, watching the way he looked, smelling him, listening to him talk.

'I was with Leo in the office today.' She winced again as the brush caught a knot. 'He seems worried about something.'

'Mmm?' from Carson, his head still bent over the book.

'Leo . . . he's worried about something; something's happening somewhere. I think it might involve us.' She waved the brush impatiently, her breasts swinging attractively.

'What did you hear?' Carson asked.

'It's something to do with Iran – we have sources there like everywhere. They're building something that seems to be worrying Haidermann and the others on the committee.'

'What are they building? Shit, they can't even get their air force up in any strength, they don't have spares,' Carson said dryly.

'I don't know, but I heard Leo say, "Yes, we are ready to go." His ashtray was full, like when he's been on the phone for hours.'

Carson thought about that for a moment before speaking.

'Well, I guess it's possible, but they certainly don't have anything warranting the Tarbaby. They have a few Silkworms, but they have an HE head. If anything, they have built or acquired some more short-range missiles that they might want to use. Loaded with chemicals they could be nasty, but I couldn't get there quick enough to splash one. They only fly a hundred clicks at most.'

'Mmm,' she said, resuming her brushing. She caught another snag and swore at it and Carson smiled, put down the book and watched her instead, her body soft in the bedside light, her curves deep and sexy.

Carson sat with Digby in the canteen after an exhausting afternoon in the simulator, the technicians throwing everything at him that they could think of, from multiple

189

contacts astern to a complete flame-out, and sipped at a glass of milk while Digby was still eating.

'If I see another cathode ray tube I'm going to go loopy,' the urbane Englishman said. 'Frigging technical types, sitting outside the bloody simulator, think they are God's gift . . .'

Carson smiled, it was the standard bitching from air crew the world over after the exhausting high pressure testing of more things than could possibly go wrong in reality. He looked tired, Carson thought, but fit. The running, the diet and the curtailed drinking had paid off.

'Get a good night's sleep and no booze tonight.'

Digby said, 'No problem, I shall simulate drinking as well! But why?'

'I thought we could go flying in the morning,' Carson said casually. Digby looked up at him, half excited, half frightened.

'Leo just okay'd it. It's time. You're ready to try your stuff in the real thing,' Carson continued. 'We'll do a short sortie at sun-up.'

'Haa! Dawn patrol and all that . . .' Digby said weakly. 'Peter, there is something I haven't told anyone here . . .' he grinned sheepishly.

'What's that?'

'Well, old chap, I'm afraid I'm not a very good passenger . . . so if you could sort of take things gently for a bit . . . you know, just to get used to it.' He grinned again.

Carson lowered his head in his hands slowly. 'Jesus . . . spare me this shit! You fucking what!' he bellowed across the table, his eyes locked on the other like radar guns.

'Well . . . my father had an aeroplane. Took me flying once, threw up everywhere, haven't been since except on big commercial ones that don't go upside down or anything. Never thought this would ever happen, old chap.'

'Well, get used to it. Get some tablets from Neilson or something. We haven't time to change and train someone else,' Carson answered angrily, walking away from the table.

Next morning as they strapped in, their bright thermo-suits contrasting with the matt black interior, Carson looked across at him.

'Try not to throw up into the mask – lift your visor or you'll splatter it all over the inside.' He passed over a brown paper bag stolen from the canteen, shaking his head. Digby looked green already.

Carson took it easy for the first few minutes then decided to give the beast its head.

'Right, we're going to run-up to ignite scrams. You just do as I tell you, when I tell you.'

Digby nodded, managing a weak smile, and Carson began, keeping his wizzo so busy he didn't have time to get sick or worry as they streaked across the sky, testing and running the laser systems, the long-range radar and the computer-activated systems. Once at 100,000 feet and Mach 10, he looked across.

'Tell me about this laser system. Assume I know nothing.'

Digby began at once. 'Forward, below and above are weapons systems powered by main engines, pulse laser from one main source with an auxiliary delivery system. The laser is an x-ray, invisible, but we can fire a visible beam alongside for effect. The pulse rate varies according to the target composition . . .' He began to slow and Carson snapped at him, 'Don't be a wanker! Keep your mind on it and it will go, believe me.'

'. . . the main computer system lines up the beam and fires either automatically or on command. One trillion watts of power for one trillionth of a second and upwards from there as we need, to a max of a second. With that we can cut through concrete, or cut the biggest ship in the world in a tenth of a second.' He was now into his explanation and it was working. His sickness for-gotten, inside ten minutes he was actually enjoying the experience. On the way home Carson put the interceptor into a series of maximum performance manoeuvres and when they landed Digby climbed from the cockpit and vomited on to the pan – not airsickness but nerves and fear mixed with relief.

Carson knelt beside him and said softly, 'Digby, that's as bad as it could ever be and you were fine, well done. Now on your feet, don't let the crew see you sick . . .' They stood and walked into the ops room passage, Digby with a triumphant if still queasy smile on his face and Carson pleased with the exorcism.

That night Leo Sagan spent another hour on the phone to Charles Haidermann and although he discussed the call with no one, the mess had an expectancy about it, the air tense, charged with conjecture and talk. Carson ate with Digby and McReadie, neither of the other two discussing anything much, so Carson did not ask what was going on. It was later that evening when, in his room, Gail, tired after a day's training with her team and undressing straight on to the floor, brought it out. She had asked Leo outright what was going down and he had confirmed the Iran problem.

'He didn't tell me what they had, but he did say we might have to activate something called the "O'Casey Alternative".'

'The what?' Carson asked with a raised eyebrow.

'The O'Casey Alternative, he said, I don't know what that is.' She looked at him, pulling a rubber band from her hair and letting it fall across her shoulders. 'Maybe we all just bugger off home,' she added flippantly, going into his bathroom and running the shower.

Carson looked after her. He knew her well now and the offhand manner was indicative of something more. She was frightened, it was her way of covering it up and hoping it would go away. That night in bed she was intense and distant all at once, like someone trying to record something, to witness something without becoming part of it, afraid to get too close to it in case the emotions spoilt the memories.

Next morning Carson walked the extra flight of stairs up to Leo Sagan's office where through one glass wall you could look down into the control room. A suite of furniture was carefully positioned so that whoever sat there could see all that happened below. Carson knew that if it ever went down, this would be the command centre. Sagan was at his desk, a cluttered grey steel arrangement that would have looked more at home in the offices of a Korean construction company. Its upper surface was covered in several neat piles of papers, tins, pencils, pens and rolled drawings. Other drawings of the base and the Tarbaby were pinned to walls and a complex flow chart outlining production periods and sources dominated the wall behind the desk, together with a large world map.

He looked up and smiled.

'Good morning, Peter. How was Digby yesterday?' They hadn't had a chance to discuss the flight the night before and Carson decided to pass over Digby's little problem.

'You really want to know?'

'Speak your mind.'

'We've talked about this before. He has improved some, but he would never hack it as aircrew. I'd rather go alone or if I have to have someone in the other seat then I'd rather have Yamashita. He is disciplined.'

'Too late for that.' Sagan fished a cigarette from a packet and lit it, leaning back in his chair. He looked tired and the bags under his eyes were proof of the late nights that Carson knew hadn't been spent in the bar.

'What's going down, Leo?' Carson asked.

Sagan went over to the window overlooking the control room and spoke facing the glass,

'The years we spent planning and building her . . . we never really thought we would ever have to launch her . . . get the base ready. Be able to react, then go home and wait.' He turned back to face Carson. 'You'll find out later today, anyway, we will be setting Yamashita and the other programmers to work immediately.'

'The Casey Alternative?' Carson asked.

'O'Casey . . . yes,' Sagan raised an eyebrow. 'Been reading the old papers in the library?'

'No . . . what's the Alternative and to what?'

Sagan lowered himself into one of the chairs and indicated that Carson should do the same.

'How do you see your brief here . . . what's your job?' Sagan asked.

'To hunt and kill missiles,' Carson replied with a shrug.

Sagan nodded. 'That was always the mission we set ourselves. Place ourselves as close to the path of ICBMs as possible and be in a position to prevent any ever getting to where they are targeted for.'

He stubbed the cigarette out. 'That's why you have the loiter facility on your Tarbaby, that's why she was designed to mid-air refuel. Just sit up there circling while the lasers did their magic. A Star Wars way ahead of its time and there for all mankind.'

Sagan paused there for a moment almost like a man defeated.

'Then in eighty-three, we had a mad crazy Irishman called Michael O'Casey who did a paper for Oslo. He was a wonderful, passionate man, a real scholar in the old sense and the finest economist that the Emerald Isle ever produced. He died a year ago. Anyway, he wrote this paper, untitled, which became known as the O'Casey Alternative. It was an alternative to the Tarbaby, a scheme of financial blackmail and coercion of staggering proportions and astounding simplicity. He wanted to hit them where it hurts and force agreement for complete nuclear disarmament in the process.'

'But the Tarbaby exists and works,' Carson said sensibly. 'Who needs any alternatives? You can't blackmail a Minuteman once it's launched.'

Sagan smiled. 'Yes and no. We have a situation in the Gulf of Arabia that may require both options . . . once the Tarbaby has gone up and the Omega Project has been compromised to the world we will have to move on the O'Casey Alternative. We will be forced to. We will have, we estimate, two to three days to force the issue before we are as toothless as the United Nations, God bless that august body, but damn their empty rhetoric,' he finished acidly.

'Say again?' Carson asked.

'We may have to do both. We may have to use you to prevent the possible problem in the Gulf and then, out in the open, force them by other means fair and foul to disarm before they find us here,' Sagan explained.

'What problem in the Gulf?' Carson asked. He remembered Gail's remark about the Iranians and felt adrenalin rising as he leaned forward.

Sagan looked back at him, his gaze measured and precise from his bright brown eyes, one hand stroking the salt and pepper goatee. Then, as Carson watched, a wave of sadness washed over him.

'We have reason to believe that they have acquired a nuclear warhead and they are going to use it soon,' he said resignedly.

'Fuck me!' Carson said in awe. 'How big, and what's the target?'

'Oh, it's big,' Sagan said, going to his desk. He pulled a roll of drawings clear and spread them on the desk, putting an ashtray on one corner and a pencil holder on another and holding the last two under his hands as he leaned forward.

Carson walked over.

'Tavis has built a mock-up down in the shop. He believes this cradle rack will hold about two thousand pounds weight. These days, they, and I mean any relatively clever university student, could build a medium-sized nuke weighing in at half that.'

'What's the delivery vehicle?' Carson asked, running a finger along one of the pale blue lines.

'We aren't sure yet, but they will definitely drop it. The real thing is being built at a place called Bandar Abbas, on one of their airbases.'

Carson nodded, his eyes narrowing.

'They have a few F-5s and a few old Phantoms. Nothing that will deliver a load that big in one piece slung underbelly. They will possibly use something larger, slower, a converted commercial maybe.' He was thinking aloud. 'That would also help them get overhead without being tumbled. That also increases the range they could operate at.' He stopped and looked up at the map behind the desk.

'Baghdad, Riyadh, Bahrain, Dubai, Kuwait, at a push even Tel Aviv . . . all possibles.'

'And then the fall-out,' Sagan said, puffing on a new cigarette. 'The fall-out with a southerly or a south-easterly would blow it back at them, so they would need a day when the wind was at their backs, from the north, that would take the cloud down over the Saudis or Egypt whatever happened, maybe the Sudan and the rest of Africa. We are talking millions at risk here, Peter . . . just not the millions we originally thought at risk.'

'What sort of int do we have, how fresh is it?'

'It's good, considering. We will know when the cradle is finished, when the crew arrives, and whatever they are going to fly – we are about an hour behind at this stage. We are getting some extra comms gear in there so our man can talk direct through the Taurus series satellite to us here when it gets near.'

'How near is it?' Carson asked, looking up at Sagan.

'Ten days, a fortnight, we aren't sure . . .'

Christ! thought Carson, it's a whole new scenario. Down in the heavy air, quite possibly a subsonic bogey, going in on a target at a height and speed unknown. Oh Jesus. The memory of the four kids in the Citroën washed over him.

Not again. It's all right. It's not kids. It's terrorism, he said to himself. These cunts want to nuke someone. I can take 'em. Talk about killing a fly with a sledgehammer, that's if Gail can find it for me. I'd rather have an EFA for this or an F-16 or something. He suddenly had a thought.

'This bomb, will it be armed?'

'Well yes, after a fashion . . . what do you mean?' Sagan asked, not sure what he was asking, but Carson interrupted.

'Armed. If we hit this aircraft will the bomb go off?'

'No, definitely not. Even the Iranians wouldn't be that crazy. It has a three-stage arming system that needs stages one and two completed immediately prior to letting one go. Without those two completed it's very stable. There are other detonation systems, but none for use in this application, thank God!'

Carson looked back down at the map and shook his head.

'We need some decent maps. Standard aviation ones, with air corridors, control zones, beacons . . . we are talking about our target being down in amongst commercial traffic. There will be a lot of clutter contacts on my screens, this will be a visual strike. Do you understand me? I must see it!'

Sagan looked at him, feeling the repugnance he felt whenever he heard talk of killing in such a casual manner, and had to remind himself that the man opposite wasn't the usual Oslo recruit. He wasn't a pacifist, or a scholar. He wasn't a thinking man's fanatic, as old Mr Chambers had once described them all. He was a professional hunter, he was a fighter pilot, a gunfighter on the payroll.

As he looked the repugnance died away and a more secure feeling replaced it. He remembered being a boy, a tall, gangly, thirteen-year-old with steel-rimmed spectacles in his brother's hand-me-down jacket, his school books under his arm, walking home along a cobbled street in Copenhagen on a crisp autumn evening. The boys had

197

come from behind the ironmonger's on the corner, big boys, all five of them. The leader, Bjørn, was the son of the local coal cart driver and had a vicious streak that had seen him in trouble with the police before. As they approached he felt his breath quicken and he held the books tightly under his arm. They cost money, but more than that, they were his escape from the greyness, his way out of the old, tired buildings and post-war depression. His way out of the smell of fish and oil and brine that was the way of life here for so many. Bjørn, a red-headed, thick-necked boy of seventeen, stood squarely on the road ahead of him, an angry frustrated sullenness to his features.

'Well, well, well, snotty Sagan, teacher's little bumboy!'

He had stood scared and outnumbered wondering whether to run or to fight. One was to be laughed at, and one was sure to end in pain and humiliation, but he was Gunnar Sagan's son, and Gunnar Sagan, watchmaker and lay preacher in the Lutheran church at the top of the street, bowed his head to no one but God, not even the Nazis. So Leo tightened his hold on his precious books and quickly pulled his glasses off, pushing them into his pocket and bunching his fist in readiness for the beating he knew was to come, scared, his heart thudding like a side drum in his thin chest. Then another boy stepped from the grocery shop. Larsens Provisions, Established in 1898, the sign said proudly. Leo knew him vaguely, he was Kai Hansen, a lithe boy a year younger than him but at the same school. Kai's father ran a fishing boat and the boy often arrived at school smelling of herring. He walked over and stood beside Sagan, a good three inches shorter but wiry and strong from heaving crates of herring about the dockside.

'So. Now we are two, you blood-headed piece of shit!' he had said, in his still unbroken boyish voice. Leo had turned and looked, astonished, thinking, now we're for it, that was very provocative to five bigger boys who want nothing more than to beat us up. Hansen's eyes burned like coals, bright blue little coals, in his white pinched face as he held the bag of flour his mother had sent him out to get, and without a second's hesitation and still holding the flour he swung his foot up, encased in a steel-capped deck boot, right into the crotch of the big red-headed boy. Leo heard the grunt of pain as the boy went down on the cold stones, his face in the slush, moaning. Then Hansen thrust the bag of flour at him and he took it, surprised and stunned at the speed of the attack, and watched as the small, tough little fellow moved forward like a mongoose, his hard fists jabbing up into the faces of his lumbering adversaries, each blow splitting the skin beneath the sharp knuckles, a wild grin on his face as his boot caught a shin with a satisfying crack. The older boys turned and ran, leaving their leader still lying on the street holding his testicles.

Hansen bent over him breathing lightly. 'Listen to me, Bjørn. This is my friend; leave him alone or we will talk again.'

He stood and, taking the bag of flour from Sagan, smiled brightly, and together they walked up the street. Sagan helped him with his schoolwork all that year, Hansen devouring the extra tuition hungrily. Once Leo's mother had said, 'Stay clear of young Kai, he is a fighter that boy, he is rough!' but while he agreed with the description, it gave Leo a nice warm feeling knowing that Hansen was around. As it did now with Carson.

The next few days went by in a blur for the teams at Omega Base. While Carson and Allison trained for hours in the simulator, honing new skills on above-positioned attacks on subsonic targets, Gail's girls waited for the technical teams to complete the links on the satellites they would need for communications and radar links in the temperate regions and the tropical areas, rather than for the polar area.

At the Deia house things were moving at an equally

hectic pace. Haidermann had called an extraordinary meeting of the policy committee and they had been in session all the previous night. Meran, the grand old man of the original group who had sat that morning in Oslo over fifty years before, had been the first to arrive, sprightly on his stick, like an actor playing the part of one so old. Cosham, a Sheffield industrialist, and Nakasa, the Japanese Under-Secretary for Defence, were next, with the Swede, Yakkonen, last. Others had come to the huge thick-walled old stone bodega in answer to the call.

There was Loren Gillivan, an expert on civil economics who had written several papers on the cause and effect of disturbances to the balance of the marketplace. Her counterpart, Oslo's expert on governmental finance, was a dry-humoured Swiss father of seven, who even with the best efforts of his tailors looked like the Michelin man. To Haidermann's constant amazement the tubby little wizard had married one of the most beautiful women in Europe, because, like the bumble bee, which flies in defiance of aerodynamics, no one had ever told Kurt Wagner that he couldn't do it. He had promptly begun breeding their bloodlines and now seven extremely bright and beautiful children ran amok in their huge Lake Geneva home. Vittorio Gorlini was a Milan-based retired diplomat, who until last year had been Italy's permanent representative to the United Nations. He was, without doubt, Europe's most talented professional observer of events and had an uncanny knack of predicting exactly what would happen next, given any scenario of incidents, no matter how unrelated they might seem. This rare talent was eagerly put to work by Haidermann who sat the three experts down in a room and gave each a copy of old Michael O'Casey's brilliant paper, his alternative to the Omega Project. At the same time a series of instructions went to the Oslo organization in Europe, America, Australasia and the Far East. These instructions were sent out from the Wall Street offices of the company Haidermann had set up back in the fifties. The dry, dusty, walnut-panelled rooms were the hub of the mightiest financial empire the world had ever known.

The instructions were in the form of warnings to directors and managers in a thousand companies that they would be receiving new policies for immediate implementation, without question. The policies were from the company's owners and on any failure whatsoever to action the new orders immediately all large bonus options and large salaries would cease to exist. The corporations, companies and conglomerates were spread across the world, with a heavy bias in high technology and media. A well-known Australian corporate raider called Matlock, who had been buying newspapers for years, was in fact an employee of Oslo, and his purchasing coups over the years were alone a sizeable slice of the western world's media. His latest ventures had broken clear of the media; he had invested heavily in AT&T and Bell Telephone and his most recent purchase had been shares in the only private organization which owned satellites orbiting the earth that sold time to the communications companies. He took a call from Haidermann himself and after a few moments of small talk they began talking business. Within the hour, Matlock had summoned his team of executives to the London office of 'his' company. That was the first of dozens of meetings late into that night employing the finest management brains in the West to launch a scheme that would horrify half of them and delight the others with its simplicity and its audacity. Oslo's activists were at work. Outside the world of commerce others started to become involved, coming active after years of just talking about it, and others still who had been overly active being reined in and redirected. Hard-core campaigners for nuclear disarmament, Greenpeace activists, churchmen, women's groups, all were briefed to expect something to happen and to support if they felt it correct. Oslo was in no doubt they would.

In a magazine subscription department in the offices of the *National Geographic* two duty operators were asked to run a program on the mailing list database with an access they hadn't seen before. The more senior of the two, a woman by the name of Beth Rudgren, nodded at the senior vice-president who had made the request and pressed the program into action. From the huge capacity of the magazine's mainframe a massive program began to run, printing a list of names, by location, by trade or profession and lastly by task. It was the only existing complete listing of anyone who had ever indicated they might be prepared to actively help an effort to get rid of nuclear weapons. It ranged from truck drivers who delivered bread to airbases, to newscasters who would drop something into their programmes while on air. It even had the name and address of a woman who years before had said she would cut sandwiches for the protesters at Greenham Common airbase in England, except that she was living in Nova Scotia.

Just after midnight that night James Kirkmill, a Scottish doctor and a very senior Oslo man, caught the Heathrow flight to Moscow. He had had a visa for three weeks awaiting this call and twelve hours later he walked through the late afternoon crowds beginning to gather in the Moscow underground awaiting the contact, the all-important contact with Gulag. If Gulag was not ready then the whole plan could fail. He was met a few minutes early by a taxi driver and driven across town by the man who managed to say absolutely nothing the whole journey, a feat that staggered Kirkmill who was used to the chatty drivers in his hometown of Glasgow. He sat in the back and packed his briar pipe tightly and lit it noisily whilst watching the buildings pass in the window. Half an hour later he had recognized the same building twice and realized the driver was doubling back, making sure he wasn't being followed. Then suddenly he did a sharp left turn off the road and up an alley, accelerating rapidly before swinging left again and into the open doors of what seemed to be a small factory courtyard.

Kirkmill stepped from the car and rubbed his ruddy features with a large meaty hand, then, jamming his pipe back into his mouth, puffed it patiently like a man given to fly fishing and old dogs, which he was. A second man waved from a door and he walked over and entered, ducking through the narrow gate, and was led up a flight of stairs into a small cheerless room with peeling paint and a smell of damp. In the corner, in a hard wooden chair, a figure sat, straight-backed, strong and exuding an aura of power that unnerved Kirkmill. He was tall, clear-faced, surprisingly young and the proffered hand wore a heavy signet ring.

'Welcome to Russia,' he said, the voice cold and full all at once.

'Thank you, son,' Kirkmill replied. 'I've been looking forward to visiting for many years ...'

'But hardly under these circumstances, doctor,' the man said. 'I am Stravinsky and, for my sins, I am the head of Gulag. Forgive the method of your arrival,' he smiled bleakly, 'but you can understand our preoccupation with security.'

'Aye, that I can. Can we talk here?' the Scot asked.

'Yes, it is quite safe for the moment. We will be warned if we need to move,' Stravinsky answered, indicating a second upright chair. Kirkmill sat, adjusting his coat and tamping his finger into the bowl of his pipe before speaking.

'Well, Mr Stravinsky, the question is this. Are you ready?'

Stravinsky gave his cold, mirthless bark of a laugh. 'I thought you would ask that.'

'It will break soon. They have some real lunatics loose there. Hezbollah extremists or something similar. We believe they are out of control and going to use the bomb they have built in the next week or so. We are going to try to prevent that, but we may compromise ourselves to the extent that we will have to keep moving while we have the ball. So, we are making plans to come out of the bottom drawer, with everything we have at our disposal. That means, in case no one has ever demonstrated the extent of Oslo, almost half a million full members and upwards of a further four million who have indicated in some form they will support whatever happens when it goes bang . . . so, laddie, what have you got available here?' The Scottish doctor leant forward, his sharp squirrel-like eyes intense.

'Mr Kirkmill, in Russia we have more freedom to speak than ever, more freedom to hold our own views, but make no mistake, this is far from ideal when it comes to raising an army. What we have is smaller, but considerably more qualified. Tell me what you are planning and we will see what we can run here in conjunction with your efforts.'

The talks ran for six hours, Stravinsky increasingly impressed with what Oslo were planning, the magnitude staggering. When he began to offer support, Kirkmill in turn sat back to listen while the Gulag facilities were paraded before him. Stravinsky played his cards slowly by nature and training, trusting no one completely, not even Oslo's senior people, leaving several trump cards up his sleeve. The meetings rolled into the second day at another location. By the morning of the third day, Kirkmill and Stravinsky had the basis of a plan, and by the evening of day four the work was done. Gulag would immediately commence preparations to move within the week against a select few targets in sequence. If they received massive public support, then all the better, but they would be prepared to go alone with Oslo's support from outside.

When Stravinsky bade farewell he finished with a remark that made Kirkmill smile.

'James, one thing, I am a humanist first, a Russian second, and a man who loves his homeland. I have no desire to do anything to my countrymen other than take their fingers off a button. If you people do the same. No more, no less. We are not interested in anything else. Do not offer it.'

'My friend, I wouldn't dream of it. Wait for our signal. It is time to forget differences. It has no place in what we do.'

'The next time we meet . . .' Stravinsky began,

'Aye. It will all be over one way or another,' Kirkmill finished.

The night Kirkmill left Russia, Leo Sagan asked all heads of department up to his office after the evening meal. When they were settled he began a briefing on the Iran situation and the progress of the O'Casey Alternative think tank. He finished by making another announcement.

'For the first time since this project's conception we are going to have two visitors who are not Oslo.'

Various people murmured around the room, some looking amazed and others angry. 'One man and a woman, who already know too much, and both have conflicts of interest. Charles thought they would be better off here where we can keep an eye on them at this critical stage. They wanted to see the Omega as part of a bargain, so they shall see it . . . and then stay here till things have blown over. Mr Van Waveren will be bringing them in tomorrow morning. Common courtesies please, no point being childish. All answers to questions, "no comment", please. I will answer anything they feel a burning need to know.'

That night, five project staffers were recalled from leave, two from Mykonos and three from Munich where they were sharing an apartment conveniently near the Hofbräu-haus. That same night the Tarbaby was towed nearer the main doors while new fuel mixes were taken onboard and left there. The kitchen staff began cleaning the 'lunch box' that would be loaded aboard the aircraft if she took off with coffee, sweet drinks, sandwiches, glucose and water. Behind the cockpit, over the bunk and chemical toilet, was a locker for the box, originally intended for the loiter over missile track period when crew who had scrambled without eating would need it. Up in his room, Yamashita began an ancient ritual of the Samurai; laying out a long, narrow piece of soft cotton, he took a soft sable-hair brush and began to paint.

9

Manu Shahazan flew home just for the Friday and
returned to the base that evening. His children, who had
seen little of him, complained loudly as small children do,
but his wife was silent on the issue. She seemed to understand he was under pressure, but knew no more. That
flight back to Bandar Abbas civil airport was the most
nerve-racking he had ever made. Security inside Iran was
as tight as in Nazi Germany or the old Soviet Union, with
all travellers internal or otherwise coming under strict scru-
tiny. Even with his military identification and his leave
papers open-ended, he was, he thought, being watched.
His concern was being discovered with the five component
parts of the new transmitter about his person and luggage.
This tiny piece of space-age technology could throw a signal straight upwards to a waiting satellite with remarkable
clarity, even under appalling broadcasting conditions. The
tiny Duracell batteries that powered the system were sitting
openly in an ageing Sony Walkman, but the other parts
were more carefully disguised. The main panel of micro-
circuitry was hidden with typical Oslo practicality in
amongst the innards of the Walkman, and the link section
was the shiny new belt buckle he wore. The batteries and
the circuit board slotted on to the inside of the buckle and
formed the base of the microtransmitter, which was, in
fact, two generations on from the type used on lifejackets
for search and rescue operations. The difference with this
one was the tiny microphone built into the earphones of
the Walkman and the four metres of thin wire that was
tightly rolled in the base of the new stem to his pipe.

Once back at the base and in his quarters he sat and with shaking hands assembled the pieces. There was no receiving facility; he would just have to trust that the tiny transmitter was working and trust the orange pinpoint light that his father said indicated signals going out. The next problem was getting near enough to the maintenance hangar to establish when the aircraft was going to go. They said they wanted as much notice as possible, with an estimated time of departure and a visual description of the aircraft. That much was easy. It had arrived the day before, an ageing Fokker F-27, its livery faded and peeling. They had begun the repaint job the night before and the drums of red and green that had come in last week meant either MEA livery or something more exotic. Either way, he could give them type and colour and there weren't that many F-27s around the Gulf. He stripped off and walked the narrow corridor sweating to the showers with a towel around his waist. He stood under the water letting the dribbling, lukewarm stream wash away the day, the trepidation and fear along with the sweat.

His father had told him what to look for if he managed to get near the secure cage in the hangars. Between forty-eight and sixty inches long and about sixty inches in circumference, matt finish alloy with conventional fins which would be added just prior to take-off. The exterior finish was the thing to notice, he said. Polished zirconium and steel alloys, the colour of dull silver plate, the casting so strong that it could withstand an air crash without plutonium leakage, just the way the Russians had built them ten years ago. They had sold this casing believing it to be bound for the Technology Museum in Munich and the real buyers had loaded the working chambers with an SS series warhead. He would keep his eye out for that but, in reality, didn't expect to get near enough to see anything.

He walked back to his rooms, still dripping water, and stood with his back to the air conditioner, letting the cold air run over him; when they worked they were a real luxury. He was thinking about the evil in the secure cage and actually accepting that he was about to betray his country, recognizing that it had to be done. Then finally, for the first time in sixteen years, he faced Mecca and began to pray to Allah to give him the strength and the opportunity to defeat the evil, with only the mat between his knees and the hard floor. When he had finished he got into his bed and a half-smile played on his lips as he thought, the Will of Allah is the Will of Allah and what shall be shall be; with a liberal dose of cunning and a little bit of luck, all will be well! He rolled on to his side and looked briefly at the Sony Walkman, now reassembled on its side on the bedside table. Allah's will and a little luck, he thought. He slept fitfully that night.

Iceland

Miller sat uncomfortably in the entrance hut, blindfolded and holding Sally's hand as they waited with Van Waveren for Sagan to arrive at the head of the tunnel. He was disorientated and had no idea where they were. The helicopter had not flown either straight or level and any attempt by him to establish direction had largely failed. They had crossed into the wind several times and he had felt the rotors change their angle in what was a stiff breeze, but with the flight duration they could be anywhere in Iceland, or for that matter, within an hour or so off Iceland on the water somewhere. That was unlikely because whatever they were sitting on was stable and without vibrations or rolling. He felt Sally squeeze his hand briefly.

'Right,' Van Waveren said. 'When Mr Sagan gets here I will guide you to a set of steps. You will climb down and once below your blindfolds will be removed.'

Five minutes later they were on the next level down and rubbing sore eyes, looking at a tall, academic type who was stroking his goatee beard and smoking a cigarette. Miller shot a look at Sally, who seemed all right.

'My name is Leo Sagan. I won't welcome you here, that would be too much to have to do. While here you will restrict yourselves to accommodation areas unless guided by myself or a department head. You will also refrain from asking questions of anyone but myself. You will also refrain from trying to leave the complex unless, once again, I authorize your departure. You will only meet the rest of Mr Van Waveren's people who have, I assure you, considerably less patience with interlopers than he does.' He paused and drew heavily on the cigarette. 'Do you understand all that?'

'Yes,' Miller answered, 'it's quite clear. How long will we have to remain here and who are you?'

'That is difficult to answer right now. A few days at least. I will explain further later. If we do release you ... prior to the Omega flying, we have ways to ensure your silence, but for the moment you will stay until the whole world knows what we have here.'

'That's what she's called? The Omega?' Miller asked. 'Is she really as fast as it seems?' His long-silent question voiced itself.

Sagan laughed out loud.

'That's correct. She is. Omega is the project name, she has recently been christened "Tarbaby" by the man who flies her. It seems to have caught on. Come, we shall go.'

As they drove along the narrow, brightly lit tunnel Miller broke the silence, asking Sagan again, 'Who are you all?'

'A group of people who don't want a world with nuclear weapons, who are in a position to make sure they never reach ground zero,' Sagan answered succinctly without looking back over his shoulder. Sally, who up until now had remained silent, more than a little scared, finally spoke.

'Are you all Scandinavians and Dutch?'

'Your accent placement is good. No, we are representing almost every country in the world. I don't think we have any members in Burkino Faso ...' Sagan said dryly.

'But you represent no government or official body?' she followed up.

'No . . . we are pacifists, pure and simple, in the realistic sense of the word. Funded from within our own holdings and enterprises,' Sagan said.

Miller looked dubious. 'And you have built a hypersonic aircraft? What for?'

'I told you. To prevent any nuclear weapons reaching ground zero. We will shoot them down over the North Pole.'

Miller still looked dubious, but refrained from comment. It was all becoming startlingly believable as they passed blast doors and storage tunnels, but his natural reluctance would not give at once. He knew how difficult it was to chase anything that went that fast, let alone catch it and get it into gunsights. They obviously had some sort of new weapons system, as conventional air-to-air rockets or cannons were only any good at sub-Mach speeds. He thought for a moment and remembered the tests done in the States by the Navy and the reports of the Russian cruisers' classified systems.

'Lasers . . . is it armed with a laser?'

Sagan said nothing, just looked ahead as another of the bright neon strip lights rolled overhead, and Miller smiled to himself and took Sally's hand.

They had dinner in their room that night, brought down on a tray by the steward, and were just finishing when Sagan phoned.

'Come up the stairs outside your door and two flights up at the end of the corridor is my office. You can meet department heads to whom you will restrict your conversations.'

Miller agreed and together they walked the stairs up to Sagan's office. There was, as Miller and Sally both expected, more of the distant hostility, more of the interloper treatment but now they understood it.

'. . . and lastly this is Tavis. He is in charge of engineering. You will accompany him in the morning to see what you have caused us all so much trouble to see.'

Miller shook the man's hand gratefully: it had been the only one offered at all. Gail had all but ignored them and Yamashita had merely bowed his head briefly in their direction.

'You can meet the crew later, they are asleep right . . .' Sagan began, but was interrupted as the door swung open and Digby Allison and his pilot entered.

Jesus! Miller thought, his mind racing back with the images of his memories. A hazy German sky and the then flight lieutenant doing his first local sortie, a milk run orientation flight with three others who had arrived at the same time. The boss, a lithe, charismatic, casual squadron leader, had stacked up behind them, the new boys very wary of his eagle eye on their performance and his own superb natural skill at the controls of his fighter. Their careers rested on his appraisal every time they were airborne, every time they reacted. The German Widowmaker had come from the side, same altitude, and he heard the barked warning and reacted instinctively, diving clear of collision. For years he had thought about the reaction speed of the man who had barked the warning, the reactions that made the difference at low level with closing speeds of a thousand miles an hour. The four of them had watched him leave the base at speed in his car before the debrief and heard the story later. He had eventually resigned his commission over the affair. Now he looked across the room into the same man's eyes.

'Well well well!' Carson said. 'Tim Miller, as I live and breathe.'

Later, back in their quarters, Sally broached the topic as soon as they entered.

'You know him?' she asked unnecessarily.

'Know him? Yes, you could say that. I worked for him

212

for a short while. He was the boss when I went on to Tornadoes in Germany.' The memories raced through his mind.

'He was RAF?' she asked.

'Yes, we have a few colonials. He was shit-hot too. Ice cold in the air, a bit of a loner, so stories went, but a real maestro. If he passed you as fit for NATO, fit for a front line job, you knew you had the stuff. I watched him take a "tomb" ballistic once. He stuck it on its tail and hit the throttle right up into the left hand corner, hit the re-heat and away he went. He could do things with an aeroplane that it was never designed to do . . .'

'And he is on the crew of this Omega thing?' she surmised.

'No,' he laughed, 'not *on* the crew – he *is* the crew. Peter Carson is a commander and a P1. He would never sit alongside anyone. He's too good, far too good for that.' He paused there for a moment. 'But he can be a real prick. Ego the size of a mountain. We haven't seen this thing yet, but if Peter Carson is up here flying it out of this isolated shithole, it must be bloody good kit. Intercepting missiles, for Christ sakes! They do Mach . . . shit, it must be Fifteen at least!' He was caught up in the concept of Omega and Sally brought him back to earth.

'Tim, have you considered what all this really means?'

'Yes I have. Someone has broached all conventional thinking on flight with this . . .'

'No, I don't mean that. I'm just as excited as you and I want to see her as much as you, I want to see her specs, her flight data recorders . . . but have you considered what this means to us, as NATO, as the West, as . . .' she faded away there and looked at him and then picking up the threads began again stronger. 'Someone here, some people right here, have just made our defence system obsolete. Doesn't that scare you just a little, Tim? We haven't been at war since the missiles went in. It hasn't been worth it. The consequences are just too much to bear, so there has been no war. There has been an uneasy truce for forty years now between two ideologically opposed super-powers, each with their share of lunatic generals and war-mongers . . . but a truce all the same. If this system takes away our equalizer, then what?'

'Stop right there. You are debating an issue that has no answer. You Yanks are so insecure! What makes you think anyone wants your way of life, your land? True, the Russians have nukes, but they are a superpower no longer. Truth be known I would rather like a world without nukes, and I'll take my chances in a conventional war because we are better equipped and better trained and we have more to lose!'

'We should make every effort to report this. Our people need to know.'

'Of course they bloody need to know. That's why we are here!'

'Oh yeah. I forgot. You the master spy.'

'We've talked about this. Every serving officer is bound to do some intelligence work at some time.'

'Bullshit,' she snapped. 'You lied to me, you bastard!'

'I didn't lie. I just didn't tell you everything.'

There were coffee sachets and a kettle on the tray by the dressing table. He filled the kettle and turned it on. Tea bags too, he was pleased to see.

Two floors above, Sagan pulled the headphones off and smiled to himself. He never failed to marvel at people, at just how quickly they would accept the principle that nuclear weapons had no place on the planet, once offered an alternative or a way out of the power balance syndrome. He looked across at Carson who sat sprawled on the sofa, one leg over the arm.

'This is a stroke of luck, you knowing him,' he said carefully.

'That's all it is, Leo. Luck,' Carson answered coldly. 'Luck and circumstances.'

'I don't much like circumstance,' Sagan replied.

'Oh, for fuck's sake, don't be so dramatic . . . it's unbecoming in you. We served together once, that's all. It's a small world.'

'I shall have to accept that at this stage, won't I?' Sagan answered.

'Yes, you bloody well will. Now did you ask me up here for this, or did you have something more constructive in mind?'

'I thought that since you had served together, as you say, you might be able to fill us in a bit. What's his motive?' Sagan began.

'You say he is now with military intelligence. Fine. But it's probably more than that. Pilots are essentially simple creatures. We operate a machine. There is a certain amount of glamour involved from an observer's point of view, but we operate a machine. We are also a little egotistical and like the elitism of the whole thing. Faster, higher than anyone else, quicker on the turn, better combat skills. Is it so unnatural to want to get up close to the ultimate machine? The fastest, the highest. Never really rated him as much. He was okay in the air, but too political for me. Squeaky clean, groomed for the top jobs. He is now flying a desk. Sounds about right,' Carson offered.

'And the girl?' Sagan asked.

'Dunno. She says she is an astrophysicist. Check her out, give her some sums or something. On the surface she's his bit of fluff.'

'Hardly,' Sagan answered, 'her father is an analyst at the Pentagon. We considered recruiting him once, but he had no real skills to offer and we have people in there already who can tell us what's going on.'

Carson shrugged.

'Well you know more about her than me, then. It looks like it's going off anyway. Just keep 'em here.' He stood and stretched like a cat.

'Peter, we think we know what your target is going after.' He handed Carson a sheet of computer printout,

'After the airbus I think you will agree it will be irresistible to the lunatic fringe.'

Carson read the message and whistled softly under his breath.

Carson was standing with Sally and Miller the next morning when Tavis threw the switches in the cool darkness of the hangar and he watched Miller's expression as the halogen and tungsten quartz lamps on the grid burst into brilliance, illuminating the pan and the aircraft he had come so far to see. He smiled as Miller's jaw dropped in stunned disbelief, his eyes taking in the sleek, long blackness of her, the huge underwing fins that channelled air into the scram jet intakes, the sheer size of her.

'Goodness me! It exists. It really exists,' he said after a moment, awed by its presence.

It was Sally Schoeman who began taking small steps closer, her mouth open. 'The channels, do they affect the airflow underbelly? They are very small.' Tavis smiled in spite of himself: she had won him over with an intelligent question about his one true love.

'Significantly, lassie,' he began, and answered her question, the first of many from one aficionado of the school to another.

When finally they had walked the underbelly side and approached the steps up into the cockpit, Carson shook his head gently at Miller.

'Sorry, Tim, this is as far as you go.'

'I understand . . .' He gazed upwards longingly. 'Glass cockpit?'

'Yeah.'

'And her speed? Missiles go fast – can you catch them, really get close?'

'In this aircraft I can stern chase and overtake and take out anything that has ever been launched,' Carson said proudly, 'Low speed, anything under four hundred knots she wallows like a pig, but above that . . .' he looked for the word he wanted '. . . she is breathtaking.'

Miller smiled at him.

'It was worth it. All the aggro, all the hassle just to see her. Are you going to fly some time soon? I'd like to watch above ground if I can.'

Carson's smile faded. 'Maybe sooner than any of us want, that's why you two are staying here for the moment. Till it blows over, one way or another.'

'Sagan briefed us last night. I really should return to my squadron in case it involves us eventually,' Miller answered.

'Nice try, Mr MI6. Stick around here and watch the fur fly. You will never see the likes of it again, not in your lifetime.' Carson looked up at the Tarbaby fondly. 'If we go . . . if we go, that is.'

'Will you?' Miller asked.

Carson grinned. 'Dunno, I'm just the jockey,' but his eyes were hard as flint and steady and piercing, and Miller knew as Carson knew, that he would fly. He would go some time soon, and Miller suddenly wished he was in the other seat when he did. He too missed the punch and the adrenalin surge.

Sally arrived back at his side and together the four walked back to the doors.

Haidermann arrived that night with his committee and the three cause and effect experts. Wagner the Swiss was excited at the prospect of visiting the base; until now he had only heard about it. Loren Gillivan and the Italian would only stay for the first day and would then base themselves in Dublin to watch and advise from there. Wagner would stay on, his wife and seven children remaining in the lakeside house. Meran, the mentor of them all, arrived the next day, eyes twinkling in broad good humour.

'So then, we are ready, are we?' he addressed the room,

peering closely at the Omega base staff. 'Young Gail. You are ready?'

She nodded twice, looking him in the eyes.

'And you, Peter, you and Digby ready?'

Carson studied him, the man behind it all, the last of the five up and walking. The man who had built a dream, a decent man, a God-fearing man, a peaceful man.

'We're ready,' he replied softly.

The fuel mixes were onboard, the aircraft rolled close to the doors, the compressor pipes for wind up laid out and checked hourly, the compressor humming softly back in the plant room. From tonight on the communications facility would be manned twenty-four hours a day by a duty technician and a member of the committee. The banks of gear clicking softly in the gentle light, but none watched more closely than the link to the Taurus satellite, the link to the frightened man at Bandar Abbas air force base. Above the receiver was a digital clock that read out local time and above it a bright cheerful little sun shone if it was daylight at the other end. It often helped those watching to orient themselves. Now it was a gentle curved sliver of moon in an inky blue background. An Islamic moon.

That night, as Gail curled into Carson's shoulder, she was once again the soft feminine woman that only he ever saw.

He slipped from the bed before dawn and ran with Digby and Yamashita, but now the banter had stopped. They ran hard and with a new strength, Carson pushing the pace and edging up the distance. This would be the last day they ran without a vehicle following. They were on an hour's notice for takeoff.

Paris

Raden leant back in the chair in his suite, his fingers pressed to his lips, deep in thought, while behind him Oxenburger sat, still bandaged, watching Chubb pace the room. Coffee cups littered the low table and outside the Paris dawn began fitfully.

'So, we don't have Miller or Schoeman's daughter any more and no trace of where they went. Italy has been exhausted, we are sure they aren't in Paris now, so what to do?' Raden thought out loud.

'Back to the drawing board?' Chubb suggested.

Raden nodded. 'Yeah, I think so, but let's narrow it down a bit, let's concentrate on UFO sightings, reports of anything interesting. The next time something happens we can get right on it.'

'We going home?' Oxenburger asked hopefully, nursing his arm.

'No we are not, you arsehole. We wait here. It's nearby. We sit and we wait for news from Langley, or NASA or the NRO or whoever sees something first,' Raden snapped.

Oxenburger had been nothing but a liability the entire mission and both his requests to have him replaced had fallen on deaf ears. He sneered at Raden's back.

'Sir,' Chubb began, 'how sure are we that this thing exists . . .'

'Two weeks ago I had my doubts, but now, with the Cassalto incident and now this Miller thing . . . it exists. Someone is going to a lot of trouble to keep it hidden; we will find it. Half of keeping something like this quiet is that no one knows it's there. Once it is known to exist finding it is relatively easy, it's just a matter of time. No one has ever looked for it before, because no one knew it was there, but now we know it's there, something is there, now we just have to locate it.'

'You make it sound easy,' Chubb said truthfully.

He didn't like Paris; people thought he was Algerian which was one step worse than being considered an American by Parisians.

'It will be. It needs a place to land, this thing, and all sightings have been northern hemisphere. That Spanish air force pilot said it was big, so we have something big, something secret. It's got to take off, but it can only do that from somewhere very private, out of the way. There aren't that many places in Europe that fit that description. We will find it.'

Indian Ocean

Admiral John B. Corey stood whipstock straight, lightly balancing against the gentle roll of the ship beneath him, looking out of the armoured glass port wing of the bridge. Across half a mile of water the destroyer USS *Valley Forge* sliced through the water like a torpedo, her engines pushed to keep pace with the Goliath she was a partial escort to. USS *Mississippi* shouldered the seas aside, contemptuous of their efforts, her huge engines giving her a steady thirty knots while her battle group, small but powerful, maintained station around her. Along with the *Valley Forge* was the *Charlestown*, another anti-submarine destroyer, and off to the right the *Morgan James*, a guided missile cruiser, ploughed her way north-west in concert, her station keeping so precise that she was more like a shadow.

Admiral Corey smiled to himself. Skip Masons, the *Morgan James* captain, was the most precise sailor he had ever commanded. His ship was always where she should have been. He had allowed a lieutenant on watch to let her slip off course one night, just by a few degrees for a few minutes, and the rest of the group had delightedly advised him of the fact by signal lamp. Corey thought the rookie officer of the watch was still probably having his arse kicked around the deck two weeks later.

He looked back to his own bridge, or more accurately, the bridge of the *Mississippi*. While it was in his group the *Mississippi* belonged to Captain Hyram 'Peg' Daniels, a crusty, salty, old navy man who inspired awe in his crews. He was called 'Peg' due to the limp in his left leg, the product of a large piece of red-hot shrapnel while serving aboard the USS *Matrix* in the Gulf of Tonkin. Then, as an ensign, he had shown the stuff for which the most powerful navy on earth selects its captains, and now, in his early fifties, he commanded the most powerful ship in the world. The *Mississippi*, recommissioned only two years before after decades in mothballs, was one of the only two battleships in service. Her sister, the USS *New Jersey*, was the other. They had been decommissioned after the Second World War; costly to run and at the mercy of the new generation of marine attack aircraft, they were considered obsolete along with the rest of their class.

Then the Argentinians occupied the Falklands and the Americans watched with some interest as the British sailed to take it back. Here would be the first air–naval action since the early days of Vietnam, with a new generation of armaments. The lesson was terrible. The fast, hi-tech, thin-skinned ships were death-traps. The French-made Exocet missiles, typical of the anti-ship weapons one could expect in an air launch scenario, were devastatingly effective. The lesson was learned, and the Americans immediately recommissioned their last two heavy ships, saved from the welder's cutting torch just in time. Re-engined, rearmed, fitted with the very latest in technology, they became the acme of the modern fighting ships. With their new weapons systems alongside the old they were indeed formidable. The sixteen-inch guns could throw their shells twenty miles using full-sized or sub-calibre rounds guided by laser. Up forward, where the old 'A' magazine had once stood, was a battery of Tomahawk cruise missiles, and aft of the after turret was the latest addition, a battery of anti-ship Harpoon missiles. She was built to take the punishment of a major naval engagement and her foot-thick armour plate would have an Exocet bouncing off like a pea. The only direct hit weapon that could kill her would be a brace of torpedoes or a nuclear strike. She was awesome, and with her battle group watching the sky and the depths ahead she was on schedule to meet up with the Arabian Gulf Task Force at 1900 hours tomorrow. She would then make her way up the Gulf for a five-day flag-waving visit. Admiral Corey and Captain Daniels were like the rest of the crew, absolutely confident that nothing could go amiss; after all, the *Mississippi* was the most powerful ship afloat.

Daniels moved on to the bridge from his day cabin and awkwardly approached the duty officer, a young lieutenant commander wearing his new stripes for the first trip.

'How goes it, mister?' he growled.

'Great, captain. The *Morgan James* is station keeping to within a micron and *Valley Forge* is, as usual, racing about the ocean like a puppy,' Commander Stevens replied.

'You ever served on a destroyer, son?' Daniels asked.

'No, sir.'

'They're good fun. Allows you to behave like a kid,' Daniels offered and, as if to illustrate his point, the *Charlestown* heeled sharply and took off after a simulated contact on her ASW screens, part of her ongoing training. Stevens turned to his captain.

'Captain Daniels, much chance of shore leave anywhere on this trip?'

'Reckon so, son. Yet to finalize details, but we can swing ashore somewhere.'

'Any idea where, sir? . . . I mean, I have a brother in Dubai . . .' Stevens finished.

'Bahrain, commander. It's Muslim and strict and there is some civil unrest at the moment. Shi'ites. The men will have to behave themselves. You could fly to Dubai, I guess.'

Stevens nodded his thanks.

From the other end of the bridge Admiral Corey watched the exchange, half an eye on the pair of young ensigns on the starboard wing. God, he thought, so long ago . . . once he had been that age, standing on the starboard wing of the bridge with another junior officer. It was on USS *Matrix*. He felt his stomach twinge in sympathy with the memory of the shrapnel, the massive blast on the bridge and his companion, Tip Saddler, braving the smoke and the flames to carry men from the devastation down the steep ladder through the attack. Tip had won the Medal of Honor for that and had scars down his back to this day. He was looking forward to seeing his old friend again as Saddler was commanding the Task Force in the Gulf. He smiled to himself. Wait until he sees my ships, wait until he sees my flagship, the son of a bitch will be green with envy! My flagship, he thought proudly, unsinkable, unbeatable, unless someone drops a nuke on her, he thought dryly.

The tension at Omega Base mounted steadily for the next two days. The teams under pressure worked longer hours than ever and reaction to that pressure manifested itself in different ways. A physicist attached to Yamashita's computer team was put to bed sedated by the doctor to avoid a complete breakdown, the other two crunching the coefficients for the fuel program had to work on to complete the new updates. Haidermann paced the office brooding and angry, pushing the team to complete their views on the O'Casey Alternative. The instructions had gone out, but Haidermann, in his long experience, knew that every new factor affected the outcome and constantly bombarded them with new scenarios.

Tavis's people were rapidly breaking open boxes of spares, items they thought they would never need because their aircraft was built for a one-time mission. Now she might need to fly extended periods, loiter and race, refuel in mid-air. She might be exposed to cannon or rocket strikes from conventional fighters, now she would be operating in heavy air conditions, low to the ground, and her conventional power systems were re-tuned to do more than lift her upward from a runway. He pushed them mercilessly, pouncing on any errors, and they responded magnificently. They fitted the never-used mid-air refuelling nozzle and increased the feeder line diameters in case they needed that option.

In the control room technicians tuned systems to give Gail Samuels and her girls big clear pictures on the display, pictures of the Arabian Gulf, and the flight simulator had its computers run the Bandar Abbas to Bahrain course seventy-six different ways, each with its flight time varying slightly. Whichever way the Iranian F-27 came in, whether over Muscat, Dubai or Kuwait, the shortest possible route gave Carson and Allison a minimum of fifty-seven minutes to intercept and shoot it down.

Carson's earlier fears about the bomb exploding on impact with the water were further allayed with the news that an accelerometer had arrived at Bandar Abbas. This meant the bomb would only arm itself once the airflow through the pedoheads indicated terminal velocity had been achieved. The possibility of a radiation leak worried them all.

Tempers began to fray and Sagan spent more time than ever adjudicating and keeping the peace. There were now people at Omega Base who hadn't been off the secure area in fifteen months and Carson's prediction was coming true. The cook muscled his massive frame in between an air-frame technician and one of the communications people who were about to come to blows over ownership of the last clean spoon on their table, applying his constant good humour and sizeable physical presence till things cooled down. Twice Digby had broken the rules and taken more than two drinks; the second time Carson saw. The English-man just turned away and continued talking to whoever it was he was with. Only two people on the entire base seemed unaffected by the strain. Yamashita continued as ever, accepting his fate, his karma, and becoming more and more professional as the hours went by. He checked his own work and that of the others, looking forward eagerly to the battle. The other was Carson: he seemed to have retreated into himself, spending hours hammering a squash ball around the court on his own, smiling pleasantly at others when spoken to, but otherwise becoming almost

224

serene in his calmness. As the pace pressured others, it seemed to feed his aura.

At nine local time, on the evening of 1 September, the tiny radio at Bandar Abbas sparked into life. The message was short. The bomb had been loaded into the fabricated bay of the Fokker.

That night, Carson and Allison sat in the hangar in deck chairs, their thermo pressure suits folded over flight boots so they could be stepped into, the ladder up to the open hatch on the Tarbaby in place and the blast doors rolled back. It was black as pitch in the hangar. Carson dozed fitfully while Digby fidgeted beside him in the other chair.

'You don't like me, do you?' he said.

'What?' Carson opened his eyes.

'You don't like me.'

'I don't dislike you. I just think you got the wrong job.'

'Look. I designed those lasers. There is no one better qualified to operate them!'

'Cut the shit. Just because you designed them don't think you are the man to be sitting in that seat. You started this so I'll tell you what I think. Up there we rely on each other. Totally. I rely on you and you rely on me. No fuck-ups. Absolute faith in each other's abilities and skills. And what do I see? A poncy bloody academic piss artist who gets airsick. You have no more right to be sitting in a cockpit than anyone else. Your have to earn the right! Every day! The truth. I would have bounced you a hundred times before now if I could. But I'm stuck with you. So you better fucking perform!'

Up in the control room they sat their own vigil.

10

Digby Allison looked across at Carson. The compact, lithe New Zealander lay sprawled in the chair, relaxed like a cat.

'You awake, Peter?' Allison called softly.

Carson's eyes opened. 'Mmmm,' he murmured.

'They are five hours ahead . . .' he paused. 'It will be dawn there soon.'

'Mmmm.'

'You and I, we are going to kill someone today. The pilot of that plane.'

Carson looked back at him, studying him in the dark. Recognizing Digby's need to talk, he let him carry on.

'I'm not sure how I feel about that, Peter. I know it's the only way, but it seems to be everything we are against.'

Carson shrugged in the dark and spoke softly. 'There isn't much I can say to that. If it's any consolation, I'm the one with my finger on the trigger. That's what I do. If we don't hit this bogey then a lot of people are going to die, so this one has to go. Could you live with yourself if you chickened out? No, I don't think you could. Anyway, it's just another plane, you don't see the people, you see a piece of steel and aluminium . . . sometimes not even that. Sometimes just a blip on the screen, a little blip. Now go to sleep.'

'I can't sleep. It's going to go soon, isn't it?'

'It will go when they are ready, it may be in five minutes, it may be five hours or five days. Go to sleep.' Carson closed his eyes himself then, knowing that his partner was wide awake, nervous and more than a little frightened. So was he.

'The things you said,' Digby finished. 'That was a shot well aimed. I'll try not to let you down.'

Deep in the rock above the hangar three communications people sat in the bright light of their hushed domain. Above them on the hillside, the huge dish antennae slowly tracked the Taurus satellite across the sky, its complex boards and circuits straining to receive the slightest signal from Manu Shahazan's transmitter. Behind the comms room in the hall-like control area, Gail's team lay stretched on camp beds beside their consoles. She alone was awake, her eyes never leaving the wall display, its geographical images overlaid with air traffic movements. A new contact entered the screen and she noted its IFF transponder number, a 747 northbound for London.

Bandar Abbas

As dawn crept over the dry red hills Manu Shahazan inched his way towards the parapet edge of the flat-roofed stores building that overlooked the hangars and main runway of the airbase. The morning was hot and sweat dripped from his face down his shirt front. He felt foolish, frightened and tired all at once. He had been on the roof all night except for the one brief terrifying walk up to the filthy windows of the hangar, where he had watched them winching the bomb into the aircraft's belly with a block and tackle. In the harsh light the aircraft's new paint job was festive and incongruous and for a moment he had been reminded of a travelling circus he had seen as a child. He had retreated to the rooftop, pulled the transmitter from its hiding place beneath the water tank and spoken quickly, hoping they were listening, praying they were listening.

Now, three hours later, the dawn was here and he knew in his heart that this would be the day. He raised the small binoculars to his eyes and studied the hangar doors, willing them to open to prove him right, but praying they

wouldn't, praying it was all some sick joke, a misunder-
standing.

Down wind he heard the familiar sound of the crew
truck and swung the glasses, instinctively watching the old
Bedford shuffle down the apron towards the line of F-4s.
They had arrived only yesterday and their crews had
remained in isolation overnight. The four fighters he could
see had missiles on the pylons and long-range tanks slung
underwing. He rolled back a few inches and drank
from the water bottle, taking several small sips, wondering what the Phantoms were doing here. They were
deployed in the north-west, usually, up nearer Iraq. He
rolled back again and swung the glasses up, trying to
see the faces of the men in the flight suits. Allah, please
no beards, Allah, not Revolutionary Guards, please . . . I
didn't warn them about an escort, shit, shit, shit. He pulled
the glasses down to wipe his eyes clear of the sweat and
lifted them again, focusing. A beard on the man climbing
the steps on the nearest. Oh shit, an escort. It's today. It's
now!

He swung the glasses back at the hangar as the doors
began to roll back, pushed by three or four ground crew,
his heart pounding in his chest. A small tractor moved into
the bright shafts of light from the dark gloom of the interior
of the hangar towing the F-27, bright in its new white and
red livery. High on the tail he could already see the green
cedar tree logo of MEA. When they start the engines, he
said to himself, when they start they will be going. Allah
is great, Allah is good, he will help us stop this abomina-
tion. He lowered the glasses and inched back towards the
transmitter where it lay in the shadows beneath the tank,
just as the footsteps began. He felt them rather than heard
them, turning fast, his eyes wide in fear, looking down the
barrels of the guns. There were five men, four green-
uniformed guards and the revolutionary mullah. The
guards had guns, Russian Kalashnikovs, and all were
pointed at him. The mullah stared with bloodshot mad

eyes, his anger and indignation spread across his dry cracked lips as spittle.

'What are you doing?' he screamed, kicking out at Shahazan, who looked up, his mind racing, God forgive me for this lie.

'Praying,' he replied angrily, 'who are you to question me?' Rising to his feet, 'I was praying.'

'With these?' the mullah screamed, pointing at the binoculars. 'WHAT WERE YOU DOING?'

One of the guards swung his rifle butt, catching him under the ear, and he went down dizzy and senseless for a second.

'Spying!' the man shouted triumphantly.

Shahazan looked up groggily at him, trying to think of a way out. Across the pan he could hear the turbo whine of the Fokker as she warmed up her engines. Oh my God, it's finished, he thought. His eyes flicked across for a millisecond at the transmitter by the tank three feet away hoping they wouldn't see it.

'You were spying for the Great Satan! You are an American spy!' the mullah screamed, kicking out.

A guard swung his rifle again and Shahazan tried to duck both blows, grunting in pain as a boot found his kidneys. A guard shouted in Farsi and pointed to the tank. Oh my God, they've found the transmitter, he thought, oh no, no, no, no. There would be no talking his way out of this one now and no way of stopping the bomb.

It was thrust in his face.

'And this? You imperialist bastard, you sucker of American cocks!' The spittle flew into his face from inches away.

Manu Shahazan looked back and, finding courage he never knew he had, he spat full in the man's face then blacked out briefly as the gun butt smashed into his cheek. He fought the waves of blackness and came back in time to hear the Fokker on her take-off run, glancing down at his watch from inches as another blow split his head open from the back.

'What is this?'

You ignorant little shit, thought Shahazan through the pain, you don't know anything. You are illiterate, you smell like a stable, you claim to represent God and yet you are everything he despises. I will tell you nothing, you fucking peasant! He spat again not caring now, knowing it was finished and he was a dead man. Knowing that he would just be the first of many today, many thousands, maybe millions. Fuck you and fuck your Revolution!

A boot swung in again and he grunted in pain. They dragged him to his feet, the bearded mullah in his filthy tattered robe screaming at him, and he was dragged down the steep stairs, spitting teeth, blood, mucus and vomit. At the bottom someone found some twine and as an unruly crowd gathered, he was bound and kicked and punched into a pick-up truck. The crowd like sharks in a frenzy rising to the exhortations and cries of the mullah, began to throw stones as the vehicle started its engine and drove quickly away. Shahazan, stunned and in pain, could only think that he had failed his father and his God and he prayed that he might be forgiven. He had become a devout man in the last few days and he did not fear death, because that was his path to Paradise. He feared for those that would be left after the day was done. In the crowd amongst the shouting men he had seen friends, shocked and frightened for him, but not daring to speak out lest they become part of the pogrom. They were also officers and although not trained by the Americans they could read and write and were educated men and so feared the hysteria of ignorance. The pain in his kidneys was extreme and he knew that when he passed water it would be red with blood, the boots and rifle butts had seen to that. He spat blood and rested his head against the bouncing floor of the truck, trying to think through the pain, the incredible waves of nauseating pain.

* * *

Sagan walked into the control room. Unable to sleep, he had paced the complex knowing he would end up there with the communications team and Gail Samuels. They would wait together. As he entered he was surprised to see Charles Haidermann sitting sipping a drink in the chair beside Gail, who flashed him a smile but said nothing. Her Polaroid glasses were pushed up against the tight bun of her hair and in the soft light she looked very young to Sagan, too young to be doing what she was trained to do.

'Good morning, Leo,' Haidermann murmured.

Sagan smiled mirthlessly back. 'I hope so, I really hope it is.'

Gail watched them both, understanding the emotions, the thoughts, the dreams and the fears that these men had planned for. She felt humble, honoured to be there and yet frightened by the humanity and fallibility they now displayed. Till now they had been godlike, but suddenly they were human.

She flicked her view back to the displays for a second and watched to see what had changed in the last twenty seconds. IFF transponders sat solidly beside the contacts identifying the aircraft, and, as she watched, a group of four military jets joined a spider web from lower altitudes. A fifth contact had appeared a minute or two before and was now making its way solidly south-east. She looked back at Sagan and Haidermann and found herself comparing them to Peter Carson. She was frightened for him. He was the one at the sharp end, the one up there where it was cold and lonely. So different from these pampered, intellectually gifted men.

She looked over to where her girls slept on the camp beds. Andrea King lay curled like a dormouse, wrapped in a thick blanket beneath an air-conditioning duct; to her left Chris Walker and Natalia, the wonderfully talented Russian girl, lay side by side, their two stretchers touching in the cramped corner. If things happened today Natalia would be watching Soviet traffic around the Black Sea and the southern republics. Chris would have the easiest job because there was no American air presence in the Gulf. She would just make herself useful. The communications technicians sat in an almost trance-like state, headphones on, eyes closed, listening for the faintest contact from Bandar Abbas. We should have heard by now, she thought, if they are going to fly today we would have heard by now. Perhaps Peter and Digby should stand down, poor dears, sitting all night in those lousy deck chairs, I'll ask someone in accommodation to rig stretchers tonight, she thought. She missed him and that was why she had opted to work the shift rather than sleep, she could be roused, dressed and at her console in two minutes, plenty of time to do her job. She looked up at the clock on the wall: twenty past one local time which made it 0320 Zulu, she added the three hours to Greenwich quickly, twenty past six in the Gulf.

USS Mississippi

Liam Kowowski, specialist fourth grade, leaned back in his chair and stretched. He was due to be relieved in an hour and he was looking forward to some sack time. The red screens, the eyes and ears of the ship, glowed back comfortingly at him as he watched the data move and shift like sand in water. He had better pictures of the Gulf air traffic than the control tower at Bahrain's airport, only six miles away across the shallow waters. He pulled on his headphones.

There were three other operators on the shift, each with his bank of electronics, screens and hardware. Behind them was a circular light-table affair where the duty officer could electronically overlay ranges, bearings and other data on to the main radar view. The two-hundred-mile radius normal when at sea had been clamped right down to sixty miles. Even so, the clutter of the Saudi Arabian land mass confused the images all the way down the left-hand side of the screen, with the island of Bahrain clear almost dead centre. The chief was at the station as the duty officer was now up at breakfast in the wardroom and, Kowowski thought, probably looking forward to getting ashore later in the day, but no more than me. He had been given the phone number of a girl by a friend who was with the Gulf Task Force. She was a stewardess with the local airline and apparently had very accommodating morals. She was English from some place called Birmingham and no one off any of the American ships knew what the hell she was talking about, so nasal was her accent. However, she did other things with her mouth that made one forget the language problem.

He looked back down at his console, pleased with the long-range view. His screens could look out two hundred miles, and although *Mississippi* wasn't a stealth ship and she was difficult to hide, here in the middle of a dozen other radars it didn't matter. Only out deep sea did she damp down her active radars, relying on her screen to watch the skies and the electronic warfare guys to begin working when any radar signal locking on to their mass with any strength was likely to become a problem whether from hostile intent or proximity alone.

He rubbed his eyes tiredly. In the sterile, air-conditioned, scrubbed environment the eyes felt it by the end of the shift. Once it would have been made worse by cigarette smoke, but not these days. Long hours, intense concentration and technically unable to leave their station without relief. They did, of course, to get down to the heads, and a blind eye was turned by the officers. He took the eye drops from the hard edge of the console and leaning back dropped the clear fluid into his eyes and blinked, looking back at the screens. It was instinctive now after three years. You never took your eyes away for more than a few seconds at a time. Four contacts appeared at the far end of his range and according to the IFF transponders they were military. He cranked his view up to the full two-hundred-mile range and, placing them in perspective to the other traffic, watched for a moment. Far out ahead of them, almost overhead Ras al-Khaima, was another contact, slower but on the same course.

Bandar Abbas

The guards had pushed the crowd of off-duty security men back with grins and excited anger and much shouting of commands. 'Yes,' one shouted, 'we have a spy, Captain Manu Shahazan is a spy!' Another said, 'I always suspected him – after all he was trained by the Satans themselves. I always knew he was a spy.'

They were pushed back by the duty guards and the mullah, and Shahazan was dragged, bloody and broken, up the concrete steps into the filthy, crumbling outer office of the base security charge room. There he was lifted and thrown into a chair as the excited mob was pushed from the office and the door slammed shut. The mullah sat importantly behind the desk, his eyes red with power and his hands shaking in anger. He had always disliked the adjutant, ever since he had his requests for cash turned down. He had not received money from Tehran for months and had been told that was a civil problem for him to address with his people in the capital.

Shahazan stole a look at his watch, surprised he still had it – it was a thing of great value to these illiterate peasants – and had trouble focusing on the face. His vision was blurred and his head pounded, piercing waves of pain, sharp shards of agony through his reasoning. Sixteen minutes, he thought, or is it seventeen, my God, I can't even count any more, sixteen, it's sixteen. He raised his head, trying to look proud and defiant and strong, like a man of the Azerbaijan and one that his children and father might be proud of.

'You don't know, do you . . . you have no idea what you have done, you simple fucking idiot?' he said to the mullah. The last two words were in English because Farsi has no equivalent richness of expression.

'QUIET,' the man snapped back, 'you will be on trial for your life as soon as the District Committee arrives. God's will will be done!'

'Bullshit! you cretin, it's your life that will go by the sword. Who do you think I report to anyway? HEY? YOU CUNT!'

The man wavered for a second and Shahazan pushed his charade further.

'Why do you think I like to lie on rooftops? HEY, DOG-BREATH!' He leaned forward, shouting with all the righteousness of a powerful official. 'I REPORT TO THE CENTRAL COMMITTEE OF THE REVOLUTION! Do you think a mission as important as this would go without being observed by us?'

The guards had stepped back now, uncertain who they were dealing with.

'Now then, I can understand you being a little over-zealous, what with a mission like this . . . do you know what the mission is? Mmmm?' He spoke reasonably enough.

'Yes, I know,' said the mullah finding his courage, 'but who . . .'

'WHO THE FUCK TOLD YOU! I WILL HAVE HIM SHOT!' Shahazan screamed. 'Now, then, shitlicker, you have one chance to redeem yourself, just one chance, or you and your thugs here will find yourselves clearing paths through the old minefields at the front. UNDERSTAND ME?'

My God, he thought, give me strength, this is working, they are bowing to their own paranoia. Pavlov, you wonderful man, thank you, Allah. He leaned forward, placing his bleeding hands on the desk.

'Now, I have to report a successful take-off to Tehran. So give me my coder device and when I've done that, then I might think about what to do with you!'

The mullah's hand snapped over the transmitter like a trap and Shahazan turned to the guards.

'If he doesn't give me back that unit in the next ten seconds, shoot him in the stomach. Understood?'

The guards, if puzzled before, were completely perplexed now and looked back and forth amongst themselves.

'Do you FUCKING UNDERSTAND ME?' Shahazan shouted, inches from one's face. The man nodded quickly and he turned back to the mullah.

'Give!'

The mullah looked at the levelled gun and reluctantly raised his hand from the transmitter. Shahazan scooped it up with a look of arrogance that changed to fear as he heard the sound of the base commander's car draw up outside. Suddenly, clearly and irrevocably, he knew what he had to do. He lifted the transmitter to his lips and pressed the button.

'It took off twenty minutes ago, repeat Oslo, it went twenty minutes ago,' then he looked the mullah in the face, defiant to the end, as the man took out a gun from his filthy robes, screaming obscenities.

'Allah Akbar,' Shahazan said, as he became the first man to die that day.

Carson lay awake in the deck chair, his eyes closed. It was cold in the hangar and the thin blankets hadn't really helped. He looked across at Digby who had pulled on his thermosuit an hour before, zipped it up and now lay snug inside its layers, asleep at last. He got to his feet quietly, stepped into the lightweight boots and pulled the suit up over his legs and torso like overalls. He sat back down and with one hand under his head, tried to relax again. So cold up here, he thought, God, I miss the islands, I miss the warmth of the wind and the feeling of the sun on my back. I miss the smell of Coppertone and barbecues and the rocking of a boat under my feet. And yet, for all that, it had lacked something. It had lacked Olivia, her laughter, her concern, her freckles and her understanding. For the first time since her departure he had begun to feel comfortable with someone else. They were alike and yet different, and both had understood the way it was. Gail was beginning to fill the void. I will take Gail to Antigua when this is over, and show her the special places, if I'm not the most wanted man on the planet, that is. He smiled in the darkness. He reached up behind his head to feel for the phone, it sat securely in its place. Why haven't we heard anything yet? I would have gone at dawn and caught the buggers at breakfast and changing shifts. If they don't go in the next hour or so, then it's probably off for today . . . and certainly on tomorrow. You don't leave a nuke in its rack for too long, not when you're loaded to go. We should hit it on the ground. Don't even let the fucker take off.

He had discussed it with Sagan and Haidermann, but they, in their academic fashion, had decided that possession didn't entail use. It had to be airborne and approaching a target before they could justify risking the Omega Project and Oslo on a pre-emptive strike. Just like the ICBM. That's the trouble with pacifists, he thought. They don't understand the principle of getting in the first punch, it makes all the difference. He smiled at the thought and relaxed into the chair.

Across the concrete, beyond the Tarbaby's tail, a sliver of light came from under the ground crew's room door. Occasionally Carson could hear some soft laughter and the door pushed open and a figure came over balancing coffee cups. He declined for Digby and accepted one for himself relishing the caffeine and the warmth as it coursed down his throat.

In the control room above, Gail jotted some notes on her pad, her eyes flicking across the radar images and telemetry projections and back to the main displays. Sagan and Haidermann chatted beside her, but she ignored them while she finished her log checks, entered the time and sat back. Every system was checked every forty minutes when they were awaiting a flight and she enjoyed the task, it helped pass the time and gave her something to do, something to take her mind off everything. She looked down over the tiered banks of monitors and equipment into the main hardware. Tucked into the corner of that haze was the comms unit. She could smell the ozone now, the gear all warmed up and humming, but silent as a grave. The listeners sat, headphones on, hunched in their world of hiss and crackle, ultra high frequencies and wave-bands.

Then, as she watched, all three sat up as if one. Two clasped their phones tighter to their ears and one turned to make sure the logging recorder was turning, watching the VU meters flick.

One turned to face her and raised a thumb in the air pulling his headphones off.

'Contact,' he shouted, 'it's gone, twenty minutes ago . . .'

Sagan and Haidermann looked up quickly, coming to their feet, faces ashen.

'Say again,' Gail said into her desk microphone, looking down at them.

'It's gone, twenty minutes ago, sounds like our guy got caught, there were gunshots in the transmission.'

Behind her Chris and Natalia began to stir, sitting up at the commotion.

'Oh Jesus, we're too late,' Haidermann said, almost to himself, then almost as an afterthought, but in more stunned disbelief, 'and they have shot him, they have shot Shahazan.'

'Perhaps we can advise the Americans,' Sagan said hope-fully, 'tell them what's about to happen.'

He looked at Gail and Haidermann. 'Well?'

'They won't believe it,' Gail said firmly, 'they certainly won't shoot down a civilian-marked aircraft on the strength of a phone call.'

Come on, she thought, come on, decision time, gentle-men, hurry up, we are fumbling the ball here. She looked at Sagan, the project director, willing him to say something, do something.

'We should try,' Haidermann said.

'Mr Haidermann, let's ask Peter,' Gail said quickly, 'we may have time.'

'It's gone, Gail, twenty minutes ago,' he said irritably.

'Oh, for Christ's sake,' she shouted, 'this is critical.' She ripped the phone off its cradle, punched the three digits through to the hangar, it was answered immediately.

'Peter, it took off twenty minutes ago . . . have we got time . . . ?'

Then she heard the phone drop against the wall and knew he was running across the pan.

'Stand back, please gentlemen, we have work to do. Natalia! Chris! let's go . . .'

They pushed their way past the two men and sat at their consoles, flicking switches and punching keys to access their fields.

'Log time at 0348 Zulu, mission commences,' Gail said into her mike.

11

Carson was already running his gloved hand over the sequence when Digby reached his seat and fumbled for his harness. Knowing better than to speak he watched, his heart in his mouth, as Carson went through the start-up drills, silently speaking the steps. Across the wraparound panel lights glowed as systems warmed up and the small cathode ray tubes began to display data. As the hatch slammed shut behind them Carson looked up to see Mc-Readie out in front of the nose below them, thumbs raised, the clear signal. Carson raised a thumb back and began to spool up the first engine, port side, then without waiting for the usual settings began on the starboard engine, releasing the brake. The huge black nose lifted a fraction and she began to roll, the jet wash blasting back into the rock face. Crew stood against the walls, hands over ears, the noise level dangerously high, and watched the Omega roll out into the night.

'Come on, lights, lights!' Carson muttered to himself and as if on command someone in the hangar threw a switch and the runway centreline appeared before them, pale green in the darkness.

'Rolling,' he said into the mike, selecting fifteen per cent power with afterburners in seven seconds, and the aircraft shot forward, throwing them back into their seats.

'Roger, you are rolling,' from the control, 'climb to sixty thousand and turn left.'

He heard the tension in her voice and without time to acknowledge he clicked the mike once and the after-burners cut in and the nose began to lift. He held it down

240

for a couple of seconds, the superheated gases leaving a bright orange flame one hundred feet out behind them and finally he rotated the column and pointed her nose at the inky black sky. She climbed at an angle of forty-five degrees, her acceleration breathtaking, and at six hundred miles an hour he tried for scram jet ignition. They faltered for a second, huge roaring crackles and he silently cursed whatever tuning had been done for low-level heavy air flight. Come on my darling, my lovely girl, and suddenly she responded to his coaxings and the computer fuel mix changes and with a blasting roar the spinning turbines raised the temperature and the pressure enough for the fuel to burn. Out behind them the simple orange flame from the primary source of afterburners was obscured by a blue-white flare, six hundred feet long as the Tarbaby blasted through Mach 1 then Mach 2, the Mach counter clicking over like a digital clock on the soft red screen. As they cleared 60,000 feet and Mach 12, Digby spoke for the first time.

It was a simple, 'Holy shit!' said with enough reverence to make Carson smile, breaking the tension in the cockpit. A few minutes later two fishermen working the deck of a boat out of the Hebrides thought they saw a meteorite streaking across the sky.

'Right,' Gail breathed, comfortable now with the aircraft on track. 'What have we got?'

Natalia came straight in. 'Black Sea routine only, some Turkish air force but nothing to worry us. East of the target zone, considerable traffic but that's into Dubai and Abu Dhabi. There is one patrol only moving south, very slow. There is commercial traffic into Muscat control zone heading west.'

'Thank you,' Gail replied. She flicked back to her primary screens and began to study the Gulf traffic. Her brow creased as she noticed the four military contacts. Okay, she thought, we are looking for a small contact and slow. It was any controller's nightmare, trying to isolate the target from the commercial traffic. The original scenario had the tracking commencing from take-off and following the flight path until intercept could take place. Now she had to isolate the one little green light from the others, all moving on different courses at different heights. The Omega would cover the course in twenty-two minutes; she looked up at the tracking screen quickly – the Omega was steady at 76,000 feet, climbing slowly to cross into Russian airspace at 90,000. With luck, and the Omega's two per cent radar signature, their north-west defence system would recognize nothing but some atmospheric disturbances and would disbelieve the speed of the contact or log it as an unidentified flying object. She flashed a look at Natalia to confirm she was monitoring border airfields and went back to her problem.

First of all she punched a series of commands into the computer instructing the machine to isolate and dim any contacts over 30,000 feet. Immediately the bulk of the little dots dimmed on the screen leaving seventeen or eighteen brightly illuminated. Next, she selected six-digit transponder numbers, normally signifying four-engine commercials, and ran a trace on all, the computer checking the data files to confirm identifications. She was left with seven contacts, of which three were way too fast for a Friendship. Come on, girl, concentrate, she told herself.

Four to go. She studied the four, looking for an indicator on instinct. One moved steadily down the Saudi coastline and she discounted it: the Saudis would have checked that very thoroughly, she thought. Three operated to the east of Bahrain, one going east towards Dubai, discounted, and the third south-west along the coastline from Fujera towards Dubai. She looked at the speed, 360 knots, 26,000 feet, looks right, the last looking on track for Doha, speed 364, speed's right, but it could be him, he could swing round at any time now. She keyed in the IFF number and the name of a transport company flicked up on the screen. Could be, she thought.

Great, just great, two profiles that fit. She looked up at the screen at the four dim contacts tightly grouped overhead Sirri Island. Definitely Iranians. Escort? Maybe, maybe not. The first of the two suspect aircraft turned to starboard. She punched in the IFF number and for a second nothing happened and her heart stopped beating for what seemed like a whole minute. Then it flashed back, MEA, home base Beirut.

'How are we doing, young Gail?' She recognized Meran's voice. Beneath the casually phrased question his voice was tense.

'Trying to find the bogey. He's here, one of these two.' She wound up the brightness on the overhead lights and dropped her Polaroid lenses. The Omega was now overhead Nizhni Novgorod, twelve minutes to intercept. She increased the brightness on the screen, rolled her seat forward and pushed the rocker switch to activate her microphone. Behind her Meran joined Haidermann and Sagan against the wall where they waited, technically impotent now it was in motion, but unable to leave the control room, even for Sagan's office and the big glass window.

'Omega, this is Oslo,' she began.

'Hello, Bright Eyes.' Carson came back strongly into the room.

'Omega, ten minutes to intercept,' she said through her smile. 'Come right five degrees,' her own tension easing at the sound of his voice.

'Roger. Do you have my bogey?'

'Negative, have two contacts, will isolate before you need it.'

'Say again, Bright Eyes.'

'Negative. We have two possibles, we will have to wait for a couple of minutes.'

'Roger,' he finished flatly.

Jesus Christ, two, how can there be two fucking targets, he thought. He understood her dilemma, but the memories of the French mountainside and the bodies in the Citroën came flooding back.

'I want a visual on the target, Bright Eyes, repeat visual.'

Carson resisted the urge to crank up the radar and flicked his eyes across the electronic counter-measures screen. His speed was steady on Mach 12 and he gently let the nose drop and eased the power settings back to start the intercept descent.

'How are we doing?' he asked Digby.

'All greens. Laser has power. Target computer is ready. All we need is the contact.' His voice shiny and metallic through the intercom. They were in oxygen masks, the feeder system pushing the air mix through under pressure.

'We will do this visual,' Carson replied.

'Why?' Digby asked aghast.

'Gail has got two contacts that are both possibles. I don't want any mistakes.'

The flight management system flashed at him, oxygen feed to the engines cutting out automatically as they entered lower, denser air. Above them, the inky blue-black sky scattered with stars began to pale and the cloud ceiling at 30,000 feet rippled beneath them. Off to the right the dark mass of a cumulonimbus towered at 50,000 feet like a giant grey swirling anvil as they flashed past it in a tenth of a second.

Digby, stunned at the beauty of the rippling pink tableau of puffball peaks and soft valleys, hardly recognized the dawn as it approached over the cloud base so far below. Ten seconds later they were in daylight with nine minutes to intercept. Carson eased the power back further and glanced across at his partner.

'Okay, let's do it. Crank up your radar; we'll be clear of Russian airspace in about thirty seconds, put it through on my primary screen.'

He stabbed at a selector button with one gloved finger and the head-up display flashed on to the windscreen leaving room for the radar image on the seven-inch primary system. The diamond hard crystal screen was steeply angled, but not so much that the head-up display was distorted. A fuzzy picture blossomed, defining itself as the southern Black Sea coast and the mountains of Zagros. With a ground speed of 150 miles a minute the scenario rolled towards him down the screen rapidly.

'Lift it a bit over the mountains, and lock it at six hundred miles.'

Digby nodded and made the adjustments as they watched the land mass sink from the screen, and on the next sweep the air activity over Iran and Iraq appeared on the top of the screen. Carson looked up at the display on the glass, checking his speed and heading automatically. He was ready to begin the intercept vector.

'Bright Eyes, this is Tarbaby,' he called using his name for the aircraft for the first time as the radio call sign.

'Roger, Tarbaby,' came the reply,

'Talk to me, I have figures five before overshooting.'

'Stand-by, two minutes.'

He could feel the tension in her voice.

'Reduce power, and move to level four five.'

'Roger.'

He trimmed the nose down and further eased the power settings back, knowing they were stalling for time, trying to identify their target. His eyes scanned his own screen for the first sweep of the target area. Where are you, you fucker? he thought.

USS Mississippi

Kowowski selected a fruit gum from the packet, choosing red after hunting in vain for a black one. Since giving up smoking he found himself ploughing through a pack of the little jelly candies a day. He popped it into his mouth and looked back at his display, sucking it and savouring the taste. He listened to the sound through his headphones, the patch from the comms suite an extra, the voices of

Bahrain air traffic clear and strength five and amused himself watching and listening to the accompaniment. Aircraft were joining the circuit at one point and then following each other like ducklings.

He looked back at the small group of military overhead Sirri and noticed that the other aircraft on the same course was now much nearer. It would have to alter course to the north to join the circuit with the others and, as if on cue, he heard Bahrain radar call the aircraft to instruct it to change its transponder number. Kowowski watched the screen. Its approach was steady at 26,000 feet – high, he thought, must be his ceiling. He had better let down soon or he'll screw up this approach badly.

He reached for the packet of fruit gums and produced a green one. He brushed off the excess sugar granules and then rolled it into his mouth with much pleasure, overdoing it to tease the other operator sitting beside him. He was junior to Kowowski by two years and two grades, but the relationship was informal. Dooley was black and from the wide open spaces of Texas, while Kowowski was a native New Yorker, his mother Irish and his father Polish. The operations centre where they worked left no room for the divisions of rank; it was staffed by specialists who had the traditional scorn for hierarchy. Dooley grinned at him.

'Man, you eat that honky shit too much and your teeth fall out,' he said.

'That one was green, the black ones were the first to go . . . as usual.' Kowowski waited for the retort and looked back at his screen, half an ear to Dooley and half on the voice of the radar controller.

He was asking the pilot of the aircraft to change his IFF again.

'This guy's got his squawk all fucked up,' he said.

'What?' from Dooley.

'His squawk – radar is giving him a hard time to change over, he hasn't, and he is way, way too high.'

246

Kowowski watched the trace, beginning to feel uneasy.

'I dunno what his intention is,' said Dooley also watching now, 'but he is gonna be in the shit. No overflights of Bahrain, standing control says go round unless you in the circuit.'

'He isn't landing,' Kowowski said with some finality, then before his eyes the transponder signal faded altogether, not replaced as requested with the new number given him.

'I don't like this,' Kowowski said softly. 'One turn left and he is all over us,' and he remembered the last time a US Navy ship had reacted to a contact at range in the Gulf. The *Vincennes*. The Iranian Airbus they had splashed. Some still said they thought there was an F-14 hiding behind it.

'Chief,' he called.

Four thousand miles to the north-west, satellite transmissions beamed the same stolen pictures on to the prime control screen at Gail's console, and from there on to the wall display. Computers enhanced and corrected the time base errors giving the sixteen by twenty high resolution image a clarity almost obscene. She watched, her brain racing, ignoring the silent bystanders and off-duty staff who now crowded the back wall. She had thirty seconds to commence her vector of the Tarbaby or put her into a loiter somewhere, burning precious fuel and revealed in the harsh daylight. Black and hugely visible, she was vulnerable at low altitudes. On the screen a transponder flickered for a second, it was one of her possibles and she eased down the brightness for a second, seeking clarity of image in the noise and interference. It flickered again and then vanished, leaving the contact alone but emitting its height. Mode two, he is in mode two, shut down his number but forgotten his height indicator, she leaned back and studied the picture in totality. Too high for Bahrain air traffic, way off course to go round the island. She pulled a list of data across the console and quickly read the details.

Come on, girl, come on, there, no overflights, traffic will pass to north. This is it.

'Tarbaby, this is Bright Eyes.'

'Go.'

'Stand-by for vector.' She quickly calculated his position from the data on the left-hand screen. 'Come round on to one two seven degrees, range one one zero miles, level two six. One bogey, speed two sixty knots, heading reciprocal at this time, over.'

'Confirm level two six, Romeo heading one one zero miles, will go for visual.'

'Affirmative, Tarbaby.'

She watched the screens, her eyes flicking back to the Tarbaby's performance data and back on to the target, willing on the close and the confirmation. Meran walked up behind her, heavy on the stick and stiff with fatigue, the years catching up with him.

'Is that the bastard?' he asked, the last word rolling off his tongue like something bitter. She answered without looking at him.

'I believe it is, but we will wait for confirmation.'

'Don't wait too long, girl . . .'

She leant forward again, ignoring him.

'Tarbaby, two minutes to visual, power back to Mach Two in ten seconds and down to level four zero.'

Carson's clipped reply was affirmative and she heard the scram jets clearly over the transmission as they fought to keep his Mach speed in the heavy humid air.

Carson reset the power gratefully. The airframe was under huge stresses and the mighty engines were burning dangerously high amounts of his fuel maintaining 9,000 miles an hour intercept speed. It was all Catch-22 for the hypersonic. At low altitudes where there was sufficient air to burn, that same air was thick and cloying against the surfaces and needed pushing aside like a ship through water. Up higher, where the thin air offered less resistance, there was less to burn and engine efficiency was affected. Optimum altitude was somewhere in the middle, for the Tarbaby 90,000 feet. Down wallowing in the heavy air she was like a shark swimming in syrup.

The buffeting eased immediately as the airspeed fell away and the Mach counter dropped back into single figures. Carson knew why Gail had asked for Mach 2: that was his critical speed for application of the slim, hydraulically driven air brakes. At Mach 2, once he was in range, he could operate the rams lifting the surfaces and sideslip the aircraft if necessary, to rip the airspeed down. It was dangerous, interrupting the airflow under the wings; jet pilots have nightmares about a flameout and Carson was no exception. The slower he could cover the final few miles the better: even at Mach 2 it meant a closing speed in excess of 1,400 miles per hour. He silently thanked the delivery speed of the laser, that was the crux of the issue. A beam of light travelled so fast you didn't experience the usual problems of ballistics at high speed. He watched the radar screen roll out before him, the first Gulf traffic solid contacts at the top of the screen, and corrected his course minutely so that his target would appear dead centre on the screen head at twelve o'clock. He caressed the red button under his thumb on the column.

'You ready?' Digby asked loudly, forgetting the sensitivity of the mikes. It was the first time he had spoken for several minutes, nervous and edgy.

'Yes,' Carson answered calmly. 'Let me have system control.'

Digby ran his fingers over the panel on his left, within reach of Carson's right hand if he so chose, and a small panel illuminated itself on Carson's side of the central display.

'You have lasers,' Digby said formally.

'I have lasers,' Carson replied. 'One minute to visual. If it's the correct plane I'm going to hit it immediately. If I'm not absolutely sure we will come back and have another look. Once we've done the job we will scramble for height, so tighten your straps now . . . Okay?'

Digby nodded, feeling sick.

Carson looked back at his radar. Bahrain was now visible with one contact dead centre, he read the transponder data. Height correct, speed correct, that's my bogey. He felt the elation briefly, but it soured as he looked further out and saw the four contacts. Oh fuck! oh fuck! oh fuck! Escort, four bogeys live and bad. As he watched two things began to happen, the four contacts altered course for the west and the primary bogey began a maximum rate descent.

USS Mississippi

'He's comin' down fast,' Dooley almost shouted over Kowowski's shoulder.

'Shit, what's this fucker on?'

'What?' A voice from behind them. The chief.

'Don't like this, chief. That's maximum rate descent. He wouldn't do that with freight or people on board,' Kowowski said, thinking aloud.

The height transmitter from the aircraft changed every few seconds bright on the screen.

'Dooley,' the chief said, his eyes narrowing, 'get the *Morgan James* on the line, see if they are watching this. Then get the OOD down here, he's up in the wardroom . . .'

'He won't like a cold breakfast, man,' Dooley said cautiously, 'but if you think it's . . .'

'JUST FUCKING DO IT! NOW!' the chief snapped not looking back, his eyes riveted to Kowowski's screen.

'Aye aye.' Dooley snatched up the handset. 'OOD to the ops room,' booming out over the main broadcast system.

Kowowski watched the figures flick over, his brain working the mental arithmetic, Jesus, that's 6,000 feet a minute, this guy has a problem or he is illegal. There is no way this is another Airbus. If he had a problem he would have called up, he would have radio traffic pouring out. He silently thanked his previous request to comms to have the air traffic channel patched through and he listened to the terse instructions. He crossed channels to Bahrain radar and listened for a few seconds, realizing that they had not yet noticed the problem, and pulling the headset clear he dropped it on the console and rubbed his eyes. Come on, come, where are you? He looked up at the door, willing the OOD to burst through, but it remained darkly empty. He looked back at the screen, realizing all his fears at once. The contact had made a hard left turn that would bring it right over the *Mississippi*.

'Oh fuck!' he muttered, and stood up. The chief did it. In the years Kowowski had been in the navy he had never heard general quarters sounded except in a drill. It was the call to battle stations and took precedence over every-thing else in the ship. It would bring the admiral at a run, have half a thousand men falling from their beds, jumping into flash gear, running to their stations, food thrown down drains as stoves were secured, medics breaking open dressing stations and the specialists, weapons operators and combat control people racing to the vitals of the warship.

The chief pressed the intercom button and on the bridge a high-pitched beep set open the speakers over the com-mand station.

'Bridge, ops room. Sound general quarters, strike inbound. Unidentified aircraft bearing zero nine four,' he said slowly and clearly into the handset. Half a second later to the command of the young officer on the bridge with the two lookouts the GQ klaxon began to blare. A second later the duty officer burst into the ops centre as a voice burst through the speakers. 'General quarters, general quarters, this is not a drill, repeat this is not a drill.'

'Speak!' the officer barked looking at the screen.

'Max rate descent, no transponder change, hard turn

251

left, brings him right over us. He's hostile, sir,' Kowowski explained in one sentence.

'I agree,' the chief responded.

The fire control alarm began to flash at the console and without asking permission Kowowski dropped back into the seat, grabbed the headset and tugged it on.

'Right, altitude thirteen thousand feet, bearing zero nine four, range two miles.'

Normally behind him an operator would have had the computer select the trace number and activate the closed-in ship's defence systems, the surface-to-air missiles that, radar guided, would have locked on to their target and awaited instructions, but the chairs were empty. Wouldn't be for much longer. Men were piling in.

The captain took the stairs up to the bridge three at a time, overtaking a rating on the last step, and burst into the hubbub of the drama.

'What have we got here?' he asked quickly.

His commander air warfare answered briefly. 'An aircraft diving at us.' He thrust a pair of binoculars at his captain and pointed to the growing speck in the sky.

'What is it?' Captain Daniels asked, lifting the heavy instrument.

'Civvy prop driven twin, sir.'

Behind him he heard someone order chaff canisters to be deployed.

'Belay that. If he had a missile he would have let go by now . . . hold your fire, this is a civilian aircraft. Let's get a look at him. Could be a joyrider . . . we don't need any problems, not after the last time, raise him on the radio, fire signal flares and put some tracer across his bows.'

The commander reached for the phone in its cradle as someone said, 'He's levelling out.'

A moment later the speaker squawked into life from combat control.

'Four contacts, bearing one zero eight, range seventy miles, speed nine hundred knots.'

'What goes on here?' said Daniels, getting concerned.

Above them a flare burst bright, even in the daylight, pink and festive.

Carson had watched the target change course sharply. This is it, he thought, what is his height now – he looked down at the small figure below the dot – he's dropping like a stone, what's his game, what's he doing?

'Bright Eyes, this is Tarbaby, confirm my target has just broken low and left, over.'

'Roger.'

He began to ease off the power, his finger hovering over the air brakes control, he was approaching at 1,200 miles an hour, positively dawdling over the last few seconds. He began to rethink the tactic. High approach for the sneaky bit, then break and drop low, why? To commence his bombing run, low also meant a delay on the weapon, he couldn't use airburst because it would blow him up as well. It all began to fit, and he was almost satisfied about the identity of the contact. The chances of a second aircraft behaving in that manner overhead that position were a million to one. It was as that thought passed through his mind that he looked back at the screen and with his heart leaping into his mouth he watched the whole image fade. He lashed out with his fist at the secondary screen, his hand moving a blur over back-up systems, but all remained opaque.

'We have lost our radar,' he said aloud.

Digby whipped round to look at the technical panel above his right shoulder, swearing under his breath, as Carson threw on the air brakes and slewed the aircraft sideways in a dangerous sideslip. Without his long-range radar he couldn't see anything and his speed was way too fast for VFR as he came down through the cloud base.

'Bright Eyes, I have lost my radar, vector me in, vector me in.'

'Oh, my God,' Haidermann said loudly, watching the

images on the wall display, a tight knot in his stomach and the helplessness giving in to fear.

'Shut up!' Gail snapped. 'Tarbaby, you have cloud base to seventeen thousand feet, let down now and come on to two eight three, you should have visual in six or seven seconds . . . come right, come right, power off, you should now be in the murk, keep coming, you are clear all-round, increase your descent three seconds . . . you should be clear now, target at eleven o'clock, low, hard on ten thousand . . .'

'I HAVE VISUAL,' blasted into the control room, the roar of the engines, the adrenalin burst and the excitement clear through the speakers.

The Tarbaby yawed dangerously, buffeting and shuddering as Carson corrected the sideslip, watching the engine instruments and pressure displays, and he brought her back on to track as they broke through the cloud with Gail's voice steady in his headphones.

He looked up, crossed the weapons systems on to the head-up and looked out of the cockpit for the first time in four minutes, the display clear and lime green against the shimmering waters of the Gulf and the blue sky through what he still thought of as the canopy, the windscreen.

Below them and dead ahead lay the huge, grey bulk of the USS *Mississippi*, surrounded by her squadron like little bathtub boats. The passive radar was functioning and the ECM gear was registering massive blasts of radar coming at the Tarbaby. Above her, and a thousand yards further aft, mid-vision was a silver speck.

'I HAVE VISUAL,' he called into his microphone.

'I'm going over the top, and hit a wing,' he said to Digby breathlessly. 'That's it, that's the bogey, but we can't do a down the throat, might hit the nuke . . .' he was panting with excitement, and could feel the adrenalin coursing through his blood '. . . give me just enough for that.'

Digby tapped keys at his front and light-emitting diodes changed on both sides of the cockpit.

'You have ten per cent for one Zulu,' he replied, surprisingly calmly.

Carson's hand caressed the red trigger button as he lined up his run. I'm a sitting duck if they let go a SAM or five he thought, they must have dozens on that big bitch down there, shit, let them be dithering as usual. As he soared over the warship closing at Mach 1 he dropped the nose a fraction and watched the bogey dance into the illuminated gunsights, the range-finder spinning over and the systems lights flashing, his flight data displayed around the perimeter of the sights, the perimeter of death.

He pressed the red button and felt the engines surge as the power drained into the laser system and back into the engines in a millisecond. Ahead, a bright shiny speck in the sky broke into two pieces.

'Splash one,' he reported, hitting the power panel and scrambling for the thin cold air she loved high above the earth.

Below on the USS *Mississippi* Captain Daniels had binoculars up to his eyes following the approach of the big twin prop, when, along with seven others on the bridge and lookout positions and roughly two hundred other pairs of naked eyes, he watched the starboard wing break away in a flash of blinding white hot air. The aircraft flipped down on that side, the other wing snapping and tearing clear as the port engine pulled the fuselage round and down. He watched it fall, holding the image in the glasses till it hit the sea several hundred yards away in three large pieces, the splash silent in the lenses.

'Who fired? Check with the *Morgan James* . . . what has happened here?' he barked.

He watched the admiral walk swiftly across the bridge towards him.

Gail leant forward, not daring to speak, and pushed the rocker switch for the intercom and PA system. She gathered herself. 'For those of you who don't know what splash

255

one means, we did it.' Her voice was tired, drained.

The bedlam was tremendous, people shouting and shaking hands, cheering in a scene reminiscent of the NASA control room after a successful launch. Meran and Haidermann came over to her and Meran swapped his stick over and put his hand on her shoulder.

'Well done, girl,' he said gruffly, over the noise and cheering. 'Leo has gone to raise the *Mississippi* and let them know they have a salvage job to do . . . well done!'

But she didn't feel the joy of the others, the feeling of a difficult job well done, and she knew Peter didn't either. They had killed someone, the three of them and the victory was bittersweet.

Tim Miller, who had entered the control room during the last minutes of the intercept, understood and walked across to her in time to see a big tear roll down her cheek, beneath the sunglasses.

'You shouldn't be in here,' she said. That was when he noticed that Natalia was still watching her screen. He walked over, his fighter pilot instincts telling him it wasn't over yet.

'Gail,' he called across, 'you have a four-ship here, paired up and hunting.'

'They've been there a while,' she said.

'Tell Carson, he needs to know,' he said firmly.

She selected Natalia's screen on her main display and studied it for a moment, extrapolating the course the two pairs were moving along. They were thirty-five miles out on the same converging course as a contact with an IFF transponder number.

'Who's on 46578?'

Andrea answered after a second of checking notes laid out before her.

'British Airways out of Dubai . . . it's a 747.'

'Dear God . . . I wonder if they . . .' Gail began, then not waiting for Meran or Haidermann to authorize it she pressed her mike switch.

'Tarbaby, this is Omega Base.'

'Go, Bright Eyes,' Carson replied, and she smiled again to herself.

Four seconds later Carson inverted the Tarbaby, whipped the power back and began a long turn back into the warm thick air of the Gulf.

'Vector me in and let me have the channel the BA guy is on,' he ordered crisply.

USS Mississippi

'Get a boat over there, see if anyone survived that,' Daniels barked at the duty officer. He didn't like things going on that he didn't understand and his crew knew it and jumped at his orders.

'Stand down,' he called. 'That was the threat.'

'What the hell is going on, captain?' Admiral Corey demanded.

'I don't know, admiral. When I do I will tell you.'

They were standing on the lookout watching the boats zipping across the water towards the wreckage when a rating stopped beside Daniels and handed him a strip of signal paper.

'What's this?'

'Beats me, sir. Just came in . . . looks weird, so I brought it up myself.'

Daniels looked properly at the man and recognized him as a communications specialist rarely seen anywhere near the bridge.

'Sir, it's in the code of the day, but it's not from Fleet and it's not from any other source who would have the codes.'

Daniels took the paper and unfolded it. Wishing he had his spectacles in his pocket, he held it away and began to read.

CAPT. DANIELS - MISSISSIPPI -
F-27 DESTROYED WAS INTENDING TO ATTACK YOUR
SHIPS. SUGGEST YOU COMMENCE RECOVERY OPER-
ATION. NUCLEAR WEAPON ON BOARD REPEAT
NUCLEAR WEAPON ON BOARD. ARMING DEVICE
ATTACHED ACCELERATOR. OSLO.

'Holy shit!' he said and read it again, giving it to Corey.
'Belay that boat party, recall 'em! I want the diving officer, the medical officer and an NCB party ready to brief
in five minutes.'

He turned to Admiral Corey. 'Who the hell is Oslo?'

The British Airways 747 had stopped on schedule in Dubai,
taken on fuel and seventy-six extra passengers, changed
crews, been cleaned, restocked and lifted off seven minutes
late. She took off with a staggering all-up weight of 376
tons, her holds loaded to capacity with freight. There were
a few empty seats in economy and including the sixteen
cabin crew and the three flight deck, there was a total of
338 souls on board. At that time she was twenty-six
minutes out of Dubai, over the Gulf and about to change
course to port which would take her over Saudi Arabia,
the Red Sea, then over Egypt and north across the Mediterranean into Europe and homeward bound into London's
Heathrow Airport.

The pilot in command was a twenty-year career man
who had learnt to fly with the Royal Navy Fleet Air Arm.
He was a senior check captain with the airline and had
logged 15,000 hours since his first breathtaking flight in
his uncle's canvas-winged biplane. Now, aged fifty-six, he
was about to retire and was secretly dreading the thought
of having to spend his days working in the garden with
his wife. They had been married twenty-seven years, but
he had been away so much in that time he wondered if
they really knew each other any more. He sat back in his
seat and listened to the banter between his first officer

and engineer. It was a big airline, and opportunities to fly together frequently were a mixed blessing. If you got stuck with someone you didn't like it could make the trip very long and boring, but luckily on this trip both his subordinates were easygoing and professional. He looked down at the inertial navigation system and watched the progressive display on the all weather loran radar. They were sitting at 36,000 feet, with clear sky ahead. Below them, with its upper layers at 22,000 feet was the scattered cloud base, and other than clear air turbulence, he could envisage no other problems.

The 747 was a very big, very safe aircraft, but it was also a very big, very vulnerable machine and utterly defenceless when faced with attack by jet fighters.

'Come on to two eight two and let down to forty thousand . . . you should have a visual ahead and below in about thirty seconds, reduce speed now, right down or you will overshoot . . .' the voice came through measured and competent. Carson watched ahead. The cloud below was rippled and white and with the sun behind them the sky ahead was a clear pale washed blue. Good, he thought, I like this. They will be coming into the sun. Cocky bastards will want to practise their down the throats.

'Roger, where are my bogeys?' he asked.

'They have done a long turn out ahead, they are paired up and waiting dead ahead of you over,' she crackled.

'Why?' asked Digby. 'What have they got to gain? Shit, Peter, that's a civilian airliner.'

'They had one of theirs shot down, remember? And they will be pissed off! We rumbled their mission, they have weapons loaded and will want revenge.'

This is fucking dangerous, he was thinking. This aircraft is not designed for any low level dogfighting shit. Rule number one is you never engage unless you have numerical superiority or you are a devious fucker. You blow 'em away from the sun, you come from below and behind and you don't let 'em get any advantage. They will be in Phantoms. Fast and very manoeuvrable. He knew Phantoms. Carry a good load and with good jocks they are about as good as any other fighter of that generation.

'We stack up behind the jumbo, up against the sun's glare, they won't even see us, they will be confident and excited. If they get stroppy . . . Look out the front, look for a flash of silver, or a shadow on the cloud, and set up the computer for a multiple target threat for fire command from my triggers.'

Digby nodded slowly and went about his task. The effect of the first kill had sunk in.

'I have visual on the target,' Carson reported to Omega Base. 'I'm going to talk to him.'

Below, nearer the clouds, the sun glinted back off something big.

'Roger, Tarbaby, he is British Airways flight zero five one, registration is Zulu Bravo Yankee.'

'Thanks, Bright Eyes, keep an eye on the bogeys.'

'Affirmative, Tarbaby.'

Carson changed channels and began again.

'Zulu Bravo Yankee, Zulu Bravo Yankee, this is a friend . . .'

Two seconds later they answered.

'This is Zulu Bravo, who is calling?'

'Zulu Bravo, this is a friend, call me Tarbaby, you have a problem, over.'

'Tarbaby, Zulu Bravo, what is the nature of your problem, over.'

'Negative my problem, Zulu Bravo, your problem, you have four hostiles on your track about a minute ahead. I am at your rear and will assist as necessary, over.'

'Copy that Tarbaby, who are the hostiles and who are you?'

'Zulu Bravo, four Iranian F-4s spoiling for a bit of action and you look like being it, over.'

'Tarbaby, are you military, over?'

'Negative, Zulu Bravo, but I can help, suggest you make an immediate left turn and get in over Saudi airspace.'

'Negative, Tarbaby, we are only permitted to enter in the corridor. We may have a problem with them if we attempt to divert at this time, over.'

'Then do as I tell you, because this is going to get terminal, Zulu.'

'Tarbaby, do you have authority to instruct course changes to other traffic?'

You fucking dork, he thought, what's your problem? I am warning you about the fact that you are about to get pounced on and you are asking about my authority.

'Zulu Bravo, I realize you have a credibility problem, but I suggest you follow my lead when it happens. I can . . .'

Gail's voice burst through his headset overriding everything.

'Tarbaby, strike inbound. Four bogeys, range four miles, speed six hundred knots, dead ahead!'

'ZULU BRAVO, BREAK RIGHT AND CLIMB,' Carson barked.

The jumbo seemed to lurch as full power went on to the four engines and she lifted her left wing and her great blunt nose to the sky, black exhaust smoke blowing back from her jets as she struggled upwards like a moose with the wolves closing. The radar lock lights flashed on the panel and as Carson watched the fighters close, saw the cannon flash and two rockets loose, he pressed his trigger.

The laser caught the first three in under half a second, blowing them to smithereens across the sky. The fourth fighter had anticipated the jumbo's high right tactic somehow and had lifted high left to intercept. The laser caught him on the next cycle, blowing him apart in a white hot air burst so close to the jumbo that wreckage in tiny pieces blew over the bigger aircraft.

The BA captain had not really believed the transmissions when they began, but as Carson had requested his compliance there, dead ahead, coming right at them were the fighters. When the command came he obeyed without hesitation, pushing the throttles forward and pulling back on the column as he heard the engineer shout 'Hold on' into the PA system.

He had illuminated the seat belt sign as a precaution at the beginning of the conversation and now he thanked his own caution as he pushed the 747 to her design limitations, dreading the sound of the cannon strikes and hoping like shit that Tarwhatever was going to help like he said. I hope he is a whole fucking squadron, he thought, Lord help me, airspeed falling off, and then the shadow loomed ahead and the blinding flash of light and blast that rocked the three hundred tons of metal.

He heard three loud bangs somewhere as he watched the engines' instrument red lining and the airspeed plummet and dropped the nose.

'Where are they?' he shouted, fighting the fear with his professionalism. 'Keep watching, they'll be back, shit! Did we take any hits?' he called back to his engineer.

'Nothing displayed here, all systems seem okay,' the man called back to him, as he watched the panels of warning lights.

'Get back down with the punters, see if anyone's hurt. See if we took a hit on the surfaces . . . move it!'

'Shall I call a Mayday?' the first officer asked, scared. 'Shit, did you see that one blow up?'

'No. I want a full status report first. Get back and watch the panels. We're not clear yet – if we have damaged hydraulics it'll take time for the pressure to bleed.'

He eased the power settings back. 'Keep watching for the bastards, get on to the supervisor, what's his name, Collins, have him put a crew member each side to keep a look out.'

'Bravo Zulu, Bravo Zulu, you can resume your track, how are you doing?' Carson's voice was calm through the speaker.

The captain thumbed the mike switch. 'Tarbaby?'

262

Carson replied positively and he continued, 'Where the hell are they? I can't see anything to my front, over.'

'You won't, Bravo Zulu, they're down. Did you take any hits, over?'

'Down? You sure, Tarbaby?'

'Affirmative, Bravo Zulu.'

'What the hell are you in? Did you do it?'

'Affirmative, Bravo Zulu. Now what is your status?'

He forgot the first part of his question thinking about the essence of Carson's and what had happened. Jesus, he's shot down four aircraft in a second.

'Not sure at this time, Tarbaby, we have no warning lights yet, but I heard three bangs, could have been cannon strikes. My engineer is down the back now having a look. Can you do a visual check of my underside and surfaces, over.'

'Roger, Bravo Zulu, I will be alongside in a minute or so,' Carson replied reluctantly. He didn't want to offer his aircraft to view, but he couldn't refuse another pilot that request.

The engineer took the stairs from the upper deck at a run, the screams and shouts from the passengers ignored. The cabin crew were moving among the people trying to calm them. One stewardess lay in pain holding her leg at the knee, a bar trolley lay on its side at her feet, the glasses smashed and fluid leaking on to the carpet.

'Sit tight, sweetie, we'll get to you in a moment,' he called as he ran past. A passenger made a grab for him and he snarled, 'Sit down!' As he moved down the aisle he was watching the bulkheads and overhead panels for splits, rents or damage, listening for the high-pitched whistle of depressurizing air, ignoring the passengers' shouts and requests for information. A woman, crying, clutched at his leg as he passed and he smiled down at her. 'Don't worry, everything's going to be okay,' and kept moving.

A group of children sat palefaced and clutching the seat arms with white knuckles, and behind them, a man vomited down his front, the smell of alcohol strong. Over everything, the voices of the crew calling for calm and asking people to remain seated.

On the flight deck the captain switched his mike over to intercom. 'Ladies and gentlemen, we have had a small problem which is now taken care of.' He knew he couldn't lie because passengers on the port side would have seen the explosion. 'We very briefly came under attack by unidentified aircraft, who have since been . . .' he searched for a word '. . . shot down by another unidentified aircraft. The engineer is moving through the cabin now, so please allow him to check for any damage that may affect your comfort.' Like gunshot wounds he thought bleakly. 'I'm afraid that all sounds a little implausible, but it's the truth. There are classified flights operating in these parts and we believe our rescuer is on one of those operations. We also believe the attackers were Iranian.' What the hell, he thought, they can't fire me, it's my last flight.

'We have asked our friend to give us a once-over underneath, and after we have spoken we will decide whether we continue on to London or divert and land at a nearer alternative airport.'

Carson eased his power back a third time and did a long slow turn to bring himself below the jumbo. As he neared the huge swirling superfast eddies of the jet wash, he called the 747 again.

'Okay, Bravo Zulu, straight and level, please. I'm just below you and moving up under your slipstream. If anything happens, I'll drop away, you pull up. Confirm you copied that, over.'

'Thank you, Tarbaby, you down, me up, appreciate it.'

Carson edged himself slowly closer, the Tarbaby wallowing at six hundred knots, the scrams barely functional, until he was below the jumbo's huge silver belly.

'Okay, Digby, have a look. You're looking for holes the size of fists, there will be a dent and some sharp edges, so look for somewhere that doesn't shine nicely,' he said, thanking the designers for the glass overhead port they had placed there for an alternative escape hatch.

'Yes, I see one, and another, they look clean, nothing dripping out or anything,' Digby reported, his face pressed to the plate.

'Look for a third, he said three bangs.'

Digby looked up the few yards again.

'No, nothing else . . . I'm looking in a line, right?'

'Yeah.'

'Nothing else.' He dropped back into his seat gratefully and locked the harness tight again. 'Some people fly this close for fun?'

Carson smiled tightly, pleased that his oppo's humour had returned.

'Okay, let's slide round the top and look for that third hole. These look like they have gone into a non-pressurized hold. Probably into baggage or freight or something.'

He dropped away and eased to his left and came up alongside the tip of the wing of the jumbo, suddenly aware of the windows and the eyes watching from inside.

The captain heard the engineer crash back into the cockpit.

'Take a look at that!' he shouted excitedly jabbing at the small window at the captain's left. He turned his head and felt his jaw drop.

'Holy Mother of God . . . what the hell is that thing, she's, she's beautiful,' he said sincerely. He thumbed the mike and, still looking out of the window, said, 'Tarbaby, I hope that's you out there, if it isn't I don't want to know.'

He had never seen anything so big and so sleek and so black and so deadly-looking. 'What are you flying, son? I have got big engines, but I could park my wife's car in your intakes and have room to open the doors!'

Carson chuckled delightedly into the airwaves for a second.

'If she drives a Rolls-Royce you get paid too much, Bravo Zulu. You have two holes in your belly, mid-section. No sign of a third, the rockets passed you by. How are your lights, over?'

'Still all green, thank you. We are going to push on for home base. If I have a problem with my gear then I want decent ground services waiting.'

'Roger that, Bravo Zulu. Good luck.'

'Thanks for your help, Tarbaby. Mind your sixes now, Bravo Zulu out.'

Carson eased away from the lumbering leviathan, his wing dropping till he sat alongside her. Stuff it, he thought, we're blown now so let them see my baby strut her stuff. He selected intercept speed and left his finger hovering on the button.

'Tighten up, Digby, let's show them how it should be done!'

'Oh dear, I knew you were going to do that,' he answered miserably.

'Bravo Zulu . . . watch this and have a good day!'

Carson hit the button and the air crackled and burned around the engines, the blue flare shot out and the Tarbaby seared and streaked her way away into the blue sky before he pulled the column back and blasted into the heavens above.

The crew in the 747 sat awed for a second and finally the engineer spoke.

'Son . . . of . . . a . . . bitch. Look at that thing shift, super-sonic for sure!'

'And the rest,' the captain said softly, 'and the rest. That's a hypersonic, gentlemen. You just saw aviation history.'

The first officer, who had been flying all the while, just shook his head.

'My wife is going to think I'm bullshitting her when I tell her about this trip!'

For Tarbaby and Oslo things would not be the same again. She had been heard overhead Bahrain, people reported hearing a deafening thundery crackle. She had been seen by three expert witnesses in the cockpit of the British Airways 747 and 300-odd other people in the cabin. One, a nine-year-old boy who needed material for his 'my holiday' composition at school, had the foresight to lift his bright yellow Instamatic to the hail-scarred window and take three pictures. It was also seen by the man in 47A who was returning from his annual holiday. He was employed by British Aerospace as an airframe design consultant and spent much of his time on Ministry of Defence classified work. A few minutes later he got up and began asking people on that side of the aircraft if anyone had taken a photograph. The boy shook his head quickly: no one was going to see these until Miss Timbrell had, so there. One passenger, drunk and bragging, said it was a SR-71 Blackbird, he knew, he had seen 'em lots of times. Another thought it was the stealth fighter the F-19. By the time they reached British airspace the reports varied wildly, with one passenger even claiming he had slept through the whole thing.

The Tarbaby's arrival home was a mixture of anticlimax, delight and concern at Omega Base. Tavis's people stripped the radar gear out and went to work and Carson, who was embarrassed by the cheering group of personnel, just wanted to debrief and then sleep. The elation of the mission's success was marred by the attack on the airliner and the unavoidable exposure to so many eyes. Haidermann, Sagan and Meran went straight into a meeting, allowing Carson and Digby time to shower and change.

At that moment an American satellite tracking infra-red heat sources flashed its recorded data back to earth, and two hours later the NRO forwarded the detail to CIA Langley, as they had been requested to do only three days before. It traced the entire mission from start to finish. Omega Base had been pinpointed.

12

Carson stripped off the sweaty damp clothing and stepped under the shower. He stood beneath the piping hot needles for fifteen minutes as if to try and wash the deaths of five men from his hair, his eyes and skin. The elation had worn off, the sharp soar of victory now become anti-climactic. He realized it himself as he turned the taps off, trying to remember the French name for it, the post-combat wind-down, when the adrenalin had done its work and the system moved down into a state of normality. It was prevalent amongst fighter pilots because they alone of the combatants in any scenario went from abject terror and split second reactions, G forces and death in the sky, back into a normal society in minutes, and they found it difficult to adjust. Gail knew this, and silently cleared up his flight suit and underwear for cleaning, dropping them outside his door. She expected silence from him and Dr Neilson had warned her to ignore any apparent depression or moodiness from him for several hours. She placed a hot cup of cocoa by his bed, pulled the sheets back and put a Bob Seager tape on his cassette machine.

'Get some sleep, I'll look in later,' she said as he was slowly drying his hair.

'I'm okay,' he said, 'just tired now – this all seems a bit weird now, too, it seems like . . . I dunno. I'm tired.' He smiled for the first time since arriving back.

There was a soft knock at the door. It was Digby with three condensation-frosted cans of beer. He offered one to Carson and the second to Gail.

'Drink and enjoy. If we are flying again soon it's the lot,

bars shut. Just a small nightcap . . .' he laughed, falsely loud '. . . sorry to disturb you both . . .'

'Cheers,' Carson lifted his can up in salute, not wanting to have Digby say it out loud. They didn't understand and he did not want to have to admit the alienation from the group.

'Well?' Digby said. 'We did it.'

'Yes, we did,' Gail replied.

Carson looked at him. 'You did well today.'

Digby smiled. From Carson, who had praised nothing about him since arriving, it was something. When Digby had gone back to his own rooms they slept, Gail pulling the blankets up over Carson and turning off the tapedeck. She fell asleep, but for a while Carson lay awake, thinking it through. I did it. I cracked it. For the first time in months he began to feel good about himself. Kids and Citroëns were now in their place, his confidence back. He slept well.

The debrief began after lunch. Haidermann and Meran had spent the entire morning with the analysts discussing the O'Casey Alternative. Yamashita was still working overtime with his programmers creating strike sequences, and he anticipated being ready by the next morning. McReadie's team had the radar set laid out in the electronics workshop and they too said they would be ready by dawn. The communications team was steadily collating and compiling data from Oslo sources the world over, transmitting instructions and establishing systems.

'We have been following *Mississippi*'s traffic all morning. They have salvaged a nuclear device from the Gulf. A warhead, Russian, off one of their SS-20s. It would have destroyed all nine American ships in the group tied up there, most of Muharraq Island, Manama and certainly irradiated al Khobar and the other two centres there on the Saudi coast. The wind was a northerly, so the cloud would have moved south. It's changing to an easterly now, so it would have taken out the Sudan, Egypt and from

269

there who knows?' Sagan continued, 'One megaton is about seventy times the size of the bomb the Manhattan Project built to drop on Hiroshima, so very well done the both of you, very well done.'

Carson and Digby waited; they both knew that there was more.

'But now the matter of the airliner, you weren't authorized to act in that instance. It was foolhardy and showed a lack of judgement. Why?' he asked. 'Why did you do it?'

Carson looked past his shoulder, an indolent expression on his features and Digby studied his nails with some care.

'You risked the Omega. You could have been shot down or damaged.'

'Well we weren't,' Carson said, 'so this conversation is academic.'

'It is not!' Sagan snapped back. 'What made you so sure they were going to actually attack and not just harass?'

'The little flashes of orange light from the cannon barrels and the smoke trail from a rocket were the give-aways,' Carson replied sarcastically.

'Don't take that tone with me!'

'Fuck you, Sagan!' Carson snapped. 'I wasn't going to have the deaths of those people on my conscience. It was a judgement call. That aircraft was under attack, so if you don't like my judgement, stuff it! Okay? JUST BLOODY STUFF IT!' he roared. 'And yes, we did get seen out of the bloody windows, so fucking what? About six satellites have got my infra-red signature blazed all over their reports and if that hasn't sunk in, it means we have about seven or eight hours before some bright little Yank or comrade is poring over the photos, and following the little images all the way to Iceland and putting one and one together. So, I suggest you clear your decks for action, because in about twelve hours a chopper is going to lift off from whatever American base is here. They know we are here, Leo, so

what difference does saving a few people's lives mean?'
He paused and then continued.

'You wouldn't know, you aren't a pilot, but you don't
leave them. You never leave another pilot in the shit,
because one day it might be you. It's a little rule we all
have. Now, is this a debrief or do you want to continue
the argument?' He was standing now, all five feet ten of
him, green eyes blazing, his bent nose thrust out like a
cock before a fight. The last few sentences hadn't been
shouted, they had barely been whispered, and Haidermann, with his long experience in dealing with men, knew
that it was time to step in between the gunfighter and the
professor.

'Relax, both of you. Peter, Leo was just concerned for
the project, that's all. Now, let's get on with the work at
hand,' he soothed.

The technical session was over an hour long, notes and
cockpit recording produced, and by four it was completed.

'Okay, that's out of the way, let's brief you on the
O'Casey Alternative. The name's a bit of a mouthful. In
his rather terse preamble to the scheme he likens Oslo to
the last of the angels in Revelations. The one who comes
at the end to say, "I told you so". So this plan will now
be known as "Angel". Your call sign, Peter, for any communications with the ground authorities will be "Angel
Seven". At precisely twelve noon Greenwich tomorrow,
we will present the Russians and the Americans with an
ultimatum. You two will enforce it by active demonstration. You will have as support on the ground, we hope,
the largest mobilization of popular opinion ever conceived
in the history of this planet. Because of the sheer size of the
project, the numbers of people involved and the amount of
initiative we are asking for, exact time frames are impossible to establish. It will be a fluid moving ground swell that
will build on itself. We will have to help it, direct it, and
harness it. Phase one will be . . .'

The briefing went into the evening, Carson making notes

on his pad, placing times against items, underlining some and marking exclamation points against others.

'We have, we believe,' Haidermann finished 'a workable plan, huge in concept and execution, but a workable plan.'

'The crux of the issue is that we have a Russian and an American president who both genuinely want to see nuclear disarmament. What this plan will do, what Angel will do, is help to convince their generals and their congresses, their committees and their senates that this is desirable,' Meran added.

'What happens,' Carson asked, 'if everyone just rolls over and goes back to sleep?'

'They won't, not with what we have planned.'

Although the NASA satellite photographs reached the CIA at Langley within two hours of exposure they sat on Edwin Raden's desk for seven and a half hours while he attended the Gulf Crisis meeting at the White House. He was one of twenty-four visitors that morning who were ushered into the big reception room in the north wing. Tables had been laid out into a hollow square and photographs and maps were pinned to the emerald green silk drapes. President Sheridan was a very practical man, and waved impatiently at the White House housekeeper when she protested at the pinning. He was a Republican and had rode to power on the wave created by the ineptitude of the Democrats, rather than his own charisma. Reagan and Bush had strained the people's tolerance of the Republicans and traditionally the Democrats were due a turn in the White House, but three Bible belt sex scandals involving Democrats and two appalling television debates had sealed their fate. Richard Sheridan, his party's nominee, had rolled into the White House like a breath of fresh air, thirty years younger than Reagan had been, attractive without being a pretty boy, and as realistic as any construction man could be.

He called the room to order.

'All right, what the hell happened? Just one of you speak.'

He pointed to Admiral Carl Creegan, who produced a pair of bifocals from his pocket and began to read excerpts from a teletext report produced by the coding room. He finished: 'The device is Russian. They were missing at least one that we knew of, maybe more. We think this is it.'

Sheridan looked at him. 'Confirmed?'

'We are sure.'

Sheridan looked back at the gathered people. 'I want the answers to the other questions as soon as possible.'

The CIA director occupying the centre spot opposite the President smiled smugly to himself as he answered, 'Mr President, it isn't quite that easy.' He was known to regard the youthful leader as overly idealistic.

Sheridan leaned forward, his eyes piercing and direct. 'Mr Gagioni, you head the CIA, it's your job. If you can't do it then get the hell out of the way and let someone else have a go. Someone just tried to mount an attack on this country. Don't you sit there like a patronizing bullfrog and tell me it ain't easy. Now get your ass on the job. I have a press conference in the morning and I want some answers. All this has been going on under our noses, for Christ sakes!' The room was hushed. This was a battle of the Titans and protocol had been breached here today with a presidential attack in such a large congregation.

'And don't let me hold the rest of you: you are all here because you got caught with your pants down.'

Round the room eyebrows were raised in indignation. 'Yes, people. It's your job to prevent this kind of thing with foreknowledge, yet did you? What the hell else is happening out there that we don't know about?'

His chief aide, David Boredean, sat at his right, jotting notes. He pushed one across and Sheridan read it quickly. 'We will reconvene tomorrow morning.'

*   *   *

273

Raden was back in his office by midnight and while his secretary was trying to raise Paul Hart in Paris he opened the envelope of prints from the NRO and knew immediately he was on to something relevant.

'Get someone up here from photo analysis,' he shouted out to his secretary, who had arrived back only twenty minutes before, called from her bed and her husband.

'Mr Raden, it's gone midnight, they will all be . . .' she tried to explain.

'Get them back here,' he said, raising his eyes heavenward, 'and where's Hart?'

She didn't answer but stood at her desk, a phone to each ear, wishing she was somewhere else.

Raden paced his office, one of the sat pix in his hand. Son-of-a-bitch, long, black, sleek and big. Crackly rumbles like thunder. Heat streaks, this is that goddamned hypersonic that old bastard at the Pentagon was talking about. He held up the photo. While the infra-red gave strength to the heat streaks, other features of the background were hazy, indistinct shapes. He wanted some news to take to the morning meeting at the White House. He had felt the pain as his chief had been berated by the President because he was a professional. He hadn't time for Walter Gagioni as a person and in his ten-month tenure of the seventh-floor office the chief had alienated many of his departmental heads, but it still hurt the Agency and the last thing they needed was another Carter who would pull the CIA's teeth.

It was another fifty minutes till his secretary ushered in two grainy-eyed men from photo analysis. One was wearing a red tracksuit and the other jeans and an old sweater. He said nothing but held up the pile of photos and as they settled at the desk the man in the sweater spoke first. 'Shit, that's hot! Infra-red is usually a pale image, but this is grey.'

'What's the source?' Raden asked.

'Hard to say,' the tracksuit answered. 'We had some

274

shots of heat emissions last year, but the whizzkids put it down to a UFO. Same colour as this. This is very high. Background heat is minimal, so this grey streak is well over normal airways.'

He reached into the heap and pulled another picture clear.

'He's lower here, see the heat traces below it there? Power station of some sort, maybe a factory.'

Raden held up the first three in sequence and selected some from the middle.

'Tell me what this is, and where it is. These are from wherever it took off, and these here, are wherever it stopped,' Raden instructed.

'Naa, it's turning here, look the trace goes off again over its original line.'

'So what does that mean?' Raden asked leaning forward.

'By the look of it, it flew down here, turned, flew around a bit in here,' he held up the next picture, 'and then went back along its original course . . . turned for home, I would say.'

'Varying speeds, too,' sweater offered.

'What?' from Raden.

'See, the heat trace changes its intensity. As it gets darker there that is less heat, ergo less speed. I agree, it came down here flew around . . . holy fuck!'

'What's that?' Tracksuit leant over sweater's shoulder to look at the print he had picked up.

'There, bottom left, about eight foxtrot.' He passed it back to tracksuit.

'Wow! That's unusual,' tracksuit said, with understatement.

'What?' asked Raden.

'That must be up at the six K mark,' sweater said.

'Could be, not much of it, but certainly hot,' tracksuit agreed.

'WHAT?' shouted Raden.

'Sorry, here.' Tracksuit passed the print across.

'What am I looking for?'

'Square 8F. A little pin-sized splinter of white, not grey, white. It's overlaid by the grey trace there, but distinct.'

'What is it?' Raden asked disappointedly. He had expected to see something clear like an image of the aircraft or something.

'The intensity,' sweater said. 'That white trace must be ultra hot, up to six thousand degrees Celsius.'

'What does that mean?' Raden asked.

'Well, difficult to say, a nuclear weapon goes off at about five, most blast furnaces at about three, the type they use for exotic metals and Kevlar and shit, testing heat tiles . . .'

'Jesus! Get to the point,' he said, exasperated. Experts pissed him off.

'Williams had a trace about eighteen months ago like this, not this hot, but up over five.'

'What was it?' Raden asked.

'Well, we weren't sure, still aren't,' tracksuit offered, reaching for a cigarette.

'What do you *think* it was?'

'Well, it's difficult . . . I'd like to take this back to the lab and have a better look,' sweater said.

'WHAT THE FUCK WAS IT?' Raden stood behind his desk glowering at them.

'Ahhh it was possibly, just possibly a . . . laser beam.'

'A what?'

'Laser. Weapons quality, but this much hotter, maybe an infra-red beam.'

'No, too hot even for infra-red,' tracksuit muttered.

'What then?' sweater argued.

'Dunno, but hotter than an infra-red beam.'

'Impossible, next one up has never been built, not even designed.'

'Look, there it is again.' Tracksuit held up another print. 'But it's bigger here . . . no, it's split.'

'They must be a hundred miles apart.'

'Yeah, but same track, same source.'

'What is it if it isn't infra-red laser?' Raden asked slowly. He considered all the Agency's experts nerds.

'Well, next level up is theory only, so . . .'

'What is it, you little shit?' he barked.

The man looked hurt and didn't reply for a second or two, then he spoke. 'X-ray.'

'What?'

'X-ray laser.'

'You say it doesn't exist?' Raden added quickly.

'Not to our knowledge,' tracksuit replied.

'But if it did, would it be this hot?'

'Shit, yes . . . no problem. Accurate, hot, and real bitchy to see, it will be fucking invisible, man,' sweater said, grooving on the science. 'We are talkin' Star Wars here, man.'

'How effective is it?' Raden asked seriously.

'Oh wow! It's so super hot it changes the molecular structure of whatever it hits. Concrete would explode like dynamite, cut through steel like ice cream, a pin-prick of this light intensity would . . .'

'Create six or seven thousand degrees of heat,' Raden offered gently.

'Yeah, no problem, man . . . no problem.'

'What if it hit something, an aircraft for instance?'

'Blast it into little pieces, or cut bits off – whatever you wanted. Just vary the dosage.'

Raden sat back, his brain racing in top gear.

'But it doesn't exist, Mr Raden. We are twenty years from x-ray lasers.'

'Neither do hypersonic aircraft. That's the heat trace you see here,' Raden answered dryly.

Neither man spoke, they just looked at each other, eyebrows raised.

'I want you to take these pics back to your place of work and return to me within the hour and tell me where this trace began and returned to.'

'Easy. This column here is a map reference,' sweater said patiently.

'So where's this?' Raden asked quickly.

'North Atlantic . . . Iceland maybe, maybe the Orkneys or one of them Brit islands. Tell you exactly in a couple of minutes.'

'Do that,' Raden said grinning. 'Molly, where is Hart?' he yelled through the door.

Four hours later Raden was back at the White House, but even so he was late for the six AM. Richard Sheridan had rattled Washington's working practices amongst other things. The others had eaten the hot doughnuts provided and were sipping coffee and Sheridan was on the telephone in his office. He had hung up and walked into the room and taken his seat only moments before Raden hurried in with another man. He looked up at the latecomers, as did the others in the room, willing Sheridan to vent his wrath elsewhere this morning, because none of them had anything to offer the meeting. All their usual sources of intelligence had come up empty.

'Sorry, Mr President,' Raden began, 'may I introduce Karl Schoeman from the Pentagon. Mr Schoeman is an air analyst.'

Sheridan nodded at the visitor who took his pipe from his mouth and smiled charmingly. ''Morning,' he said.

'I asked him to join us this morning, sir – he is cleared to level five.'

Walter Gagioni was looking alarmed. He had not been briefed by anyone at Langley and was holding what he thought were the only notes on the issue that the Agency had available. Raden noticed and, with his career on the line, smoothly crossed the gap with a polite nod. 'With your permission, Mr Director, we will commence the briefing on what we have.' Raden had tried to contact him without success since three AM. Some director of the CIA, he had thought; you can't find the fucker.

278

Gagioni, politically astute, nodded smiling, trying to look as if he was aware of the whole thing. He had spent the night rampaging around his sealed suite on the seventh floor at Langley shouting at his senior assistants and directive heads, his phones off the hook.

Schoeman looked at the President, grinning hugely and enjoying himself. He loved it when the unbelievers and flat earthers came to realize the faith. It usually took a dynamic enigma like Sheridan to do it. 'No shit Sheridan' his college classmates had called him, he seemed to remember.

'Well then, let's get on with it,' the President said tersely.

'We got some satellite pictures yesterday. They indicate a heat source travelled south from Iceland over the Gulf and, using what appears to be a laser, fired five times in two locations, before returning home. That is what we believe the big, black, sleek aircraft was.' Raden began to distribute copies of the photographs.

'The aircraft is what we think is a hypersonic,' he continued, before being interrupted by Schoeman.

'Not think, Mr President, I am sure this is a hypersonic and have been for months.'

Sheridan looked sharply at him. 'Explain please, Mr Schoeman . . . months?'

'Yes,' he said, removing the pipe, 'months. Your defence budget pays me to analyse these things and we said months ago that someone had built a hypersonic. There it is.' He jabbed at the photos in the President's hand.

'Why the delay in us getting on to it?' he asked to the room in general.

'Snafu!' Schoeman replied delightedly. 'I was pulled off it by my boss. Told not to waste any more time.'

'Well at least you talk straight!' Sheridan muttered. 'Carry on, please.'

'It would seem to be the aircraft that splashed the twin turbo that was going after the *Mississippi*. It then turned, gained height, then came back and here,' he pointed to the photo, 'took out the four Iranians. The people in the Brit jet got a good look. They said it looked like Concorde, but longer, wider and with engine intakes from midwing to midwing. When it left, it did a one to one power climb. Stood on its tail and went up like a missile,' Schoeman said, shaking his head in wonder.

Raden picked it up there. 'The message that *Mississippi* received was signed Oslo. It would seem they built it, they operate it', he paused, 'from Iceland. That's where the heat sources originated, we back-checked old material. We have three other sets of pictures with similar results dating back four months or so. They were never thought unusual because UFOs sometimes leave heat sources. There are plenty of those so it's understandable. We don't know who they are, what they are, what they do, other than protect our ships and civvy jets. Mr Schoeman can tell us a little about hypersonics if you wish.' Raden sat down with sigh, wondering if he had a career left.

'Before we get that far, what have you done about this?' Sheridan asked.

'I have had a man in Europe for a while looking for this thing; he will be in Iceland this morning.'

'So, we know where it came from, we know what it is, what we don't know is who are Oslo . . . I can't believe an organization that can build something like this and mount an operation this complex has never been heard of. Do a search, someone must know who they are . . .'

'Sir!' Raden answered.

'Okay. Mr Schoeman, what is a hypersonic, what will it do, who makes it, what is your judgement here? Is this a threat to us?'

Schoeman repacked his pipe, but didn't light it. 'Well now . . .' he began. He was worried he hadn't heard from Tim or Sally for over a week.

280

The nine-year-old boy who had photographed the Tarbaby walked, clutching the film in his hand, down the wide Chichester street. He had the five pounds his mother had given him to pay for the developing and as he walked he enjoyed the sensation of the secret bursting in his heart. He looked up at the shop signs for the familiar bright yellow of the high street 'Super Snaps' shop and eventually crossed the road and waited patiently in the queue for service like a good English person. His father had mentioned this several times on holiday, how wogs and chinks didn't queue and they were rude. Nice people queued up. The woman ahead of him, bulky in her herringbone overcoat and smelling of mothballs, inched forward steadily as if he might try and push in. He smiled pleasantly at her, thinking unpleasant things and wishing she would hurry up.

Eventually at the counter he put the yellow Kodak roll on the flat surface by the assistant's hand. Funny, he thought, yellow camera, yellow film packet, yellow Super Snaps shop sign. He wondered if it was his lucky colour and decided that it could indeed be, if he wanted. He thought about Miss Timbrell at school, how she would be proud of him when he showed the pictures of his holiday and the sharp black spacecraft. He was sure it was a spacecraft. He had seen the shiny suits of the aliens with their dark helmets bobbing through the window. He did like Miss Timbrell. His friend said it was a crush and sometimes teased him about it. He just smiled shyly and blushed and sometimes denied it, knowing it to be true. Miss Timbrell was so pretty, with hair the colour of milk chocolate and white, soft-looking legs. She wore glasses, but he didn't mind, and behind the lenses her eyes were violet and large and moist. He even liked the little scar on her knee where she had fallen on the hockey pitch, and when she smiled his heart thumped in his chest and he would have died for her if she had asked. He had accepted with the fatalism of young boys that she was too old for him and that she would probably marry Mr Ford, who sometimes came to collect her from school in a battered old Golf. She had said he was a reporter.

His father called them both 'lefty bastards' whenever they came up in conversation and he ignored it, having already understood that his father called people names whenever they didn't agree with him and that it didn't actually mean anything. Miss Timbrell had spoken to them once in class about the women at Shoreham Harbour and tried to explain what they were protesting about and how it affected the government and the people and the animals and everything. He didn't really understand the fuss, though he didn't like cruelty. But when he had asked his father it seemed he disagreed, because all he had said was not to listen to that sort of thing and phoned the head-master. He had said the same when he had asked him about algebra. Which was why he had not said he had a photo of the spaceship.

The assistant smiled and pushed a small chequered piece of paper back at him and said when to come back.

'Please be careful,' he said, 'it's my special pictures . . . miss.'

She winked back at him and feeling that she understood he left the shop. Carefully folding the receipt he put it in his top pocket and patted it, smiling to himself. Damien Potts was a happy young boy and Miss Timbrell would be in class tomorrow and the world was a good place to be.

Reykjavik

Raden's message had arrived only two hours before and by more luck than management Hart and his team had found themselves on a flight within minutes to London Gatwick where a driver had met them and driven them to a private airfield where a CIA executive jet was waiting

282

to fly them to Iceland. A tall, thin-faced customs officer had cleared them in, ignoring the diplomatic passports, the smoke from his cigarette curling up into his eyes. An embassy car was waiting and as they cleared the airbase Hart unfolded the relief map he had requested the driver to bring, spreading it over his knees in the front seat.

'What are you looking for?' the driver asked.

'You cleared for this?' Hart asked.

'Yo,' the man replied laconically, 'but suit yourself.' He yawned as he drove, seemingly uninterested. Hart wanted to smile.

'Okay, maybe you can help.'

'The boss will be pleased, he hates to be left out. He is bucking for something in Washington,' he grinned. 'I will have to tell him.'

'Fine,' Hart said. 'Career or political?'

'Neither, the man is a lightweight,' his tone saying he was beyond caring.

Hart laughed out loud.

'We are looking for a secret base, somewhere an aeroplane could operate out of, somewhere quiet and lonely.'

'Shit, this place is half the size of Missouri,' the driver said.

'I know, but lots of it is mountains and lakes and hot springs and land unsuitable for a site.'

They stopped for coffee and pastries at a roadside café and the man began to mark likely places on the map. Hart would then request satellite and reconnaissance photos for comparison. Oxenburger and Chubb sat and watched, Oxenburger with bored indifference.

The driver, a lanky grade three junior operative from a small town in Alabama, had the unfortunate name of Cleatus Dray. He explained to Hart that right throughout school he had been called 'clitoris', and if he ever saw his father again he was going to punch him in the mouth.

'He pissed off when I was about three, so if I appear antisocial at times it's because of a broken childhood . . . I

283

would look to the north up here. Lots of little fishing villages, but not much inland at all and enough valleys to be interesting.' He smiled easily, even teeth showing.

Hart liked the man's relaxed manner and the self-control was evident and strong. That night when they pored over the map marking likely places he phoned Washington and after a conversation with Raden, Dray was transferred to his team. He proved an immediate asset. At six the next morning he woke Hart, banging on his hotel door.

'We've been looking at new maps,' he said, holding out an old tourist guide. 'This is about six years old. Have a look at this!'

There, on the map below the small fishing village of Husavik, a small old airfield was marked.

'They've taken it off the new maps, obviously,' he said, reaching for his pocket, 'and here is the reason.'

Hart took a small tape recorder from Dray and pressed the play button.

'I taped it last night. Phoned a guy I know at the government printers here, he agreed to go back to the office last night, this is his voice.'

Hart listened to the squawk and then the strong even Icelandic accent in the English.

'. . . it was ordered removed from all maps since ninety-two. The order is from the Ministry of Interior, but it's yellow, which means it's from security. They will have taken their instructions from the Prime Minister's office in this case. That makes the area classified for some reason.'

Hart nodded pursing his lips and sliding his hands into the pockets of his Calvin Klein jeans as he walked to the window. Outside the day had dawned bright and cool and the soft fog over the harbour was lifting as the day warmed.

'That's interesting,' he said, 'interesting enough to go and have a look at it, anyway. They wouldn't be inv . . .' he turned to look at Dray and at that moment Chubb walked in, sweating and tracksuited, after his morning run,

'. . . naa . . . couldn't be involved,' he tried to convince himself.

They left forty minutes later, Oxenburger, one hand still bandaged, sitting in the back with Chubb, Dray driving with Hart sitting in the front seat deep in thought. In the boot of the car they had hiking boots, warm jackets and packs to look like hikers, if stopped. Hart had also asked for a detachment of SEALS to be on standby at the American base in case they were needed.

He didn't get very far. He and his three-man team were arrested by the Icelandic military police at a point seven miles from the disused airfield. They had been walking, packs on, moving fast, when around the corner had come the light truck. The officer had been pleasant but firm. The area was restricted and no one was permitted to enter. They were escorted to the edge of the area and watched departing.

'If at first you don't succeed . . .' Hart said, and set off on a longer, more roundabout course to arrive at the same place, this time slower and more carefully. Only half an hour later a second vehicle spotted them on the short tussocky hillside. This time the officer in charge was not so polite.

'You were only seen off the area a short time ago, by my brother officer, why did you come back?' he had asked.

'We got lost,' Hart replied. 'Sorry about that. Which way to Husavik?'

'You are hiking?' the officer asked.

'Yes, you have a lovely country,' Hart smiled back.

'Why are you hiking with an injured man? He doesn't look like he is enjoying the experience.'

'Ah, well, he hates to be left behind. Very keen hiker is Mr . . . Oxen.'

'In the truck,' the officer said tersely.

'What?'

'You may tell my commanding officer about Mr Oxen's

likes. Does Mr Oxen like prison food? Does Mr Oxen want a call to the American embassy? Get in the truck! You are under arrest!'

'Have a nice day,' Dray said from behind Hart, the beginnings of a smile on his face.

'Do not make funny,' the officer warned.

'Joke,' Hart said, 'not funny . . . joke.'

'I speak Icelandic, Norwegian, Swedish, Finnish, some Russian and English, thank you for correcting me. How many languages do you speak?' the officer said frostily.

'I apologize,' Hart said seriously.

'In the truck, now.'

As they climbed into the back of the truck Hart regretted his impulse to retry the entry. But it had proved a point, and they would be released before too long. Next time they would do it properly, low-level chopper approach with night vision gear.

Damien watched Miss Timbrell as she spoke to the class. Her hair was tied back with a bright yellow ribbon, his lucky colour! Today was the day: he had collected his photos, rushing into town before school, and now the morning break was coming up. In a few minutes he would show her his spacecraft. One shot had a bit of his finger in it and one had glare off the scratched glass of the window, but one was wonderful in clarity and showed the big black thing entirely. He was a little disappointed that the tiny spacemen didn't come out, but he had clipped the newspaper story detailing the drama to back up his story. It said MYSTERY RESCUER IN UNKNOWN PLANE, but it was a spacecraft for sure. From his seat, four rows back, he watched as she finished illustrating her point with a smile and out in the hall the bell rang. They had to sit with straight backs and arms folded quietly for five seconds before she dismissed them and then, as the other kids struggled and giggled and shouted their way out into the playground, he was suddenly alone in the classroom with

Miss Timbrell. She looked up, large moist eyes smiling at him.

'No French cricket today, Damien?' she asked brightly.

'Miss Timbrell, I've got something to show you, can I?' he asked quickly.

'Yes,' she laughed. 'What is it?'

He got up, clutching the envelope with the photographs and the news clipping and threaded his way between the desks. Dust hung in the still sunbeams, suspended like his heartbeat for the moment. He stood by her desk respectfully until she had finished packing her books and folders back into a large purple sling bag.

'All right, Damien, what have you got to show me?'

He was disappointed because she seemed somewhere else, but he pressed on regardless.

'We were on holiday and when we came back we were on the plane,' he began, 'the plane that was attacked!'

She looked up at him, eyebrows raised over her glasses, trying to see if this was another fib. The kids always had stories, some beyond the realms of possibility.

'Were you really?' she asked.

'*Yes*! And a big black spacecraft came down and blasted the Japs.' He was confused a bit there. To him any attacking aircraft was Japanese and the good guys always won. Men like Sergeant Rock sitting in Mustangs came blasting out of the pages of comics into his memory confounding the more recent reality.

'What Japs? Which plane was this, Damien?'

Miss Timbrell had been teaching long enough to know when a thread of truth was there to be reeled in.

He pulled the clipping clear like a prosecuting attorney and held it out to her, the judge of all things, his teacher and his first puppy love. She took the jagged square with one hand and raised her glasses up her nose with the other.

'This plane, miss,' he gabbled. 'Mum, Dad and my sister Cheryl, she's only four and couldn't see and started to cry!'

'Shhh,' she murmured reading quickly. She finally

finished after what seemed a lifetime and looked up.

'Were you really on the plane, Damien? It must have been very exciting! Were you scared?' She asked the question carefully.

He looked at her, knowing better than to lie; Miss Timbrell knew when you told a fib.

'A bit . . . when it went up. Some people were screaming, the lady next to Dad was sick on him,' and she knew he was telling the truth. Little boys never admit to fear unless it was real. She remembered the stories in the daily papers.

'But then IT came!' he demonstrated with two bony hands, 'right along the side of us,' his excitement mounting, 'it was big, miss, and black and, and . . . and I GOT A PHOTO!' he roared triumphantly.

Omega Base

Haidermann looked around the gathered faces in the main recreation room. It was the entire staff of the base less a handful of Van Waveren's team who still stood guard above ground. Engineers, admin staff, control room personnel, catering, medical and technical teams, and of course, the flight crew. Carson sat on a table, his feet clear of the floor, Gail on a chair between his legs.

Digby Allison looked across at them and Carson winked. He had changed, relaxed somehow, and the mood between them had improved overnight. The mission had been his test, he knew that. He knew he hadn't let anyone down, but there was more to it; that he also knew.

'Today in precisely one hour, simultaneously in both Moscow and Washington, Oslo people will begin to offer our ultimatum to those governments. While they are talking softly, we will carry the big stick. You all know why you are here, you are all here because you believe in what we are trying to do with enough passion and with enough professionalism to see it work. You are all the very best at what you do, there has never been a gathering of such skill or talent as this. This is the culmination of fifty years of planning and dedication and effort, but there are those who will try and stop us, make no mistake of this. We have received word that an American guided missile cruiser has been despatched to the waters of the north coast of Iceland. They know we are here. The Omega . . . the Tarbaby will come up against the best they can throw at us, but we must win.'

Meran, leaning heavily on his stick, cleared his throat and looked up, his clear old eyes commanding still. 'You are the young lions. Now you have the chance to undo what I and my colleagues did all those years ago. Oslo on the outside is ready and waiting to begin. You handful are the spearhead of a dream, the dream of millions of people. We are ready, we are committed, we are about to begin, we are formidable, and we shall win!' his voice quavered, but his gaze was firm and his presence was powerful against it.

'Your job here is to keep Peter and Digby airborne, to guide them in, to be their eyes and ears, to maintain them and protect them as best you can. They will become in the next days a symbol of what can be accomplished by people who want something badly enough.'

'We shall fight them on the beaches and on the landing fields,' Digby mimicked perfectly and, the tension broken, several people chuckled quietly.

Meran smiled. 'I heard that speech live. He would have been a member of Oslo – said he was too old when we asked him. So. We are ready, let us begin.'

13

Mikhail Chekhov had turned sixty-three four days before. He was lean and healthy, if one discounted the diabetic condition that had manifested itself seven years earlier. He had controlled the condition with strict dieting and insulin, but admitted to close friends that occasionally he slipped on the drinking rules that limited him to one vodka a week. The expert care was excellent, as one would expect for the President of the Russian Republics.

The dacha he had retreated to this Friday was not the same as the one used by his predecessors. This building was older and without any palatial extras. Chekhov was a simple man, a pragmatic man, moderate in the face of extremes, a widower, a father, an achiever and, above all, a survivor.

Olga, his housekeeper and senior staff member in the dacha, moved about closing the windows. It was getting cooler, and although the sun was not yet setting over the heavy firs behind the log-walled low-eaved traditional Russian building, the five fireplaces in the residence were being prepared, along with pots of the strong American coffee and heavy dough cakes that Chekhov preferred.

He entered the room behind her; she felt him there rather than heard him. He had that charisma, and many had felt it in the fifty-three years he had been involved with the Party. He had joined the Young Communists aged ten and stood proudly in his red beret to recite his oath. He had never forgotten it, even through the hell of Stalingrad and that bitter winter of death and starvation. His father had died in his tank leading his regiment and the young Mikhail had promised his mother that he would make his father proud. She had grieved in silence and died the following year and Mikhail, now alone, threw his life and his formidable will and strength into the Party. He was loyal but he was also a revisionist, a liberal, and when Gorbachev ushered in the new age of Russian policies Chekhov was there in support, driving through the reforms that he knew were essential. Now the links of blood and iron and fear that had held Russia together were strained to breaking-point, with organized crime and corruption rife throughout the country. He was the man who was to hold it all together, to some as corrupt as the system he ran. No longer was the Russian man a peasant free from the Tsarist yoke, or a simple socialist. He was educated and ambitious, modern, and with a different set of aspirations. To Chekhov the way was simple. Drive the reforms through, but drive them with people in mind.

Provide food for the people, jobs, security and a better future for their children; but simple in concept was not necessarily simple in action. Power was still in the hands of very few and they headed what were called the clans, the powerful pressure groups, lobbyists representing the major industries and affiliations. This was still a country barely able to feed itself, reliant on American grain every year. The exhortations of the Party faithful had never worked, and now it was the time for western ways. Market forces. But they needed time to work, time to change. He realized it, so did working people, but not the Red Army, the clan leaders or the new extremists. The army was on its knees, never having recovered from the ignoble pull-out from East Germany. The sight of Russian soldiers selling their equipment to the highest bidder was one he would never forget. And then there were the extremists, men who didn't like the reforms, hard left and hard right. His support from the Council of Ministers depended on providing them all with what they wanted, keeping the peace between them like some godfather figure. True support was limited to three men, all his protégés. Younger men, clever men, but without the necessary power to take on Smetlov, the ultra right winger, or Kraskin, the old-time Communist and Red Army man. Both had growing followings and the next election was going to be touch and go. Smetlov was the danger. A fascist.

One of the three was coming today: he had granted a rare hour of his private time to Yuri Ustinoff. He had time for the younger man, one of his personal protégés and, at forty-nine, very young for the cabinet post he held. In time he might become President himself. He had claimed it was important and confidential, so Chekhov's personal security team had been advised to allow Ustinoff's big old Mercedes through the gates.

'When Ustinoff arrives show him in here please, Olga,' he said pleasantly.

She nodded as quickly as her tired old neck would allow. She had worked for him for the best part of twenty years and although the same age, she regarded him much as she had done her father. She was one of only a handful of people in all the world who would address him with the western diminutive, when no others would hear.

'*Da*, Mike.'

He smiled at her and poured himself a cup of coffee from the ornate heavy silver pot. His daughter would be coming tomorrow and bringing his grandson. Yelena was his pride and joy. She was like her mother, strong-willed, beautiful and intelligent. Too much for her foppish husband, whom she ran roughshod over any time it suited her. As head of the Agriculture Ministry he was well paid and had all the privileges of power, but Chekhov had decided that was the last move he would help him with. The boy was another matter entirely. He was a sturdy little chap with bright, quick eyes, a ready smile that usually meant mischief, and a huge appetite for the stories that Olga recited at bedtime. He knew them all by heart and would brook no diversion from the plot. To Mikhail Chekhov it was reason enough to keep his country safe that his grandson had to live there.

Ustinoff arrived at three o'clock precisely.

At the same time two other events occurred. The nearer was at the Red Army computer headquarters at Novosibirsk, where it was nearer six o'clock. A tall man in the immaculate uniform of a full colonel of the GRU, the army intelligence organization, entered the installation with a series of passes that could only have been genuine. He had cold eyes and an even colder voice and behind him walked a duty technician carrying the new program tapes that had been escorted from Moscow that morning.

The other event took place in the small breakfast room in the White House. President Sheridan, from the day of his arrival in Washington, had ignored the heavy walnut table in the dining room with its chafing dishes and formal layout, and chosen to eat bran cereal and drink coffee in the sunny little alcove alongside the kitchen. It was there that his senior aide found him that morning. Peter Kramer was three years Sheridan's senior, a Republican all his adult life, an attorney, and arguably the most gifted political analyst in four decades of post-Korean War administrations. He was a confidant of the President's, a lifelong friend, and Sheridan's daughter's godfather.

Kramer tried to judge the President's mood as he entered the room, Sheridan stolidly munching his way through a bowl of something and absorbed in the morning newspapers, his jaw muscles tensing and relaxing in his perfectly cleancut face. The tan was natural, as was the salt and pepper effect in his hair.

'Peter, good morning! What have you got that drags you out so early? Something earth-shattering or just insomnia?' he called.

Kramer smiled, relieved to find him in good spirits, and pulled out a chair from the table to sit in the bright sunshine that beamed in the large window.

'Richard, how long have we been friends?' Kramer asked, reaching for the coffee pot.

Sheridan looked up, 'Best part of twenty years I guess . . . why?'

'In that time have I ever given you cause to disbelieve me, or to distrust me?'

Sheridan was interested now and put the *Morning Post* down. Watergate had destroyed Nixon, Irangate nearly got Reagan. Scandals, the bread and butter of Washington, were the death of administrations.

'Can't say you have, Peter. What's on your mind?' His hazel eyes were steady across the table.

Kramer sighed and passed across a bound dossier. 'Read this, it's a preamble to a statement I have to make.'

'What is it?' Sheridan asked taking the document.

'Read it, Richard. Then we will have to go to your office.'

'That sounds like fighting talk. Is this my aide talking or someone else?' Sheridan asked with remarkable intuition.

'It's Peter Kramer. Your oldest and most trusted friend.'

Sheridan opened the first page, looked across at Kramer for a full three seconds, his eyes displaying his disappointment.

'Oslo . . . that's the outfit that . . .' he began.

'Correct,' Kramer said.

'What are they to you? Where did you get this dossier? It wasn't put together overnight.' He hefted it in his hand.

'No, it wasn't. Read it, Richard, and then I will answer any questions you may have about it.'

Sheridan went to his study, Kramer following, and there he settled into an old club chair originally bought by Ladybird Johnson and began to read. He stood once, collected a pencil from the rolltop desk and, returning to the chair, began to make notes in the margins. Kramer sat and watched him, taking the calls on the internal phone and putting everyone off. The door wasn't a problem; when Sheridan closed the study door it was off limits, something even his daughter respected. Kramer watched him jotting the pencil notes, his eyes flicking across the pages, and knew he was absorbing every word and every phrase, just as he had done as the highest paid corporate lawyer in the country in the days before politics. Thirty minutes later he was through.

'You are part of this organization, this Oslo?' he said the last word with incredulity.

'I am, and have been for six years,' Kramer answered.

Sheridan looked at him as if seeing him for the first time, seeing something he had never seen before.

'Do you remember,' Kramer continued, 'about two years ago, up at the lake? We talked about the nuclear issue, do you remember that?'

'I have a memory like an elephant. My God! You were trying to recruit me!' he answered, the realization slamming into him.

'I was feeling the water,' Kramer said. 'We try to get people who can be effective. You could have been, you can be now.'

'What do you want?' Sheridan asked.

'It's quite simple. You and Chekhov, you both want disarmament, nuclear weapons in particular, so do we. We want you to immediately begin dismantling the ICBMs, recall the missile subs and strip the nukes from them, get rid of the air launch cruise missiles . . . we want nuclear disarmament. Right now. This is an ultimatum.'

'Ultimatums have a threat attached, what's yours?' Sheridan asked distastefully, looking to destroy his opponent as he did when debating.

'Don't misinterpret me, Richard, I'm serious. I am not some junior staffer you can browbeat. I would like to discuss this in a businesslike manner . . . it would be in your interests to take this seriously. At this time in Moscow, Mikhail Chekhov has a similar meeting taking place – you can do it, the pair of you! Think about it, Richard, you can be the President that brought nuclear peace!'

'What is your ultimatum?'

'Do I really need to present it?' Kramer asked. 'Isn't it enough that we have one hundred and fifty thousand Hiroshimas waiting to happen? Let me tell you about a nuclear explosion . . .'

'I'm not a child,' Sheridan snapped back.

'Then I'm sure you will be able to concentrate on what I have to say.'

'I will not.' Sheridan stood, his face reddening with anger.

'Oh yes you will. It's me. Peter. The one that got you into politics. The one that got your daughter out of a drugs bust. Your fucking *friend*. Now you *will* listen!'

Sheridan reeled under the onslaught. In all the years he had known Peter Kramer he had never heard him swear or raise his voice. It gave the whole nightmare credibility, and he settled back into his chair.

'It's here, Richard. The best opportunity you ever had to do something decent for this planet. You are a good man, take this opportunity to get rid of these things for ever. You and Chekhov, you have begun it with the medium range treaty, pick up the ball and finish it. Today. Now!'

'Even if I thought it would work, it would never get past Congress. I have opponents there who think we should nuke Nicaragua for Christ sakes. Be realistic, Peter . . .'

'. . . I am realistic. The consequences of Congress not ratifying the programme would be disastrous. You can either be the President that ended the nuclear arms race, or a President that brought the most powerful nation on earth to its knees in twenty-four hours. Congress will ratify it. They will be tainted with the same brush.'

'What do you mean, to its knees?' Sheridan asked. The ultimatum.

'If you don't agree to commence within twenty-four hours the complete dismantling of all nuclear weapons, cease testing and production, we will force you to,' Kramer said softly but firmly.

'How?'

'The laser-equipped hypersonic . . . the one that was over the Gulf, the one that saved the lives of the entire Gulf Fleet and half of Arabia and North Africa from a nuclear blast,' he let that sink in, 'it will come overhead this country and begin to take out these targets.'

He unfolded a sheet of paper from his pocket.

'We will commence with the Pentagon. That will be followed by the IRS computers and data banks. How many honest Americans are going to pay their taxes after that little number? All the IRS records, Richard. We will then take out Wall Street and the financial district, General Motors, General Electric, Lockheed, Boeing, Pacific West Telephones – the others are ours anyway – the utilities companies, the broadcasting networks . . . do you want me to go on? We will have America an economic basket case in just a few hours. We are going to hit America where it hurts, in their pockets. More? Okay, how about Fort Knox? All the gold reserves melted!'

'This is madness,' Sheridan said, aghast. 'Sheer madness!'

'No. Nuclear war is madness. This is your ultimatum. Do it, or perish. Not much choice, is there, really? Just get rid of the bombs, the warheads. If you don't you will be the President that destroyed the American economy. The phone will go soon. Mikhail Chekhov will want reassurance that you are not behind his ultimatum. He will say "angel" and you will reply "seven". Then we'll all know that you two are talking and understand each other. Oslo is powerful, Richard, we will have our way here. You can either benefit by our strength or . . . well, that's being negative.'

'We need those weapons to redress the balance, their conventional forces are bigger than . . .' Sheridan began.

'That's hackneyed and you know it. You have demolished the same argument a dozen times. The Russians don't want America, they have problems of their own. It's that kind of bullshit paranoia that has driven us into this mess in the first place. Anyway, you know that American know-how and technology will beat the Russians hands down every time ... with conventional weapons! Shit, they don't even have a decent computer that we didn't build for 'em!'

Ustinoff was ushered in by Olga who had dismissed the bodyguards with a wave of her arthritic old hand.

'Come in, Yuri, would you care for a cake? I need to eat about this time of day. No?' He indicated the chair opposite.

Ustinoff accepted coffee and he filled his own cup while Chekhov watched him. He was tall, with wavy fair hair just beginning to streak with white. A large, friendly nose was slapped across his face after nature's original issue had been adjusted by a lost bout in the university boxing championships. For Ustinoff the boxing was secondary to his prime love of history, and he had been a brilliant scholar, his intellect only hampered by his impatience. Then, as he had matured, he had found the time to do things right and somehow, to his friends' amazement, he had begun to move up in the political machine. He wasn't a normal piece of the apparatus and had been lucky. At each critical stage of his career he had found the right mentor, someone who had seen the promise and the same charisma they had demonstrated at his age, and been in a position to guide and influence his life.

Now his mentor was the most powerful man in Russia and Chekhov admitted things about his charge. Ustinoff was a potential leader of tomorrow. He had not dedicated his life to the Party, as Chekhov had done, but then, the requirements had changed. This young man had not stood in the ruins of Stalingrad amongst the frozen corpses and the rubble, he had not seen his homeland invaded, nor had he seen the fear and exhaustion on the faces of his comrades when confronted with the awesome power of the United States of America at the end of the war.

He himself, like the others who had been leaders so far, had helped to chase the Nazis back into the guts of Berlin, beaten and tired but with the tenacity of a thousand years under the Tsars and hatred of tyranny giving them the strength to see it through. Then the first views of the mighty American armies, with their chocolates and cigarettes and equipment and their wealth and their open dislike of Communism. He and his friends had agreed that never again would the land they loved be invaded and they agreed that the only people strong enough to do it were the Americans.

Those years had bred intractable leaders, powerful men moulded by what they had seen. Now times had changed, fifty years had rolled by and the huge American ogre was little better understood; soon it would be for younger clever men like Ustinoff to lead Russia as she took her next lumbering steps towards betterment.

There were other things with the new Russia. No longer just the problem of too many roubles chasing too few products, or the corruption, or the organized crime that spared no one. The simmering nationalism from Armenia and Georgia and further north in Estonia, Latvia and Lithuania was returning to haunt him, and in the south, in the Muslim states, it had exploded. There had been Abkhazia and now Chechnya was on fire. The Orthodox Church was about to celebrate its thousandth year in Russia. Many Russians hated the southerners, the Christians, the Muslims, each other. The ones in favour of reform fell foul of reactionaries like the Lubyerites in Moscow. The Lubyerites disliked everyone, it seemed, the smattering of punks and hippies in Moscow taking the brunt. It was a minuscule problem by Russian standards, but indicative of other, deeper currents.

The young veterans who had returned from Afghanistan were angry and gave no thought to Pamyat, the old school campaigning for the restoration of national values. *Blat*, bribes, were so commonplace that there was now a price list. A few dollars in real currency could get you a parking ticket removed from the records and at the other end

$2,500 could get you a building permit to erect something that was nothing if not dangerous anywhere you liked. Yesterday's paper had a story of one soldier who, after he hadn't been paid in months, was furious when expected to pay the traditional *blat*. He had dragged the official out into the street and pushed his face into the filth in the gutter. Angry young men, and a country with technology and its economy falling further behind the West and nearer to the Third World it had tried to dominate for so long. A country where its workers traditionally revolted for only one reason, food shortages. It was coming again this winter, Chekhov knew that already.

Agriculture estimates from the ministry were predicting a shortfall again and last winter the riots in the bread queues had raged uncontrolled in six Russian cities. The long summer was coming to an end and winter was just around the corner. With factories now self-financing, no state help for those that failed and the staff paid only if they performed, it had been a bittersweet step towards capitalism. The only people so far unaffected by perestroika, the reconstruction of the old Soviet system, were the rich and the criminal, and Russia had both, Chekhov mused.

The Soroki Hills in Moldova were as exclusive as Beverly Hills in California, and it was partly in reaction to that that he chose to weekend in this simple dacha. Chekhov was only too aware that many of his predecessors had lost touch with the real Russians within weeks of assuming the supreme role. He had not, and in fact six weeks before had put on a false beard and stood in a queue on a cold Moscow street, clutching his *avoska*, his string bag, like any other shopper, and listened to the talk of his people. The complaints had been by and large good-natured, but summed up with the simplicity of youth by a child who had looked up at his mother and asked why, if they had money, could he not have a new pair of boots. His mother said there weren't any and he had asked why not. Why

300

not indeed, Chekhov had asked himself. They were the largest country on earth, could amass armies like others amassed litter, put men into space before the Americans. Yet they had a real problem just feeding themselves, providing health care for their people, consumer goods, a decent quality of life and even children's boots. He had his bodyguard follow the woman home and the next day he had sent a dozen pairs of boots of different sizes and colours for the child to choose from, feeling impotent that there were other children who would have cold feet this winter.

'So, Yuri, what brings you out here today?' he began.

Ustinoff looked up from his coffee.

'When I tell you, Mikhail, you may well wish I had never come. You may also want to throw me into the Lubyanka.' His gunmetal grey eyes blinked over the broken nose.

'Sounds like you had better begin at the beginning,' Chekhov said without a smile.

'Read this. It will explain much. Then we can begin at the beginning.'

Chekhov took the dossier and began to read.

Novosibirsk

The GRU colonel escorting the new computer tapes stepped from the elevator at level three and watched the man carrying the heavy lead-lined case exit behind him. He then walked the seven feet to the fifth security check since entering the complex. This one was manned by a GRU major and four soldiers. The major stood and saluted, as did his men.

'Stand easy,' the colonel said, handing over his batch of papers.

The major took them and looked up at the senior officer.

'Major Bogovich?' he asked. Bogovich was the officer who was routinely involved in escorting the tapes.

'Unavoidably detained,' the colonel said pleasantly. 'Hurry up. I want to be back in Moscow tonight.'

'Detained, where? I only spoke to him last night.'

'Did you? Well you'd best report that when you go off duty. He is the subject of an investigation,' the colonel replied crisply.

The major nodded quickly and dropping his head began to check the papers in a perfunctory manner.

The last thing he wanted was to get involved with a GRU internal investigation. They were brief and terrifying and usually ended with the guilty, and they always were guilty, going off to the Aquarium. He had never seen the Aquarium; few of them had unless they were specially picked for overseas duty. It was the headquarters of the GRU and men who went there for investigation usually never came out again. The Red Army intelligence machine was awesome and the GRU had vied for power with no other group in the whole of the USSR after the demise of the mighty KGB. The animosity had been legendary. Often at loggerheads and constantly crossing swords, each organization resented the other's power. Each had its leaders in the Politburo and divide and rule was the system. Let neither get too powerful lest they swallow up their creators. Now, with a slimmed-down service, the competition was over but residual distrust remained.

The major signed the authorities and handed back the papers. One of the soldiers smiled to himself. The colonel took the documents and walked straight past the post and down the long brightly lit corridor towards the main computer room where Igor sat quietly clicking and whirring his way through his programs. The technician moved ahead, pushing the double dust-proof doors aside with his hip, and led the way into the complex. There, at consoles across the room, the duty operators sat, the bulk of Igor's CPU in front of them. Above them on the next level the operational people watched screens of data that Igor produced.

From there they and their group of officers in the glass booths behind them would control the missiles and interceptor squadrons for the entire north-west sector. These people rarely left the complex, eating and living underground, watching the films sent in and looking forward to their next leave. Here, deep underground, they were shielded by three hundred feet of rock and concrete, safe from even a large warhead.

The colonel knew that standard operating procedures insisted that he view the tapes loaded and the system locked down, so he stood to one side, his hands behind his back, as the lead-lined box was opened and the tapes were loaded into upright cabinets. From there they would dump down the new program on to the disks. It would take about forty minutes and the colonel accepted coffee from a slim girl in a corporal's uniform. Sipping slowly, he watched the reels spin and stop, the megabytes surging from the tapes into Igor's main disks, a slight smile playing on his lips. The operators and their supervisor checked the job and announced it finished. Not a minute too soon, he thought, pulling on his cap. He nodded to the staff and began to retrace his steps, the old program tapes in his briefcase. As he passed the major who had questioned his replacement of Major Bogovich, he stopped, turned and crooked his finger. The major hurried over.

'You look like a decent sort. I won't report your conversation with Bogovich, they may not notice. After all, you can't be held responsible for another man's foolishness.' His voice was cold.

'Thank you, colonel, sir!' the major said, relieved. The colonel walked away in measured strides, arrogant and strong. The major never saw the wintry smile on his lips and certainly never dreamed he had just allowed the head of Russia's most secret subversive organization into the most secure complex in the country.

Once above ground the man travelled to the civil airport, changed his clothes in a disused shed near the car park, re-emerged in the uniform of a colonel in the FSB, the security service. In this he was far more comfortable – after all, that was what he was. At the ticket counter he glared across at the clerk.

'I am Colonel Rordino, I want a seat on this flight to Moscow.'

The clerk hurriedly cancelled the booking of some unfortunate and entered the officer's name. He already had a ticket to travel from Moscow to Minsk in his pocket. He was pleased. Suki Yalta and Pyotr Rabanov had done well on the program changes: now Gulag was ready. Ready for Oslo and the Tarbaby. He looked at his watch. Yuri Ustinoff would be with the President now, he thought; he did not envy the job Ustinoff had. He was also pleased because the years of work had paid off. In his day-to-day work he had been looking for the men behind the theft of the warheads for what seemed like a long time. He had found them. But one was high up. Very high up. In the Kremlin itself. Not even an FSB colonel would survive making a claim like that. Ustinoff could do it. Do it from within. But even he would need to get his timing right, or the clan would wipe him out.

Chekhov slammed the dossier down on the hardwood table and sent crumbs of the dough cakes flying across the polished surface.

'You must be mad!' he muttered angrily. 'You, with the brightest future in Russian . . .'

'Not mad, Mikhail. Angry, yes, concerned, yes, enlightened, yes. Not mad,' Ustinoff said gently.

'What is it you hope to achieve?' Chekhov shouted frustratedly.

'A world free of nuclear weapons,' Ustinoff answered honestly and simply.

'And you want to disarm Russia? What of the Americans, the French, the Chinese, the British, the Indians, the Israelis and the rest?'

'President Sheridan has a similar meeting taking place at the moment. The British will disarm with them, the French we will force, the others the same.'

'Sheridan? He is tougher than you think. So am I. You naive fool!'

'Think of me what you like, but take the desire seriously. We mean to win and we shall.'

Chekhov studied the younger man's eyes for guile or weakness, but found only strength and a gaze of iron as he finished the statement.

'So, you want us to disarm the missiles,' he said moderately, preparing to debate the issue.

'Not just the missiles in the silos: the SS-20s, the sub-launch, everything must go. None of us are safe while they exist,' Ustinoff said. 'You began it, Mikhail Mikhailovich, you and Sheridan, now you can finish it. You know we are right in our cause, you believe it too, so help us finish it once and for all.'

'You want to take our teeth. You want us to become vulnerable again? Twice this century we have watched invaders roll across the steppes, twice this century we have eaten rats and frozen while the guns roared and the dead mounted up unburied because the ground was too hard. No, Yuri, never again, never, never again!' Chekhov answered venomously.

'That argument was true once, but no more. We mass more conventional men and arms than all of Europe put together. We are the largest military machine on the face of the earth. We need fear no invader ever again, and we need no missiles to protect us,' Ustinoff argued.

'Next you will want to disband the Red Army . . .'

'Never! They need tempering to our control, but never disbanding. They are Russia's security, not missiles. We are Russians, not spies or agents or anarchists. We are patriots! We do not want to control Russia, we do not want to change it. All we want to get rid of are the nuclear weapons, that's all. It isn't much, is it?'

'Yuri . . . Yuri, Yuri.' Chekhov shook his head. 'In my heart I agree, no sane man could not. These weapons hang over us like a sword we can't wield because it would cut us down too . . . but it's not me. The Duma . . .'

'The Duma can't do this and you know it. The reforms haven't gone that far. You have the power, Mikhail. No elections for another two years.'

'And the cabinet,' Chekhov countered. 'Powerful canny old foxes, men like me who have survived the decades, can move and shift opinion, but control it? Never. I am President. I have a certain influence, but I can't do this. This would need the consent of the group and that you will never have. Not with Kraskin and his followers: he is powerful and these missiles are his toys.'

'Tough. He can't challenge you on his own. You would just fire him and he knows it.' Chekhov sipped at the cold coffee as Ustinoff continued, 'And Smetlov? Smetlov will side with you. Anything to break the stranglehold Kraskin has. If Smetlov comes on to your side, then Sivlat and the Ukrainian will follow. You have me and I will promise Gordin as well. He will follow you. I guarantee it . . . it could work. Mikhail, we live in a country that is on its knees. Look at us, my friend. We have a crime problem so bad that western businessmen need bodyguards just to survive a three-day trip. The mafia control too much of life now. What's happening to us? The other day there was another case of cannibalism. Shit, Mikhail! Cannibalism! I walked through the park last week. A crowd had gathered. Know what they were watching? A dog fight. Mikhail, we live in a country where people go to see two animals tear each other apart for entertainment in public parks. Let's get rid of the missiles. Spend the money where we need it. On education, on jobs, on law and order. Let's spend it on people, on quality of life, on decency. Not facing some imaginary foe.'

'I hear you, Yuri, but let's keep the emotions out of this. Fact: the medium range treaty cost me dearly. Fact: Kraskin has not forgiven me for that. I am President, but fact: only so long as I win elections. He has growing support out there. Hard-liners. Fascists. People fear him.'

'Kraskin will be begging for an agreement by the time we have finished with him. But we need your agreement that you will act then,' Ustinoff pushed.

'You seem confident that your plan will work. What have you to play with? You think Sheridan will bow? He works for the will of his electorate, more so than us. You and your people are – what was it you said, enlightened? So am I. So is Richard Sheridan, but between your team and mine and Sheridan's there is a large block of powerful men, men with cast-iron views who have no more vision or imagination than that of a large stone. It is they that need convincing, it is they who are the real influence . . . so, Yuri Ustinoff, you think you can walk into the private dacha of the President of the Russian Federation and tell him to disarm because you and a few people want to see that happen. It is not that easy. Now, the question is, do I hand you over to the security people and the Lubyanka for treason, or do I have you committed for insanity, or do I just forget all about this? Mmmm?'

Chekhov looked across at Ustinoff who burst out laughing.

'Good try, my benevolent Uncle Mikhail. Now listen carefully and listen well. We can destroy Kraskin. We can bring the Red Army to its knees, we can do the same for Russia! DON'T PATRONIZE US! Now, you can side with us on this, retain your power base and survive the changes and be the Russian leader who gave the world a nuclear-free existence, or you can watch Russia bend its head. I know what I want. I want a strong, proud Russia, bowing to no one! But by God we will do it, DO YOU HEAR ME? You have the power. We will take Kraskin to pieces, and have the others begging you for a solution to it all. WE CAN DO THIS! WE SHALL DO THIS! WE MUST FOR THE SAKE OF OUR CHILDREN DO THIS! You will call Richard

Sheridan in five minutes. You will say "angel" and he will reply "seven", that means he has had his ultimatum, and you two must begin agreeing to disarm. We will provide the support. We will take out the Red Army payroll system, we will hit the GRU headquarters and the Security Service headquarters, we will take out the communications systems. We will have strikes and civil disobedience so bad it will make the Uzbeks look like a picnic, and you won't have an army to control it. You will have Russia breaking apart at the seams, one hundred separate racial groups at each other's throats, years of frustration unleashed, years of bullshit flung back at you. You know it's there, just below the surface, waiting. So what's your choice? That's just the beginning, Mikhail. Support us – you agree with it anyway, we know that. Russia can take punishment like no other country ever, but she wouldn't survive this, not as a Federation. Call Sheridan . . . now!'

'Don't force me into this, Yuri. You leave me no way to win,' Chekhov warned, his voice low and menacing. Any ordinary man would have wavered under his gaze. Not Ustinoff. He launched back.

'You can win. Disarm the missiles, stick HE heads in them for all we care, but no thermo-nuclear, no chemicals and no bacteria. You can win, Mikhail. You put an end to this senseless waste of money and redirect it at the economy and ordinary people's needs and you win the next election. I'd guarantee it and I've never been wrong reading the water. But it's more than that. Mikhail, you can win the most important issue of our time.'

Olga shuffled in bearing fresh coffee and the two men fell silent as she placed the tray on the table and took the old one, clucking to herself as she wiped the crumbs clear. Eventually Chekhov waved impatiently at her and she scuttled back towards the door. His secretary appeared and waved a pile of documents at him. The man, a bright, career acolyte, needed only to see Chekhov's expression to close the door again and leave it closed.

'Call President Sheridan,' Ustinoff said gently. 'Reassure yourself that this is not an American plot.'

'I did not think it was,' Chekhov snarled. 'They have more acumen than to hatch something as harebrained as this – and what about the breakaway states? Half of our arsenals still sit in their soil! They see it as a bargaining chip! Do you think they will give those up just for your cause? They are unstable enough as it is.'

'Then we need to get rid of them more than ever,' Ustinoff countered. 'They will co-operate. They will get soft loans, technology, aid they never dreamed of.'

'From who?'

'From us. From the power and influence we bring to bear. We have it! Don't doubt us for a second.'

'Oh but I do,' Chekhov said quietly.

He stood and crossed the polished wood floor to the cabinet alongside the huge hearth. He opened the heavy old scarred door and there, inset in complete contradiction to the wonderful warm, smoky atmosphere of the room, was a communications panel. Five telephones, three conventional and two cordless, sat on the upper metal shelf. Below that a facsimile machine, computer printers, radio communication panels with decoder units and a video camera recessed above a small monitor formed the main bank of gear. In the trees behind the dacha a satellite dish squatted amongst the aerials and cable junctions. From the panel Mikhail Chekhov could communicate with anywhere in the world, any of his Politburo colleagues in their cars, homes or offices. Below the video screen was a perspex panel that slid back to reveal a red telephone without dial or buttons. When he arrived in office the hot line was in fact an ominous black instrument and he had had it changed: he had always felt it should be red. He had used it three times in the four years he had been President. Once when Russian fighters had come close to shooting at American F-15s over the Aleutian Islands, once when a Russian submarine had been caught loitering in a

Norwegian fjord by an earnest American ASW aircraft, and the last time when, with four shots of a Highland malt in him, he had called to wish Sheridan merry Christmas.

He lifted the handset and waited, his expression wreathed in contempt as he caught Ustinoff in his vision.

Washington

'So then, tell me who we need these missiles to protect us from,' Kramer argued.

'The Russians, you arsehole,' Sheridan burst back, throwing his arms up in exasperation.

'The Russians? And what if they didn't have any? What if they could only muster tanks and men and aircraft and ships and guns and things? We wouldn't need them, would we? Well the Russians will be disarming their stockpiles and their front-line-deployed nukes,' Kramer offered reasonably.

'Bullshit! Who the fuck do you Oslo people think you are dealing with? The Russians will not give in like a kid in some alley fight ... they will fight this with all the tenacity they have and let me tell you, fella, it's considerable. If ever there was a bunch of tight, intractable bastards it's them. So, even if your scheme has all the moral virtues, this is the real world, and let me tell you, I'm not going to Congress or the American people to say, "let's disarm", if the Russians have the motherfucking things bristling up like the quills on a porcupine's back!'

'Calm down, Richard,' Kramer answered gently. 'They will be disarming at the same rate, we will ensure that, we will monitor it, as will your own observers.'

'Peter, I run this administration with one thing in mind. This democracy is the finest on earth. It's had its problems, but it works! I represent the best will of the American people.'

Kramer smiled then, a delicious, slow, secret smile from his childhood in the wheatfields of Kansas.

'The will of the people? . . . oh dear, Richard . . . we will show you the will of the people. Oh just you watch!'

At that moment the door burst open, one of the staffers from the aide's office panting after a short run, behind him a secret service man, a radio to his ear.

'Excuse me, Mr President, the hot line, sir . . . it's ringing!' he panted.

'Thank you, Eddie, we have been expecting the call,' Kramer said pleasantly, and then to Sheridan, 'Shall we answer it?'

Kramer picked up the handset and spoke without looking at Sheridan.

'Mr President, my name is Peter Kramer. I am a White House aide to President Sheridan and I am also here making an ultimatum on behalf of the organization I represent. I believe you have my counterpart with you?'

There was a considerable pause, then, 'I wish to speak to President Sheridan,' Chekhov said tersely, his English excellent, if accented, unable to believe the audacity of the man.

'After I have spoken to Ustinoff,' Kramer replied.

'Very well, speak, it may be the last time you two have the chance.'

'I think not, Mr President,' Kramer answered coldly.

'Mr Kramer, Yuri Ustinoff . . .' a new voice clean and crisp.

'We have got to stop meeting like this,' Kramer said smiling to himself. Ustinoff laughed, delighted, on the other end, his exposure to the West complete enough to understand the joke.

'You have spoken with the President?' Kramer asked.

'I have, and you have spoken with your President?'

'Yes. It would seem we are ready to let them talk.'

'*Da, tovarich*, let us finish this. All the best from Gulag.'

'And from Oslo, Yuri. Take care now.' Kramer handed the phone to Sheridan and stepped back.

Sheridan took the phone and without prompting said one word in reply to something he heard.

'Seven.'

His voice came through into Chekhov's phone clearly in reply to 'Angel'.

'President Chekhov?'

'Let us dispense with the formalities, Richard. How are you, my friend?'

'Great until about an hour ago,' Sheridan answered honestly. 'And you, Mikhail?'

'I am fine, thank you. So. This is delicate, this problem I have. I have a man here, a man I trusted and nurtured and supported, who is making an extraordinary demand of me. All my instincts tell me he is mad. All my instincts tell me that you and your country are not involved in this conspiracy . . .'

'Mikhail, I am going to ask you the same question. I cannot believe they put this plan together without help. You have my word, as President of the United States of America and as Richard Sheridan, that I was not, was never, and do not intend to ever assist these people. Now, you have never lied to me yet. You just say nothing rather than do that, that well I know you. What say you now, Mikhail Chekhov?'

'I did not partake in this project and knew nothing of it until today. Yuri Ustinoff, however, is a full member of the Council of Ministers and did know and did actively work for it. He is as senior as you can get in my country and I wonder how many others there are. I cannot but respect their ideal, but Richard, you and I know just how difficult it was to push through the medium range agreement. What they want of us is too much too soon.' Chekhov probed for Sheridan's feelings, gently laying his own on the table.

'I agree. But they are powerful, and I think we are going to find out just how powerful they are. The threat they have laid before me is considerable. If they carry it out or are capable of carrying it out it will be another issue entirely.'

'What are you saying?' Chekhov was lost in the English and for a second wished he had his interpreter there.

'They have threatened to destroy the American economy. Something not even your most zealous colleagues would advocate, not while you need trade and technology. It would affect the whole world. It's not a threat I can shrug away like I can most I get.'

'I have had a similar scenario placed before me. A toothless blind army and civil disturbance on a massive scale. A nation split by a hundred old hatreds – they could do it with enough planning.'

'I think we should get together now, tonight . . . can you meet me halfway?'

'Where are you suggesting?' Chekhov quickly asked.

'I'll call you back. I must have a carrier somewhere halfway. Bermuda, perhaps?'

'I'll be there. Are you suggesting a joint reply?'

'I'm suggesting we need a few hours to think this through. Then a meeting face to face, you and me. See what we can come up with.'

'I will be there. Come alone, we don't need this thing confused by bad advice from others who have other motives. I don't know who I can trust any more, anyway. My people are either hard-liners or, in the light of this possible thing, members of this Gulag.'

'I know how you feel.'

Ustinoff indicated he wanted the telephone and Chekhov gave it to him as if it was of no consequence.

In Washington Peter Kramer took the other instrument.

'Yuri, do you have a problem if this meeting takes place?' he asked.

'No, but we may have a problem getting a representative there,' Ustinoff answered.

'We will have someone there, Haidermann perhaps, certainly one of the committee. They won't want to miss this opportunity to discuss our proposal with the other two.'

Sheridan shook his head at the casual reference to him and Chekhov.

When Kramer put the phone down he turned and looked at the President.

'I have somewhere you can meet. Majorca. We have a villa there. I'll make the arrangements now.'

He called in two aides and issued a complex set of instructions, then asked to see the head of the Secret Service detail that would be on duty that night. They would need all the few hours available to muster their men to accompany the President on this brief unplanned visit. Kramer then placed a call to King Juan Carlos of Spain, who could ease the necessary hinges to allow the American President and the General Secretary of the Russian Communist Party to meet undisturbed and in secret. That done, Kramer said, 'Right, let's get you some things in a suitcase. I will make your apologies to the Senate Committee and the others. You will be taking a break at Rancho Cabaldo, we will get someone who looks like you to walk out of the chopper with Claudia. I'm sure she will co-operate . . . one last thing, Richard, call off your dogs.'

'What!' Sheridan asked nonplussed, stunned at the speed things were moving.

'Call off your dogs. The missile cruiser you have steaming towards Iceland, call it back!'

'Or what?'

'Or we will blow it out of the water! Do you want the deaths of those men on your conscience?'

Kramer had no authority to threaten that act but he knew it was all that would force the issue to a close.

'I'll meet you halfway, for the sake of good relationships,' Sheridan answered. 'I'll have it heave to, for the moment, but recall? No way, bucko!'

Kramer nodded. 'That will do for the moment.'

Sheridan walked towards the hotline.

'Where is this villa of yours?'

314

14

Carson sat in his room, the BBC World Service hissing softly from the big radio in the corner, a cup of cocoa steaming at his side, engrossed in the latest papers that had arrived. His mail lay opened and discarded to one side, one or two letters from friends, a bank statement, a few printed circulars and the like.

Gail lay sprawled across the big bed, her hair spread across the jumble of blankets and sheets and wrinkled, sweaty pillows. Her eyes were closed, her cheeks flushed with afterglow and the warmth of sleep and the security of lying in his bed, his smell on the sheets and Tabac on the pillows. He sat naked and sipped at his cocoa and read the centre pages of the *Telegraph*, his jaw working angrily for a second at something he read. He put the paper down and closed his eyes, stretching like an old tom cat. The phone rang shrilly in the warmth and he snatched at it as he sat up.

'Carson.'

'Peter, it's me.' He recognized Digby's voice. 'Apparently Haidermann is going to a meeting. We are to stand down till further notice. Probably tomorrow morning at this rate.'

'Meeting with whom?' Carson asked.

'Dunno.'

'What about the cruiser?' Carson asked.

'It's been told to hold on where it is, apparently . . .'

'Shit! That's something at least. I didn't fancy taking off through a screen like that thing can make. Okay, I'll see you topside for some food later, eh?'

'I thought you were living off the fruits of love,' Digby answered dryly.

'Piss off,' Carson chuckled.

He immediately felt better. He needed a good night's sleep before they flew again. God knows when we'll get more than an hour then, he thought, looking at the bottle of Benzedrine tablets he had taken from the pharmacy. Flying stoned, he thought, is only one better than flying asleep, but at least I will be awake.

'What was that?' Gail asked sleepily.

'Stand down till tomorrow.'

'Oh goody, come to bed then,' she muttered.

Tim Miller was climbing into bed with his woman at the same time two floors above. Sally Schoeman was sitting bolt upright in the bed, a sensible pyjama top covering her breasts. Her hair was up in a bun, but one long wispy tendril had fallen over her eye, softening the effect. Her arms were crossed angrily and she glared at him.

'Well?' she said.

They had been arguing most of the day about why she should have waited outside when Tim crept into the control room during the Tarbaby's intercept.

'I've got to get word out somehow,' Tim began again.

'You've said all this before,' she said tiredly.

'I know I have. Either be constructive or . . . look, I'm sorry,' he said gently.

She turned to look at him as he brushed back the blond hair from his forehead and slipped lower into the bed.

'I forced this situation,' he said, 'but now we have seen it, I have to report it somehow.'

'What's going to happen now? To us I mean?'

He sat up and put his arms around his knees like a boy watching cricket.

'I'm not sure. They are about to take on the world, and while they do that, we are to wait here . . . right in the thick of it. I rather like the idea, myself. Beats sitting in the fun factory watching your dad froth with frustration while the flat earthers quote from the Old Testament. Well, I'm not sitting around doing nothing. There must be a way.'

'Oh grow up, Tim. We are watched like hawks, under what is virtually house arrest, miles from anywhere. You're not James Bond.'

'No. You're right. But I'll have to try.'

There were only three large dark sedans with tinted windows on Majorca and the local police commandeered all of them to receive the visitors they had been warned to expect. No names were given, but they were warned that any indiscretions would result in those guilty patrolling roads in the Basque country. King Juan Carlos may have been a simple figurehead compared with the absolute power his predecessors enjoyed, but he was certainly influential and much loved by the Spanish people. The discreet escort waited in the shadows of the main cargo sheds at Palma International Airport and watched the four-engined military jet settle on to the runway, American markings evident on the high tailplane. Almost right behind it an Aeroflot marked civilian aircraft of similar size landed and taxied in towards the cargo facility behind the American. The inspector whistled softly to himself as he recognized the markings on the two jets, and watched the service truck with the boarding staircase trundle its way towards the American. He waved into the dark and one of the limousines moved forward and stopped by him. He lit a cigar and pointed at the moving staircase.

'Pick up the Americans,' he said through the smoke.

The car drove away on to the pan, oily and slick in the moonlight, towards the deep pool of dark at the big silver jet. He waved to a second car and as it pulled up he pointed to the Aeroflot Ilyushin.

'Collect the Russians, there will be only two or three. Head back here and join up behind the other car. I will be

317

in the lead with you and Manolo behind me. Keep your distance and just follow.'

The man nodded quickly. He had been driving government cars for years and knew the drill. He accelerated away towards the Russian aircraft and left the inspector smoking in the gloomy warm evening by the last limousine.

They arrived in Deia just over a hour later, both Sheridan and Chekhov having enjoyed the drive up through the hills and terraces of vines, olives and fruit trees. Sheridan had a team of three Secret Service men and Chekhov had two, both alert, very professional men. They shook hands in the moonlit drive of Haidermann's villa beneath the bunches of grapes hanging from a trellis above their heads.

'You look fine, Mikhail,' Sheridan said. 'Holding the diabetes at bay?'

'I am, yes, thank you, Richard. You are greyer than when I saw you last . . . your daughter or affairs of state?' Chekhov asked smiling.

'I'd like to think it was my daughter,' Sheridan laughed back at him.

In the background the security men had stopped eyeing and circling each other like wary dogs and had now turned to concentrate on the darkness around them. One of Sheridan's men coughed politely and nodded at the doors and the light that beamed out into the night. Sheridan took the hint and touching Chekhov's arm moved towards the house as the men surrounded them, hands in pockets. An ageing Spanish retainer met them at the entrance to the house. He bowed his head respectfully and spoke.

'Mr Haidermann sends his apologies, he will be here as soon as possible. In the meantime, there is food ready for you and your staff and I have prepared suites for your comfort and a room for you to meet in. Follow me, please . . .' he turned and walked quickly down the long cool passage ignoring the security men as best he could.

Once they were alone Sheridan poured himself a drink from the cabinet and waved his glass at Chekhov.

'Perrier, please,' the Russian said.

They settled down and began to talk.

Haidermann, running late with bad connections from Reykjavik, hired a helicopter at Palma. Meran had accompanied him and now sat alongside in the clattering machine as it gained height over the bright lights of the town. Off to the left, the ribbon illuminations of Palma Nova and Magaluf jutted out into the dark sea. Meran smiled grimly to himself at the thought of the tourists below, ignorant of what was happening to the world. But not for long, Meran thought. If you never thought about it before, you will now. If you never stood up before, you will now. We are offering you something wonderful, but you will have to reach out and take it from us, and once you have it, guard it, because it is a very precious thing. He looked across at Haidermann.

'I have waited almost fifty years for this meeting, Charles,' he said over the engine noise, 'and now it is upon us.'

Haidermann smiled across at him. Meran was still very much an academic, a thinking man going to a meeting, a man who grew roses and never went anywhere without a handkerchief, a brilliant scientist and yet a man who had never learnt to drive a car. For the thousandth time since they met he acknowledged the differences between them. If Meran was the scholar, then he was the warrior. He did nothing by halves: if it hadn't been the stock markets and Oslo's investments, then it would have been something else. A corporate raider, a career naval officer, not stopping till he was a full admiral, or perhaps even a politician. A life where he could fight and win for his ideals whatever they might be. If Meran was the thinker, then he was the doer. To Haidermann it wasn't a meeting, it was a confrontation, a contest to be won like any other, but the most important contest ever.

'. . . so it is, Alexander. So it is,' he said, his eyes glittering, relishing the contest and the attainment of the dream.

He stood in the doorway for a second, looking at the two most powerful men on the face of the earth and determined not to allow that thought to intimidate him. He quickly pulled them down to mortal status with the observation that Mikhail Chekhov, the President of the Russian Federation, looked older in the flesh than in photographs. He walked forward into the room, Meran following, leaning on his stick.

'Gentlemen, thank you for permitting me to offer you a venue for this meeting and allowing us to attend. My name is Charles Haidermann and I shall be your point of reference to Oslo and Gulag, the sister organizations we are here to help.' He turned and introduced his companion. 'This is Alexander Meran; he is here because he is Oslo in its purest form, the last of the original five men who swore to make a better world. A concept we are here to agree in form and action.'

Sheridan stood. 'And you, what are you to this concept? You give it a vaunted feel, you give it lofty noble virtues. You are nothing more than blackmailers . . . you are the leader of this misguided venture?'

'No, we don't have leaders. I am a stockbroker, actually. You used the word blackmail. How else are we to get this accomplished? How else could we get a meeting around the table with you two! You don't even meet each other, let alone the representatives of an interest group! So let's stop the petty heckling and get on with it. You have both had your ultimatums and you have had time to discuss them . . . What we want is quite simple. We do not want money, we do not want to impinge on anyone's sovereignty, we want no changes in government nor do we want recognition in any fashion. What we want is a world free of nuclear weapons and it must begin with you two. It is possible and it can start immediately. Are you prepared to agree this in your official capacities and commence?'

Chekhov smiled grimly across the room at him. 'You think that you can take on the combined wishes of the United States of America and us?' he asked.

'Yes. It will be easier with your support, but we shall do it anyway.'

Paul Hart lay on the narrow bunk above Chubb. Across the other side of the big holding cell Oxenburger slept the sleep of the innocent. Between the bunks sat an old pot-bellied stove, cold now in the last days of summer. At a seat near the stove the cell's last occupant sat. He was a man of indeterminate years, a long hooked nose proud over his white lips. His eyes, deep-set over high Nordic cheekbones told tales of past glories and he stroked a white beard with an arthritic old hand. He glared up drunkenly at Oxenburger and mumbled something into his beard and rubbed his hands at the cold stove, as if willing it to glow warmth. They had talked for a while, ignoring the old man.

'Jesus, when are they going to get us out of here?' Oxenburger complained.

'When they can,' Hart answered dryly. He had misjudged the seriousness of their incursion. They had been in the cell most of the day and all the night. Embassy attempts to get them clear were failing, that was the best indicator they had. The Icelandic government were involved in this somewhere, or if not the government, then certainly people well placed in the administration.

'Then what?'

'Then we go back,' Hart replied almost to himself.

It has to be the place, he thought. You could hide a whole town up there and no one would be any the wiser. It's sewn up like a glove, but oh so carefully – unless you stumble across the patrols you would never know they were there. And what of the interior of the zone? If Icelandic troops patrolled the perimeter who was inside? Could be listening posts, cameras, anything. The feeling was different, areas controlled by military usually got busier as you went further in, but this place didn't. Just more snow grass, volcanic rock, streams and the old airfield. He tried to remember the map in his head. To the immediate west of the airfield there were steep hills and gorges: that will be the place to go in next time, he thought. By chopper, low and fast and close, over the patrols and right into the thick of it, have a quick look and then get the hell out before everyone comes running to the noise. All he wanted was to see recent wheelmarks on the runway, to see where they might be hiding the goddamned thing. Shit, it's as big as a B1, so it's sitting somewhere. Dug into a pit in the ground, ramps perhaps, maybe even into the hillsides somewhere, certainly something more substantial than nets covering her.

The cell door clanked open and the old man got hopefully to his feet.

'Not you!' the guard said in Icelandic, then in English, 'Americans, come!'

Oxenburger stood up eagerly, followed by the others stretching cramped limbs and looking forward to a bath and some food. The old man muttered at the guard, who laughed at him and turned to the Americans, miming pulling his pants down.

'He shit on the officers' club steps . . . ha ha,' obviously delighted with the charge and wishing he had done it himself.

Hart ignored him and pushed his way to the door. The American ambassador was waiting in the charge room. Christ! thought Hart, he's going to be pissed off having to come out here. But that was not the case. Once in the car and heading back towards town the ambassador looked back from his seat in the front.

'I've been told to give you whatever help you need. Anything! I don't like it, but that's it . . . someone in Washington is real keen to see what you can dredge up out there,' he said.

322

'Oh . . . who?' Hart asked, thinking maybe the Director was getting involved.

'The White House,' the ambassador answered firmly. 'I don't know what you are on to out there, but remember this is a friendly country, we have a military base here, this is the key to supplying Europe, so don't mess it all up, will you?'

'Aye aye, sir.' Hart grinned, delighted with everything suddenly. If the White House was becoming interested then things were hotting up considerably.

'Now what do you want?' Ambassador Caley asked.

'An intro at the base. We will need a chopper and some SEALS.'

'What?' Caley burst back, 'SEALS? What for?' He had seen the heavily armed raiders at the base, shinning down ropes and playing in rubber boats and things. They seemed terribly warlike.

'They will go the other way. Any interested parties can follow them instead of me and my boys. Don't worry, they don't need guns or anything, in fact I'd rather they didn't have them, just a few fleet feet to confuse the other side.'

'The base commander is a fellow called Henry Willis,' the ambassador said, somewhat mollified. 'He's a one star general, West Point in sixty-six, nice man, married to a girl from Boston, one of the . . .'

'. . . thanks, ambassador, but if you'd make a call for me?'

'Yes, of course.'

Ye gods, thought Hart, he was going to give me the social low-down on the general. We go in today.

The talks had been furious for over seven hours. The old Spaniard had brought food and coffee twice and the debris littered the old walnut table. Chekhov had left the room once to take his tablets and see to the welfare of his body-guard and had come back washed and refreshed. Sheridan seemed tireless, and often he and Haidermann stood like gamecocks, thrusting and parrying across the table, while Meran dozed in the corner and Chekhov waited his turn to speak. Then Sheridan would settle frustrated into his chair like a coiled spring, and the Russian would take over, wily and experienced, stabbing at any flaw in Haidermann's reasoning.

'Look,' Haidermann said, 'both of you have agreed more than once that what we want is in essence a good idea. You have both agreed that given the right circumstances it's feasible, without any unpleasantness, so what is the problem?'

'The problem is easy to see. You are an American,' Sheridan snapped, 'you know that I have no absolute power. Whatever I commence must be ratified by Congress, it must be generally agreed and accepted. This concept will scare the living shit out of half the Congress because they are voted into their seats like I am. If their voters believe they are being left defenceless you will have these men out on their arses, and a new breed of ultra-right-wingers suddenly in the Senate and Congress. That, mister, scares me more than nukes in Russia, because then the Russians would be justified in having them. Right now we have the medium range treaty. Hell, our cruise missiles have left Europe. Let everyone get used to that first, then we can proceed . . .'

'How long will that take, President Sheridan? Another five years, ten? We don't have that long any more, and quite frankly your electoral problems haven't even begun. Imagine if you were the President that brought a nuke-free world? Imagine if you had the chance and let it slip away? You wouldn't last five minutes in the next election, neither would your party. Why are we even talking elections? This issue is bigger than any election, it's the most important issue of our time. You two men can address it once and for all . . .'

'Mr Haidermann, listen to me now,' Chekhov said gently. 'Richard and I realize the importance of what you

324

are trying to achieve, you and all your people. I wish that I had so many genuinely concerned about such a thing in my organization. But the realities are different. I am here because you have made an ultimatum. You and your organization have threatened to carry out certain acts that will bring my homeland to its knees. We have been on our knees before. We lost fifty million dead in the last war – one was my father – but we survived that, we survived the Tsars, we survived every winter since time began, and until you have wintered above the Arctic Circle you won't understand that, but, but, there is nothing you can do that will last. So while your technology may inflict damage in the end, we shall still be there and, as you said to Richard, would you want to be the man that did all these things to two countries and gained nothing? I am convinced of the basic concept. You are preaching to the converted here, I put my signature to the medium range treaty willingly, but there are others less willing, others who would fight you. Like Richard, there is only so much I can do in time.'

'President Chekhov, I mean what I say. Time is running out for all of us. You have an army that resents even reporting to your parliament, an army that feels they are the ones who should dictate policy. American Presidents are shot with tedious regularity. You two men agree in concept, but, what about the next two men? You are diabetic, you are sixty-three years old! You won't be here for ever, who will follow you? Who will follow Richard Sheridan? We don't have time to let this problem meander its way to its conclusion, because there are two possible endings to this. We can do it now while we have two men who agree in principle, or wait. For how long? For how long? We have waited. Fifty years now. It's long enough. Long enough with this monstrosity hanging over us all. Gentlemen, we are talking about the ability to destroy the planet Earth. What choice do we have for Christ sakes?' Haidermann was standing again, his eyes sharp, his tie askew. 'What will start the new world war? Saddam

Hussein? The oil? Hunger in your winter, or just good old-fashioned imperialism? How many times did your generals wish they could irradiate hillsides in Afghanistan? How many good, reasonable, thinking men in America said "Let's nuke Hanoi!" and meant it?'

He turned away and ran his hands through his hair tiredly, stretching his arms. Meran sat up in his chair, pulled himself to his feet and shuffled across to the table.

'You weren't there when we did it. The Project. And then we took them and dropped them on Japan. My God, the deaths we are responsible for. But they are dead, gentlemen, we can't bring them back, all we can do is stop it ever happening again. One hundred and fifty thousand of those little Hiroshimas and Nagasakis are waiting for us . . . the end of the world as we know it, for how many years? No one knows. We created this monster, we can bury it . . .'

Haidermann turned back into the fray.

'What do you want from us? What can help? We are big, we have resources that not even you two men can muster.'

'Like what?' Sheridan replied.

Chekhov shook his head.

It was dawn before they finished talking. Tired bodyguards came back on duty and the limousines were called for the return run to the airport. Haidermann wasn't beaten yet, and he drove himself, Meran sitting deep in thought beside him thinking about the phone calls they had just made and what they had set in motion.

Dublin

People later said they thought that they had moved in a couple of weeks before. The big old building on Wisher Street had been vacated by the Cornerstone Insurance Company the previous year and had sat empty. Then, one

326

day the vans arrived with desks and chairs and cabinets and computer screens and hardware and the new telephone system was installed, all seemingly overnight. The word was they had two whole floors of facsimile machines and personal computers linked to modems and another larger room of computers that talked to others around the world. They were an investment company, so the man on the front desk said, and they were sure to be employing local people in a few months' time. They seemed to work odd hours because the last couple of days the lights had been on all night and there had been comings and goings at all hours. One local lad helping with the moving said they had an area like a money dealing room with banks of screens and telephones and clocks around the wall telling the time in different parts of the world. It was just like *Wall Street*, he had said, and he had just rented the video. They employed a lot of foreigners, too, people from America, Japan, Britain, France, Germany, other European countries, Singapore, Hong Kong, Australia, and even two from Africa, one of whom spoke French with a big toothy smile as he helped the lad carry in a box of computer stuff. When someone asked what was going on the brass plate he was told it was 'Global Futures (Offshore)'.

Haidermann arrived just after six that morning at the new Dublin office where the Oslo effort would be co-ordinated. He smiled grimly at the new brass plate on the door, took the stairs up past the security man three at a time and edged his way through the hubbub of people at the main communications consoles. Electricians were still installing wiring at one point and he stopped.

'What's not ready?' he asked, concerned.

'Coffee machine,' a bearded young man answered. 'Everything else is tested and ready to go.'

Haidermann nodded and walked through to the large room at the back where his team of managers waited. They were men selected from the huge organization who had displayed consistent skills over the years, skills at achieving the impossible with other people and tools. He looked around the room.

Powerful men, respected in their fields, each and every one an Oslo member. There was Yushi Uhara, sent as a donation by the chairman of Shamatsu Industries of Tokyo. Shamatsu had said he was too old to come himself, but he would provide Haidermann with three men who could do anything they needed and Uhara had brought with him a team of two of his operations specialists. There were four Americans, each with his backup team down on the next floor. Haidermann knew the pyramid effect from these men, all actual employees of Oslo who could effectively muzzle and redirect the bulk of America's national media. There were five Europeans, three West Germans, a Frenchman and a Dutchman, not one of whom, when given resources and a task, had failed to meet the objectives.

Only the Dutchman was new, recruited the week before, and he had the dubious distinction of being the only man in the room who had been in prison. While a student at university he had successfully accessed the Shell Oil Company's computers and redirected a substantial sum of money into the bank account of a children's charity. He was now the guru of the Holland Peace Movement, a self-made millionaire and hugely influential outside his own borders particularly in Belgium and Denmark. He was a maverick, delighted with the chance to help Oslo – if nothing came of it, he had said, then they had tried.

The Singaporean banker was alone from his part of the world, but held enough of the media stock in the region's newspapers to be able to establish editorial content in any process where Oslo didn't have people.

Lastly was the Australian, another Oslo employee, who controlled vast resources in both Britain and the Antipodes. A colourful figure in his own right, his personal purchases of paintings at auction in his homeland made the news every time, as did his beautiful wife's parties.

Haidermann looked around the room. Here was gathered the media might of Oslo. Between them they controlled sixty per cent of the daily national newspapers in the world, forty-six per cent of the commercial broadcasting and all the commercial satellites. Thirty years of investment and planning around the room, and a full twenty per cent of Oslo's actual resources represented.

'Thank you for coming . . . all of you. I have just come from a meeting with Presidents Chekhov and Sheridan. They have seen fit to turn down our demands. We will now commence with Phase One of the O'Casey Alternative. The Omega Project, of which some of you were aware, will work in indirect support of Gulag and then, if needed, be moved westward to support Oslo. I envisage a symbolic role only, supporting your work.'

'And Phase Two?' one of the Americans asked.

'What's the matter? The IRS inspecting you?' another asked and people round the room laughed. The sound was tight and tense and already the room was charged with adrenalin.

'Phase Two may never be necessary. It depends on how effective we are with Phase One, but we have planted the seed in their minds. Sheridan is in no doubt that we will do it if we have to,' Haidermann replied. 'You have all met Darby.' He indicated an elegantly dressed Frenchman sitting in one corner. 'He was, until recently, heading up the biggest public relations company in Europe. He has planned the campaign we are about to action. Those of you who have read the entire brief will see how fast it moves and the positioning we will attempt. The scale of the campaign and the content will roll from one country to the next with differing approaches in differing areas. It is something he is very good at. His organization was responsible for the re-election three times of the Conservatives in the UK . . .' muffled cheering from the Europeans and Darby smiled '. . . and the relaunch of Mitterrand in Paris . . .' more cheering and one raspberry '. . . and last, but not least, the acceptance of the NATO principles in

Spain.' The Frenchman rose and bowed formally to the group.

'I am honoured to be 'ere with such a collection of talent,' he began sincerely. 'Each of you 'as a programme for your teams, each differs slightly, but basically they all start with the Omega exposé, roll into a description of its builders and its reason for being. That done as the introduction, the world is hungry for more . . . then we give them the demands and support them with lots of gritty material, documentaries, pre-prepared articles and a list of experts available for panel shows, discussions, phone-ins and the like. That will be the beginning. The campaign will then roll on from there, feeding itself on its own momentum. Active pressure groups will begin their routines then, with prepared material, march routes, etc. Even so, this is the most ambitious scheme I have ever been involved with and it is absolutely reliant on the ripple effect. We can expect active support from many groups once the ripples arrive, and they in turn will add their own momentum. For example, we know that Greenpeace will support us in an instant. Even the Catholic Church.' He looked at Haidermann.

'One of our people is there tonight, Cardinal Juan de Cueva from São Paulo,' Haidermann replied. Darby nodded and gave a very Gallic shrug. To the room in general he asked, '*Ça va?*'

Cardinal Juan de Cueva had been a member of Oslo for fifteen years and always knew that one day his role would be decisive. But he had never realized just how important it would be as he walked down the long, ancient passages of the Vatican towards his meeting. The other party had traditionally been a thorn in the side of many a leader in the last two thousand years. The aura of the position had long ruled the men entrusted with it, but in this individual, de Cueva felt, the Church had at long last found a man as uncompromising as he was decent. The product of a Polish peasant background, he was a shining example of the power exerted by Christian faith.

He was strong, astute and glamorous all at once and revered by five hundred million people across the globe; he was probably the single most influential man on the planet.

He was Pope John Paul II.

De Cueva often likened the process of gaining an audience with His Holiness to running a marathon when they kept moving the finishing post. Even he as a cardinal had to go through the process, but admitted that knowing where he could take a short cut made it bearable. His audience of three days before had been cancelled at the last minute to allow the pontiff to have time to offer prayers for the victims of a landslide in Chile. Now with the Oslo campaign in full swing he was determined to have the chance to plead his case before another incident interrupted the routine running of the Church and his audience.

De Cueva was not a man who found it difficult to reconcile his Oslo activities with his calling. To him they were one and the same; he considered halting the arms race and ridding God's world of nuclear weapons as important as he did guiding the Church of his native Brazil, conducting communion or hearing confession.

At fifty-six he was a young man for the role, and representing the Catholics of that large country he wielded considerable power in the Vatican, but even with that, and his resolute convictions on the Oslo issue, as he walked the age-old flagstones of the inner courtyard he felt the butterfly nerves in his stomach.

15

Commuters at London's underground stations queued up in milling lines to buy newspapers. Every paper that morning, with the exception of a blue-collar tabloid, carried the Tarbaby's photo across the centre of the front pages. The wire services who had supplied the items had provided a selection of pictures, but most opted for a three-quarter view, impressive with her huge engine intakes like double garage doorways. The headlines screamed various messages: MYSTERY RESCUER REVEALED and STAR WARS IS HERE was carried by the *Independent* and the *Telegraph*, with the *Daily Mail* more jingoistic, their headline reading, NUKES LOOK OUT, OMEGA'S ABOUT.

Beneath the sensationalistic follow-up to the intercept story in the main body of the copy came the first references to Oslo, some of the publications boxing it as a sub-story in support of the main leader. One small paper in Chichester led the world with new pictures taken by a child passenger on the rescued 747. His photographs, although blurred, carried a new angle of authenticity, and a second picture of him standing proudly with his teacher and the little yellow camera carried the heading, LOCAL BOY SNAPS PLANE RESCUE DRAMA.

Morning conversation in offices and homes around the land was dominated by the stories. In Paris and Bonn as well as other European cities similar interest was generated. In Brussels a weekly colour magazine held its presses and slapped a full colour picture of the Tarbaby on the cover. By eight AM correspondent teams from *Time* and *Newsweek* had been put on to the story and artists were

332

already drawing up the sequence of events graphically. *National Geographic* editorial teams decided to go for the hypersonic in their next issue, and archives were ravaged for material on modern aerospace technology for the evening news on television. Conveniently, there were experts available, but thankfully for Oslo, no one had yet put two and two together.

The Ministry of Defence in London hit the panic button with accusations being stabbed up and down the corridors over who should have been aware of this development and wasn't. Already the follow-ups for the evening editions and the early dailies in other countries were coming off the wire. Suggested headlines read: PEACE GROUP BEHIND OMEGA and ICBM INTERCEPTOR.

The American press, while not getting the first grab at the story like the European papers, prepared to do it justice for the next morning's editions with in-depth material that just seemed to arrive on time. One paper, deciding a communist plot was afoot, said they would not run the story; a call from their owners put paid to that, much to the relief of the journalistic staff who saw the best story of the year unfolding off the teleprinters. In cities all over America and Europe, pressure groups were contacted a second time and told to prepare. It had begun.

In London the Campaign for Nuclear Disarmament was absorbed gleefully into Oslo's ranks in one six-minute meeting at Hyde Park Corner. Oslo, for all their expertise, had no experience in organizing protest marches and rallies.

'Leave that to us,' the cleric said.

At the Dublin office the telephone teams were working at a frenzied pace, each calling a list of members who in turn had other lists to call. The ripple effect was electric and by mid-morning most of Oslo's active members worldwide had been contacted. Some were given specific tasks, others told to wait, still others asked to assist where possible, any way possible as the campaign unfolded. The lady in Nova Scotia who had offered to cut sandwiches began going through her attic for warm clothes to give peace marchers, talking to her cats and singing merrily. A rock singer touring America sat back and thought about his gig the next evening and a beatific smile creased his lips. A radio DJ in a small Australian commercial station jotted some notes, and a power station supervisor in Scotland checked some calculations. Two engineers loading programming for a satellite transmission changed tapes and smiled at each other, and a stunt pilot with a Pit Special equipped with skywriting canisters doodled a design on a pad.

In Iceland, Paul Hart was thrown the morning paper by Oxenburger. It wasn't in English but the photograph was unmistakable.

'Holy fuck,' he said.

'Does this alter anything?' Oxenburger asked.

'No,' Hart replied, still trying to puzzle out the report, 'we go in as planned.'

He looked at his watch. 'The car should be downstairs, let's go.' Chubb swept up his shoulder holster and slipped it on, adjusting the straps under his arms and then reaching for a windbreaker. He looked at Hart.

'Do you want a piece?' he asked.

'No,' said Hart, 'I don't like guns, you know that . . . keep an eye on Oxenburger. I don't want him shooting at anything, either.'

'Yo,' the black man replied.

'It doesn't say where this thing is based,' Hart said still reading, 'so let's go find out,' he finished smiling.

Carson let the hot needles of water sluice over him. He had done a fast workout with Digby and Yamashita in the gym, running on the machine, press-ups and sit-ups, followed by a light breakfast in the mess. Now he stood in the shower washing the bright sheen of sweat from his skin. Gail had laid out his flight suits on the bed, and when she had left he had changed the way they were arranged, his ritual preparation as important to him as Yamashita's boken was to him. He turned the taps off and stepped from the cubicle, dripping water on to the floor as he reached for a towel. Russia, he thought. The big black bear herself. The briefing the night before had been expert and informative. According to Gulag the computer at Novosibirsk was as good as down and that meant most of their air would be blind. The Tarbaby's pre-selected target pattern called for an approach at 90,000 feet and then hold there while the machine did the hunting; the complicated gyro-compasses crossed with the satellite vectors would place them to within a metre overhead the target for the lasers to burn.

He would only need to override the system if they were rumbled, and then they would fight manually if necessary. He didn't like that at all. Easy on the fuel would give him anything between fifteen and eighteen hours, but if he had to scramble up to her ceiling then that calculation would be a joke. He would need to rest, too, the Benzedrine would only hold off fatigue for so long and pulling Gs was exhausting. He hoped that the autopilot system was as good as Tavis said it was. He would sleep with Digby watching the systems.

He walked out into his room and looked at his gear, the bright shiny thermo pressure suit stark on the rumpled bed, his chamois gloves and the silver pressure gloves side by side. He shouldn't need those today, not intercepting anything over Mach 3 with luck. He began to dress, wondering how many MiGs they had available to throw at him. Although he had no obvious radar signature they would eventually tumble to the hole on their screens and that, backed up with infrared scanners, could mean a running dogfight from one end of the old Soviet Union to the other. He pulled on the specially softened lambswool underwear and eased the old comfortable green RAF issue overalls on over it. He looked down at the faded wings over his left breast and let the memories flash back for a second – Tim Miller, strong in the images of grey German skies.

He folded the thermosuit down over the boots and stepped into it, leaving the airtight zip open to the waist, bent and picked up the heavy helmet. Something white and colourful flashed back at him from the inside and he put his hand in and pulled it clear. He smiled widely and folded it into his pocket, it was a *hachimati* from Rikio Yamashita. Warriors wore it as a headband and the two symbols painted either side of the red sun read *Hittsu Shou*, roughly translating as 'never-give-in' or 'to-the-finish'. He thought again and taking it from his pocket wrapped it round his neck like a cravat. Twenty minutes to take-off. Gail was standing in the doorway when he turned the handle. There was not much more to say that hadn't been said already and now it just felt awkward to discuss it, so they walked together in silence up to the control room.

They had lain awake before the dawn, both knowing that it might be their last night together, the talking finished and the feelings strong as the clock had ticked its way into the O'Casey Alternative. He had said that when it was over he would introduce her to an old dog and take her to Cades Reef, and she knew that from a man like him it was as near as she would get to a planned future. She had cried quietly into the pillow when he finally stood and slipped into his training gear. Then she had dried her tears angrily and gone back to her own room to change before she was expected up in the control room. Activity up there had been constant and feverish, as the new links had laid the great mass of Russia across her screens. All the previous day they had plotted the deployment of the front line interceptor squadrons along the display with intelligence inserting whatever data was available. Natalia and Christine estimated upwards of sixteen squadrons available to be arrayed against Peter and Digby, but doubted they would all be committed at once. They were more likely to stern chase and harry the Tarbaby into specific quadrants where others would wait, new MiG-29s tuned with exotic fuels and anti-satellite missiles. If she had to fight, then ground targets that were unessential to the success of the initiative would be missed out, and if she didn't fight she would die, chased above the earth's atmosphere to burn her critical fuel reserves running for home, where it was possible, they had agreed, she could be prevented from landing by either the Americans or Russians.

Moscow

Perhaps the most efficient system for the dissemination of illicit information exists in Moscow.

A hangover from the pre-reform days, handouts printed on backstreet presses, illegal photocopies and the like are passed from hand to hand on the metro, at street corners, left on café tables and pasted on to walls. The rumour machine is second to none in its scope, and Gulag used the system devastatingly that morning.

Workers coming off night shift crossed tracks with those arriving for the day and the circulars changed hands. Many were talking about the pirate transmission that morning on the radio and even more about the television signal that had laid itself over their screens like a blanket, crushing the morning news and fitness programme with a darkened, unfamiliar face speaking in measured, scholarly tones.

'Good morning, my friends. This is the voice of a friend, the voice of the people. Today Russians will join the people of the world in protesting against the presence of nuclear weapons in our world. We of the Gulag,' he smiled grimly for a moment, 'are good Russians, your friends and neighbours. We just have one desire. To see the missiles and nuclear bombs disposed of. We cannot afford a war where these will ever be used and neither can the Americans. We need them no longer . . . they wait above us like death, it is time to see them go. At this moment in America and

Britain, in France and the rest of Europe, people are saying enough! Now we join them. Today listen for word in your workplaces. Today we of the Gulag will begin to destroy the missiles and the factories that make them. Listen for the fire alarms in your workplace. When you hear them you have only a few minutes to get clear. Russians, Uzbeks, Ukrainians, Chechens, Tartars, Kirkiz, Turkmen, Armenians, Slavs, Balts, for once in your life you now have something in common with others under this mighty flag of ours. Christians, Muslims, Jews, atheists, for once in your lives stand up for something other than your loaf of bread and your religions. Let us be rid of the missiles. Do you know how many billions of roubles they cost each year? To do what? Let us have the government spend that on us, the people, on jobs, invest it in our economy. Let us feed ourselves each and every winter. It's your Duma, let them know how you feel. Wait for the signals in your area. Discuss it in your places of work. The time has come, it is here, it is today . . . I shall talk to you again. Until we have a nuclear-free world . . . good-bye, and remember Chernobyl.'

The FSB, stunned into action, tried tracking the broadcast until they realized it was coming in from somewhere in India via satellite and broadcast over their own government-owned transmitters. Angry and impotent, they made sweeping arrests at the broadcasting stations and questioning began. Everywhere on the streets the word was the same, 'for Russia and for the world'.

The GRU, the Red Army intelligence machine, was caught completely off balance and reacted with typical measures. Spetznatz units, the Soviet special forces, were deployed in strength at all installations and factories producing component parts for their nuclear capability. Their own sources were tapped for information, informants pulled in and pressured to come up with something. GRU hostility to the FSB rode supreme on their paranoia and reached a climax that day when they received a warning to clear their infamous Aquarium headquarters before nine that morning as it was going to be destroyed. The FSB, the security service, themselves pulled out all the stops in their attempt to locate the groups responsible and as the target lists came in they noticed that the broadcast warning was holding true. The first target listed was Pavlobad, the SS missile solid fuel motor factory in the Ukraine, south-west of Moscow, with others following seemingly at random across central Russia. There were other targets listed, the GRU headquarters, Red Army communications facilities, railheads, the computer centre in St Petersburg responsible for the army payroll. Northern fleet communications, responsible for the Red Banner Fleet, was conspicuous by its absence. At the time the warnings were pouring back into FSB headquarters in Dzerzhinsky Street, meetings were taking place all over Russia. Fast, furtive meetings in cars, offices and buses. The Gulagists were calling in the favours they were owed. Many community leaders were immediately drawn in, long having been avoided due to their high profile, and asked to use their influence among their own people to support the Gulag attempt. Across the length and breadth of Russia people talked, worried, did what they could and waited, waited for the Tarbaby. They would not be waiting much longer, they hoped.

Facsimile machines between Russian embassies abroad and Moscow ran hot with copies of the morning's papers. It seemed it wasn't only a Russian problem but right throughout the developed world; out of nowhere people were coming forward saying, 'enough'. All that differed was the method. In the West the free press provided an organ for the commencement of the campaign. In Russia, without the sophisticated media of the West, they had to use another channel, the underground.

'It's orchestrated,' FSB General Bushirov said. 'They have planned this on an international front and caught us all.'

His Directorate, the First, was responsible for domestic security and he quickly contacted the heads of the other three Directorates for whatever they had.

The klaxon started to blare three seconds before the blast doors triggered by electric switches began to roll shut at specific points around the Omega Base.

'What the hell is that?' Carson barked.

'Intruder alarm,' Gail answered. 'Let's go.'

Carson pushed past her and ran for the hangar. Jesus, don't let them have got into my way, keep 'em back, Pauli, I'll be up in three minutes. As he ran down the long corridor, from a door at the end a voice called a farewell, and from the corner of his eye he saw Yamashita, running towards the alarm, dressed not in his training gear but in something baggy and black and with what looked like his boken under his arm.

Carson took the stairs three at a time, protecting the helmet from bumps where possible. Digby was waiting nervously and panting for breath when he burst into the hangar.

'Where's Tavis?' he shouted. 'Let's go . . . MOVE, MOVE.'

The door leading to the workshops burst open and the technical teams, pulling overalls on over naked shoulders, ran on to the pan beneath the Tarbaby, as Carson and Digby ran awkwardly in the pressure suits towards the steep cockpit access steps.

The Oslo security man had seen the helicopter coming low and fast from the south, and had watched frustratedly as it had dropped out of sight behind a spur from the main ridge. He had got up from his position and begun to run towards the top to try and see over. He knew the sound of a helicopter hovering when he heard it. He arrived breathless as it lifted off again, and caught the movement of six men in uniform moving off to the east. He didn't see the other four hidden in the rocks close by as he reported the occurrence to Van Waveren by radio.

'Are you sure they are moving away?' the Dutchman had asked.

'Affirmative,' he replied.

'Okay, return to your post . . . good work.'

The young man grimaced to himself and walked back down the ridge towards his shelter.

Hart and his group moved immediately to the camouflaged ventilator shaft they had almost jumped on to and were forcing the grille when the alarm began.

Van Waveren put the base on alert and the young guard, realizing he had been duped, grabbed his weapon and ran back out towards the shaft head, the klaxon loud over the radio on his hip.

'They are coming,' Van Waveren said. 'The men Simon saw moving east were a diversion.'

'And now?' Sagan said, 'We must give Peter time to get up!'

'They won't get that far,' Van Waveren replied. 'We will stop them at the shaft head.'

Neither man saw Yamashita as he moved past the door, and neither saw the weapon in his hand. It was not the familiar boken they had all seen him with. It was a *katana*, a samurai sword, manufactured by the finest craftsmen in Japan some time in the summer of 1562, and loved and honoured and honed razor sharp by ten generations of warriors since.

Van Waveren scooped an Uzi from the rack on the wall and ran down the corridor thirty seconds behind Yamashita.

'Shit!' Hart snarled, 'that's fucking torn it.'

He looked quickly around, thinking fast.

'What now?' Chubb asked, pulling his gun clear from its holster. Oxenburger had his out already, Hart noticed.

'Let's get into the place – we're committed anyway,' he answered, pulling a small tyre iron from his pack. Jamming the chisel edge under the riveted rim of the ventilator screen he threw his weight on it, Chubb joining his effort.

It was then that the young guard skidded to a halt and quietly went to ground twenty yards away, fumbling for his radio and bringing his gun up at the same time. Oxenburger saw something move in the rough tussocky hummocks, and swung the big heavy Magnum to point at the spot. Without calling a warning to either the figure he had seen or to Hart and the others, he snapped a shot off. The big calibre gun bucked upward and the sound slammed round the hills.

'Got 'im,' he shouted, his face suffused red with excitement, 'I got him.'

Hart, who had rolled into cover, jumped to his feet as Oxenburger rose from his crouch and Cleatus, the Iceland station agent, still fumbling for his weapon, swore softly to himself.

'GOT WHO?' Hart shouted. 'Shit, who did you shoot at, you fucking dumb redneck?'

'I got him, so fuck you. He's over there.' Oxenburger gestured with his weapon at the place he had fired into.

Hart spun around, his eyes searching, the klaxon sound coming up the shaft, but now there was another sound, a soft moaning like a man in pain and rustling in the grass.

He was about to send Chubb to investigate Oxenburger's folly when he heard the screen on the shaft rattle and turned, all his instincts aroused, in time to see a shadowy figure emerge like a fleeting ghost. He knew instantly what it was and as Oxenburger turned his gun at the threat he bellowed 'NO', but the man never heard it, or chose to ignore the shout, and completed the turn, again firing his weapon.

Yamashita had cleared the vent only two seconds after hearing the gunshot, and rolling on to the ground the *katana* safely above grass level he rose in one fluid extraordinarily fast *kata*, the silver blade a blur.

He saw the threat from the big man, feinted to the left, dived forward rolling to his feet, the sword in his double-handed grip, sweeping round from the right in an upward slash that opened Avery Oxenburger's torso from waist to shoulder, severing muscle, bone, organs and tissue alike. He followed through the stroke and the return strike, this time from the left. It severed the American's head from his shoulders and it rolled and spun, a Catherine wheel of blood hitting the dry grass at Hart's feet.

Chubb's stunned disbelief was suddenly a burst of action and he turned on the small figure in the black baggy pants, white top and headband, comical if not for the bloody blade.

'NO!' Hart bellowed again. Chubb fired twice quickly, his Browning automatic kicking in his fist, and although sure that he had hit his target he didn't stop coming. He fired his third round from only inches away, aware at the end that it was too little too late, thinking, my God, these people are prepared to die for what they have here and dying himself as Yamashita's *katana* hissed from above, chopping through his skull.

'NO . . . NO MORE!' Hart screamed. Cleatus and the swordsman faced each other at three yards distance. 'Put down your weapon, Cleatus . . . he won't harm you if you lower your gun.'

'Jesus Christ, did you see what he did! A fucking sword! I'm not putting my gun down, sir, no way, sir!'

'Put it down, son,' Hart said quickly. 'He is honourable. It is their way. He won't strike down a unarmed man.' He looked at Yamashita. 'Don't shoot. There has been enough of that.' Yamashita stood stock-still, his *katana* straight out before him in the classical opening stance. He was bleeding heavily from two gunshot wounds in his abdomen and already his face had taken on the paleness of death, but he stood ready for combat and Hart knew he could still get to and kill Cleatus, irrespective of how many bullets were in him.

'Enough, *sensai* . . . enough killing here. Put down your sword.'

Downwind he could hear jet engines spooling up and he knew they had lost, and above that sound was the rattle of the ventilator screen again and a tired Dutch-accented voice said, 'He won't put down his sword until your guns are down and your hands are over your heads . . . I have an Uzi pointed at your backs, and if you look on the ridge above you you will see others. Enough of the attempt . . . eh, Mr Hart?'

Cleatus bent slowly and placed his cocked gun carefully on the ground, stood and stepped back from it raising his hands high. Hart watched Yamashita for a second before following suit, hating the blood and the death, but his own martial skills allowing him silently to recognize a real master of the art.

'That's better,' Van Waveren said, before bending to speak into a small handheld radio. 'Now slowly fall face forward, arms outstretched, palms upward, legs bent, feet raised one inch above the ground . . . now!'

Only then did Rikio Yamashita lower the *katana*, slowly settling to his knees as his strength finally gave way to the terrible wounds, his face raised to the sky long enough to watch the Tarbaby scorch her way upward. Van Waveren later said he thought he had smiled.

The control room had been frantic. Natalia and Andrea had arrived half-dressed on the heels of a dozen technicians, the klaxon alert bringing forward the take-off time by forty minutes. Gail had watched the system lights glow on the Tarbaby's duplicate control panels as Carson began his ignition sequence.

'Come on, move, all of you!' she had ordered. 'Tarbaby is rolling!' She flicked her eyes back to the computerized overlay screen that would give her weather, traffic and geological images on the same display, as the other two girls dropped in behind her at their stations. The tension was rich in the air like the ozone from the instruments.

'Log time. Mission has commenced,' Gail said.

She watched her prime screen closely, reading off the height and direction telemetry data to herself for a full five minutes before speaking aloud to Sagan.

'Speed Mach Four and accelerating, seventy-eight thousand feet and climbing, coming on to track for Pavlobad.'

She raised the Polaroid glasses and looked across at Natalia and Andrea King, both deeply immersed in their hazy green images and computerized overlays of what was to become their battle zone. This is it then, she thought, what we have worked for and trained for. This is what we are here for. This is what we do. Pavlobad, where the Red Army have their solid rocket fuel factory for the SS-20s.

'Let me know the moment we have anything,' she said to Natalia, 'anything at all.'

The Russian girl nodded, her eyes not leaving her radar screens for a second. Sixteen squadrons, Gail thought, my God, sixteen squadrons.

Hart and Cleatus were taken down into the accommodation area and locked in a store room, the big bolt pushed across from the outside.

'Well, we know it's here,' Cleatus said. 'Now what?'

Hart looked at him. Two of his people dead. One of theirs dying. All because of guns. He disliked guns for that very reason. They upped the ante every time. It was fruitless. A complete waste. And now they were captives.

'I don't know,' he replied honestly.

'What do you think they will do to us?'

They both remembered the last time a CIA operative had been caught and imprisoned. Beirut. They tortured him to death and then kindly send a cassette of his screams back to his employers.

Hart shrugged and tried the door. It didn't budge an inch.

Carson let the nose begin to drop at 110,000 feet and eased the throttle settings back on the touch panel. He looked across at his systems operator.

'Well. We're up and safe,' he said. 'Now let's just hope we have a base to return to.'

'They knew about it very early this morning. There were only four or five of them. Pauli's people were confident they could contain the problem,' Digby replied, his voice tightly normal. Carson recognized the tension the moment he began to speak.

'Relax, Digby, we are going over very high and very fast. With a bit of luck the only place you will see something is on your screens.'

'You think so?' Digby asked hopefully.

'Yes,' Carson lied, thinking, like hell you will. We are going to have them buzzing around like angry bees down there. Just watch the rearward defence screen because all we need is some clever little bastard with exotic fuel, an interceptor and an anti-satellite missile and we will have do some fast footwork. They will have Sukoi 15s, MiGs, the twenty-nine, the twenty-five, everything except a slingshot. 'Okay then,' he continued, 'let's do it. Point Alpha in ten minutes.'

'We're early,' Digby said. 'Will they be ready?'

'We haven't the fuel to waste stooging about. They better be,' Carson replied.

He ran the Kevlar seat forward under the instrument panel and lowered the angle a few degrees. Finally he checked the heating panel and, once comfortable, checked the instruments for the umpteenth time since lifting off. They were now cruising at 110,000 feet, just below where the Tarbaby would need to start using the precious supplementary oxygen. This was her optimum altitude, 60,000 feet above normal traffic, her exotic mixture of propellants, stabilizers and fuel thrusting her easily where no other aircraft had ever gone in horizontal flight.

In the cockpit the glass screens had bathed Carson and Allison in soft green and orange light, but now as the nose dropped the rising sun stabbed light in through the crystal windscreen, warming them as the flight management systems made millimetric changes to course and nose attitude.

Carson felt slightly impotent with the mission as it was planned. The complex computers were now flying the aircraft, they would place it exactly overhead the target, they would initiate the laser sequence, they would move it on to the next target, and again fire the lasers. He knew that in that role they were essential, no man could make the necessary calculations fast enough to be effective, but even so he had every New Zealander's inherent distrust of machinery. Everything broke down sooner or later and if it couldn't be fixed with a bit of ingenuity and a length of No 8 fencing wire then you were likely to be in the shit, as he had once explained to Digby.

'Let's hope this hardware does its job,' he said across the cockpit, 'or there are a lot of people down there who are in big trouble.'

Digby who was watching the system management screen smiled dryly.

'The gear will be okay ... what happens if we get attacked? Do we break and run or what?'

'Yeah, just long enough to lose them then come back and go back on to the sequence.'

'We are now in Russian airspace and it's too late for me to back out or crack up ... so level with me here,' he said sincerely.

It was Carson's turn to smile dryly.

'Estimates as you know are ten to twenty squadrons, that's twelve or thirteen to each. Realistically they will have non-operationals. Natalia thought sixteen squadrons might be accurate. Sixteen times twelve. It seems like a lot of aircraft. What we will have is a few minutes, maybe up to forty or so where they are looking for us. Then someone will tumble the radar hole and check infrared, then they have a trace. But all that is academic if they can't get up here. They will be swarming around between thirty and fifty thousand feet, they may try missiles but we can outrun those. Our problems will begin if we have to go below this height. If the gear packs up and we have to go in visual. Then they will be all over us like a pack of dogs.'

Digby nodded almost to himself.

'I'm still scared,' he said softly.

'So am I,' Carson replied. 'Scared is good.'

A series of lights on the control panel lit up, two new images flicked on to screens, and Carson felt the decrease in the engine thrust as the Cray computers settled the attack format.

'Here we go,' he said.

Pavlobad

Svetlana Mirov was a senior chemist at the factory once officially designated No 289. Now it was just called Pavlobad works. It was in fact the Red Army's solid rocket fuel facility and produced to a rigid schedule ninety per cent of the requirements for the SS-20 series missiles, and fuel for other smaller launch vehicles as required.

Mirov had been recruited by Gulag two years before and was now finally to play her part.

She looked at the clock on the wall. Two minutes to go, then she would activate the fire alarms on the wall in the passage outside.

The plant could be evacuated in under a minute, and the drill was practised frequently, as might be expected. Then they would have twenty minutes or so till the place went up. The drill required that all staff moved quickly into the car park where every available vehicle was used to get clear. The safety area was two kilometres and from there the fire investigators moved slowly back. The only problem was the group of soldiers that had arrived the night before, rough-looking men in camouflage uniforms. One of the security guards said they were Spetznatz, special forces, and the camouflage was Afghanistan issue. Now she would have to make a real fire to get the plant evacuated.

She lifted the beaker off the bench, looked around to see if she was being observed and tipped the hydrochloric acid into the large wastebin. Earlier she had sprinkled a good quantity of a water purifying mixture into the bin. The two compounds reacting would make a very satisfactory fire, and as she watched the bin began to issue great gouts of acrid smoke. Very good, she thought.

She called out a warning, picked up an extinguisher, to prevent anyone else using it, and watched her four colleagues following the drills: one ran to the phone, one to the alarms on the wall. The last two ran into the hall as Mirov pressed the extinguisher into action against the bench away from the now bright hot flames. At last, the cylinder empty, she too ran from the room and joined the people running for the car park, the alarm bells loud behind her.

At four other facilities in the area similar scenes were taking place. While the Spetznatz troops did not try to stop anyone leaving, they themselves remained, some laughing scornfully at those escaping, others more convinced that something was actually going to happen, cocking weapons and taking cover, not sure what the threat would be but following orders not to leave the plants deserted and to watch for saboteurs.

Precisely thirty-six minutes before schedule, and only a minute after Mirov had climbed out of the panel truck she had driven to the safe zone, the Omega Project arrived in Russia.

People later said it seemed like three blasts in succession moving across the plant from north to south. Others said they remembered nothing, just the flash a millisecond before the plant exploded in a massive rumbling orange blast that shook the ground many miles away. The air rushed past the waiting people, blowing dust and leaves and papers in towards the massive fireball, sucked in by the vacuum. Thick black smoke billowed and swirled into the sky, towering over the fields and roads around the plant site. It would be a full day before anyone could get near enough to actually establish what had been spared.

'They were right,' people said, 'those on the television.' Svetlana Mirov knew she wouldn't have to report the success of this to anyone. The whole of Russia would hear of it.

Miles above them Carson felt the engines momentarily falter as the laser generator took power, and watched the lights on the panels glow bright and fade.

'Was that it?' he asked.

'That was it,' Digby replied. 'One down, thirty-six to go.'

As if on cue, the laser fired again and seventeen seconds later a third target was eliminated.

A communications technician waved at Gail from his console below hers. She patched him into her headphones.

'Lots of traffic in the Ukraine . . . I think we've been sussed.'

'What exactly?'

'Red Army comms to interceptor bases round Minsk, Moscow. They are confused, they know they have a hostile, but they can't see it.'

'Thanks,' Gail replied. 'Natalia, anything yet?'

'No, nothing at all . . . wait . . . yes, confirm we have a flight airborne from Vinnista. They will be MiG-29s, probably six in the flight, with another six on the ground to take over . . . update, we have a flight lifting off from Saratov. They will be Sukoi-15s.'

Gail flicked a rocker switch and took Natalia's data on to her screens. Saratov is ahead of track. They have our track.

'Tarbaby, Tarbaby, this is Omega.'

'Bright Eyes, this is Tarbaby.' His voice metallic and crisp.

'Tarbaby, you have bogeys ahead and behind,' she said.

Carson wasn't overly concerned about what was behind him.

350

'What have we got in front, over?'

'Tarbaby, believe one flight possibly six Sukoi-15s . . .' as she was speaking a second large blip appeared on the screen, '. . . sorry, make that two flights, one squadron, over.'

'Let me know if they get above level five zero, Bright Eyes.'

'Roger.'

Twenty seconds later she was back telling him that interceptors had lifted of from Volgograd and Penza. They were stacking up and waiting for him. Carson, aware that his infrared signature was being traced, cranked out his radar to full range. They knew he was here now and there was little to be gained by flying blind. The picture was not good; in his 600-mile sweep he could now count six squadrons.

He resisted the urge to take command from the computers. The sequence was now into its third strike run with six to go. Strike five was the critical one: the underground silos that threaded their way across Russia's beltline all the way to Novosibirsk where their air tactical command mainframe sat awaiting its application.

He checked the height again, running his gloved finger over the instruments as again the laser fired and the engines missed a beat.

Moscow

'Come on, let's go,' Chekhov shouted to his driver through the window. The driver was startled. He had never seen the President run before, let alone to his car. He started the engine and pulled away the moment the second bodyguard was in the follow car.

'Begin,' Chekhov said to his aide, as the big limousine powered its way on to the main road towards the Kremlin.

'They have hit nineteen targets so far. Probably more by now. We aren't sure how, but it's certainly tied in with a very high-flying aircraft. Red Air Force has the sky covered, but they can't actually see anything yet. It's following the warning to the letter.'

'Any fatalities?' Chekhov asked quickly.

'A handful of Spetznatz troops. The staff all heeded the warnings and got the hell out of the way.'

'Recall the troops. Let's not waste them if they can't actually do anything'

'Yes, sir.'

'What is the reaction on the streets?'

'Local FSB report disbelief initially, with other more reactionary displays almost immediately.'

'What kind of displays?' Chekhov asked quickly.

'Some cheering, some shouting, but what disturbed them was the silence in most places.'

'Silence?'

'Yes. They said it was unsettling.'

The calm before the storm, Chekhov thought. I'll bet it was unsettling, like watching the first trickle of water through a dyke.

'There have been reports of gatherings of people in Pushkin Square,' the aide continued.

'Not Democratic Union?' Chekhov asked.

'None of the usual faces, it would seem. Also gatherings in Minsk and St Petersburg, other centres.'

'All of this in under an hour?' Chekhov remarked almost to himself. 'I want to see the army and FSB separately. Then the full Council meetings. I don't want anyone over-reacting to this thing.'

'There's more, Mr President,' the aide said.

'What?'

'The Christians and the Muslims in Azerbaijan have issued a joint statement supporting this Gulag group . . . who are they? You haven't been surprised at one thing I have said so far.'

'They are an anti-nuclear-weapons group. Apolitical, but powerful as you have seen. That's why I don't want anyone doing anything silly. This is an internal problem, with limited assistance from outside, a similar group in the West, but essentially an internal problem. I don't want tanks and troops in the streets. This would be foolish. Pass the word – I know you talk to other aides and secretaries. Let it be known that if anyone overplays this I will take a dim view of it.'

The aide nodded. Twice before Mikhail Chekhov had warned he would take a 'dim view' of a particular scenario, and twice before reshuffles had changed the order of power on the Council of Ministers itself.

From the corner of his eye the aide watched as Chekhov bit into a soft cake, his dietary discipline as rigid as ever even in the speeding car. The general conference of the Party was coming up in less than a week. The aide was confident that Chekhov could dominate the events without a problem, but now on top of the separatist troubles and the Democratic Union, the coming winter and certain food shortages, this Gulag could have the pack turning on its master.

Minsk

Stravinsky, the Gulag chief, otherwise known as Colonel Rordino, listened to the radio traffic as he read the morning's telexes.

It was as effective a means of monitoring the Gulag efforts as any. As head of FSB in the Minsk area there was little that didn't come over the wires regarding the mysterious blasts at the nuclear manufacturing facilities, or the groups of people massing in the country's parks and squares. Brave people standing up and facing the machine that had dominated their lives for so long.

He looked up as a figure came through the door. It was a tall, slim young woman, long hair caught back in a ribbon and full rosy cheeks over a square jaw.

'Tell your people they can begin,' Stravinsky said. 'They have begun in Moscow and St Petersburg. Don't keep an audience waiting.' His cold voice softened briefly and his smile was warm. 'Remember, tell it how it is, don't lie to anyone.'

She smiled back, nodding.

'The Oslo people, are they here?' she asked

'Up there.' His thumb pointed upward towards the damp ceiling. 'Yes, they are here. They have hit over a third of their targets already and they are early, and the hornets are rising to greet them. Let us not depend on them entirely. They are about to enter the Novosibirsk control area. It is the most heavily defended zone in Russia, maybe even the world. They may not come out of it alive.'

The girl nodded again.

'Go now,' he finished. 'My time safely here is limited.'

Carson's eyes flicked across the screens, the tactical radar displays a festive Christmassy glow of green and orange. They would be within reach of the first of the arrayed squadrons in about ten seconds. The altitude was their only safety at this stage, that he knew. Fighter controllers below would have tagged the hole on their screens, scanners would have snatched up the infrared flare and now they would be tracking him. On a course as straight as this it was inevitable, and with the Tarbaby's speed a sluggish Mach 5, they would believe that with a vectored maximum rate climb and anti-satellite missiles they could hit him. He watched the screens carefully, his pulse rate increasing, his hand hovering over the throttles, as again he felt the engines falter and the laser fire at some target way below the clouds. He wanted to break and run, all his combat instinct telling him this was madness.

'You never, never engage the enemy unless you are numerically superior, or have some other advantage,' the instructors said. 'You come from below and behind, or above and behind, you get sneaky and you get clever, you come out of the sun, you gang up on some poor bastard who has lost his wingman. You do not engage unless you are sure you will win! Understood? Why, you ask your-selves? Because you take too long to train and you take too much money to re-equip just because one of you thinks he is Douglas fuckin' Bader. Remember, up there in aerial combat, there is no honour, no decency. There is only who gets to come home.'

He remembered smiling at the time, looking at the weapons instructor with the jagged scar down his neck, wondering where it came from, if the story about the crash on a Trucial Omani hillside was correct. The Air Combat Manoeuvring classes were intent on that lesson.

Now he was about to ignore it in favour of his altitude superiority and hope like hell they didn't have any fancy weapons slung under the pods on the MiG-25s.

'How long till Novosibirsk?' he asked Digby.

'Two minutes.'

Carson missed the reply, his eye watching the prime radar. A tiny contact had broken from the main group immediately ahead, and seemed to be falling behind. You had to try it, didn't you, you little Russian shit, he thought.

'Here comes an intercept attempt,' he said quickly.

Digby had seen the change also.

'He's slowing down, isn't he?'

'Negative, max rate intercept climb. He has his burners going.'

'Oh my God,' Digby murmured, 'what now?'

'We see how far he can go. He should blow out at about eighty-seven thousand feet. Turn up that rearward defence howler. If he bangs a missile at us I want to know.'

'Tarbaby, this is Bright Eyes,' the radio squawked harshly.

'Go, Bright Eyes,' Carson replied, quickly turning down the speaker.

'One bogey about to break through level five zero, dead ahead. Three others lined up in the other wings.'

That Natalia is good, Carson thought, as he thumbed the on button.

'I have him on echo, watch my sixes, Bright Eyes.'

'Roger.'

On the screen the blip was getting larger. Now I begin to earn my money, he thought dryly, his palms sweating in the chamois gloves. Suddenly the missile lock alarm, many times more sensitive than those in current use, screeched for a second.

'Oh shit, missile lock,' Digby said quickly.

'Negative. Freak signal, he's too far away, that will be his prime radar trying to lock on to us. If he's gonna let one go it will be in the next twenty seconds, that will be his max ceiling for about three seconds till he falls out of the sky.'

Carson could imagine the pilot having pushed his fighter to its maximum speed, almost Mach 2.8, pulling the stick back into his guts and going ballistic, the needle nose pointed upwards at the deep blue, engines screaming, bursting upwards trying to get as much altitude as he could before the thin air and the gravity bled away his airspeed and the nose dropped in a wonderful terrifying parabolic curve back towards the earth's surface. If his on-board computer giving him his vector intercept was good, that would be the time he would let go a missile, he thought, at the peak of the climb. Again the engines surged as the laser fired, and together they counted the seconds, and then almost anti-climactically the dot began to fade and pass rapidly beneath them.

'Next time they will try something else,' Carson said.

'Like what?' Digby said, breathing again.

'The MiG-25 has cracked through one hundred thou'. If they strip one down, they might get it up there in front of our nose long enough to let a burst go.'

The Red Air Force general stood straight-backed and angry, watching the tactical fighter controllers on the level below him.

'How long, dammit!' he snarled at the colonel.

'General, it will be seconds only. Then he will be in our control zone.' The colonel was confident they could kill the intruder and it showed in his smug expression. The Novosibirsk defence systems were advanced indeed. Linked up with the infrared detection systems they had been tracking the intruder for the last twelve minutes. The huge computer was now waiting to churn out intercept vectors for a dozen squadrons, the pride of the Russian Air Forces, all there to protect the intercontinental missile silos that sprawled east to west around them.

'He will be in our web in moments, general.' They stood in tense silence, the ozone smell strong, the massive ventilators unable to clear the air completely this third level down, listening to the soft voices of the tracking teams as they watched the bright flare of the intruder on their infrared displays.

'Who has got the ice-queen?' the general asked, not mollified one iota by the colonel's confidence.

'The OC from the 325th Tactical, sir.'

The general grunted a reply. The ice-queen was the latest series of anti-satellite missile, very expensive and in very short supply. The price of a main battle tank each, the central supply people had allocated only four to the Novosibirsk area, and none at all for training purposes. It was said that there were only a dozen in all Russia.

The colonel leant forward, his nostrils flaring. One of the computers was churning data noisily, but above the noise was the excited call of the systems operators.

'I have the intruder. One zero seven degrees. Very hot trace moving at very high speeds.'

'Contact the interceptors,' the colonel shouted. 'Patch

them through. Quickly, let's not let him get away!'

On the next level down the huge Data General main-frame machine whirred almost silently into life and in a tenth of a second data began to flash on to the screens in the tactical control centre above. Less than thirty seconds later the duty supervisor ran up the stairs from the level below to look in disbelief at the displays.

'We seem to have a problem here,' the technician said.

16

The Ishim Steppe is a bleak place. In the winter freezing winds sweep south from the Siberian plains, winds that cut through clothing, bringing bone-numbing temperatures that freeze the ground hard like iron. Small towns dot the railway line to the west, towns of hardy folk and soldiers who watch the trains in the night, heading ever westward.

Most of the townspeople and all the soldiers are there to service and protect the zone. Buried beneath the steppe in a broad belt running from Kuybyshev on the western side of the Ural mountains to Novosibirsk itself lies the heart of Russia's offensive intercontinental ballistic missile capability.

The silos are scattered in groups, each protected by the Red Army with the usual GRU presence and small groups of local militia. During the construction of the silos in the sixties and early seventies, cost overruns plagued the uninterested hurried construction crews. Engineers called in to finish electrical wiring and control and communications systems found conduits going nowhere, shafts completed to the wrong specifications, and in one instance a complete group of silos installed six miles from its designated site.

In desperation they, with their own target completion dates, had to improvise on the original specifications to give the Red Army operational systems in time. The army was all-powerful in Krushchev's administration and the engineers knew better than to fail to complete on time.

Instead of ordering the return of the groundwork

contractors they relocated the launch initiation and control facility to ground level where shafts and conduits were unnecessary. Cased in bombproof concrete under a few inches of soil and the brown sad cold grasses of the steppe, they awaited their ultra low frequency instructions from the main facility at Novosibirsk. The back-up system of land lines had been unserviceable since the previous spring and the new microwave transmitter was yet to be commissioned. If anything happened to the ultra low frequency transmission towers with their UHF tandem signal in the six relay stations, then the missiles were unlaunchable.

Gulag had established this fact three months before and given Oslo the exact co-ordinates of the relay stations, which were protected by the pride of the Red Air Force and the massive computerized air defence screen from Zone Control at Novosibirsk.

A MiG-25D, an ice-queen missile slung underbelly, swept up off the runway at Omsk airbase, his escort ranged out above and behind him, while a controller at Zone tried to vector him on to the intruder without benefit of the computer-assisted intercept profile. The major's real concern wasn't missing the intruder as he lifted off into the chilly bright morning. It was the fear of mid-air collision with one of the hundred-odd fighters seeking the same target.

Sally had crept into the Omega control room. Tim had disappeared. He had helped carry the mortally wounded Yamashita down to the surgery, and watched as the two Americans were led towards a store room, now converted to a temporary cell, their dead comrades still lying in the grass above. As they walked past one had looked at him and nodded. 'Tim Miller I presume.' She was still angry with him, angry with him for lying to her and for his pathetic boy scout jingoism.

Now she stood in silence against the wall below the big picture window, watching the seemingly mismatched battle over the computer-imaged Russian landscape on the wall display opposite. Jesus, she thought, the place is swarming with them.

Below them Natalia fed Gail data as fast as she could as new squadrons lifted off, the radar screens and satellite images offering sharp new green contacts on every sweep. Above them, white and solid and moving as if on rails, was the Tarbaby's signature.

'New bogeys, lifting off from Omsk at this time. MiG-25s. I have one flight airborne.'

Sally stepped forward, not believing what she was about to do but rationalizing it as the opposite to what he would have wanted her to do. So goddamn, do it!

'What type of MiG-25?' she asked Natalia.

Gail didn't look up from her console, but her voice was an angry lash: 'Get out of here!'

'No I won't ... it's important. What kind of 25s are they? Do we know?'

Natalia noticed the we, even through the tension, and relented.

'Yes. Omsk has the D series and a handful of Es.'

'The D with the new engine upgrades will give some sustained flight over one twenty thousand. They did it in seventy-three with a thousand kilo payload,' Sally said quickly, looking Gail in the eyes as she raised her head. 'I suggest you advise Carson.'

Gail pulled the Polaroids off and looked Sally in the eyes, relying on her intuition to tell her if the other woman was lying.

'I know more about modern military aircraft than all of you put together. It's what I do,' Sally said, angry and defensive without understanding why.

Gail held the look for a second before turning back to her prime displays. 'You'd better pull up a chair,' she said.

High over the steppe the Tarbaby flew, her complex gyros and inertial navigation systems constantly cross-matching

satellite data to give her millimetric accuracy on her prede-
termined course.

Carson smiled to himself in spite of the scene his radar
portrayed.

'That tactical computer. Whoever did the job on it has
done a goody!'

Digby looked across. 'There must be hundreds of them,'
he said, not understanding Carson's remark.

'There are, but they don't know what the hell is going
on. They'll be colliding with each other soon, they have
no effective control. They'll all be so busy watching out
for each other they won't have time to watch out for us.'
He paused. 'It's a shit fight,' he said delightedly.

'What will they do?' Digby asked

'It may have already started. Keep enough at low levels
to keep us high, and then throw in a few real hot shots.'

The duty sergeant at Number Three relay was a grey-haired
veteran. He had seen active service on the Chinese border
and in Afghanistan when he had been in a motorized regiment. Now in the last years of his enlistment he commanded a twelve-man section that rotated with four others
to guard the five-acre barbed wire enclosed site. It was, he
said frequently, the most boring posting he had had in
thirty years of serving the Motherland.

Within the wire tall camouflaged masts of differing
heights supported by a complex spider's web of wire stays
stood aloft and alien to the stunted windswept fir trees
and tussocky grasses.

They had a small hut in the trees seventy yards from
the wire where they could boil up water for tea and an old
table had seen thousands of ration packs opened, sniffed,
abused and reluctantly eaten. As sergeant he pulled rank
and got to sit on the old car seat that lay scarred, torn
and weary against the far wall of the hut away from the
draughts. In the three years he had been on the relay guard
he had only twice had to move people on or actually report

anything. Once his detail had found two homosexuals in a compromising position in the cab of a truck and once an insane old woman had appeared from nowhere and offered to buy the UHF relay which lay solid and square in the centre of the site beneath the masts. She said it would do fine for her dog to live in. Someone had told her to fuck off and thrown a can at her. That was all.

'What do you think, Dimitri?' his corporal asked.

'About what?' he asked, scratching his cheek, listening to the high soft roar of another jet going overhead. There were a few about today, he had noticed.

'You know ... the Gulag thing. They reckon they can destroy all the nukes. That will mean us, won't it?'

'How are they going to destroy all the nukes? You are so stupid I wonder why that girl is going to marry you.'

The corporal grinned sheepishly, and took a mug of tea from a private who stood stirring the pot with a stick. 'Well,' he persisted, 'it was on the radio today, and I saw the handouts at the barracks before we left.'

'You'll get in trouble reading that shit,' the sergeant replied.

'It's public enough,' the corporal argued, lifting the hot mug to his mouth to blow on the contents exactly as three microsecond bursts from an x-ray weapons laser hit the ground inside the wire.

The 12,000-degree pencil-points of impact burnt craters nine feet deep and seventeen across, melting granite and sandstone into white-hot globules of glass approaching the hardness of cubic zirconium.

The centre black smoking hole also contained trace elements of pure steel from the two towers and the UHF relay that had been transformed by the super heat into a fine dust of silicon carbon that glowed for a second almost blue hot and cooled into a grey ash.

The other towers that had escaped the three blasts collapsed as rivets and bolts rapidly expanded, their molecular

363

structure changing, leaving them brittle and fatigued and unable to hold the weight up.

The laser's heat was, however, so intense and localized that grass within six feet of the smoking craters seemed unaffected other than that it had been blown flat by the shock wave of air rushing into the centre of the micro-second inferno.

One soldier was burned up his arm as a shard of white hot steel hissed through the air, but otherwise no one was injured. The corporal also burned himself, but that was on the tea he spilled when he heard the strike. It sounded to him like a cross between the white-hot crack of a lightning bolt and the sound a fly made when it flew into the ultra-violet fly trap in the canteen at the camp.

The sergeant struggled to his feet and ran to the door of the hut, looking in stunned disbelief at the three smoking craters inside the wire.

'Jesus Christ on a crutch,' he said softly, thinking, I will have something to report tonight after all.

'Tarbaby, this is Bright Eyes.'

'Go, Bright Eyes,' he replied, his eyes not leaving the displays but pleased to hear her voice.

'Tarbaby, suggest you climb to level one three five immediate.'

Digby shot a look across the cockpit that said yes please.

'What's my status, Bright Eyes?' Carson asked calmly, his eyes flicking across the defence screens for the threat.

'Tarbaby, believe Delta series two fives coming your way from zero nine zero degrees may be high altitude rigged, over.'

'How high?' he snapped back.

'Level one two zero sustained for unknown time, stand by . . .' she paused there and Carson looked across at Digby. '. . . possibly two minutes, over.'

His eyes flashed at the directional bearing on the radar.

There out ahead was a large contact from the west.

'Digby, if we climb will it alter anything?'

'Yes . . . we will have to reprogram the machine, about ten minutes but no problem . . .' he said, too quickly.

Carson had made his decision.

'Negative, Bright Eyes, don't have the fuel to waste at this time. Let's see what happens,' his eyes never leaving the contact from the west.

Washington

President Sheridan was finally woken from a light troubled sleep by a call from the Director of the CIA Walter Gagioni.

'What is it, Walter?' Sheridan asked, already knowing what the news would be.

'It would appear from satellite reports that something cataclysmic is taking place in the Russian Republics.'

'I'm listening,' Sheridan said, sitting up in bed. 'Go on.'

'Explosions across the country. From the smoke clouds they seem to be sourced in some very strategic places: three factories in the Ukraine, then along into the Volga Command and it looks as if it might even hit the Zone itself. We will know that on the next pass.'

Holy Mother of God, they have actually done it, he thought. Oslo have actually gone ahead and attacked Russia.

'Who have you advised?' he asked quickly.

'Other than you, only the NSA and the State Department.'

'Not the chairman of the Joint Chiefs of Staff?'

'Not yet,' the CIA Director said.

'Keep it that way,' Sheridan snapped. 'They will only exaggerate things. Get over here for a meeting at nine, bring the guy who is running your team looking for the hypersonic.'

'You think it's the same people?'

'Yes I do,' Sheridan answered carefully.

365

'Mr President, sir, can you advise me why you believe that to be the case?' Gagioni asked.

Sheridan knew that tone of voice. The formality suggested that the new name of this game would be pass-the-buck.

'I'll tell you later.'

He hung up, put on a dressing-gown and went downstairs, past the duty secret serviceman and into the Oval Office. He opened the cabinet in the walnut sideboard and picked up the telephone. Six seconds later it was answered.

'Good afternoon, Mikhail, I see it has begun.'

Carson watched the series of blips coming from the west. With his Mach 5 speed and their intercept from the opposite direction the contacts were approaching very quickly with a closing speed approaching 6,000 miles per hour. The heavy green contact had fractured into nine smaller pieces and as he watched four of them seemed to stop on the screen.

'Here we go,' he said to Digby. 'The second attempt.' His tone didn't encourage a reply so Digby, his hands sweating in his gloves and the fear real in his guts, said nothing. Carson was thinking fast, assessing the threat.

Four bogeys intercepting across a thirty-mile front, assume they have the MiG D and can vault up to me for a few seconds, so who is better placed for the first shot? He flicked his thumb over the battle management console allowing the laser computer to isolate the contacts and prioritize them. Course height and speed projections overlaid themselves over the blips as Carson watched. The contact on the extreme left seemed to be in the best position to initiate the battle. Now all you need is the altitude, he thought. Come on then. What's your little game? What kind of shitty surprise have you got up your sleeve?

'Tarbaby, this is Bright Eyes.'

'Go,' he snapped, not wanting the interruption.

'You have four bogeys coming up through five zero.'

'I have them,' he replied, thinking, get off the air, I want room to think here.

The four blips had distanced themselves from each other now, the first three almost evenly spaced ten or twelve miles apart to position themselves across his line of flight. The fourth was setting back, his climb slower for some reason.

Ten seconds, he thought.

'How long till the next ground target?' he snapped to Digby.

'Six minutes.'

I don't like this. Three alternatives. One, increase height now, two, bug out and go home, three, attempt to maintain altitude but engage if necessary.

'Give me combat lasers,' he said. He flicked down his tinted eye shield, and ran the seat forward into the ACM position, Digby's seat moving in concert. He jabbed at a button and the combat head-up display danced on to the crystal canopy. The pressure suits automatically began to expand with compressed air and tighten around their limbs. He selected the F&B, forward and below option, on the laser battle management system and instantly the first three blips flicked into view before his eyes. The first MiG was now crossing through 106,000 feet, still climbing but very slowly, her original Mach 2.8 now bled back to a mere 300 knots as she struggled to maintain manoeuvrability in the high thin freezing air, her methanol-injected jet engine screaming to find the thrust to climb those last few thousand feet.

Two seconds. She appeared as a thin bright sliver of silver, a flash in the harsh ultraviolet light of the ozone layer, off to Carson's right. His weapons systems had been locked on to the MiG for the last three seconds, but instead of firing he hesitated, knowing the MiG pilot had left it too late for a real intercept, too close to a fast target, marvelling at the skill and courage it took to fly a conventional fighter that high, that fast, that bravely.

He was willing it to fall from the sky, its nose to drop, to give him an excuse not to fire. Come on! Stall, you fucker, tuck your nose and fall, you don't want to die up here, but the MiG seemed to find its balance and Carson heard his missile lock indicators screaming, and suddenly he was past it, and the threat was gone, falling away astern.

He heard Digby breathe out for the first time in about thirty seconds.

'The next guy might be better,' Carson said.

With his F&B option and the head-up display locked on the final two, the Tarbaby's hardware was not geared up to watch from the side. The side where the major commanding the 325th Tactical Squadron was still climbing his MiG-25 D. It was slow because although his load only weighed 2,000 kilos it was bulky and offered bad airflow resistance under the fighter's sleek belly. Only once she was launched would the ice-queen fly as she was designed to, with the required speed to break the earth's gravitational pull and enter space. As he crossed 65,000 feet he activated the launch sequence, the missile's complex targeting system already having located the 'satellite' moving in a steady slow orbit over eleven miles above.

He moved his hand over the throttles to ease back the power once the missile had launched, and pressed the three matt black buttons on the small temporarily fitted junction box in the right bulkhead, counted to three and pulled the control column back into his stomach, feeling for the heavy missile dropping away and the shudder of the broken airflow as her ignition systems activated.

Carson watched the final two on the head-up, the battle management system placing them in order of attack, the little digital meter counting down the seconds to intercept. He noticed immediately they were not climbing as fast as the first fighter had done only seconds ago.

Sixteen seconds to intercept and they were still way below 90,000 feet. His thought process raced through the possible reasons and he discounted the performance aspect. If they had one MiG D rigged to fly high then they should have others. So why wait down at that level? They must be expecting me to go down there. Why? What is up here? He checked the management screen again, almost feeling his hackles rising, all his instincts screaming at him. He flicked the F&B screen on to his secondary display and punched up rear defence; old habits dying hard, he whipped his head around scanning the sky, and suddenly the rear defence systems began to report, the missile howler shrieking its warning and Gail's voice crashing through the speakers: 'ASAT INCOMING BREAK LOW LEFT!'

His foot jabbed at the left rudder as his hand forced the control column over into the top left corner, and as the nose dropped his right hand hit the power settings and the Tarbaby rolled over, pointed her nose at the earth's surface, the mighty scram jets roaring, and passed through Mach 6 in an inverted dive, Carson knowing that the only thing an anti-satellite missile couldn't really do is turn back downward, his heart in his mouth, the G forces coming on, watching the missile track him on the screen, trying for the falling power on turn, and his hand jabbed against the G forces, missed, jabbed again and hit the rearward defence multi-option and the light flashed as the chaff and flares fell away, and pulling the nose up, power back, oh Jesus, that's what they were waiting for, the motherfuckers, the howler still shrieking but fainter, and his hand flicked the menu back to F&B and he saw the flash of the cannon fire along the silver streak ahead and he fired his lasers allowing the battle management systems to aim and blew the MiG into a million superhot globules of steel, aluminium and titanium, and heard the bangs of the cannon strikes.

His breath exploded out, the adrenalin racing in his blood as he pulled the nose up and scrambled for height.

'We are hit,' he hissed through clenched teeth, and as he spoke the warning lights on the central display began to wink, and an audible alarm began to ping behind them.

'Have a look, Digby, see what's down,' he said. He levelled the Tarbaby off at 120,000 feet and watched as Digby ran his seat back on the electric runners, easing backwards to look at the engineering panel above his head, his hand shaking and breathing in short sharp pants, trying to remain professional but really feeling frightened and sick and not wanting to die.

It was Sally Schoeman who identified the threat from the last of the MiGs. Gail, who had the benefit of all the Tarbaby's systems all the time, forward and rearward systems active, had seen the interceptor's track, but had not given it threat status because it was about to fall behind the Tarbaby and thirty-odd thousand feet below.

'The one on his sixes,' she said, 'it's too slow and too low. Uncharacteristic. It's almost as if . . .' then the tiny blip had separated from the main contact. 'ASAT! It's an ASAT LAUNCHED!' Gail had hit her mike open and called the warning as the missile had streaked inbound and they had watched as Carson dropped his nose and been forced into the same flight level as the remaining MiGs. The whole control room had been terribly quiet for the next few seconds. They all knew the Tarbaby wasn't designed for air combat manoeuvring, for a dogfight.

All at once the little solid white blip on the wall display and Gail's main console display, and the reporting systems and flight management screens faded.

'Tarbaby, this is Bright Eyes, do you copy, over,' and the silence was thick like the ozone smell.

'Tarbaby, do you copy, over.' Oh my God, no, she thought, please no.

'Tarbaby, this is Bright Eyes, do you copy,' and the tears began to well up in her eyes and she choked back a sob, but the airwaves just hissed.

'Tarbaby, this is Bright Eyes, do you copy, over?'

Behind her Sagan's hand fell to her shoulder. It was Sally who broke the silence.

'He's not down till he's overdue,' she said softly.

'What?' Sagan said

'It's not down till he's overdue.'

'What are you saying?'

'I'm saying he might have a tech problem. A dicky radio or transmission gear.'

Tokyo

Not surprisingly it was the government of Japan which led the official support for Oslo. With men in government who remembered Hiroshima and Nagasaki, their support was immediate and devastatingly effective. The nine executives of the Japanese ministries of Finance and Trade dominated the meeting with a policy of iron. Across the table senior men from the three major money-broking houses and the stock exchange sat in stunned silence as the government's new policy was made clear in a fast, furious thirty-six-minute meeting. By the time the exchanges opened for the afternoon's trading they were ready to begin dumping American stocks and selling dollars. The impetus was further fuelled when the Central Exchange Bank of Japan put their entire dollar fund on the market, forcing the price down. Singapore followed suit with Hong Kong and by four that afternoon the mighty greenback was reeling; without the American market awake to trade and support it, the Europeans began to offload their dollars to anyone who would buy them.

The Japanese press threw its not inconsiderable weight behind the effort and ran all the Oslo stories in the late editions and by six that evening 40,000 peace protesters had gathered outside the American and Russian embassies.

Washington

It was three AM when Sheridan, finally showered and dressed, made his way back down to the Oval Office. The telephones had begun to ring already and the White House's seventy inward lines had been busy since the evening editions the night before. The inward log, long a measure of public opinion for those in the know, showed that six thousand calls had been logged on the system since seven the previous evening. Sheridan was sure they were all inspired by the Oslo media effort.

His comments the night before about muzzling the press had his aides shrieking the First and Fifth Amendments and preaching doom. He pushed the page aside and called the Chief of Naval Staff at home, ordering the Guided Missile Cruiser presently holding station in the North Atlantic to proceed with her orders and make for Iceland with all speed.

He then placed a call direct to the American ambassador in Reykjavik, a serious breach of protocol, and instructed him to deliver a message to the Icelandic government immediately advising that the American ship was no threat to Iceland but would maintain station for the security of America itself, four miles off their northern coast. It would be there that evening.

Further than that the US government was not prepared to discuss the issue. Lastly he summoned the Secretary of State to the White House.

St Petersburg

The priest stood on the altar steps, his worn robes brushing the stone floor as other robes had done for seven hundred years, his eyes on the faces of the people before him. The ancient Russian Orthodox Cathedral had not seen a congregation like this since the Nazis were at the city's gates, and certainly not since it was reconsecrated after its Soviet days as a technology museum. Word had passed from one to another, and Christians who had long worshipped in the privacy of their own homes or in other smaller churches found themselves in the ancient cathedral and kneeling to pray with the young priest.

He was in no doubt as to the reason for the turnout and from training and habit dropped straight into the role he saw himself fulfilling, as shepherd to his flock. He turned, settled to his knees before the altar and began to pray for nuclear peace, his voice high and strong and leading the thousand-strong congregation.

Only minutes into the prayer a small group of uniformed militia men arrived at the vestibule door and with the arrogance of atheists sought to make an example of the young robed man on his knees. They were only feet away from him when the prayers from the solid mass of people turned to something else, and they saw some deep under-current of something that scared them.

They turned and left the building, the priest having never faltered in his prayer. This itself earned him vast and immediate respect from the gathered people, and the acolytes had to break out more wine and small portions of bread for the communion. There were similar scenes in other churches across Russia that morning, as thousands stayed home from work, universities and schools.

In Pavlobad, the scene of the first tremendous blast that day, six thousand people had gathered in the city's central park to hear a nuclear physics professor from the university talk about radiation. It was inevitable that at some stage the Red Army backlash would commence, but here in the warm sun of the summer morning something remarkable happened. Troops called by the local militia for assistance were met by the local mayor as he walked into the park. He politely informed them he was coming to listen to the speaker and sat down beside a concrete worker and his daughter.

The officer commanding, unsure of what to do, stood

for several minutes and then frustratedly re-loaded his men into trucks and drove away, the crowd laughing and cheering.

Carson had swung the Tarbaby back on to her course and gently allowed the computer to attempt re-entry into the sequence. He was unsure what damage had been sustained by the cannon strikes and was unwilling to give control over to the machine until it had proved its operational status. He had no warning lights or alarms going off. Jesus, what a fluke, he thought, closing speed near enough to Mach 9 and I fly into his cannon fire. Digby had now pulled himself clear of his seat and had opened up two wiring panels in the tight bay behind Carson's seat.

'The transmitter is buggered,' he eruditely reported.

'That's why I haven't been able to raise Gail. How bad?' Carson asked.

'Can't tell. But this panel has no signals moving through it. It's the test circuit from the main units back aft . . .' he slid back into his seat '. . . could be like that BA jumbo, a couple of holes in the fuselage.'

'Let's test lasers first,' Carson said.

Five minutes later he eased the nose up and punched a new course into the navigation system. The Tarbaby was homeward bound, her entire data transmission system unserviceable, her weapons computer suspect and a certain two holes drilled into her underbelly by the MiG's thirty-millimetre cannon shells.

She was losing fuel. Quickly.

Below her the Russians watched with some relief as the infrared trace moved north-west.

At Novosibirsk the general who had stood watching the débâcle as technical teams tried to unravel the corrupted software took a phone call from Moscow. He listened, saying nothing, and finally replaced the handset.

'We have chased him away, general,' the colonel said proudly, 'the Zone defence system is . . .'

'A piece of useless shit!' the general finished angrily. 'Now, get the computer up and running before he comes back to finish the job or you will be commanding a shit-house cleaning detail in Kamchatka. Do you understand me?'

'We have new software coming from Moscow General, it should be here in a matter of hours,' the colonel said in a placatory manner.

'How? Tell me that? The weather is closing in, you fool!'

'Well, that means the Americans . . .' the colonel began.

'A, no one said it was the Americans, and B, this thing, whatever it is, flies higher than the weather, so don't even suggest it,' the general finished. Bastards. All his life had been spent in the military. First the Red Army, the mightiest army ever seen on earth, and now the Russian Army, the linchpin of the defence of his homeland. He was not going to be rolled over by something like this. There were others who thought like him, the most powerful in the Kremlin itself. Kraskin, ex-Marshal of the Army and head of the military clan. He went to his office and closing the door made a phone call.

The Icelandic government's reaction to the American stance was typical of their Norse forefathers. They didn't even ask to discuss it. They simply ordered all American troops to return to their bases till further notice, putting police round the bases to make sure their requests were complied with, and closed the airport to US air traffic, civil or military. They then moved troops into the area long ago loaned to Oslo and secured it to prevent any further incursions. It was their first overt support for the effort, and was followed by the arrival of two fisheries protection vessels four miles off the northern coast to await the arrival of the American missile cruiser. The small old patrol craft were no match for the might of the USS *Bunker Hill*, but they would serve to demonstrate Iceland's official stance to the world.

At the Omega Base despair had replaced the previous hope instilled by Sally's remark. The control room was still alive with lights and people, but it had lost its spirit along with the banks of performance indicators and the small white blip.

Natalia remained at her station because she was too well-disciplined to leave it without permission. Gail sat staring at the wall display, trying to believe Sally and hoping that Peter Carson was still safe, the mission forgotten for the moment.

Sagan went to his office to call Haidermann and advise him that they believed the Tarbaby had been damaged or shot down over Russia.

'It was never designed for air combat, Charles,' he finished, 'so we have to consider the possibility that we no longer have an Omega Project.'

In the crew room Tavis and his team sat drinking tea, the talk awkward and forced, and up in the clinic the doctor was performing complex abdominal surgery on Rikio Yamashita, trying to piece together the remnants of his liver and spleen, torn apart by the heavy wadcutter rounds favoured by the dead Avery Oxenburger. The doctor was being assisted by the gay cook who listed amongst his considerable talents Royal Marines medic training, but his relaxed banter over the table did little to dispel the gloom. The guard hit by Oxenburger's first bullet sat in a comfortable position in a bed against the wall in the other room and smoked constantly. In the steel-lined pantry Paul Hart and the local CIA man sat cold and huddled in the corner under the harsh white fluorescent lights. Outside a guard waited, but down the passage Miller, who had worked out where they were, awaited his chance.

London

The Campaign for Nuclear Disarmament had pulled out all the stops for their first rolling demonstration with a full 7,000 protesters crowded between the elegant windows of

376

Oxford Street as they marched towards Hyde Park, the by now familiar death masks and skeleton suits in abundance. But this time the atmosphere of protest had an immediacy never before seen in London.

Three women had flown from Japan the night before carefully carrying the photographs of their dead left in the irradiated ash of Nagasaki. They planned to announce a hunger strike to the death in the park and the protesters bore a small Shinto temple on poles across their shoulders and the wood for the funeral pyre.

The evening editions of the newspapers all carried, in addition to further updates on the Tarbaby stories, the first word that Oslo had directly confronted the Federation of Russian Republics and that the United States of America was next. It was nuclear disarmament or ruin. At six PM the House of Commons was scheduled for a full emergency debate, the tumbling dollar threatening to pull down whole economies and the Japanese bankers threatening to bring sterling down with it.

The Independent Television network rolled with the flow and planned a special debate of their own, with a Labour minister, his Conservative counterpart, a university lecturer famous for his stance on the nuclear arms issue and the editor of a right-wing magazine. They planned to follow the debate with a re-run of a made-for-TV movie called *The Day After* about a nuclear strike and its effects.

After peace activists had announced a national strike by teachers the BBC, reluctant thus far to give voice to a pressure group, recognized the mood of the nation and decided to cover the events in some depth on their late evening news programme.

New Zealand would begin an all-night debate in their House, long anti-nuclear, on both their foreign and domestic policy. Local press speculated that they supported the Oslo and Gulag effort and would offer help for the hypersonic if needed. They predicted that they would offer sanctuary to any activist who felt they needed it in the event the effort failed. The O'Casey Alternative was gathering momentum.

The Dublin headquarters of the Oslo effort was still largely undiscovered by the press. In the old stone building the telephone teams had been working at full stretch for the last five hours while all active Oslo members had been contacted, and they were now into the second stage of the roll-out, the full 'dramatic' media as they had termed it. Television, radio, stage, public appearances and the spectacular wherever possible, because people love the spectacular.

Haidermann walked out of the committee room, now the coffee room, in answer to a call by Darby, the French PR whizzkid. He was studying the fast computer message coming out on one of the bank of machines.

'It's on the Reuters screen too,' he said pointing at the small VDU in the corner. His tone was merely unsettled because he was too experienced a journalist to be upset by anything any more.

'The Russians have claimed they shot down a high-speed aircraft engaged in attacking their sovereign territory.'

Haidermann read the text fast, his frown increasing.

'Well?' Darby asked.

'Well what?' Haidermann replied

'Don't bullshit an expert. I'm here because that is my job. Is there any substance to their claim?'

'We lost contact over an hour ago. Nothing at all. That's all. She is not overdue yet,' he replied tiredly.

'Where there's smoke . . .' the Frenchman replied.

'Where does this leave us?' Haidermann ripped the text clear of the roll.

'We must deny it. Make a counter-claim. Then if she pitches up all well and good. If she is down . . . then we need to keep that quiet till we are finished.'

'How will this be treated by the media?' Haidermann asked.

'The independent media? Not ours? They will have a field day. They thrive on this sort of scenario . . . but if the Tarbaby's okay . . . how about this as answer?'

Haidermann listened with a wolfish grin.

'We're still pissing fuel!' Carson snapped. He had powered his engines right back to subsonic and moved on to the take-off units to try and conserve his dwindling fuel, but it wasn't looking good. Conventional fighters had self-sealing tanks and some had the ability to pump fuel from one side to another, but not the Tarbaby. She was never designed to have a holed tank and the trim computer automatically pumped fuel across the airframe to level her out. Pumped fuel straight into the holed area.

'How much?' Digby asked quickly.

'Heaps,' he replied. The computer threw up a new flight duration figure and moments later changed it, re-calculating constantly.

'Do we have an alternative?'

'Negative.'

Digby looked at the flight duration readout. They had five minutes.

Moscow

Ustinoff surveyed the ten other men and the one woman around the priceless polished table that had been com-missioned by Peter the Great and now sat in the centre of the graceful old high-ceilinged room in the Kremlin.

This was the Council of Ministers, the twelve people who were put in place by Chekhov to make day-to-day policy, execute that policy, and govern the nation. There was no real power in the Duma, the lower house, and even less in the House of Representatives. The power lay here, with these few people and the vested interests they represented. Ustinoff studied them as they settled in their chairs. Some of these men dated back to the old days, before the reforms began. As in the West lobbying had become commonplace, but here in Russia it was different. The real power really was held by a handful. Through the clan system each person in the room represented their own interests. There was the Moscow clan, the agro clan, the military and the munitions manufacturers, the oil and gas clan. Although the external lobbyist had fewer people to try to influence, they were infinitely more difficult to sway, forming if they had to uneasy alliances to further similar aims.

Occasionally two or three of the elite group would gather together, plan a united stand over some issue or other, flex their muscles and oppose the President and those close to him, but it was a risky business. There had been many who had tried it on with Mikhail Chekhov and lost. They got to where they were by being canny and strong and reading the subtle signs and hearing loud and clear what was never said. One needed to be noticed as strong and independent, worthy of the seat on the Council, but only enough so to be considered neither a weakling nor a fool.

Make your stand then concede graciously, had been his advice from Chekhov, then run your department and run it well. That had been on his first day at the table, immediately seen by the few as a Chekhov protégé. But to take on the combined ranks was to lose and in Yeltsin's case earlier in the year, it had been a swift fall from grace. He wondered who round the table would try it today.

They had listened to the reports from the Security Service, the military and the militia who had tried to piece together the fragments of civil disobedience, the attacks, the meetings with dissident speakers, the Gulag. Now, with the doors closed and the security people, personal staffers and aides having left, the discussion would begin in earnest.

Ustinoff knew that Chekhov would need to be very careful here. As President he was powerful and they all knew it; only an election or a complete coup could topple him, but it was theoretically possible if all other members round the table directly confronted him and presented their case to the nation. Much would depend on whatever support he could offer Chekhov from his small sphere of influence. He could give momentum to any motion and could suspend the meeting by calling for a recess if things began to move the wrong way.

I walk a thin line today, he thought. I am an extreme disarmamentalist on the one side and three men who would bomb America tomorrow if they thought they could get away with it are over on the other; tucked into the middle are the Ukrainian and the others that owe me or owe Chekhov.

Chekhov, he thought, so much depends on Chekhov. With my support here at the table we are powerful enough to win this, but only if it is what he truly wants. Defence Minister Kraskin sat at the opposite end of the table. He was a hard-liner, straight from the senior ranks himself and brought in after the Chechen débâcle. He was a big man who moved surprisingly fast, his head snapping back and forth like a snake when he spoke, his heavy florid cheeks swinging like an afterthought. Now his cold flat eyes were locked on Ustinoff. He was an old campaigner and represented the military and the munitions makers. He had already assessed the younger man and had established where his threat lay. He had taken the call from the Zone earlier. Agreed. Supported and endorsed the secret orders. The submarine on routine patrol in the North Atlantic had new orders and was now deep under radio silence and running for Iceland. Her small contingent of Spetznatz troopers would handle this.

'Let's get on with it,' Chekhov said firmly.

At the Omega Base a technician leaned over his infrared scanner and watched the real time pictures they were stealing from a French satellite. The control room was very quiet with just Natalia watching the Russian high-level radar pictures as the interceptor squadrons headed home, Andrea marking them on her chart.

Gail was up in Sagan's office with him, talking to a contact in Bergen to see if he had patterned any kind of search for wreckage on the Russian side. The Scandinavian radar network covered most of northern Russia west of the Urals and he was their first attempt to pinpoint the extent of their problem.

The technician watched the screen for a moment longer and plotted the course of the trace, then spoke into his throat mike, looking up into Sagan's window where he knew the wall speaker was live.

'I have the Tarbaby inbound on zero two zero degrees,' he said flatly. 'Long finals in approx three minutes.'

Gail Samuels squealed delightedly and took the stairs at a run, not bothering to go to control but heading straight for the hangar.

'Are you sure?' Sagan asked quickly, as he himself arrived smiling widely in the control room.

The technician, who had been plotting infrared since leaving UCLA, regarded Sagan with the kind of look he reserved for morons. 'Does a bear shit in the forest?'

Carson taxied the Tarbaby straight into the hangar on her primary engines, the massive roar in the cavern bringing Tavis and his crew shouting and cheering from their crew room. Within minutes they were swarming over her still hot surfaces, looking for more damage. Tavis was confident he could repair the two nine-foot gouges in her belly, seal the fuel tank and have the communications systems working by midnight. When they drained the remaining fuel there was only forty pounds left, in theory not enough to even provide pressure in the lines.

Carson and Digby, both dog-tired, went straight to bed leaving the computer tapes to be studied by the analysts, who would then program the second flight to complete the mission.

In the cool darkness of his room Carson held Gail closely and whispered to her as she cried.

'I told you I wouldn't crash, didn't I? Well, I didn't. So stop being a silly goose and smile.'

'I love you,' she said miserably.

'I love you too,' he replied. She did smile then, bravely through the tears of her relief, and within minutes he was asleep and she sat and watched him breathing and occasionally touched him gently just to make sure he was real and there and safe.

USS Bunker Hill

She was a state of the art Aegis class missile cruiser only four years old and the pride of her breed, her captain and her crew. Right now she was steaming at a very gentle three knots barely under way in the heavy rolling northern seas, while her engineers made repairs to drive shaft bearings that were due for replacement when she was diverted north. Her captain had chosen this time because without a full briefing he wasn't sure what her role was to be and if her maximum speed of thirty-three knots was called for the old bearings wouldn't hold up. It was a seven-hour job, the engineering officer had told him, and now five hours later he was impatient to be on his way. He had wanted to be on station off Iceland by midnight, but now it would be nearer full dawn the next morning.

His orders were to maintain station and be prepared to shoot down an aircraft. Orders from the President himself. They are going to need to be, he thought, after that fuck-up in the Gulf. I'm not carrying the can for this one. The last captain who had fired at a civilian aircraft had lost his command, the *Vincennes*, over the issue, and rightly so. He had been too gung-ho, too eager for a fight, he had put too much faith in his officers and the battle control systems they were unfamiliar with. With a nasty little firefight at water level not thirty miles away, the forty-three-foot

Iranian gunboats whizzing in and snap shooting at another ship, he had given the command to launch his SAMs at the contact.

The Aegis system is good but not that good, he stood thinking. The epilogue to the story as far as he was concerned was the humble pie the crew had to eat every time they went ashore. To the world it was an Aegis class US Navy ship that shot down a civvy airliner. Which didn't matter and that pissed him off.

He stood down from his self-imposed watch, handed over to the duty officer and made his way back to his night quarters.

The chief was waiting in the passage. They had served together a long time, the chief having transferred to be with his skipper.

'Spare a minute, captain?'

'Sure, Barney, what's up?' he replied.

'Got a rating here, sir. Think you should listen to what he has to say . . . talk below decks.'

The captain nodded quickly. A modern warship was no different to an old ship of the line. Crew morale was important and every captain had his sources of information on the mood below decks.

He looked at the man beside the hulking chief.

'What's on your mind, sailor?'

The boy, he was no more than twenty or so, gulped. He had never addressed the captain of the ship before. This aloof figure in his crisp uniform ran their lives, their hopes and dreams.

'Captain, sir . . . the rumour machine, sir . . .'

'Spit it out, son,' the chief growled good-naturedly.

'Sir, talk has it that we are gonna blow away that hypersonic. The one that saved the *Mississippi* and the *Morgan James* and them other ships in the Gulf Task Force . . . sir.'

'We just follow orders, sailor. You know that. Sometimes we . . .' the captain began, but he was interrupted.

'Sir, my brother was aboard *Vincennes* when they

splashed that Iranian plane, sir. They were shit scared, sir . . . they were scared of just what they tried to do to the *Mississippi*. And okay, they made a mistake and people died, but sir, I ain't happy about this whole thing, no sir . . . why are we going to try and shoot down the good guys, sir?' He paused and licked his chapped lips quickly. 'If it weren't for them, sir, half our Gulf fleet would have been nuked. This just don't make no sense, sir.' He stopped and stood to attention expecting a sharp reprimand and a lecture on doing his duty. He got neither.

The captain looked at the chief. 'Is this boy's feeling indicative of the other men?'

'Yes, captain, pretty much. Some are sullen, some are more mouthy about it, but it's pretty much the same throughout the ship.'

He thought for a minute. 'Okay. Get one man from each accommodation deck up to the hangar. Include a marines representative and two officers. Let's clear the air here a little, and when the smoke's gone we can all see things a little better.' He turned to the young sailor. 'That took courage to speak out, but let me ask you this, would you ever disobey a direct order from me?'

The sailor looked at his captain and thought carefully for a moment.

'I don't think so, sir . . . but I would expect you to be able to answer for it at the end of the day,' he answered bravely.

'Oh? To who, son? To you?' the captain asked, interested by the reply, a half-smile on his lips.

'Oh no, sir . . . to your conscience and to the Lord God,' the sailor replied with an equal smile on his lips.

'Fair enough,' Captain Hendricks said. 'Fair enough.'

Moscow

Kraskin was almost thumping the table in anger as he belaboured his point to the Council.

385

'Never in all my years of serving the Rordina have I ever seen such behaviour on the streets of Moscow! Dissidents and long-haired students who should be in school, people absent from their jobs, marching in the streets, in parks listening to reactionaries! Discussing the smoking ruins of our national defence systems! And we do nothing! Let me sort it out. A couple of motorized regiments will have these antisocial elements where they belong!'

'And where is that?' Ustinoff asked dryly. 'This is 1997, Kraskin. Democracy is here. You can't quell your own people with soldiers any more. You have to listen to them. See what it is that has taken them from their homes, their workplaces. It is they we represent here.'

The old minister seemed to go red in the face at the thought of representing anyone other than his armed forces, but toned down his argument to suit the mood.

'I realize that, Ustinoff. But the Americans can . . .'

'You keep harping on about the bloody Americans – this is a Russian problem! Here in Russia! The people of Russia are that pissed off with this issue. They are out there in the streets! Next you will be blaming the Australians for a failed wheat crop . . .' the ageing old-guard Agriculture Ministry head lifted his eyes with a plea to be left out of this one '. . . or the British because we can't meet demands for fresh fish. This is a local problem and not just ours! The Americans and the British have the same thing in their streets and parks. Has it not occurred to you that the whole world has just finally had enough? And Russians have had enough? Is that so difficult to understand?'

Ustinoff paused there for a second.

'Anyway if your Red Army is so bloody shit-hot tell me how this Gulag outfit managed to wipe out ninety per cent of our nuclear production capability and seventy per cent of our front line arsenal? Mmmm? Tell me that! I know your problem. It's that if we disarm, your people are out of pocket. No nice lucrative contracts for replacements. So don't give me motorized regiments attacking good Russians on our streets simply because they don't want another fifty billion roubles squandered on nuclear weapons when they have to turn to crime to earn enough to buy a bloody car.'

The others had sat back and watched the leaders of the two factions fight it out. Chekhov had remained largely silent and that was not a good sign. When he let his Council tear each other to shreds he was about to launch a crusade of his own, watching the lie of the land, who really stood where and how much they meant what they said. This was the heart of Russian politics, wearing the others down. The final say was his and his decision absolute. Yeltsin had challenged and lost. No one would be keen to make that same mistake.

He would hear the debate and he would decide.

'It was Sally who identified the MiG Ds, and realized you had that goddamned ASAT on your tail,' Gail said. 'She's good. Knows her stuff.'

They lay wrapped in the sheet on Carson's bed, he smoking and she with her head on his chest. They talked for a while longer and then Carson showered and dressed for his next briefing. With the last of the silos on the Ishin Steppe in Siberia as the target for this last run over Russia, they could make the pass as early as they liked, with no workers or civilians at risk.

Sagan's part of the briefing covered the intended arrival of the USS *Bunker Hill*.

'Sat pictures put her still four hours away, but she is under way now after being stopped for a while, we understand for repairs.' He paused and looked at the flight-suited pair. 'You realize that this means they may prevent you landing.'

'Ironic, isn't it?' Digby said in his best Cambridge manner. 'The same class of ship that propagated all this is the one they send to try and finish it.'

Carson who had not said much at all spoke then.

'They better not.'

'What?' Sagan asked.

'Try and stop us landing.' His voice was dry and brittle with threat.

Sagan stood to full height and glowered down at the fighter pilot.

'You will not, I repeat not, engage the *Bunker Hill* under any circumstances. She is not a nuke-equipped vessel.' Carson just looked. 'We have made alternative arrangements, that should suffice.'

'They better,' Carson replied. 'I'm coming back here and if they get in my way I'll blow a hole in their hull. Do you copy me? Tell 'em that. Tell 'em that if I come back in then I am committed, and I will land. If they wish to survive the experience then just leave me alone.' Sagan was shocked at his attitude and Carson, immediately feeling guilty, tried in his own way to explain. 'Pilots like their runways. It's how we walk away after stopping an aeroplane flying. It's also the only way in for that one.'

The plan called for them to fly higher than ever before for this phase of the mission. Even allowing for incredible bad luck and flying into the MiG's two cannon rounds they had decided not to risk the Tarbaby again. She would complete the mission at 160,000 feet, burning precious fuel and making a mockery of her flight duration figures, but safely above anything except another anti-satellite missile.

She took off at two AM local time, her sleek black nose pointed at the black sky and the flares of her afterburners bright in the darkness.

In Moscow it was already eight on the Saturday morning, but it was no normal Saturday. By five the crowds of peace protesters had begun gathering outside the GUM department store on Red Square. A second major group had descended on the American embassy and by seven police and militia estimated the crowd at 30,000 in the surrounding streets and growing as the minutes passed. A third group had begun to form outside Spaso House, the official residence of the American President on his last visit to Moscow at the time of the Mid Range Nuclear Arms Limitation Talks. That crowd the police estimated would link up with the Kremlin crowd by mid-morning, and be a solid moving mass of over half a million Muscovites.

The group outside the American embassy had already begun to sing. The song was John Lennon's 'Give peace a chance', sung by everyone who knew the words, and picked up by those who didn't.

The scene was the same in Minsk, St Petersburg, Volgograd, throughout the Crimea and Armenia where the locals forgot about their hatred for the Azerbaijanis long enough to join in the first real spontaneous demonstration seen in Russia since the failed coup and the storming of the White House.

In the USA the Oslo effort, twelve hours behind the rest of the world, suddenly gathered momentum and in the true American way passionately strove to compete.

17

Oslo's North American effort was the real powerhouse of the global campaign. Their absolute and complete domination of the media and communications was apparent from the start, with both major networks running anti-nuclear programming from early evening through until the day's transmissions ceased. Some of the material was visually disturbing and they made no excuses. It was designed to be.

They showed footage of donkeys and pigs that had been irradiated in experiments and of children with radiation burns. Experts on panel shows talked of the nuclear winter and of mutually assured destruction being just that, for the entire planet. Interspersed throughout the evening on the networks, and on local channels in most areas, the same call went out: phone the White House, phone your congressman, America is a democracy, tell them you don't want nuclear weapons, not now, not ever. Celebrity guests, actors and well-known, respected people, took cameo spots urging support. Four West Coast channels broke the law and used subliminal techniques, fast flashes on the screen conveying messages that the brain cannot consciously recognize but will take in anyway.

News programmes went on air as usual but reported the mounting campaign nation-wide, and gave heavy air time to the rolling-out of the efforts in Russia and Europe, the Icelandic decision and the fact that the New Zealand government looked like coming out in support of Oslo.

In a major coup Haidermann's past spadework came to life: calling in past favours the Teamsters Union applied pressure to their colleagues in the steel and automotive industries.

By midnight Oslo had convinced the air traffic controllers that their support was essential and they agreed to strike unless the as yet unnamed American Navy ship was withdrawn from her questionable mission to Iceland.

By eight that evening operators at the Oslo-owned telephone company were offering to connect callers to the White House or to congressmen at no cost and by nine the White House's seventy incoming lines were hopelessly jammed with people wanting to tell President Sheridan they didn't want nuclear weapons in the USA.

In Edinburgh, Illinois, a stone's throw from Springfield, the townspeople proudly hung banners proclaiming their support for Edinburgh in Scotland, the town they were named after and the town that built the Tarbaby.

In the Midwest, the home of the silos that hid America's ICBMs, people long used to their presence began to question the soldiers and airmen who staffed the facilities and that night those personnel were advised by the military not to venture into the towns till the current situation had died down.

At a rock concert in San Diego the performers, now nearing middle age and a product of the Vietnam era, announced that the proceeds were to go to Oslo and their live broadcast was now a benefit concert. At one stage they had the audience holding up lighted matches in the dark, just in case the Tarbaby was overhead.

A radio station DJ in Albuquerque, New Mexico, called for his listening audience to switch off their lights at home as a sign of support for the movement. He was delighted with the response since it included the nuclear testing site, but unknown to him he was assisted by an operator at the local power station grid, who began throwing the micro switches on his panels and shut down half the lights in the state for two minutes.

An eccentric man with a sandwich-board caused much

amusement on the streets of Kansas City. He had been predicting doom from the warheads in the soil around the state for many years but tonight his sandwich-board was changed and read 'Omega-Master Blaster!' on the front with 'Minuteman you gonna get yours' on the back.

In New York, Boston, Cleveland, Philadelphia, Chicago, Los Angeles, San Francisco, Denver, Houston and Washington massive rallies were planned for the following day, the largest in Washington itself. The police, fearing numbers they couldn't handle, asked the army for assistance in crowd control. At nine PM local time in Washington, President Sheridan called a meeting of his staff, and they set out to schedule an Address to the Nation. His aides told him, Peter Kramer in the background, that in their opinion nothing since VJ Day came near to approaching the public excitement over the issue.

Edinburgh

Stuart McKay sat at his kitchen table cleaning his kit for the parade. Every three years or so, the five or six pipe-bands in the district would be amalgamated to form a massed band for a special occasion. This year his pipe-band had drawn the straw to lead the massed band, and he as drum major would lead the lot. He was proud. He had been one of Scotland's acknowledged talents for some years, but it wasn't every day a man got to lead the pipes and drums of the Edinburgh and Districts massed band up Princes Street in Edinburgh in a civic procession.

He rubbed the blanco up the wide white belt again and pushed on. He still had brasses and puttees to do, and then give his kilt a final press.

Against the wall the heavy mace-like baton stood in its protective walnut case. For practice he used a lighter pewter model, but in a few hours he would heft the real thing. It was sterling silver and had been presented to the city's band by a group of men who had survived the Crimean

War and never forgotten the welcome home the band had given them. Its ornate carved head was valued at £70,000, and Lloyd's took a dim view of its public use for anything but very special occasions.

He looked up as his wife began to move about the kitchen making tea. She was never a woman who spoke much, but since the night before she had been ominously silent. That was usually a sign that she disapproved of his behaviour, and the small, serious little woman was the only thing on earth that Stuart McKay was afraid of. He also loved her as you can only love someone who has stood beside you for thirty years through hard times and good.

The argument had been with his two daughters. A year apart in age, they were both at the university and both what he termed left-wing wallies. They had argued with him all evening about the Oslo thing, he staunchly defending the Conservatives and their policies on defence.

She had listened the way she did with these things, quietly sipping her tea and making up her own mind. At the end of the discussion as the girls were going back to their flat she looked up at him.

'Stuart, they are right,' she had said.

Now she was making tea and moving about and he knew why. She was going to join Jennifer and Morag at the demonstration in Princes Street Gardens.

'You're going then, lass?' he asked.

'Aye,' she said.

He polished the belt wondering what possessed them, this day when he would lead the massed bands and they would not see him do it.

London

CND activists and volunteers were laying out tapes in Hyde Park, making every effort to assist the police where possible. They had been granted permission reluctantly for their demonstration and rally, on the grounds that here the Metropolitan Police could at least keep an eye on them and they would not be in the way of the traffic. Oslo had just advised that they would have their senior spokesman at the rally and he would hold a press conference after it was over. This was to be Oslo's first live statement, and already at four in the morning, camera crews were laying out cables for their outside broadcast units, to the left of the hastily erected scaffolding stage. This was no longer just Oslo's press influence at work. It was the news story of the year, and accredited journalists from all over Europe were scurrying to get to London in time for the event. The morning editions were carrying the Russians' statement that they had shot down the Tarbaby and the Americans had denied it even existed, saying they were at the forefront of aerospace design and while hypersonic travel was possible it was yet to be tried.

The Trades Union Congress was meeting that day to answer a call for a general strike from the Labour Party, who saw political mileage in the hammering the Conservatives were taking every minute. Oslo were not going to turn away any help they could get, but the morning editions had already printed their own ridicule of the Labour Party for their almost too hasty jump on the anti-nuclear bandwagon, saying the party leader was thanking his lucky stars he wasn't in power and taking the brunt of Britain's new sentiments on the issue.

The Prime Minister was on her way back from Chequers, her country retreat, with the Chancellor of the Exchequer, who was a long-time confidant, and her heir apparent, the Foreign Secretary. All three had their dispatch boxes and the two men took turns to brief her in the stretch Bentley as it powered its way through the pre-dawn darkness.

The Politburo meeting had been going all night, Ustinoff with seemingly endless energy attacking and counter-attacking the conservatives led by Kraskin. Three times Chekhov had broken to eat, his diabetes ever present, and at one stage he had taken a call from the American ambassador on behalf of President Sheridan. Sivlat and Bushirov, the two members who owed Ustinoff their support, gave it early, but Peter Gordin, the manufacturing clan leader, waited till Chernyavin had committed himself before he himself lent his backing to Ustinoff. Now there were five of the eleven in favour. Everything rested on the last man, Smetlov, the extreme right-wing Minister of the Interior, and Chekhov himself. If both of them came in, then Ustinoff's 'I will if you will'-type offer to the Americans, British and French could be made without reference to the Duma, but presented rather as a coup, a gift for the nation and the world. Ustinoff watched the leader of the Nationalists carefully. This debate and discussion could go on for hours yet. All rested on Smetlov. He was as uncomplicated a man as had ever held the post, but that meant nothing. He was still a formidable adversary and if he sided with Kraskin events would get bloody, literally.

Ustinoff's one hope lay in the inherent dislike and distrust the pair held for each other. If I were Smetlov, he thought, what would I do? We know that all too often the GRU had run unaccountable to any but their own. They were arrogant and unpopular, with their rigid, uncompromising style of intelligence gathering, but more to the point it was a powerful machine not answerable directly to the state. Smetlov hated that. Ustinoff knew the one consistent fear that Smetlov held was that the Red Army, conservative in the extreme and essential in his vision of a strong Russia, would atrophy under weak leadership and budget cuts. They must be strong, but they must report to the state.

Smetlov was once head of the FSB. As head of the

security service it was his job to protect state security both internally and externally unless armed conflict arose, and he would do the job as best he could. If I were Smetlov that would mean clipping the wings of the GRU. Then best get it done now. Come on, Smetlov, you fascist Nazi pig, he willed, do the right thing for Russia and for the world.

Sitting next to Smetlov at the table was the Estonian. A hard old-school type, it was he who had dropped his eyes when Ustinoff had mentioned the agriculture programme. He had spent all his life in the Party and was wily and experienced, and Ustinoff knew he would not lend his support willingly to anything that would undermine their own power base. He had stood and clapped when the Red Army had rolled into Afghanistan.

Time, thought Ustinoff, to start playing dirty poker. He signalled to Chernyavin to join him at the table against the wall where the heavy ornate coffee-pots stood on almost priceless antique burners liberated from Berlin, having in turn been liberated from Paris.

Ustinoff poured himself a cup and waited for the old man to shuffle across. Kraskin watched from under hooded eyes as one of his faction argued with Peter Gordin about mutual deterrence.

'What is it you couldn't say over the table, Ustinoff? Wanting to change horse mid-stream?' Chernyavin said smugly.

Ustinoff looked at him, the deep bags under his eyes and the broken veins in his nose the legacy of a lifetime of vodka and over-indulgence.

'No, but you are.'

The old man chuckled. It was a flat, mirthless sound like bones rattling. 'You have shot your bolt. Admit it!' his old hand shook slightly as he held his cup under the jug that Ustinoff held for him.

'I think not. You will lend my plan your support immediately or things in your life will change,' Ustinoff said conversationally.

'Oh?' again the bones rattling.

'Yes. Or the pictures I have of you entertaining your nephew and his friend will be all over the streets tomorrow.'

Ustinoff had been given the photographs by Stravinsky as ammunition and had been appalled. The eight by ten colour prints showed the old man's wrinkled, liver-spotted body receiving the ministrations of two known male prostitutes, both of them very young indeed.

'We both know how Chekhov feels about this kind of thing. You would be out tomorrow. Disgraced.'

'You wouldn't dare,' Chernyavin began, the shaking hand worse than ever, the blood rising in his face. As head of the agro clan he was a powerful man and no one had spoken to him like this for twenty years.

Ustinoff leaned close, very close, his voice almost a whisper. 'The Americans have a saying, you disgusting old pervert. Loosely translated it says, "Don't fuck with a man on his way up". That's me! Support me or I'll crush you like an insect.' He turned and walked back to his seat as Chekhov re-entered the room.

Novosibirsk

The software writers had been working all night on the bug in Igor's program. The one woman, who had spent fifteen hours on the problem, wanted to give in and wait for the new tapes to arrive from Moscow.

'No! I forbid it,' the colonel snarled. 'Keep going. What is written can be unwritten. I know that much about computers.'

'Colonel. Whoever rewrote this software had access to the passwords. That makes them a Grade Seven and there are only a dozen in all Russia. If I am lucky and work very hard for another three years I might make a seven. These people are clever and I am tired. There is only one place

397

that could hack into this in the next hour and it's not here . . .' she replied

'Where?' the colonel asked hopefully

'Where I studied,' she said. 'MIT.'

'What's that?'

'It's in America,' she told him, tired of it all.

'Don't be insolent,' he snapped. 'Now get on with it.'

She did and twenty minutes later she began to find a pattern on the screen. Working calculations on her own personal computer, she began to input sequences and slowly but surely the solutions began to offer hope. Oh boy, she thought, I'm in. This is it, I've got past the loop. It was a time bomb activated by the operational status. She keyed in her routine access code, expecting the screen to give her the operator menu. Instead it danced symbols for a second and settled into a message on the screen.

> IGOR HAD A LITTLE LAMB,
> ITS SCREEN WAS WHITE AS SNOW
> AND EVERYWHERE THAT IGOR WENT
> GULAG WAS SURE TO KNOW.
> YOU THOUGHT YOU WERE IN DIDN'T YOU?
> SORRY. BETTER LUCK NEXT TIME
> NOW BACK TO OUR LOOP!

The woman watched the screen, reading the English quickly, and in three seconds it dissolved back into the logic loop that had stymied its multi-megabyte capacity for the last eighteen hours.

She put her hands to her face, the tiredness and frustration welling up and she began to cry.

Carson tapped out the new altitude requirement into the flight management system and settled back. Once again the computers would fly the hypersonic over the target sequence. They were hard on 160,000 feet, the scram jets burning only with the help of the oxygen supplement and the retuning that Tavis had completed in record time.

'First target in twenty-two seconds,' Digby said. 'Overhead Kuybyshev now.'

'Okay,' Carson replied, activating the automatic laser. 'Let's dance.'

His eyes scanned the all-round radar every few seconds now. He was not going to be caught napping again. He could see the contacts on the screen as the interceptors again lifted off, and he knew that Natalia was watching Omsk where the MiG-25 Ds were based. Down on the ground he knew that his minute radar trace was being ignored and they would be concentrating instead on the bright hot trace of his flare. With the Tarbaby nudging Mach 10 the scram jets would produce a hot spearhead of burning exhausts two thousand metres out behind her track. This was also her effective height limit for the x-ray laser, which dissipated badly in the atmosphere.

'Half an hour overhead the target zone should see us through,' he said, 'then we'll need to head back and refuel.'

Falkenburg, Sweden

Lars Eriksen stood in the Saturday morning quiet of the crew room and pulled the flight overalls over his long lean frame. Beside him his engineer, a smaller, darker, heavier man, did the same.

'Come, Gustav,' Lars said consolingly, 'we have discussed this a dozen times in the last few days and we both agreed it was on.'

'Lars, it's our careers we are talking about here,' the smaller man said. 'Not just in the shit. We are talking general courts martial.'

'Would you feel better if I order you?' Lars said seriously.

'No . . . yes . . . I don't fucking know, do I?'

'Consider yourself ordered,' Lars said, pulling up his zip. 'Let's go.'

They took the long maintenance passage down the back

of the hangars. At weekends it was normally deserted.

'I have filed for two hours thread the needle,' he said to Gustav.

'Oh great. Now we have filed false flight plans,' Gustav said miserably.

The two men had flown together for four years and the only reason Lars Eriksen had cajoled his engineer into the crime was that he couldn't do it alone. This was a two-man job. Gustav knew that and in spite of his complaints he didn't really mind. He would have followed Lars Eriksen to hell if necessary. Four minutes later they were airborne.

The aircraft they were in was a multi-engined Lockheed L-1011 with a standard Marshalls conversion for mid-air refuelling and she was heavily loaded with over 100,000 pounds of Jet A fuel. It was not an ideal fuel mix for the Tarbaby, but it would keep her airborne anywhere under 120,000 feet, and considering that beggars can't be choosers and that the entire aircraft and its fuel load had just been stolen from the Swedish Air Force, Lars Eriksen, a new Oslo recruit, thought they had done very well.

They had been airborne less than a hour when someone at the base wondered who they were playing thread the needle with, since there were no over-water fighter sorties logged that morning, and contacted the base commander.

Novosibirsk

The Officer Commanding the Zone was a full Marshal of the Red Army. His rank had been confirmed three years before and there were only two others who were more senior in the entire Red Army's complex command structure. For that reason there were few men he feared in Russia, but he had not risen to his present rank for nothing. He was an achiever in the system and in his thirty-four years' service he had never failed to deliver the goods or complete an assignment on time.

He was also a fighting soldier, frustrated with his current command, and missed the hiss, static and excitement of commanding a battle. The last time had been hunched over his maps, his aides around him, cold and tired on an Afghan hillside. That was his only regret, that he had never been allowed to confront the enemy as it should have been done. He had learned to respect the mujahedin, and finally understood the futility of fighting an irregular war with regular troops; he understood the way the Americans had felt in Vietnam. When his promotion came through he had handed the Afghanistan area over to a junior colleague and travelled to his new command. The Zone. There were only four big jobs in the army: the West, where NATO lay scant miles away, the East, where constant Chinese probes over disputed territory gave a shooting war every few months, the Ukraine, where the Red Army based itself in peacetime, and the Zone.

Today another regret to add to his list. He watched with hooded brown eyes as his intelligence staff reported back to him on the condition of his command.

'We estimate, Marshal Rostov, that we have as little as four per cent of our nuclear strike capacity left. The hypersonic is overhead again this morning finishing it off. Any minute now we won't have a capability at all.'

'Have they missed anything?' he asked acidly.

'Not so far. Near as our scientific people can establish, the speed of the individual strikes means it's all computer controlled.'

'Is he still above our range?' Rostov asked

'Yes, marshal,' the senior officer replied.

'How much longer? Do we know?'

'No, sir, we are not sure. At this rate he will have hit all six repeater stations and all the ground-level silo electronics in the next ten minutes. What else can he add to his target list? He's already hit the railheads at Petropavlosk and Sverdlovsk. That's the SS-18 maintenance depots . . .'

'I know,' Rostov snapped. He stood and walked the

room, his polished boots squeaking on the linoleum floor.

'We take the battle to him.' He turned and smiled at the gathering of men. 'When he lands we will hit him. I don't care where it is.'

'Sir . . . can we do that? It may mean war if it's a NATO country. Certain problems may be . . .' The speaker was a full general.

'My command is no longer. I didn't like it, but it was mine,' he replied acidly. 'I won't have some bunch of *hippies*' – he used the western word – 'attacking my backyard and getting away with it!' No one spoke, the room hushed with tension.

'Get Admiral Kibinski on the line. Let's see what we can do to follow this . . . this *thing* back to wherever it comes from. And get me a line to Kraskin.' Time to be a bit more obvious. Screen the other previous orders.

Rostov had always wanted to disturb a full meeting of the Council of Ministers.

'That's it,' Digby said cheerfully. 'Sequence completion.'

He keyed into the computer as Carson gratefully took the stubby control column in his right hand and eased it over for a long gentle turn to the north and home.

'Bright Eyes, Bright Eyes, this is Tarbaby.'

'Tarbaby, Bright Eyes,' Gail's voice clear over the high cold air and into Carson's headset.

'What's my situation? We're coming in.'

'Negative to that, Tarbaby. We have company here. Standby for an alternate, over.'

Digby looked across at him, the elation at the successful completion draining from his face.

'The *Bunker Hill* . . . she's there,' he thought aloud, looking at Carson.

'Yeah, looks like it,' the New Zealander replied.

'What now?'

'We see if we like the alternate.'

'If not?' Digby asked. Carson didn't reply, so he repeated the question. 'If not?'

'We see how she floats with a few square metres of her hull missing.'

USS Bunker Hill

Captain Hendricks stood on his bridge, knees bent against the swell as it rolled under the *Bunker Hill's* high sharp prow.

Ahead in the dawn of a cold overcast day the two brave little Icelandic fisheries vessels coursed back and forth ahead of the area the American warship patrolled, harassing her each time she hove to.

Their first encounter had been almost comical. The tiny boat bobbing on the rollers like a cork, and the bearded captain, for all the world an image of his Viking ancestors, standing on the wing drenched in the wind-driven spray coming alongside the Goliath of the missile cruiser, a megaphone held to his lips. He had barked his statement across the foamy water between the two surging ships, the extended middle finger of his right hand unmistakable in case the Americans misinterpreted his instruction to leave Icelandic territorial waters forthwith.

Hendricks had instructed the officers of the watch to avoid any collision with the aggressive little patrol boats but maintain station, and now he stood in the funereal gloom at the rear of the bridge to await the outcome of the day, whatever it might be.

He was a worried man. His meeting with the crew representatives in the mess hadn't defused anything. If anything it had simply illustrated the extent of his problem. He had a crew that didn't want this involvement, that didn't want this fight. In all his years with the Navy he had never ever seen a ship's company that had been anything but eager for action, trusting the system to be right, to be noble and to be honourable. Somewhere that trust had been shattered, maybe here tonight when asked to engage a concept they in their all-American wholesomeness believed good and correct.

For the first time in his career he doubted his ability to command effectively, and he felt like a priest who has lost his faith. Now here in Skjalfandi, four miles off the Icelandic mainland with the arms of the bay around him, he had a decision to make.

If he gave the order to launch missiles at the hypersonic and his men refused to carry out the order, he would be technically correct but nevertheless guilty of gross mismanagement of the situation. With conventional weapons systems he could perhaps rely on a few stalwarts like the chief and his senior officers to actually operate the systems, but not with Aegis. It needed a full complement of highly trained experts to be effective. He accepted a steaming cup of coffee from a rating with a nodded thanks and when the man didn't walk away he looked round at him. It was a grizzled veteran sailor, the oldest man aboard and a real character. He had been made up to non-commissioned rank no fewer than seven times in his chequered career and each time his fondness for the bottle had assured his demotion.

'You have something to say, Eddie?' Hendricks said softly, not wanting to attract the attention of the watch.

'Pardon me, cap'n, but they don't mean it, cap'n,' he said.

'Mean what, Eddie?' he said into his cup as he lifted it to his lips.

'No offence, sir. They mean no offence.'

'Why are you telling me this?'

'So you don't get upset, sir . . . when they go deaf on you.'

The old sailor saluted and walked away across the rolling bridge, leaving Hendricks alone in the gloom.

That's it then, he thought. They have decided. If I give

the order then I will have a mutiny. A mutiny on an American ship. Sweet Jesus.

He put the cup on the gimballed shelf attached to the arm of the high battle chair, itself a traditional relic of the days when captains ran their ships into action from the bridge instead of the muted haze of the operations room, and walked back to his day cabin.

He ran his hands through his hair and began to compose the most important signal of his career – probably his last, he mused. Below him fore and aft the surface-to-air missiles that were the heart of his anti-aircraft firepower stood sleek but impotent in their launchers.

'Tarbaby, Tarbaby, this is Bright Eyes.'

'Go,' Carson replied. He was getting impatient with the waiting, his fuel reserves settling by the minute as the scram jets blasted them through the uncertain sky. Already he had let down to below 100,000 feet to conserve his oxygen supplement.

'Come round on to two five two. Intercept with a tanker overhead the following position.' She read the co-ordinates aloud twice and as Digby tapped them into the inertial navigation system Carson did some quick geography in his head.

'Bear Island,' he muttered, then tapped the mike button.

'Roger that, Bright Eyes. What then? I could try an over-land approach if the locals wouldn't mind.'

'Negative, Tarbaby, have a new mission. Awaiting the details now.'

'What am I looking for at the Romeo Victor?'

'A Swedish Air Force Tristar, over.'

Carson looked across at Digby, grinning. 'They on our side?' he asked.

'Negative, Tarbaby,' Gail replied clearly. Carson could hear the smile in her voice.

'You mean someone nicked it?' he asked.

405

'Affirmative.'

The audacity appealed to the buccaneer in him and he laughed delightedly.

Washington

Sheridan glared at the men around the room. They did not represent the cream of his aides and advisers, but if nothing else they could all be trusted to keep their mouths shut. Kramer was not included in the group.

'Is this the best advice you can muster? I could have thought of all this myself! I want a press conference in a few hours and I want to say something sensible.'

'With all due respect, Mr President,' one of them said, 'that's all you have done. Kept this to yourself.'

'I hardly call the beginnings of what looks like a general strike private,' he answered.

'No, but your meetings with President Chekhov were,' the man countered.

Sheridan's eyes narrowed and those that knew him recognized the sign.

'Listen, mister, I don't pay you what I pay you for this! You either contribute or get the hell out of my office,' he growled.

'Sorry,' the man said contritely.

'Accepted,' Sheridan replied, his anger dissipating as quickly as it had risen. 'Now what's the situation at this time?'

'Air traffic have just gone out, teamsters and metal workers, as you know, yesterday. New York City garbage men, and a few others have joined in. The big unions like the Electrical Workers vote today. Kansas, New York, Detroit and Chicago want to call out the National Guard to assist police with their peace rallies.'

Someone at the table guffawed at the term and the speaker looked up at him. 'That's what they are calling them, here's the report at this time. Oh, by the way, the switchboard here has broken all the records. Thirty thousand calls overnight.'

'Jesus Christ,' someone said.

'How seriously do we take their threat of this Phase Two?' another asked.

'Very,' Sheridan answered. 'They have actually done it in Russia.'

The Security Council man looked up from his notes. He wore a pair of tortoiseshell spectacles and an expression of studied arrogance. 'This is a golden opportunity,' he said softly, watching the expressions of the others round the room. Two or three of them looked at him, their faces saying they had thought of it too.

'Bullshit,' Sheridan replied. 'They still have their SS-20s pointed at Europe, and the biggest conventional army ever massed. You haven't grasped this, have you? That hypersonic has just made intercontinental missiles obsolete, they would be shot down before they got there. Besides, if you really think we should start a war with Russia because she was unfortunate enough to catch the brunt of this Oslo campaign before us, then you are stupid.' He paused to allow his feeling on the issue to penetrate. 'We are here to discuss their Phase Two. This Angel Seven is in a position to make an assault on the American economy that we would never recover from. We would be a third world nation overnight.'

He stopped again to refer to notes.

'Support is growing at international level. The New Zealanders are expected to support out in the open. Iceland already has, our people there are restricted to base, and so far the dollar has fallen twenty-seven cents against the Deutschmark and the yen. That is a result of systematic dumping by the Japanese central banks overnight.'

'Christ, it could be another thirty cents by tonight if everyone jumps on the wagon,' someone muttered.

'Angel Seven rings a bell for some reason,' Tortoiseshell said. Sheridan smiled grimly.

'I looked it up. The Bible, Book of Revelations. The destroyers of the earth ... I never saw myself as that.'

Edinburgh

Princes Street was bright with colour, bunting and flags suspended from lamp-posts, and people had already gathered to watch the parade. The procession was gathering at the bottom end of the street, the organizers marshalling the groups into order and finishing the last-minute details.

McKay stood and watched his massed pipe bandsmen as they fiddled with their kit, tightened straps, adjusted the hang of kilts and sporrans, the pipers warming up to the dry rattle of the side-drums.

He wondered if this would be a record size for a civilian band. By his count there would be 326 members marching this morning. He looked at his watch, then at the organizers who were scurrying around wearing orange plastic tabards like the men repairing the motorway.

They couldn't organize a bloody riot, he thought. He was still unhappy about the previous evening's events. His family had never been divided on an issue like this and it was unsettling. He had never before questioned the wisdom of nuclear weapons, leaving that to other men in London, but now he felt he had to and today of all days.

He looked at his watch again and realized that if he didn't get his men together now the wheels were going to fall off the procession.

He took the heavy silver baton from its case, adjusted his traditional bearskin, and walked to a spot in the centre of the car park, his pace measured, hefting the baton.

He stood for a second, his own bandsmen watching him fondly, put his whistle to his lips and blew a piercing blast that cut through the noise and chatter of the thousand-odd people milling round the area, lowered the base of the baton to the ground at forty-five degrees and stood at ease facing the crowd to watch his band fall in. They would be seven men abreast and forty-six rows long with two boy pipers at the rear, boys who would proudly remember this day for the rest of their lives.

Family members clapped politely as they formed up, calling encouragement, and the usual group of pipe-band fans stood and watched, small children pointing gleefully at a bass drummer as he twirled his stubby heavy drumsticks over and under his hands.

McKay walked the rows, gently moving men here and there. Finally satisfied, he nodded at them and walked to the organizers.

'My band is ready,' he said. 'If yon Provost gets a move on then we can march before my laddies want to go home.'

'Yes, of course,' the man replied, wondering what was eating the normally gentle-mannered McKay.

Half a mile up Princes Street in the park below the high battlements of Edinburgh Castle 12,000 people had gathered and more were arriving every minute. Scaffolding stage work had been erected overnight and ice-cream vendors plied their trade in the crowd as the first speakers began to address the issue, between the rock bands and musicians. Princes Street was unusually quiet for the parade, with most of the people who would normally have gathered on the pavements now in the park, beneath the CND and Oslo banners, basking in a warm September morning.

'That's her, with a bit of luck.' Carson pointed to the strong contact on the radar F&B screen. He quickly confirmed the tanker's position and radio frequency with Gail at Omega control and eased back the power settings. Below them the sea was slate grey through the broken, scudding clouds, and the Tarbaby began to wallow through the thick cold air as she eased down towards the 36,000-foot flight level of the tanker.

'Rainbow Warrior, Rainbow Warrior, this is Angel Seven.' He smiled at the use of the illustrious name and didn't think its real owners would mind at all.

'Angel this is Rainbow, I think you must be thirsty, *ja*?' The voice was confident and humorous. In the cockpit of the Tristar Lars Eriksen grinned and raised a thumb to his engineer behind him.

'Roger, Rainbow. What speed? The more the better,' Carson came back.

'Angel, can give you six hundred knots, holding one eight zero degrees at level three five.' Carson was delighted with that: it meant he could keep his scram jets running during the operation. He felt very vulnerable at this level and scanned the radar screens constantly.

'Rainbow, will be with you in one minute, over. How much can you give me?'

'Lots, Angel. Figures one zero zero zero zero zero pounds, over.'

'Nice one, Rainbow!' Jesus, thought Carson. Almost a full load. 'Reel it out. I have onboard pumps. You blow and I'll suck.'

He heard the other pilot laugh.

'And to think I hardly know you, Angel.'

Fifty seconds later he eased the needle nose of the Tarbaby up and under the broad tail section of the Tristar and watched the fuel management panel light up as his coupling dropped from the nose seven feet back from the tip below and forward of his left-hand window.

It took three attempts to achieve the mating of his male section and the trailing cone-shaped tip of the feeder hose, but in seconds he was talking direct to the engineer on the tanker.

'I have a green on my pumps, Rainbow,' he said.

'Roger, Angel, max flow rate coming up in three, two, one, now.'

Carson's hand dropped to the computer trim and activated the system. As the fuel weight increased, so the computer would alter the trim of the aircraft to keep her straight and level.

It took twenty-eight minutes to transfer the load, Gustav the engineer unable to believe the power of the Tarbaby's pumps, and it was just as they were about to uncouple the link that Gail came through on her channel.

'Tarbaby, Tarbaby, Bright Eyes.'

'Go.'

'You have company. Lifted off from Murmansk and heading your way.'

'How long, Bright Eyes?'

'They have been airborne forty minutes. They have just Romeo Victored with what we think is an Ilyushsin tanker out of Kirovsk. This is not a routine patrol. They will intercept with Rainbow in half an hour at this rate.'

Bastards want to follow me home or splash my tanker, he thought. No bloody way.

'Tarbaby, come round on to one seven one. Instructions follow,' she said.

'Negative, Bright Eyes. Let's see Rainbow safely home first.'

Five minutes later, Sagan angry and Gail caught in the middle, the Tarbaby was sitting at 90,000 feet, way above the tanker as she headed for home base and, Lars thought, a general court martial. What Lars and Gustav didn't know was that Oslo in Sweden had just thrown their not inconsiderable resources into preventing that, but right now they had other worries. The four Sukois had just appeared on Carson's radar and there was no mistaking their objective. As the tanker gently turned east for home the fighters swung menacingly south-east.

Carson eased the throttles forward and chose his intercept spot some two hundred miles ahead of the tanker as she lumbered home.

Only a couple of minutes later he knew his infra-red trace had been tracked because the four Sukois suddenly turned northwards for home. They were bugging out. He now knew the Russians had accepted they couldn't get to him, not with conventional weapons. But they would wait and attack his support systems. That was certain.

'Rainbow, you are clear for home. If you can manage to help again I'll meet you closer to home.'

'Appreciate that, Angel, but I think we will be in jail. Stick it in for all of us. We will be thinking of you,' Lars answered seriously.

'Thank you for your help, Rainbow.'

'You are welcome, Angel. Good luck and good day.'

London

It was twenty past ten in the morning and already there were 200,000 people jammed into Hyde Park and scattered through the surrounding streets, with more arriving every minute.

The Japanese hunger strikers sat in a small roped-off area alongside their Shinto funeral pyre, reading, praying and handing leaflets to the people who crowded the edge of their little patch of grass. Alongside them a group of hard-core CND campaigners dressed in skeleton suits and horrific masks carried out the death watch with a large hourglass representing the world's time running out. An active Geiger counter buzzed ominously whenever held near the ancestral ashes in the urns.

On the stage an Irish rock band played traditional music while they waited for things to begin, and police in their hundreds patrolled the largely peaceful crowd. They made several early arrests, mostly of a group purporting to be members of the British Nazi Party. They had been catcalling and shouting anti-communist remarks at all who passed them, and waving a banner that said NUKE EM. The police thought it best to remove them from the area altogether.

Television camera crews huddled on to scaffolding towers and ITV had a cherry-picker hoist arrangement that they used to begin their transmission with crowd shots.

At ten-thirty the band fell silent and the Oslo public relations machine kicked into high gear.

On to the stage walked a man who was a household name in the music world. He was an outrageous, flamboyant individual who was a master showman. He wore a tight white catsuit, his black hair slicked back, and as he walked on the band struck up the opening bars of one of his gold selling songs.

He waved at the massive crowd.

'NICE DAY FOR IT,' he shouted

The crowd roared back at him.

'WANT ANY MORE?' he asked, holding the mike towards them.

'Y-E-S' they screamed back.

'THEN STICK AROUND AND LET'S DO IT FOR THE WORLD!'

'Y-A-A-a-a-a-' The crowd rolled and moved for him, the band began again and the maestro strutting across the stage began to sing.

Five minutes later they would have torn down Whitehall if he had asked, and he stopped dead, mid-bar in his second song.

'But we aren't here to hear me sing. There's better men than me, so will you do something for me?' he asked the by now quarter-million-strong crowd.

'Y-A-A-a-a,' they roared back, swaying still to the rhythm.

'Listen to THE MAN, and do what he asks. DO IT FOR THE WORLD. Remember we only have one. ONLY ONE WORLD,' he screamed at them as they moved and jumped excitedly. 'HOW MANY WORLDS?'

'W-U-N . . . W-O-R-L-D' they roared.

'ONE CHANCE,' he called and they screamed it back at him.

'ONE OSLO!' Again it came flooding back like an echo, the cherry-picker sweeping low over their heads, the cameras rolling live to most of western Europe.

'PLEASE WELCOME DOCTOR MERAN!'

The applause, whistling, clapping and cheering was thunderous and from stage left the crowd saw an old man enter the hotpotch of cables, instruments and cameras. He was bent slightly over his stick and wore an old tweed jacket, and as he approached the microphones he coughed genteelly into his closed fist.

Finally he stood and looked them in the faces, his eyes piercing, and when he spoke his voice was strong.

'Thank you, young man,' he said, looking off-stage at the entertainer, his voice carrying over the speakers to the world. He said it like an old Oxford don to a student who has just helped in some minor chore, and the crowd with their British taste in understatement loved it.

He began without notes or rehearsal, speaking from the heart, and they knew it and listened. He did however keep half an ear cocked to his rear for his ten-second cue.

Edinburgh

The Lord Provost as was customary led the procession, behind him the ranks of baillies and other city notables followed by three floats.

Stuart McKay was pleased that they had stuck to the agreed pace, for it was difficult for a band to march at half speed. It should be either a full march or a slow march. Out behind him his band waited for his signal: as they turned left into Princes Street he raised the baton high above his head, and knowing that not everyone could see the signal again blew the whistle, dropping the baton at the same time.

The sheer volume was nothing short of staggering: six bass drums, sixty side-drums and 260 sets of bagpipes breaking into a quick march were enough to give him goose bumps. He set the pace, the baton swinging as the massed band finished its crocodile turn on to the parade route, his ancient Celtic blood rising to the call of the pipes.

414

Up ahead he could see the high walls of the castle and the banners that were strung over the old grey stones, and he thought about his wife and daughters there in the park.

He loved them dearly and yet they felt strongly enough about the disarmament issue that they were now in the park and not on the street to see the band march by. My God, he thought, was this such an issue, to break up a family? He began to think about where his priorities lay and almost absent-mindedly led the band into the next tune, thinking about his wife, the woman who had shared his bed and borne his children, the woman who had wept at his side when their wee baby boy had died in the winter of '62, and been with him when the girls had been sick, and there with him proud when they had received their scholarships to the university.

The park was near now, the trees and flowerbeds beginning on his right, and he had several thoughts simultaneously. He thought the parade was a non-event because most of the city's people were in the park, he thought how the park in spite of all the thousands of people lacked something inherently Scots, and he thought it was about time to stand beside his wife again. He glanced up at the high stage against the castle walls trying – stupidly, he thought – to see them in the crowd and then he made a decision.

He raised the baton high above his head and blew the whistle, counted to three to be sure the band was watching and dropped the baton to the right, holding it at ninety degrees to the road surface. Reckoning that the band was seven men wide, which would leave enough room, he led the 326-strong Edinburgh and Districts Massed Pipes and Drums down the wide steps into Princes Street Gardens.

The crowd began to part, cheering and clapping, some dancing, and behind him McKay could hear individuals in the band laughing round their mouthpieces, obviously delighted with the change of route either because all pipers

415

love an audience or because they were sympathizers with the cause.

On the stage a man with a microphone boomed a welcome at them over the cheering and shouting, calling for the crowd to make room.

Suddenly Stuart McKay found himself at the foot of the stage and raising the baton he brought the band to a halt, wondering what to do next. He was saved the embarrassment as his band finished the tune by the faint wail of pipes on the battlements above them and, identifying the strains of 'Scotland the Brave', he looked up. There, a hundred feet up the wall, was a long-haired young man in jeans and an old grey jumper, his pipes under his arm proudly marching to his own tune. McKay raised the baton, blew the whistle and allowed the massed band to ease its way into the lone piper's windblown skirl, the crowd roaring its approval, and McKay looking to the left for some reason saw his wife and daughters standing proudly watching his band. There was a tear in her eye.

The Lord Provost was not amused, but he was politically astute, and as soon as word arrived of the missing band he turned the procession and headed for the park, reflecting that Britain was still a democracy and if he wanted to be in office this time next year he better bloody well get himself down to the park where the bulk of his electorate was gathered. The poet who was due to get the keys to the city would have to wait.

London

Meran paused briefly as someone handed him a note. He had been speaking for twenty minutes, hard-hitting, precise reports on the state of the nuclear arms race. One reporter whispered 'Gutsy stuff' to himself as Meran looked up.

He waved the note, a broad smile on his face.

'The government of New Zealand has joined us!' he

416

called. 'They have offered all assistance and safe refuge if we fail . . . thanks but we don't intend to fail!!' His voice boomed out over the park, and the crowd cheered their support. Behind him he heard his cue and he stood tall.

'I have told you of the Omega project. The peace umbrella. The Russians say they shot her down! The Americans say she doesn't exist! Do you want proof?' He paused, then said it again. 'DO YOU WANT PROOF?'

The crowd sensed that something sensational was about to happen and answered, 'Y-E-E-S!' It was a long-drawn-out moan from a quarter of a million throats.

'SO BE IT,' he answered.

The crowd fell silent as if by command and followed Meran's eyes upward. The silence was total and then over the soft rustle of the wind in the trees and the distant traffic noise they heard it. A dry, crackling noise like sheet lightning, building, rumbling into a full ear-splitting tearing sound across the skies. The ground seemed to be reverberating beneath their feet and finally the Tarbaby broke through the cloud, her sleek blackness a blue-orange-flamed blur against the grey scudding cloud, even those watching closely not seeing the spectacular four-point roll executed at Mach 2 one thousand feet above central London.

'WE ARE STRONG . . . WE ARE ALIVE!' Meran shouted over the thundering echo. 'BUT WE NEED YOUR HELP FOR A SAFER WORLD . . . WILL YOU HELP US?'

There was only one answer to that and he got it.

The Tarbaby did one last display that day in Europe, one that delighted Carson more than the London low pass. He called West Drayton radar and advised of his intent regardless to do the two passes, and they reluctantly cleared him an airway. His next destination was a short way to the south, where the Farnborough Air Show was taking place. Traditionally Farnborough is the place to show off whatever is new in aviation, probably the most famous air show of its type anywhere in the world. Carson took the Tarbaby on a low slow pass over the airfield, then returned and ignited the scram jets overhead for his finale. The knowledgeable crowd was informed of the display five minutes before by the commentator after a call from Oslo taken in the tower. Now there was no doubt that the Omega project was alive and well, in spite of what the Russians and Americans had said.

As the Tarbaby turned towards America, in Hyde Park Meran drew things to a climax. 'When you leave here, get your friends and your families, get the people who live on your street, who you work with. Bring them to Westminster. We will stay there until the government agrees! There are eleven million people in London. Let's get them to stand up and be counted. Those of you in Paris, Stockholm, Madrid, Rome, Brussels, Bonn who are watching this, join us. We only have one world. Please God, let's not lose this opportunity to ensure it's here for our children. THIS IS OUR LAST CHANCE.'

Six minutes later as the first of the thousands began to march towards Westminster, Alexander Meran seemed to stagger, then he collapsed on to the wet muddy grass by the stage.

18

Stockholm

Amongst the thousands of individual efforts two other events of major significance took place that day. Lars Eriksen and Gustav his engineer arrived back at their base in Sweden and were placed under house arrest for the unauthorized use of the aircraft and the theft of the fuel load, pending an inquiry. Although the perimeter fence was jammed with Oslo supporters and activists, the major response was outside the Prime Minister's office. There thousands had gathered to ensure that Oslo's efforts weren't forgotten in largely neutral Sweden, throwing pressure on to the government. It didn't take long. Sweden's most famous Prime Minister had been Olof Palme, a statesman much respected for his solid views on the arms race. He was still revered, his assassination still fresh in the minds of his people. The emergency cabinet meeting had been in session since the air force had advised them of the unauthorized mission of the tanker and the ensuing Soviet protests that had been flooding in for the last hour.

In a move that surprised even Oslo, the Prime Minister announced that while the mission may have appeared unauthorized it was in fact retroactively approved, and furthermore a second mission would be flown if they felt it in the interests of Sweden. The second mission would also have a squadron of Saab Viggens as an escort and the Swedish government reserved the right to carry out mid-air refuelling exercises over international waters wherever and whenever it liked.

One Reuters journalist phoned his office in Paris with the following excited statement.

'The Swedes are in with Oslo. They have just told the Russians to get stuffed after a mid-air refuelling incident over the Arctic Ocean. Get this! They refuelled the hypersonic! And they have said they will do it again if necessary in the interests of world peace.'

Lars Eriksen, as officer commanding the mission, received a severe reprimand behind closed doors, and was then told to go and reload his tanker, fly it to Reykjavik and await instructions. The delirious crowd at the fences had broken through the wire and, shoving flowers down the guards' gun barrels, crossed to the pan and sprayed a huge bright pink peace symbol on the tanker's side, before being chased away by confused guard reinforcements.

At two that afternoon Eriksen, Gustav and a second pilot taxied past the crowds waving to them, gloved thumbs up in the windows, and took off fully loaded with Jet A for Reykjavik where Oslo would meet them and mix the additives.

Rome

With the governments of Sweden, Iceland and New Zealand having announced their support openly, and the far more damaging economic support from Japan, there were many large groups as yet uncommitted to the fray, either for or against.

In the Vatican Cardinal Juan de Cueva waited nervously for his audience. In all his years serving the Church he had never challenged its leader, but now he knew that time had come. Twenty minutes later he was lifted from bended knee by the man himself, his old, worn, comfortably creased face open with a welcoming smile.

'Holiness, forgive me, for I come not with the state of your flock in Brazil in my heart . . . but for the world,' he began.

'Ah, Juan, my son . . . are you here for this Oslo group?'
De Cueva nodded.

'I wondered who it would be,' the pontiff said, smiling.

'You knew, Holy Father? That one of us was with them?'

'I would be surprised, Juan, if it is only one of you.
Come, sit.' The old man indicated a hard-backed chair
against the windows in the warm afternoon sunshine, 'and
tell me what is happening out there. But first, you are the
official Oslo representative?'

'Yes, Holy Father, why?' Cardinal de Cueva asked.

'Because, my son, Mankiewicz and Cortisa have already
been in here in . . . how shall we say . . . an unofficial
capacity.'

De Cueva said a quick prayer of thanks for the cardinals
of Spain and Poland.

New York

From the CBS news helicopter Central Park was one heaving mass of humanity. City officials put the numbers somewhere over one and half million. A touring rock band had
put their sound systems and technicians at the disposal of
the rally organizers and a team of engineers from a Japanese electronics corporation were fine-tuning the huge
screens that would carry live pictures not only of the
speakers, but of the rallies in London and news coverage
of the Moscow protests outside the Kremlin and the US
embassy. There were similar arrangements going on over
on the West Coast for rallies in San Francisco and Los
Angeles. The Los Angeles effort was being hyped as a glittering showbiz event with celebrities arriving in limousines
and spotlights in the sky. Oslo had pulled every string
they could this day and now it hinged on the American
people.

The evening papers had screamed the headlines
RUSSIA DISARMED and NO RED ICBMS. Now it was up to
America's people to follow voluntarily. The alternative was

O'Casey's, but so far only the President and his immediate staff knew that.

The only larger crowd in America had formed outside the White House, overflowing into a score of streets and blocks around the area. They had been gathering since before dawn and nervous National Guardsmen and regular army personnel were attempting to keep sidewalks open for emergency services vehicles and catering franchisees who had been brought in to supply food and drink to the huge gathering before the demand became difficult to manage. One enterprising man was selling what he called peaceburgers at $5 a throw inclusive of the little Russian flag memento that came pierced through the bun.

President Sheridan was watching the television news pictures in the almost besieged White House with Peter Kramer and four other top aides. In one of the other rooms the rest of his team and a group of representatives from the Senate and Congress were snatching a quick meal.

One of the aides, a middle-aged admiral who had retired early, turned to Kramer.

'You ought to be arrested and charged with treason! Shit, look at 'em.' He pointed to the screen as the helicopter pictures came in from New York.

'Never mind New York,' tortoiseshell glasses said. 'Look out the window.' He carefully lifted a pizza slice to his mouth.

'Now, now, gentlemen,' Kramer replied evenly, not trying to disguise his smile. 'What you are seeing is democracy at work, so let's stop feeding our faces and get this resolved.'

'He's right,' said Sheridan, 'we aren't the only people watching. I'll bet half the country is glued to this. Let's reconvene next door, and if that arsehole from Nebraska asks again what we are doing about compensation for lost earnings after the missile pullout he can get the hell out.'

Tortoiseshell nodded. He would warn the man to keep to the subject.

A junior aide entered the room quickly, miming holding a phone to Sheridan. The President nodded. Chekhov again.

'Richard, my friend, by now your intelligence people will have told you that the Gulags and your Oslo have largely achieved their short-term aim,' Chekhov began. Sheridan noticed the fatigue in his voice.

'Yes, Mikhail. I have been briefed twice since midnight. I would not have thought it possible. Have you seen any news pictures from here?' Sheridan asked. He knew that Chekhov watched satellite television, but, more importantly, the Russians monitored American broadcasts ceaselessly.

He was back ten minutes later in the big darkened conference room where Senator Bradley of Illinois was up and speaking.

'Gentlemen, we have to consider that if we don't disarm our missiles, now that Russia has had it done for them, they may just force us to.'

'Bullshit, Howie,' his Michigan counterpart snarled. 'How the hell are they gonna do that?'

'By threatening to use the remainder of their SS-20s on Europe or a conventional land assault. Don't forget the estimates to rebuild their Zone are put at sixteen weeks minimum. They aren't gonna want to be vulnerable for that time, not with the internal problems they have. They will see themselves as real close to the water on this patch of ice.'

'Well I still see our problem as being out the window on the streets. Not in the Kremlin,' someone muttered.

The congressman from Texas cut in there, a man with a mind like a steel trap but more famous for his down home on the farm image.

'For Christ sakes, son, they are related. The two issues here are welded together like marriage and mortgage. If you can't see that, then you should go home to your mama . . .'

Sheridan listened in the dark, his thoughts on the call he had taken and the conversation with an exhausted Mikhail Chekhov, now in the thirtieth hour of his Politburo meeting.

'Now, the way I see it,' the Texan congressman continued, 'is we have three choices here, we do nothing and by the look of it out there get voted out next time round, and get slathered as the people who didn't want a nuclear-free world, as warmongers and the rest of it, plus get our economy wrecked by this Oslo outfit, and they look like they can do it. Or we disarm gracefully in the spirit of a better world, and I kid you not, gentlemen, it would be just that, and we all know it. Or we initiate a first strike ourselves right this minute which would be as dumb a thing as I ever heard, about as dumb as doing nothing.' He paused there and stood, easing the creases from his suit, looking round the faces at the table.

'Now you all know that I have long viewed missiles as a expense we can't afford, both in real terms and humanitarian. We need 'em less than ever now. My vote is for disarmament forthwith.'

He was the first of the men in the room to make a stand on the issue and he sat down to an uneasy silence. Sheridan watched Kramer silently raise a fist in triumph. An aide entered the room and passed Sheridan a note. He read it and passed it back to the aide, shaking his head.

The young man began to read the situation report. 'Gentlemen, the governments of Norway, Switzerland and Denmark have just joined the game on the other side. So have Nukualofa, Fiji, and half the island states in the Pacific ... Singapore has just asked the captain of the *Boston* to anchor outside their limit, after he refused to say if he had nukes on board ... Belgium, France and Holland have called for emergency meetings of their cabinets.'

'Anything from her Britannic Majesty's Government?' Bradley asked.

'Who, sir?'

'The Brits son, the Brits!'

'Oh . . . sorry, sir, been a long day. No, sir,' the aide said, 'not yet, but our ambassador there reckons it isn't far away, not with the pressure they are under in London.'

'I believe he might be right,' the Texan said almost to himself.

In the corner Kramer looked at his watch and got to his feet.

'Gentlemen, just so none of you are in any doubt that we will carry out Phase Two, I have arranged a demonstration for you. Help you make up your minds . . . so to speak. Now, we believe in audience participation, as is apparent if you look out the window. I'd hate to leave you all out, so now, the fun bit here is you get to choose the target . . . you have a choice of three. The IRS West Coast computer, the IRS Midwest computer in St Louis, or our very own IRS computer right here in Washington. Personally I'd take the St Louis one. I'd hate to see all those rich film stars getting away with their taxes this year if we take out Orange County, and then there's all the fat cat politicians here in Washington.'

'Sir, I resent that remark,' the Texan said in mock anger.

'Oh why, Morgan?' Kramer asked. They had been friends for years.

'I pay mine in Dallas. Can't that go on the list?' he asked, chuckling.

'What the hell are you laughing at?' Bradley demanded. 'It's outrageous, it's blackmail, it's the most preposterous thing I have ever heard!'

'Grow up, senator. Goddamn! They have our collective nuts in a crush. It's brilliant!' The Texan began to laugh again.

The pilot was a forty-three-year-old ex-air force Vietnam veteran who thought of himself as a professional reprobate, something his mechanic and his wife agreed with. They followed him and his pride and joy to air shows across the country, his pride and joy being a bright red and white chequered Pit Special fully aerobatic biplane, now warming up on the oily pan.

The airstrip he was about to take off from was close to the Virginia–Maryland state line and only seventy-six miles from Washington DC.

Thirty-five minutes later he was airborne. As he checked the electrical switches on his smoke canisters, raised his nose and increased power he smiled to himself; the conditions were perfect with still air and a warm cloudless sky.

He pin-point navigated his way over the Potomac and moments later, after a quick look at the ground to orient himself, he jabbed the left rudder, pushing on the power, and threw the Pit Special into a gut-wrenching hammerhead turning climb as he hit the white smoke. He climbed hard for a few seconds, flicked the nose over in a second breathtaking hammerhead turn just as he was about to stall and finding airspeed began a graceful full inverted loop, full power on over the White House, two million rollicking cheering screaming protesters watching awestruck from the ground. At the top end of the loop he shut off the smoke, dived down the side of his first upward line and then, turning left, started the smoke again and added a tangent line, rolled, turned at the bottom, and came back up to complete the symbol.

But he wasn't finished. He used the old sixties ban the bomb symbol as an 'O', then hit the red smoke and finished the display to the crowd's hysterical chants with the letters 'S-L-O', before dropping his nose and flying by to do a full victory roll low over the crowd.

Inside the White House secret service agents were urging the President to take the stairs down into the bombproof basement, but he wasn't having any of it and stood watching as various men from round the room pulled back the blackout curtains to watch.

'That boy can *fly!*' someone muttered in awe and then withered as he realized what he had said.

'Let's get on with it, can we?' Sheridan said.

All across the nation the campaign had been gathering strength overnight not only as the result of America's free press at last turning and attacking its creator, but around and intertwined through the efforts of many. Churches were packed with record congregations as many ordinary people caught up in the fever wrestled with reactions they didn't understand. To some the thought of questioning the American dream had been unthinkable and now they were not only questioning it, they were positively dismantling it and seeing how it really worked.

University campuses that had been the base of the surge were now hectic or had been forgotten in favour of the local city hall and suburbs. The only airline flights allowed to operate by the air traffic controllers were into Washington DC, and the following Monday morning was promising to deliver the first general strike in American history. The dollar had been plummeting since the Japanese coerced the world into dumping the currency, and while that promised to be good for American exports abroad, one economist was booed off the stage in a live television debate for saying so without admitting to the effect on international purchases. In a major development the cities of San Francisco and Portland announced that they were henceforth nuclear-free, and would ban nuclear-weapon-equipped navy ships from their civilian ports. In Nevada, the scene of so many underground tests, a group of protesters, six hundred middle-aged retired Americans who normally toured the country in big luxury motor homes and Winnebagos, stopped their vehicles and made camp in the test site, their spokesman saying that they would stay there because there would be no more bombs and no more tests because, mister, the place is just too beautiful to ruin any more.

There were too many for the local sheriff's office to move along, and one was a retired judge who had some interesting papers to serve on anyone admitting to be from

427

the authorities. The outnumbered deputies departed without a word, leaving one of their group who had crossed the floor to join with the relaxed crowd. That was not the only instance where civil and military authorities had members of their forces crossing to join the protests. Not only in New York and Washington, but all over the country young and not so young soldiers, National Guardsmen and police had the issue forced on them, not in the tense anger of most street protests, where their own training and esprit de corps demanded cohesion, but in the light-hearted, almost carnival atmosphere that characterized the day.

There were obviously problems. Neo-Nazis and the Ku Klux Klan had arrived at early protests in the southern states expecting to find the usual gatherings of what they termed niggers and hippies and commies. What they found was their neighbours and workmates, wives, children and families alongside each other. A very tense situation in Cleveland was diluted by the arrival of marching girls, the product of a phone call from a very quick-witted mayoral aide. In Georgia police attempting to move a group of extreme right-wingers off a protest route had unusual assistance. The two motorbike cops were sure they were about to take a beating when from behind the angry mob their help arrived in the form of the Atlanta chapter of the Hell's Angels who later said that bikers were bikers and you have to help each other, and besides the wife and two little boys of a member were in the protest march.

In San Diego a frustrated National Guard officer watched over half of his platoon cross into the happy beer-drinking crowd outside City Hall, and after ordering them to return pulled his firearm from his belt and threatened to shoot. He was grabbed by two plainclothes men from Fort Bragg who were moving through the area keeping the peace in their own special way. They cuffed him to a tree to await their vehicle and moved off into the milling masses, leaving him to be offered a milkshake by a teenage girl who felt sorry for him.

Throughout the demonstration areas Oslo supported the speakers and bands with literature, films, documentaries and where possible witnesses from Hiroshima and Nagasaki. The sheer size of the nuclear overkill was demonstrated over and over and a team of people based in a large West Coast movie library had constructed, under the guidance of an expert, a fifty-minute view of the nuclear winter and what it would be like.

In Los Angeles and New York lasers were being set up to beam the message on to the clouds that were expected that evening. To those at home the networks and radio stations carried the message, if not voluntarily then because it was the news story of the day. As night fell the East Coast radio stations picked up on the Nevada announcer's gimmick: 'If you are for Oslo, turn off your lights' and 'If you like the trees and flowers and clean air do the same'. The freak load pattern on the utility grids had engineers concerned most of the night, because when most people went to bed and the usual load dropped, announcers had people turning everything on again. A British Airways jet outbound from Antigua flew up the American coast to touch down in Montreal before flying on to London. The passengers said the entire East Coast from the Chesapeake up to Boston was like a Christmas tree with fairy lights blinking on and off.

Carson had taken the Tarbaby scrambling up after the living proof scene over Farnborough and settled at 90,000 feet, the scrams shut right down to minimum in the loiter mode, the big black hypersonic barely sitting on Mach 3, the onboard computers working the canards for the most efficient flight.

Digby had crawled back, broken open the cold box and dragged it back with him on to the flight deck, opening sandwiches and packets of fresh and dried fruit. There was a bank of thermos flasks containing neatly labelled COFFEE, TEA, SOUP, WATER, and a mixture that was identified only xxxx in red and a label saying 'don't drink this till told'.

'What's this?' Carson asked, sniffing at it.

Digby took the flask and peered into it.

'Looks a bit healthy to me. Probably some concoction of the quacks – best leave it, methinks. Probably to keep us regular or something. I'm not drinking it,' he said with a tight smile. Carson rummaged in the bottom of the box and produced a cold tin of Coca-Cola.

'This is more like it,' he said.

They ate quickly, both men hungry, peeling back sandwiches to find the ones with their favourite fillings, and sipping the drinks.

'Only one fizzy one each,' Carson warned.

'Why?'

'We are pressurized to hell. If we lose pressure or the system changes the rating, you'll be doubled up with wind as it is.'

Half an hour later he looked across at Digby.

'You have control,' holding his hands clear of the column.

'WHAT?' Digby recoiled visibly.

'Just shout if anything happens to that panel of lights,' Carson said, pointing to the autopilot. 'I need a leak.'

He climbed awkwardly out of his seat and moved back to the chemical toilet that was hidden discreetly under the bunk along the right side of the access tunnel.

When he had finished he took the opportunity to stretch his tired muscles and began a short series of sit-ups and knee bends lying on the access tunnel floor. Ten minutes of that and feeling much better, he clambered back into his seat.

Digby made to hand back and Carson shook his head.

'Not yet, sport,' he said. 'Need a kip, then your turn. Just give me a shake if anything looks like happening. The radar is cranked right out, so just relax.'

They alternated sleeping and relaxing for the next six hours until the radio hissed into life.

'Tarbaby, Tarbaby, this is Omega.' It was a new voice, not one Carson had heard over the air before.

'Omega, go,' he said, looking across at Digby, his eyebrow raised.

'Polly Smith,' Digby said. Carson nodded quickly, remembering her voice. She was Gail's relief controller.

'Tarbaby, still have company here. How is your fuel, over?'

Carson knew they were watching his gauges down there, and asking was simple courtesy. Shit, he thought, the bloody *Bunker Hill* is still waiting to have a go at us. Bastards.

'Omega, I never say no to fuel. Have you an alternate yet?'

'Negative to landing, Tarbaby, but Rainbow is now legal, loaded, on the pan and waiting for a Romeo Victor, over.'

He smiled widely in the cockpit, delighted the pair of Swedes hadn't landed into real trouble, and even more delighted they were back to help.

'Okay, Omega, give me a place and time, and watch out for bogeys. We had four sniffing about last time.'

'Tarbaby, be advised Rainbow has an escort, repeat an escort. Figures six Viggens of the Swedish Air Force, over.'

'Roger that, Omega.' He chuckled softly. '. . . aaah . . . where is Bright Eyes, over?'

Polly laughed softly into her mike.

'Taking on fuel and some sleep . . . the doc wants to know if you have drunk the weird stuff in the thermos, over?'

'Not yet, Omega.'

'Be advised it contains Benzedrine and stimulants. Only one cup per three hours. Did you copy that, Tarbaby?'

Digby sat expressionless, but Carson smiled. 'Roger, Omega. Do you have my next target?'

'Negative. They are still trying to decide.'

Three doors up from where Gail was asleep Tim Miller let himself out of his room. In all the drama they seemed to have forgotten about him and he walked confidently up the passageway towards the service area where he knew the two Americans were being held. Incredibly, there was no guard on the door, just the heavy bolt pushed across. He looked both ways, up and down the corridor. Nothing. What to do, he thought? This was way out of his area of experience. There would be all sorts of inquiries after this thing had run its course. If it was found that he did nothing when he could have, that would be a career limiting move. But then if he blew it, it could have the same effect. It seemed the least he could do was get the door open. The Americans were the pros. They would know.

He slid the bolt and stepped into the small room, pulling the door to behind him and putting a finger to his lips.

Hart was coming to his feet and nodded at the signal for silence. 'You must be Miller,' he said softly. Miller nodded. They spoke for a few moments, Hart thinking quickly.

'Okay. No point us moving now. Go back out, lock the door. Then come back when the aircraft is back. Then we can do something. Okay?'

Moscow

Ustinoff nudged the man beside him awake. The meeting, now in its thirty-sixth hour, had drained even those long used to the marathon sessions. Chekhov had spoken many times, always to bring them back on to the subject and away from personal attacks that habitually crept into the sessions, and now he was looking as if he was about to talk again.

The council was still evenly split down the middle on

the issue. The younger men, the vanguard of reform and those with least to fear from democracy, were supporting Ustinoff in his call for complete nuclear disarmament. The old brigade of men, youthful and zealous in the days of Krushchev and Brezhnev, viewed the concept as suicidal; they enjoyed the sense of security brought about by the vast belt of missile silos buried deep below the frozen steppe. They were advocating immediate repair and upgrades to the system and missiles with multiple re-entry warheads complete with decoys, the latest that money could buy. Ustinoff knew that Kraskin's military and munitions clan were buying in favours from the others. Rearmament would be worth billions to them.

Chekhov was looking his age, and twice Ustinoff had seen his private doctor in the anteroom, trying to convince his patient that it was in his best interests and those of Russia to halt the meeting and rest. The bags beneath his eyes seemed heavy now and his skin was wrinkled and grey. But his eyes still carried the bright Chekhov flame.

Don't fade on me yet, Mikhail; I need you, Ustinoff thought.

Chekhov looked at each man in turn.

'Enough of the debate,' he said. 'We have two groups here, both of which have Russia's best interests at heart. I hope,' he added dryly. 'I am lucky, I am young enough to understand Ustinoff's call, and yet old enough to fear it like you, Kraskin. We sit here in Moscow with half the world wondering what takes place behind these doors. They assume us monsters or, worse, saviours . . . They believe us gifted men who don't make mistakes, who have every answer. Men scheme to learn what we speak of as if it were all gold, and yet who among you has ever read Plato or *Faust*, or even this Toffler man's *Future Shock*?' He stopped there and stood, raising his tired frame from the high-backed chair, his eyes disappointed and wise all at once.

'I look about you and I see ambitious men, greedy men,

men who lust for the privilege that a chair in this room will bring. And yet there are those who have willingly offered their lives for Russia, who have dreamed her dreams and struggled for her ... There are those of you who believe that you have a better world waiting, and others who fear that world for what it will bring.'

He walked round the table behind Ustinoff and the Ukrainian, the eyes of those opposite fixed on his face, the old Chekhov magic as powerful as ever.

'So what do we do? We mortal men ... we men who shit with our pants round our knees like everyone else ... must make this choice. The decision made here will take this nation we serve and love another step. Let us not urge her into a lumbering stride on a path we are not convinced is correct.'

Ustinoff watched him as he walked round behind Kraskin, looking for a sign, a clue to the way he would move.

'This meeting is adjourned. We will meet again in twelve hours from now. Think carefully on what I have said, because before the next meeting ends we will have chosen our path and we will have to walk it regardless, because there will be no turning back. For the sake of time, Kraskin, you and Ustinoff will present the cases. Closing statements, if you want to call it that.'

Chekhov had arrived back at his chair where he stood stock-still and faced the ten men and one woman.

'I have one other small change to make. I am not sure that the pressure and favour calling that takes place in these meetings is healthy. What is acceptable with routine matters is not necessarily appropriate to this issue, perhaps the most important of the decade ... Comrades, the vote on this issue shall be by secret ballot.'

Kraskin and Ustinoff both looked stunned at Chekhov. He had thrown seventy years of tradition out of the window, tradition which allowed the combatants to not only marshal their forces, but watch them play their role. The strong survived and the weak were vanquished. It was the way it had always been, but not any more. Jesus Christ, the old bugger has actually done it. Ustinoff's mind was racing with the possibilities. His allies may now turn and support Kraskin, not for Kraskin's sake but to preserve the status quo, but equally so, Kraskin's support may waver as new alliances were foreseen. All the old allegiances had been thrown to the wind. The issue would stand alone and be decided that way. My God, it's brilliant, he thought. Chekhov, you devious son-of-a-bitch. It was the only way to get a completely impartial vote and he had done it, something every leader since Stalin had been frightened to do. Hand control to the majority.

'What is more,' Chekhov said, 'I have taken the liberty of ordering food here, and bringing some of your things into the building. You can sleep, shower, eat and rest in the guest wing. One thing, however. This vote will remain impartial. I must ask that you do not speak to each other until the next meeting. The two of you preparing your closing remarks will find stenographers and supplies in your suites.'

With that he turned and walked out of the room leaving Ustinoff silently saluting the strategy.

Rome

Pope John Paul II stood framed in shadows cast by the light from a priceless gilt desk lamp, his hands clasped behind his back, his eyes on Cardinal Juan de Cueva.

'Juan, do you know what you are asking of me?'

'Yes I do, Holy Father,' he replied sincerely.

'Do you know how long the Church has remained clear of politics and why?'

The question was rhetorical and de Cueva knew better than to answer.

'For four hundred years we have remained largely impartial. Ever since Michelangelo was painting in the chapel. And why? Because it was a requirement for our

435

very survival. The days of the church ruling or establishing policy are over. We were troublesome priests for too many years,' he said. 'The best we can do is guide and comfort. Although individual priests follow their beliefs and act in politics, as a church we do not get involved at this level, Juan . . .'

'Holy Father, may I speak?' de Cueva asked, rising to his feet.

'Of course, of course, speak!' the pontiff replied, already tired of the formality of the audience.

'Holy Father, this is not politics any more. It became political because it was politicians making the decisions. But it is now more than that. It is survival! It is the survival of the planet God created, and the survival of his children. The Vatican must take a stand on this issue. Millions of God-fearing Christian men, women and children are out there now, standing up for something they believe in . . . but further millions are waiting. Catholic millions who believe that this earth of ours has no place for nuclear weapons. They wait for us, Holy Father, they wait for you as their spiritual leader.'

Pope John Paul studied him through guileless eyes, remembering when he was this age and a cardinal to another Pope, the first cardinal from communist Poland, and finely aware of the delicacy of his faith in the eyes of the Party. It was something he had never forgotten, not for a second.

'As much as in my heart I believe in what you are seeking to do, we cannot risk the Church. We have slender enough footholds in Eastern Europe, without labelling ourselves as disruptive or dissident. In the West members of the Church are free to speak and vote for those they choose.'

'There was another long ago, Holy Father, a man who spoke things that were unpopular, who moved to change the world for the better, who was seen as a dissident and who died for it,' de Cueva said bitterly.

'Don't presume to quote me biblical history, young man.'

'Holy Father, I don't presume anything. I merely want to illustrate that dissent is nothing new in Christianity, that the very foundations of our faith were given to us by a man who defied the authorities for something he believed in. Holy Father, it is not risking the Church! In the name of God, surely it is the foundations of the Church?'

'No, Juan, the foundation of our Church is the implicit belief in God the Father. Do you really think he would allow such a thing as you suggest might happen with these bombs?'

'Holy Father, we must take a stand here, for our faith, for our God, for the decency of life on his earth!'

'Juan, your Oslo has a forceful advocate in you. They chose well. But I have told you our position. We shall not become involved.'

'If Christ had said that . . .' de Cueva began.

'How dare you compare us!' the pontiff snapped.

'I dare in the name of God the Father, in the name of my belief in him. Holy Father, you must take a stand here! You cannot ignore the issue. It is out there tonight, bringing nations and families together. You can no more ignore this than could Christ ignore the money-changers in the temple! IN THE NAME OF GOD, DO SOMETHING!' he bellowed.

'Get out of here and come to your senses, man,' the pontiff snapped, pointing to the door.

De Cueva stood stock-still for a moment, his passionate Latin blood now cold, an awful realization in his heart. Finally he pulled his cardinal's cape from his shoulders and threw it with his other tokens of office at the pontiff's feet.

'I think I just have,' he said softly, tears in his eyes. 'You care no more than anyone else.'

He turned and strode from the chambers, his simple

black cassock flapping round his long bony legs, with his very faith in doubt.

Pope John Paul watched him leave, and with great sadness in his soul he knelt to pray. Beside him de Cueva's cape was a vivid reminder of the man and his cause, a cause that the Pope knew could divide the Church as swiftly and as effectively as it had divided them.

That evening the governments of Ireland, Andorra, Liechtenstein, The Netherlands, Denmark, Austria, Italy, Spain, Greece, Jamaica, Trinidad and Tobago, Venezuela, Bolivia and Colombia announced their support for the disarmament proposals.

Canada, Australia, Brazil and Argentina, under enormous pressure from their own populations, were expected to make statements soon. The Greenpeace ship *Son of Rainbow*, fresh from her protest voyages in the French nuclear testing sites of the South Pacific, sailed into the port of Marseilles to hand over half a ton of radioactive coral to the people of France. They had been warned not to expect the usual hostile officials, but in no way were they expecting the thousands of people who lined the wharfs waving banners and placards. The coral was accepted in its lead-lined canister not by the reticent mayor of that city, to whom it was offered, but by the mayor of Cannes, a flamboyant character who, ever mindful of what was a vote-winning issue, accepted it cheerfully, saying that in doing so he absolved France's national guilt and made an apology to the people of the South Pacific.

Across the US and Europe at switching centres for the Internet late changes to the programming allowed Oslo to have a home page that fronted every other site. No one could access the world wide web without getting their message with a clear call to action.

In West Germany the Green Party, which had thrown its weight behind Oslo from the first day, staged a spectacular protest on the site of the now dismantled Berlin Wall. The Green Party support spectacular involved $30,000-worth of pyrotechnics, lovingly prepared that morning by two English experts. They were set off after a three-hour concert, three famous tenors singing opera, the huge speakers carrying their voices out over the city.

Australia was only holding out against her people's pressure to take an anti-nuclear stand as a show of allegiance with her old ally the United Sates of America. Her government had proved its ability to move quickly with the wishes of her people before, and that she would fall in with the movement there seemed little doubt.

Down in New Zealand, the first country in the world to ban nuclear-armed ships years before and whose people were still unaware that it was a countryman of theirs flying the Tarbaby, life was reverting to normal. They had had their say, and all that remained were the good-natured jibes across the Tasman Sea at the Australians: had they become the latest American state yet, and didn't this just prove once again that not only could they not play decent rugby, but they didn't have the balls to stand up for what they believed in.

In the United Kingdom the staggeringly successful rally in Hyde Park had picked itself up, multiplied and moved to Westminster where its component parts slept in makeshift tents and ate over camping gas stoves in their thousands. They were hard up to the doors of the Houses of Parliament, and when a policeman asked the nearest to move back, they smiled and said where? pointing to the shoulder to shoulder mass of humanity moving behind them. Again the carnival atmosphere was strong, with any hint of trouble stamped out by those nearest before it could gain momentum. Skinheads stood alongside pensioners, young unemployed alongside affluent yuppies. A journalist described the crowd as like that at the royal wedding, but intoxicated with its own success. One person was notably absent. Alexander Meran, the grand old man of Oslo was in an intensive care unit listed as critical, his great-granddaughter at his bedside. The prognosis was not good.

Haidermann stood, his jacket off and his sleeves rolled up, in the first-floor viewing room at the Oslo headquarters. The banks of television pictures were being beamed from all over the world and collected by the satellite dishes on the roof. From where he stood with Darby, Haidermann could watch forty transmissions simultaneously, and of those thirty-four contained their material either pre-programmed or as news footage.

'Well?' Haidermann asked. 'Rate the effect so far.'

'A first ever,' the Frenchman answered. 'There has been talk of the global village in the marketing world for years, but for the first time its power has been seen. This concept will change the way politics is worked, it will change the way globally important issues are decided. Geldof with his Live Aid began it, of course. No doubt about it. It's working.'

'I agree,' Haidermann said. 'All that now remains is to see its impact in the Kremlin and the White House. France and Britain will fall with them, if not before.'

'The Chinese?'

'They have made it known they will halt their pro-gramme. I think they are pleased. They can't afford it, anyway.'

'What of the White House? Have they made their choice yet?'

'No, we had to do it for them. They couldn't agree the same flavour milkshake ... it will be Sunday morning there now.'

It was then that one of the girls working the phones downstairs pushed her head round the door and handed Haidermann a note. He read it and sat back heavily into a chair and for the first time since he was twelve years old allowed the tears to come. Alexander Meran, his friend and mentor, was dead.

* * *

They had rendezvoused with the Swedish tanker two hundred miles south of the southernmost tip of Greenland. She had swung into view, her six-fighter escort above and behind her, their weapons loaded.

Carson had taken the Tarbaby in a long gentle turn above and behind and slid down through the escort like a huge black shark in a school of minnows, to take up her refuelling station below the Tristar's tail.

Half an hour later she let slip the hose and again Carson used his scram jets for no other reason than as a show of appreciation to the brave Swede and his escort, and after running up to 110,000 feet, now possible with the correct fuel mixes, he turned for the American mainland, the inertial navigation system fixed to take them in on the next target, the Inland Revenue Service's Western facility in Orange County, California.

Both Carson and Digby were tired now. Sleep before take-off had been snatched and light and they had been airborne for over twenty hours. Their short naps were no substitute for a decent night's rest, and although Digby had held out until he had to be woken by Carson, both were now drinking the Benzedrine suspension every three hours. Muscles were cramped and tight after the hours in the seats and in spite of the exercises in the limited space of the passage, Carson felt stiff and sore.

'We'll come in from the south,' he said, easing his leg into a more comfortable position and running the seat forward into the battle position tight under the dash. 'If you want a piss have it now. Another ten minutes and we can expect Eagles any time.'

'Expect what?' Digby asked.

'Eagles. F-15s.'

'Are they better than the Russians we came up against?'

'Bet on it! Better aeroplane, better drivers, better avionics, better controllers, better ASATs, better everything.'

'Oh shit.'

'Naaa . . .' Carson said. 'They are better, but I am the best.'

'And the most modest,' Digby added dryly over his nerves, tightening his straps and running his seat forward under his tactical displays.

As if on cue the radio crackled into life over the cockpit noise.

'Good morning, Tarbaby, this is Bright Eyes.' She told them about Alexander Meran.

Moscow

Ustinoff had dispensed with the stenographer the moment he arrived in his room. He showered and dressed again in casual slacks and sat at the desk and began to write the most important address of his career. Two hours later he rolled exhausted into bed, too tired to even check in with Stravinsky.

Defence Minister Kraskin, after arriving in his suite, had walked to the window and looking down into the wide street below waved to someone. The man nodded in acknowledgement, climbed immediately into a military vehicle and drove away. Kraskin stared from the window for some time, now irrevocably committed to his plan. The submarine was on clandestine operations anyway, but this larger effort could not be concealed. Not with an aircraft carrier.

On the next floor down Ustinoff woke when his call came through. He showered, shaved and, gritty-eyed and still dog-tired, he made his way, his notes in his pocket, down to the council chamber.

Washington DC

Sheridan looked up tired as the aide entered the room.

'Well, is the son-of-a-bitch coming?' he asked.

'It appears so, sir. NASA have the infrared trace on real time,' the aide replied.

'Are we rigged to talk to him?'

'I'd best ask the comms people, sir,' the aide replied, picking up one of the pale green internal phones. He spoke quickly and quietly and then just as suddenly replaced it. 'They say they are ready to give it a go, sir.'

'Good. Kramer, you come with me, the rest of you gentlemen wait here if you will.'

The basement of the White House contains far more than the much speculated about bunker. There is bulk storage for the family wing's kitchen, and the main production kitchen. There is an extensive wine cellar, maintenance workshops, air-conditioning plant, and other utility rooms. There is also the communications facility, from where the Oval Office and rooms of state can be linked through to anywhere on any channel known to radio waves.

Sheridan had chosen to speak from the main facility rather than his office. He wanted a clean new environment without the clutter and sham of the meetings upstairs. He strode in and rolled one of the chairs, mounted on steel castors, up to the main desk. The gear was a ham operator's dream, with everything from simple SSB radio through to the identical rigs used by modern naval ships that, boosted by satellite, could cover the globe with their signals.

'What are we on?' Sheridan asked the long-haired young man.

'Standard aviation frequency one three five decimal one. It's a few bands of routine traffic from Andrews, but his people will be monitoring it. That's for sure, man.'

The operator was a honours graduate from MIT cleared by the CIA for sensitive work, and was reputed to be able to rescue a signal falling down a well. Sheridan found his casual disrespect refreshing and smiled to himself as he pulled the mike forward.

'What's your call sign?'

'What?' asked the President

'Your sign? Gotta have a name. You go on and say this

is the President, you'll have every turkey in six states wanting to chat with you.'

Sheridan looked round the room and spotted the American seal on an equipment case. 'Eagle,' he said.

'Eagle it is. Okay, we are gonna roll the bands here, you keep calling and when something comes back in I will lock in on it. Then with a bit of luck they will either give us his operating frequency or get him to call us back.'

Kramer, standing back, was not authorized to offer Carson's frequency to anyone, but there was little he could do to stop them trying.

'Angel Seven, Angel Seven, this is Eagle . . . Angel Seven, Angel Seven, this is Eagle . . .'

Six minutes later, with a surprisingly good signal, Sheridan managed to talk to Omega Base who had a listening watch on most military aviation channels in North America that morning.

'Either I talk to Angel Seven or it's off. It's all off. Do you hear me, Oslo? Do your damnedest. That's my deal. All I want to do is talk to your man.'

There was a pause while Sagan thought and then he came back.

'Call off your ship and you can talk. The moment I am told that the *Bunker Hill* is moving off permanently, you get your talk.'

Shit, that's easy, thought Sheridan; they had agreed to that this morning to try and get the air traffic people back to work.

'Okay. You have my word on it. Consider the order given.' Sheridan looked up at the aide and nodded. 'Now, what's his frequency?'

'We will have him call you, Eagle. Stay on this channel.'

Not thirty seconds later a new voice, a strong voice with the flat vowels of the Antipodes, came through the big wall-mounted speakers.

'Eagle, this is Angel Seven.'

'Angel, this is Eagle. Do you know who is speaking?'

444

One hundred and ten thousand feet over the Appalachian Mountains, Carson smiled at Digby before replying.

'Well, well, well, Mohammed has come to the mountain. What can I do for you, Dick?' Carson asked casually. Sheridan hated the diminutive and the world knew it.

'I'd rather you didn't use that name, Angel . . . You don't have to do this, you know that. You will be risking lives, over.'

'Negative, Eagle. You have been warned. Anyone on the target now and it's your problem.'

'You can stop this now.'

Carson thought about Meran, the charming old man with the great-granddaughter at London University, who had developed a taste for cricket and given his life for nuclear peace.

'Negative, Eagle, only you can do that. Agree to disarm and I will turn for home. You don't and this is the start. You have a list. I have a list. We can check them off together.'

'I will stop you with anything and everything at my disposal.' Sheridan's voice had hardened.

'Listen, you want to save lives, Sheridan? Then keep your fighters out of my way. They can't fight me and win up here and you know it. You have one way out of this . . . I have a message from Oslo. When I have finished this demonstration you will have six hours to give us your decision. If it is not agreement, then we will commence with Phase Two in its entirety. That means the list you have. Before we commence, however, we will advise the American people of what we regrettably must do . . . Angel Seven out.'

The main Inland Revenue Service facility is a little like the CIA at Langley, surrounded by trees and trimmed lawns. The National Guard had moved people back to a three-mile radius and waited half-bored, half-excited for something to happen. They had heard the air force jets overhead at varying heights most of the morning, but heard nothing prior to the massive string of blasts that shook the earth beneath their feet just seconds before nine AM. The building just seemed to collapse on itself, the laser, at its lowest setting, having cut through the load-bearing walls.

The computer disks were saved, moved in the evacuation the night before by the night staff, but Oslo had made their point. Even with two squadrons of Eagles as top cover their hypersonic could still go so high and so fast as to make any building in the USA a target, and there wasn't anything the authorities could do about it.

Arctic Ocean

The Russian Northern Fleet carrier *Kirov* gently lifted her huge bow as the monstrous roller moved beneath her. She was making four knots, her massive engines on barely ten per cent power, cruising in a twenty-mile circle, her escort deployed protectively around her and awaiting orders. The orders they were waiting for in computer-generated codes had come through *Kirov's* secure communications facility from Murmansk and the captain, ashen-faced, looked across at his commanding officer, a full admiral, as the fleet intelligence officer checked the orders one last time.

The captain's eyes were pleading.

'Nicolai, this is madness. There must be some mistake.'

It was stuffy and warm in the carrier's operations room and sweat ran in an uncomfortable trickle down his neck under the heavy starched collar. He couldn't believe the orders he had just read. This was a routine exercise, a shakedown for the new ECM gear on the *Bolshoi*, the sleek new cruiser that was now three miles off the *Kirov's* port quarter. The sea trials were not going well and the new systems had been plagued with problems. Now the new orders were to make for Iceland, a neutral country with NATO connections and American bases, land whatever Spetznatz troops the group had, in conjunction with his own aircraft, support a second Spetznatz team already

446

deployed to destroy a facility on the northern coast. The orders were irrevocable, and with the G-RT-3 prefix they were final and absolute. Any counter-instruction was to be ignored, and the *Kirov* and her group were to maintain silence till the mission was complete.

'Nicolai,' he repeated, 'these orders? I must question them. This could start something. It is an act of war.'

'Maybe we are at war, sir,' the intelligence officer suggested.

'With Iceland? Don't be stupid,' he snapped back.

The admiral took the decoded pages from the desk and studied them again, the awful weight of responsibility on his shoulders.

'The codes are correct. The prefix is plain, the message is clear. Captain, you will obey them, as will I and every officer in the group.'

Six minutes later the *Kirov* began to swing her mighty bulk due south, and into the teeth of the storm that had been building since that morning, her escorts battering their way through the mountainous grey seas.

The submarine was already there. In the sheltered waters of a bay six miles to the west of where they believed the aircraft to be based they put ashore their detachment of Spetznatz, the Russian equivalent of Britain's Special Boat Squadron. The ten special forces men had been given their task. The aircraft was to be destroyed, but if possible they were to strip it of selected components before they finished the job. They had been told what to look for and were now making their way to the beach in inflatable boats as the sub settled into the deep waters of the bay and made her way slowly out into deeper water where she would sit on the bottom and await the outcome.

19

Ustinoff watched Kraskin as he rose at the end of the table. He had chosen to wear his medals on his clean suit. There was the Order of Lenin and the Hero of the Soviet Union, the two highest decorations in the land, with, as lesser offerings, campaign medals from the eastern border that on any other chest would have been impressive on their own. Ustinoff was in no doubt that even with his Aquarium GRU headquarters in smoking ruins, his railheads destroyed and the Zone inoperative for the next few months, more than ever he had everything to lose and would be a formidable opponent in this debate.

As the Defence Minister arranged his notes on the table Ustinoff looked at the faces either side of him trying to judge the mood of the moderates. Smetlov was still an unknown quantity. His flinty eyes betrayed nothing of his stance and his demeanour was that of a predatory animal waiting for a calf to be separated from the herd. He had contributed little over the last two days. While his fascist nationalists were a growing force, he lacked real support round the table or in the communist-dominated Duma. He believed his old service could have sorted this out, got them to the heart of the Gulag group. He would have preferred a return to the old ways just this once – the Lubyanka and its basement chambers could still deal with this kind of thing – but Chekhov was adamant. This was a new Russian problem to be solved the new Russian way.

Valeria Kramsk was the council's only woman member. Strong as she was, and determined to remain impartial and equal, Ustinoff knew she felt she owed her position to Chekhov himself. She was a wide-faced academic with torpid eyes that hid her lightning intellect and sarcastic wit. Her hair, brown and braided, was said to be long, and it was also said that in the privacy of their bedroom she danced naked for her husband. Ustinoff could not picture it and fancied the stories to be just that, men's fanciful images of the council's only woman.

She ran the Health Ministry and ran it well, with the support of the pharmaceutical and scientific industries that formed the least powerful clan. Ustinoff knew that if the original two groups of four adversaries remained constant then Smetlov and Kramsk would tip the balance one way or the other. If their decision took them different ways then it would be Chekhov's vote that would carry the day.

Kraskin would be first to speak and had, Ustinoff felt, two disadvantages. First, like the attorney who has to sum up first in a trial, he would lose the effect of the last word. Second, the two people to influence were on his left and right and he would not be able to make eye contact with them, but would have to rely on his physical proximity to achieve the effect.

Chekhov raised his eyes and the room fell silent.

'Defence Minister Kraskin will address the council.'

Kraskin nodded formally to Chekhov and faced his colleagues round the table, his lined weathered face hard even in the soft light.

'I ask that you forget who I am or what I have become. I ask that you forget my record and my career,' he began.

Very shrewd, thought Ustinoff, that will draw their attention to it, you wily old bastard. *Et tu Brute* coming up, no doubt.

'. . . see me only as an old man, a man who has seen and learnt much. I am a communist and have been for almost seventy years. I remember as a boy in a small village outside Smolensk, my father telling me of the frosty crisp morning that the Tsar's cavalry had put down a popular protest in the town, workers and peasants were dead, and

449

as they rode past on their big horses, horses that seemed to breathe smoke from their nostrils, one man pulled his mount to a halt and laughing he wiped the blood of his sabre blade on the shawl of a woman, a neighbour, as she stood respectfully in her doorway. It may have been the blood of her son, for he died that day in the square. That was tyranny and he fought it. Then it was my turn ... I fought it then. Hitler.' He raised his clenched fist, his eyes alive and burning with the memories, casting a glance at Smetlov. 'I am one of the last of the old school, one of the last old comrades, and as I stand before you I have seen tyranny. I have seen it. I saw it in the eyes of the Waffen-SS. I saw it but we survived. We survived because we were strong. We as a people have absorbed more punishment, more death, more cold and more fear than any people should have to do. How many millions died in the Great Patriotic War? I will tell you that we don't know. Fifteen, twenty, thirty million? But I ask you this. Should we ever have to put up with that again? How many times must Russia bend her back to throw off the European invader? I have seen it in my lifetime. I was there when Hitler's panzers stood at the walls of Leningrad, and I will tell you something else. The German soldier is outstanding and his officers are second to none. We only held them back because our old friend the winter arrived to help, and we had people to spare. Lots of people. Gun fodder. But how many times must good Russians be fodder for the guns? No more, I say, because we now have another way! We have an arsenal so powerful no one will dare attack us ever again!'

He stood tall and proud, the image of the undefeated, his fist rising and falling to punctuate his words. Christ! thought Ustinoff, he is good. Not the simple soldier he loves to portray.

'We are not perfect. If I was in charge of heavy industry or agriculture I would be concerned for wheat and steel, but I am not. I am responsible for the defence of the Rordina, so I am concerned with that.' He raised his hands modestly and with an uncharacteristic display of humility. 'There has been much discussion here of Ustinoff's desire to disarm the Zone. Ustinoff, our young lion! Our young man with a bright future, who wants to offer complete disarmament to the Americans. The Americans are weak and ill-disciplined, they have had their time as a world power. Our future threat does not come from the Americans! Anyone who believes it does is a fool! There are two threats for us. A new power in the Far East that in the next few years will produce more people, more money and more industry than the Americans ever could. We must watch the East. And we must watch the West. But not America. I have stood before you here many times and protested with all my heart against the reunification of Germany. Even with controls a unified Germany could rise against us! Divided was the only way to keep them. Again they are one. The trade barriers drop in Europe. Bit by bit, little by little we are seeing a united Europe develop and, comrades, it frightens me. They will have a domestic product that will be awesome. They have technology we haven't even started with, they have a workforce second to none in the world, they will be productive, powerful and rich, and they have always been our enemy! Twice this century! Twice the Germans have nearly beaten us on the ground. What if a combined European military force were assembled and trained? The British, the French, the Germans, the Italians, the Austrians, the Spanish, the Belgians, the Dutch, the Baltic countries? Must we be fodder again? Must we allow the cream of yet another generation to be ground to mincemeat under the tank tracks?'

He slammed his fist on the table, leaning forward and angry, and paused there to allow the image to sink in.

'The nuclear missiles in the Zone we can point anywhere. I say they should be kept and pointed at wherever the threat lies, and let's keep the motherland safe. Think of this when you vote. Think if you are to risk another invasion and another generation of Russians with no sons. There have not been another fifty peaceful years in Europe for three hundred years. Why do you think that is? Because now the risks are too great. It is peace or annihilation, so peace reigns! So vote for peace, or vote for the young lion ... and then prepare for war in the next decade!'

Glowering at Ustinoff he lowered himself into his chair and with mounting despair the younger man sat through the hand-clapping, awaiting his turn to address the council.

Jesus, that was brilliant, he thought, he has turned the tables completely! Now I am the aggressor, I am the man who will bring war, and Gulag is the worst thing since Hitler. He put his notes aside and prepared to ad lib his response.

Rome

Pope John Paul II moved slowly through the long walkways of the Giardini del Vaticano, the Vatican gardens, towards St Peter's where he would conduct the morning mass. He had sent his assistant to see de Cueva and ask if he would attend mass that morning and now could only wait and see. It was normal for a crowd to gather in St Peter's Square to hear the mass over speakers, but this morning he had been told the square was full to bursting, and people had spilled over into the streets of the Angel and the Spirit and were massed shoulder to shoulder along the Via dei Conciliazione. It had been remarked on at breakfast, that that didn't even happen at Easter.

De Cueva opened the door when he heard the knock and stood dressed in a plain black cassock like the priest of some simple rural community. The arrival stood large in the door. Monsignor Pellini was a very big man who towered over most, but like so many very big men he was gentle of voice and deed.

'Cardinal de Cueva, His Holiness asked me to give you

this and also asks if you will be attending mass this morning?'

De Cueva looked at the parcel and knew it contained the cardinal's cape, sash and hat he had rejected the night before. He shook his head.

'I am cardinal no longer, monsignor. I am barely . . .'

'He knows what you think,' Pellini interrupted. 'Tell me, cardinal. Have you seen the square this morning? Quite a crowd gathered there. Some since last night. If it were up to me I would attend mass just to see them from the balcony.'

That was as direct an invitation as anyone ever received to join the pontiff on the most famous balcony in the world. It was a peace-offering and de Cueva knew it.

He nodded and leaving the door open he pulled more formal attire from his wardrobe and walked with the monsignor towards the palace's side entrance to St Peter's.

Carson let out an audible sigh as his main bogeys touched down on the runway at Omega Base. They had been airborne over twenty-three hours and his eyes were grainy and his nerves jittery and tight from the dexedrine. They had passed right over the *Bunker Hill* on their way in, the American ship sitting solidly to the north-west having received her orders to clear the area. Carson had decided that if they tried anything he would retaliate, though he was too tired for anything fancy, but it hadn't been necessary and now he taxied quickly towards the hangar doors and the waiting ground crew, fuel, real food, sleep and Gail Samuels. As he shut down the engines the crew swarmed over the Tarbaby with their preallocated tasks and he climbed stiffly down the narrow ladder with Digby, pale and drawn-looking. Carson's eyes looked outward at the gathering storm to the north.

Sagan and Neilson, the doctor, met them at the passage doors, Sagan smiling broadly. 'Debrief later . . . get some sleep now. The doc will give you something to bring you down from the dexedrine. How are you both? Well done, well done.'

'How are things going?' Carson asked tiredly.

'Both the Council of Ministers and the Oval Office are still in meetings. The Brits are holding out with their NATO commitment so far, but under a barrage from the opposition . . .'

'Not so good then,' Carson said quickly, his nerves still jangling from the drugs.

'Not bad either. People the world over are involved now. I'm afraid I have some bad news. Yamashita died an hour ago.'

Carson's eyes, hard and cold like jade, looked at Digby who was opening his flight suit as Neilson was putting a stethoscope to his ears.

'Get some sleep . . . we may have to go up again.'

Half an hour later Miller made his move. With everyone down in the operations areas the accommodation area was almost deserted except for two people in the kitchen. He went straight to the makeshift cell, slid the bolt on the door and slipped inside. 'It's back,' he said. 'Now what?'

Hart had been wondering the same thing. His brief was to find it. And find it he had. This gave 'Technology with a Military Application' a whole new meaning. The ramifications were staggering. The next phase was to report in.

'Now I need to get to a phone.'

'And then?'

'Not my call. I'm the who why when what how guy.'

'There's only two outside lines. I know that much.'

'Any idea where?'

The office above the control room, Miller thought. 'Maybe,' he said.

Washington DC

'When I was a kid I joined the marines and went to Korea.' The congressman speaking was a tall man with thin greying hair and red-rimmed eyes. He had contracted cancer seven months ago and the chemotherapy had taken its toll. He had contributed little, preferring to sit and listen and husband his strength.

'We were in the cold rain and the fella I was with looked down at his rifle and said, "Shit, look at this thing. You can't eat it, or sleep in it, it won't keep you dry. I have to carry it everywhere and it weighs fourteen pounds, and all it will do, all it will do, is kill." Now we are talking about these Minutemen and suchlike and I believe the same statement can be made. They are pretty much useless unless we plan to attack someone with them. Hell! I signed off on that last budget and, fellers, let me tell you I would love to have seen that money go to something we ARE gonna use!' He paused there to cough painfully into his hand. Someone went to interrupt, but Sheridan silenced them with a glare and a few seconds later the old man continued.

'Now of all you people gathered here, I am probably the best equipped to give you an impartial view, because it looks like I will be dead by Christmas, so what we decide here does not really affect me. But I am thinking about my sons and their sons and your sons and them Russian kids and French and so on. It always amused me that we who decide to go to war are never the men at the front being shot at. Maybe if we were we wouldn't be so warlike . . . now, we have an opportunity here to reverse that process a little. Let me ask each one of you in turn a question and each of you answer honestly.'

He looked right to left and settled on Sheridan's youngest aide, a thirty-three-year-old political science whizzkid from Yale.

'Son, would you like to have your family die in a nuclear blast? Yes or no?'

'That isn't a fair question, congressman. Of course I . . .'

'What do you mean, fair? Since when has war been fair? Now you answer me, and remember what we are talking about here. Nuclear war, assured mutual destruction.'

455

'Why bring families into it? Let me answer for me personally.'

'Bombs kill families, so answer for yours! Well?'

'No I wouldn't,' he replied, somewhat miffed.

'Then how the hell can you endorse their existence? They will be the very thing that kills you!'

He turned his eyes to the next man and in the gloom Kramer thought he saw Sheridan smile. The congressman addressed each in turn, spurning attempts to qualify the question, quashing rhetoric and forcing a one-word answer. In each case the men agreed that they didn't want themselves or their families to die.

'Now after all the bullshit, we are getting somewhere. We have agreed that we want to live with our families. So why is the rest of America any different? Look out there ... that's all they want. Kramer's people have presented a legitimate cause to government, and are supporting its discussion. So here is the question that needs answering. Do we offer to disarm our missiles?'

The debate became fast and furious, Kramer now actively involved in the talk, leaning across the table, jabbing a finger to emphasize his point

'There is no real choice here,' he said. 'We disarm for all the right reasons or we keep the nukes and lose America as we know it. Make no mistake, gentlemen. Our people will be back and we will finish the list. Fort Knox, Wall Street, the IRS – and this time we will make sure the computer tapes go as well! We can destroy the American economy as easily as we destroyed the Zone ... enough is enough, gentlemen, make your minds up!'

Rome

De Cueva had reluctantly joined the line to take communion with the others in the huge church, the other cardinals noticing his attire and his deliberate choice to be part of the congregation rather than officiate in the service as was his privilege. Outside in the square of St Peter the vast crowd was silent as they listened to the service, waiting to hear the voice of the pontiff.

The Brazilian, still deeply upset by the Pope's refusal to make a statement, moved slowly forward with the line towards those kneeling to receive the sacrament, feeling hypocritical for even being there. Since he had been a small boy he had believed in the church and its inherent goodness. He came from a country where priests did not stand back and watch harm befall their flock. There they delivered babies, tended the sick, wounded and dying, they stood up and faced political persecution and corruption. They raised money for medicine and schools, raised blisters on their hands in the fields at harvest time, and they praised God.

De Cueva, at the age of nineteen and still in the seminary, had stood between five drunken policeman and the prostitute they were about to rape. They had laughed and thought him easily dealt with, but the young Juan de Cueva was a different breed, a young man brought up on stories of the soldier priests, and the days when the church was to be reckoned with. He had stood his ground, the girl, thin from perpetual hunger, lying in the mud behind him and tried to reason with them, to appeal to their decency. That failed as he knew it would, and when they swung their clubs a cold anger welled up. They were about to attack him and therein the Church itself and therein God. He balled a fist and the years of surviving the streets of São Paulo flashed back. Now he had a nose that was flattened, a scar like a boxer over his left eye and a shoulder blade that gave him trouble in the damp.

The priests had set it because he could not go to the hospital and for all their efforts they had not done a good job. In the hospital were three of the five policemen, who more out of shame than anything had reported the attack as carried out by many unknown assailants. That incident demonstrated the courage and conviction that was to mark his vocation, and everywhere he went thereafter the story followed. De Cueva was a man who got things done, a man of God with a will of iron and a heart that embraced the common people.

Now he stood silent at the base of the great staircase to await the pontiff's party as the congregation filed out to find places in the square or push their way home through the crowds.

A few minutes later he followed them up the stairs to the balcony landing and at the top the pontiff turned and faced him, his worn face smiling a greeting like a father to his son. In his arms was the parcel that the monsignor had offered de Cueva earlier.

'Take it and put it on, my son,' he said. Their eyes met over the brown paper and for a full three seconds de Cueva fought with his pride. Finally he took the offering and ripping the paper he pulled the cape over his cassock, took the heavy red hat from another hand as it was offered and put it squarely on his head.

He then looked at the pontiff, his eyes saying everything he had spoken the night before, silently pleading Oslo's case, and he followed him out on to the balcony.

Below them in the square over a million people looked up and crossed themselves in respect for Pope John Paul II as he moved to the front of the balcony.

'In nomine Patris et Filii et Spiritu Sancti.' He paused there and turned and looked at de Cueva and then back at the masses below, raising his hands for a blessing.

'Beati pacifici,' he began and behind him de Cueva, tears welling in his eyes, his spirit soaring, silently translated the Latin to himself: 'Blessed are the peacemakers, for they shall be called sons of God,' and with the Pope's voice carrying over the masses below, Cardinal Juan de Cueva, holding back his tears, began prayer of thanks as the Catholic Church in the form of Pope John Paul II stepped solidly behind Oslo, and with it its five hundred million members.

Chekhov watched Ustinoff stand up at the table. The beginnings of the iron grey in his hair seemed more noticeable today and he knew the Gulag man hadn't slept much in the break if at all. My God, he thought, what courage he has displayed. Even if this campaign he represents works he knows he could be in the Lubyanka any minute: treason is unforgivable even in the new Russia. Smetlov knows and he waits for my nod. Could I allow the end of one so strong and so brave and ever look my grandson in the face again? Could I ever walk the streets among the people and know I had taken one so good from them? The children with no boots need a man like this. So here, Ustinoff, is your chance. Fail this and you fail everyone. Fail this and I will have to give you to the wolves.

'Marshal Kraskin has offered one argument for the decision on our nuclear arsenal. He is a fine soldier and a brave man. He has the Order of Lenin and is a Hero of the Soviet Union and so is worthy of your time and your consideration. But he asked us not to consider that, so we won't. He likened me to a young lion. I am honoured: I have never heard a shot fired in anger, while he has been serving Russia for sixty-odd years. A considerable achievement, a man who has seen much. But with due respect to him, I had to wonder what the Tsar's soldiers had to do with our problem here. He spoke of tyranny. Tyranny is not the issue here. Neither are the days of the Tsars. This is an issue of today. The today of the microchip and the semiconductor, the day of the Internet and the modem, the mobile phone, of global trade. We are here to decide something quite simple. Do we need a nuclear arsenal we will never use? Do we need a nuclear arsenal that costs us a trillion roubles a year to update and modernize? If we really have so much money to waste why not just give it to some African state? But no, we pour it into missiles every year, missiles that will never be launched, missiles pointed at some imaginary foe. Yes, we have been invaded twice this century. And we threw them back twice this century, without nuclear weapons! We are the most powerful conventional military power on earth. WE NEED FEAR NO ONE! . . . except ourselves. The only thing we need fear is death by our own hands . . . for that is what those missiles mean. As long as we have them, the NATO alliance will have them. They genuinely believe that we are a threat, and looking at that it's not surprising. We and America have rushed into the sport of acquisition like some board game and we have both been burnt, both of us have had our Afghanistans, and suspicious of each other we have missiles pointed, fingers on the triggers.

'I'm not saying roll over and die. What I am saying is let's go to the Americans and NATO and let's say, "You disarm and we will." Imagine what we could do with a trillion roubles a year. We could modernize factories that are long overdue for it, build new factories so we can produce enough cars for people to buy, build new hospitals, invest in computers and technology, invest the money here, in Russia! Where we need it!

'We have been told it will take four months to rebuild the Zone. I say, let's not rebuild it at all! There is no room on this earth for nuclear weapons. We all know why, we have all become aware of the size of the world's total nuclear arsenal and what will happen if it is ever used. We had them, yes. But now they are gone. Let's not make the same mistake twice. We have a chance here, a chance to do something decent. If we don't need the nuclear weapons then why have them? For God's sake, we have people in our military that haven't been paid for four months! And we want to rebuild a nuclear arsenal? Let's take the money and pay our people what's owed to them. Let's invest in Russia. In the economy.' He stopped for a moment and walked slowly round the table, allowing the words to sink in.

'I am not an ex-Marshal of the Red Army. I do not have

a chest resplendent with medals. I do not remember the invaders. Why? Because I was born after that. I am of a new generation, like those people on the streets out there. They are not subversives! They are Russians, people like you and me. They just want peace and they want to be able to go to bed at night and not worry about who is going to push a button that can destroy the world. We have a dialogue with NATO. They have seen our newest bombers and we have seen theirs. We accept American aid, we have their businessmen operating here, trade going on without suspicion. Never before in the last fifty years has there been a better time to talk to each other. Now is the time . . . for a better world . . . and you people can do it with a simple vote. Vote to agree nuclear disarmament with NATO.'

He flicked a look at Kraskin who nonchalantly looked down at his watch and smiled smugly.

'This is more important than two sides beating it out in this chamber. This is more important than clearing an owed favour with a vote. Ask yourselves the real question and decide. Remember! This is the long-term survival of the planet we are talking about here, and the long-term survival of Russia itself. We simply cannot afford these weapons. We need the money for other things. Rebuilding the Zone would cripple our economy, and then our problem would not be invading armies. It would be wheat and grain for the winter. It would be the mafia and their black markets. We need factories producing things that we can export, we need money to spend on our cities, on law and order, on education, on new hospitals. Not new missile systems.' He raised his hands in appeal. 'Surely that's more important than one man's memories of another time long ago.'

He looked at the General Secretary, nodded and sat down in an atmosphere that was thick with tension, and absolutely silent.

'Congress will ratify whatever we decide here,' Sheridan said firmly, 'that's why you people are here. So let's not have any armchair theatricals about the constitutional legalities. They are awaiting an emergency session right now.' The Colorado representative had been quibbling over minor issues since the meeting began and Sheridan had had enough. 'So if you don't like it, mister, then get the hell out of my office.'

An aide came through from the Oval Office, a blue confidential message sheet in his hand.

'Read it,' Sheridan said standing and stretching. Each time the group had recessed for food or a break he had been on the hot line to General Secretary Chekhov from the privacy of his office, and now he was tired.

'It's from Ambassador Craig in Rome. Message reads quote in ex cathedra address Pope John Paul II has offered prayers and support for nuclear disarmament movement. St Peters balcony speech televised unquote.'

'That was all we needed,' the Secretary of State muttered, looking at Kramer. 'He one of yours, too?' Every man present was either a politician or a political appointment and knew never to underestimate the influence of the Church.

'He is now,' Kramer replied.

'Shit,' someone said. 'That means every Catholic who wasn't out on the streets will be now . . . how many Catholics in the USA?'

'About fifty million,' another answered quietly.

'Let's get a consensus on this,' Sheridan said, bringing them back on track. 'We know the Russians are hurt. This meeting proposes that we remain silent on the issue until they make contact. If and only if, they propose a full and unconditional nuclear treaty we are ready to talk.'

'Not just talk,' Kramer said crisply. 'Comply in full.'

Their eyes locked across the room like radar-controlled

guns before Sheridan spoke again. Out in the streets, across the immaculate lawns of the White House, they could hear the crowd singing something, a brass band in there somewhere, the wind plucking at the sound and distorting it.

'Those in favour say yea, those against say nay.'

Then the wind dropped and the melody became apparent. It was 'America the Beautiful' and over its strains the men at the table gave their replies.

Moscow

Chekhov's eyes took in each in turn as he spoke.

'Each of you has in front of you a slip of paper. Complete it, entering yes or no, and go through into my office and drop it into the sealed square box on my desk. My vote will not count unless we are deadlocked, where it will be the decider. One last thing . . .' he paused there, steepling his fingers before his face, powerful and confident '. . . this decision will be final.'

Ustinoff, expecting the statement, looked quickly at the others in the room. Chekhov who had remained almost aloof for so long, gently guiding the discussion and keeping the peace had finally prioritized the events. This was it. If he lost then he would be out of a job and certainly under arrest.

Chekhov looked at Valeria Kramsk. 'Ladies first?'

It was Natalia sitting in the post-operational quiet of the control room who took the call from the breathless, frightened man in Finland. He had asked for Sagan and when told he was resting didn't wait for him to be roused but blurted his news.

'The *Kirov*, she has been sent to your area.'

'You are sure?' Natalia said quickly in Russian.

'*Da*,' he replied. 'Eleven hours ago she turned from her routine patrol.'

463

Natalia knew the *Kirov*. She was the pride of the Northern Fleet, Russia's newest aircraft carrier.

'Thank you. I will inform Mr Sagan,' she said in a measured tone. 'Duty satellite tech to control please ... quickly now,' she said into the handset. She dialled again. 'Mr Sagan? Problem. The *Kirov*, a Russian carrier. We just had a call she's heading this way. I'm waiting on satellite confirmation.'

Seconds later a tall young man pulling on a shirt burst through a door. 'Yo,' he said.

'Satellite data for sectors three seven and three eight, please. Surface up to thirty thousand will do.'

'What am I looking for?'

'An aircraft carrier possibly with her battle group,' she replied.

Three minutes later Natalia bent over the big tactical image display screen.

'That's her,' she said. 'That's the *Kirov*.'

Sagan joined them, rubbing sleep from his eyes, his suit rumpled. He listened to Natalia's appraisal without interrupting and then shook his head.

'They tracked the infrared traces. But they won't attack us now ... it's too late,' he said.

'Some would. The military. They are not going to take our attack lying down. It's not their way,' Natalia argued. 'I know. I am Russian.'

Sagan thought for a second, accepting her conviction. 'What will they do?'

'She's in the heart of that low pressure area. When they can get their aircraft up, runway denial weapons, possibly smart bombs.'

Sagan needed no more. There were no contingency plans for this. The hypersonic could simply move to a new base, but without her sophisticated maintenance support and her tactical controllers. They could save the aircraft, but in so doing limit her ability to function by ninety per cent.

'All right, how much time have we got?'

'They are in range now and getting closer,' Natalia replied.

At that moment Van Waveren came through the door. 'We have trouble. Visitors.'

Sagan looked at him. 'Who?'

'Not sure. Our friends spotted them. They are military. Eastern bloc weapons. They have been playing hide and seek with Icelandic patrols, but they have slipped through.'

'How many?'

'A handful. They saw five. I'm going out with the watch. I think we can intercept them.'

They had slipped down the passage and were now in the deserted gym, Cleatus watching the passage through the slightly open door. Miller had explained where the ops room was, where to find the office, but Hart hadn't let him off that easily. 'I'll need a diversion. Just long enough to make a call. Cleatus goes one way, you the other. Help me out here.'

Bollocks, Miller thought. You're on your own. I got you out. This isn't what I do. It's what you do and it's resulted in three deaths so far. 'Sorry. This is as far as I go.'

Hart gave him a withering look and tapped Cleatus on the shoulder. Miller counted to thirty, followed them out and made his way back to his room.

Twenty minutes later Carson was in the ready room pulling on his flight suit, his hands fumbling the zips, tired and groggy. Gail, also tired and looking worried, was helping him.

'Where's Digby?' he asked.

'Problem,' the doctor answered. He was preparing a hypodermic laced with a stimulant.

'What problem?' Carson snapped. 'Get him!' He stopped there and shook his head. 'No. That was unfair. He has done well. He's a good lad. He all right?'

The doctor looked at Sagan as if looking for a lead. 'He couldn't sleep, I gave him a sedative. He will be asleep for the next three or four hours and I can't chemically alter that state without damaging him.'

'Shit! ... I'll go alone. Once I'm up and they know, then it's unlikely they will attack the base. Not with the Icelanders as stroppy as they are.'

'You don't have to go up. This hangar was designed to withstand an air attack. Get some sleep,' Sagan said.

'No,' Carson said quickly. 'I can't risk her being damaged. Not now, not so close to so much ... and if we wait that storm won't make it any easier to get her off.' He had a look in his eyes that Sagan hadn't seen before.

'I feel I must warn you ...' the doctor began, holding the needle up.

'Yeah, yeah, just stick it in,' Carson interrupted.

'... that this will only keep you going three hours at most. Then you will fall asleep regardless, and you risk damage to the central nervous system if you attempt any more barbiturate introduction.'

In the control room Hart, who had slipped in through the back door, was awaiting his moment to take the five stairs up to Sagan's empty office when a young voice, strained and frightened, burst through the speakers. He couldn't help but hear it and in the background there was a burst of gunfire. He ran lightly up the stairs and lying on the floor took the telephone from the desk and dialled. It was answered immediately.

In the ready room the telephone bleeped. Sagan answered it. He listened for a few moments before saying, 'Oh my God.' Carson stopped dressing and looked at him as did Gail.

'I'm not sure. Perhaps ... yes, alert other watch. They won't be long now.' He put the phone down. 'Van Waveren found them. They fought. He is dead. Two of them got away. Our people have lost them. You must get airborne as soon as you can.'

466

Carson looked at Sagan. 'Miller. Tim. Get him down here. He can help.'

'He is not ours. Why should he? And besides he isn't rated on the aircraft or the systems,' Sagan replied.

'Look, if Tim comes we can stay up till we need fuel. If I go alone . . . you heard the doc. Three hours, and Christ knows what will happen then. Three hours. Yeah, he's not rated but it's got wings and engines. Straight and level won't be a problem for him and we don't have any bloody choice.'

'Out of the question,' Sagan replied. 'Absolutely not.'

'Let's leave it up to him!' Carson snapped. 'If he agrees to go you agree to let him! Yes?'

Sagan thought quickly. Why should he? No reason to. No chance of it. Agree. 'Agreed.'

'Let's get him down here, then.'

It was then that the door was pushed open and Paul Hart entered the room.

'Who let you out?' Sagan snapped. This was all too much. He had enough to worry about.

'Never mind that,' the American replied. 'I was in your ops room. I overheard. You have been rumbled.'

'We are aware of that.'

'I'd like to help.'

'Don't be ridiculous. You are here to . . .'

'I got into your office. Made a call. I have new instructions. That aircraft is not to fall into Russian hands. Under any circumstances. I can either try and blow it up, and that option is a little unrealistic, or help you to get it away. I am to assist you,' he finished dryly.

'We have no intention of letting that happen.'

'Whoever is out there might just disagree.'

'There were five of them. Two got away. We shall . . .'

'Five? No way,' Hart replied.

'How do you know?' Sagan snapped. 'They were seen. Get out of here.'

'I wasn't always in this job. Before that I was military

467

intelligence. Those people out there must have been landed by submarine. That makes them Spetznatz, Russian special forces attached to the navy. They don't operate in fives. Minimum is ten men. That's also the standard troop deployment on a submarine. It's not five out there. It ten minimum. And you think you got three.'

Sagan's head dropped, his eyes closed.

'Where's the guy who got us? The Dutchman. I'll brief him. Do what I can.'

'He's dead,' Carson answered. 'And the rest aren't up to it. Young. Keen. But ex-policemen, not soldiers.'

'How many?'

'About fifteen on each watch,' Sagan replied. 'Mr Van Waveren took one watch out with him.'

'Shit,' Hart said. He was getting in deeper by the minute. He looked at Carson. 'How long do you need to get it up?'

'Ten minutes from the go.'

The door swung open and Miller was escorted into the room. He was worried, thinking that Hart and his partner had been missed already and they had worked out who had released them.

He saw Hart. Carson looked at him. 'Never mind him. I'm taking her up again. Clear the area. My oppo is flat out on his back. I've got three hours and then I crash too. I need a number two. You on for it?'

'What?' Miller asked, astonished. 'You must be kidding. I'd be history. And anyway I've never even seen inside the cockpit. Your . . .'

'Straight and level. Nothing skoshey and, besides, if I don't get her up you might be history anyway. We might all be. There's a Russian battle group heading this way and some of their special forces people out there somewhere.' Carson's voice lowered to a rasping whisper. 'You owe me one, Tim. Remember? You owe me!'

The grey German skies. The local cross-country familiarization sortie, the West German fighters streaking in at the wrong height, the barked warning all came flooding back in a microsecond. If it hadn't been for Carson's reflexes then he would in all probability have been killed. Not many pilots survive a high-speed mid-air collision at low level.

He nodded. 'I remember.'

'Do it,' Hart said. 'I'm under new orders. That thing must not fall into Russian hands.'

'You may be, but I'm not,' Miller replied.

'You always did lack initiative,' Carson snapped. He looked at Sagan. 'Get Rainbow somewhere clear of the weather where she can service me, if you will please.' He stood legs apart, aggressive like a bantam cock. 'Can we get Digby down to the aircraft? He can sleep in the seat. I can use him later. We'll go as soon as we have him dressed.'

Neilson looked at him, a sadness in his eyes. 'I'm afraid,' he began, 'I'm afraid that won't be possible. Digby won't. Digby won't be going with you.' He looked at Sagan again. Angry now. He looked back at Carson. 'The drugs. I warned him often enough. He knew the risks.'

'What are you saying?'

'He suffered rheumatic fever in childhood. The drugs you two have been using to stay awake . . . his heart gave out. I'm afraid he died about an hour ago.'

Carson just looked at him, stunned. 'Oh Jesus . . .' memories flooded back. Murphy, his first mate in the air force, his face overlaid with Digby's. 'You say he knew? He knew the risks?'

'Yes. He knew. So did Yamashita.'

'You can't go alone,' Sagan said. 'You will fall asleep and crash. Enough people have died. We shall try and defend the base. Negotiate . . .'

'No. I'll go,' Carson replied. 'You're right. Enough people have died. Too many. Too many to give up now.' Jesus, he did know. He remembered the look on Digby's face when he had taken the stuff. What faith! What commitment! All of them. Rikio Yamashita, Pauli Van Waveren, Digby Allison. 'Too many good people. Can you find somewhere I can take it. Sweden? Will the Swedes . . . ?'

'I can try,' Sagan said.

'I'll come,' Miller said.

'What?'

'I said I'll come. Got some gear that will fit me?'

Carson looked at him, not sure whether he was serious, but Miller's look said he was.

'Yeah. Digby's will fit. Welcome to the world. We go in ten minutes.' He looked at Sagan. 'Don't bother with Sweden. We'll loiter. Refuelling only.'

'Hang on,' Hart said. 'Give me time to get to where we think these people are. I'll try and keep them clear of your runway.'

'Can you?'

'All we have to do is slow them down. These guys won't like being shot at any more than anyone else. Once you are up they will reassess.'

The security man who had delivered Miller led Hart away. Fifteen minutes later, having looked at plans of the tunnel complex and the exit points, he decided what he was going to do. Leaving one man to operate the alarms desk they climbed into the golf carts, an M-16 203 between Hart's legs and his time with the Rangers flooding back. The first bunch had come in from the north-west. What would I do? Split my force and have the others come from another direction. Which? Take too long and be too exposed to swing all the way round the south. I'd have gone round to the north-east. Come in from the opposite side. Wait and see. They would trip a silent alarm somewhere and one of the mikes and cameras would find them. Then intercept them. They pulled over at one of the tunnel intersections.

'We are under the hill above the base now,' the section leader said to Hart. 'That up there . . .' he pointed to a ramp '. . . is the way up. There is another further along and two behind us.'

'How long to get to the other side?'

'Three or four minutes. Pauli . . . Mr Van Waveren didn't take everyone on the watch. There are three of them still out in the quadrants. One in each.'

Hart nodded and glanced at Cleatus. He looked as miserable as the rest of them. Hardly surprising, he thought. They were going up against professionals. Soldiers trained to assault installations like this.

A minute or so later the telephone on the wall shrilled. The section leader snatched it up and then slammed it down.

'South-west!'

'Let's go,' Hart said. That was good. It meant they were south of the runway. Could they be held there? Three or four minutes to get there. Find them. Engage. They don't know how many we are and they have already lost a few of theirs. They will break off and move round. We will be frigging about probing at each other for at least twenty minutes. 'Get word to Carson. He can go in fifteen minutes.'

At the security station the duty guard simply pointed to a nine-inch monochrome screen and traversed the camera to follow the movement. They watched them on the screen for a minute, five men moving slowly, well camouflaged, below the ridge line.

The section leader pointed to a map on the wall. It was rather like the map of the London underground, but overlaid on a geographical survey map. 'If they keep going they will pass this point. There is a tunnel ramp here.'

Ambush, Hart thought, the Rangers training flooding back. Ambush. Don't bugger about seeing them off to reassess. This was too good an opportunity to miss. Tactically sound.

The section leader led them up the ramp and they slithered out of the trap door into a depression. Hart pointed silently to the men, selecting eight of them and pointing along the depression. He and Cleatus would take the top end. He crawled forward and parted the tussock grass.

There below them and approaching from the right, the five Russians.

Along the line the others were moving up, slowly, silently on their stomachs, their weapons pushed forward ready to fight.

Come on, Hart thought. The first was past him. Then the middle two, the last approaching. He took up first pressure on the trigger, sighting on the farthest of the last pair and fired, the rounds ripping out into them. He swung back on to the other man as the others along his line opened up; three of the five falling hit, two going to ground, spinning in the air trying to return fire, screams and yells, but the fire poured into them and as the last rounds of the first heat of the engagement died away Hart heard the deafening crackling roar of the hypersonic.

'Do any of you speak English?' Hart called.

One of the men nodded.

'Tell them it's over. The aircraft is gone and won't be back. Okay? Won't be back. No more fighting today. If they want to go freely back to their pickup they must put down their guns. Okay?'

The man nodded and began to shout in Russian down the tussocky slope.

As the Tarbaby scorched off the runway and gathered height, buffeted and harried by the brisk first feelers of a full Arctic cyclone, Miller sat in the right-hand seat and Carson talked his way through the take-off.

20

Chekhov had asked them one by one by name to go through the wide double doors into his office and place their votes in the box. Even with the doors open for security a confidential secretary stood either side of the box.

Ustinoff was last and as he stood to walk through a member of the Head of Kremlin Security's staff put his head round the door from the main administration section.

'Excuse me, Mr President,' he said.

Chekhov looked up. 'President Sheridan?'

'No, President Chekhov, it's coming through from the communications centre . . . he says will you talk to Oslo?'

Chekhov looked quickly at Ustinoff as he walked past towards the ballot box.

'I am coming. Remain here, all of you,' he snapped. He was tired, his temper worn thin and along with it his habitual courtesy.

'This is Chekhov,' he said, dismissing the technicians with a wave of his hand.

'This is Richard Haidermann of Oslo,' the voice said.

'Mr Haidermann, how are you?'

'Good. You trying to start a war?'

'Don't be cryptic with me. What are you talking about?' Chekhov replied, rubbing his eyes with the back of one hand. The radio carrier wave hissed back at him before Haidermann replied.

'Your Northern Fleet carrier *Kirov*. She is heading towards Iceland with a small group. We believe she intends to deny the Icelandic government the use of one of their military areas and destroy facilities. An act of war. One the USA will not take lying down.'

Chekhov's thoughts raced ahead. Kraskin! You stupid, ambitious, bitter old man. You ordered the Northern Fleet into action against another state without consultation or permission. You thought you would succeed in destroying them and perhaps even me in the process.

'Haidermann . . . I know nothing of this. You have my word. If this is true she will turn back immediately,' he said.

'You didn't know?' Haidermann asked. 'If that is so then you have a problem there . . . however, I believe you. But if she doesn't turn back, or launches her aircraft, well, anything could happen. Things are very tense.'

'Do not do anything. I will fix it.' Chekhov straightened his back and glowered at the microphone. 'I have given you my word!' He threw down the handset. 'Quickly, get me Naval Command,' he barked to the communications officer.

Twelve minutes later, his face sagging in disbelief, he lowered himself into a chair to think. My God, this is how it happens. This is how wars start. I ordered the irrevocable codes system to be abandoned seven months ago for this very reason. There was no way he could order the *Kirov* to return.

He stood, walked quickly from the room and going straight to his office picked up the hot line.

At 120,000 feet over Greenland, Carson looked across at Miller.

'You okay with the basics?'

Miller nodded. 'Affirmative.'

'Okay. Lift that panel between your knees.' Miller lifted the Kevlar panel and the sides dropped away revealing the second control column.

'You have control.'

'I have control,' he repeated.

474

Sheridan excused himself and crossed to the Oval Office where an aide held the handset out to him.

'Good afternoon, Mikhail,' he began.

'Richard, my friend, we have a problem.'

Sheridan could tell by his tone that something was amiss. He nodded at the aide, who pushed the record button on the big tape-deck.

'What kind of problem?' he asked carefully.

'I have a man who has let his ambition cloud his judgement. He has given a G-RT-3 order, something I expressly forbade some months ago. You are familiar with this type of order? It is the same as your "No recall" of the 1960s.'

'Yes, I am familiar with it,' Sheridan answered quickly. 'What was the order, Mikhail, and to whom was it given?'

'A battle group of the Northern Fleet. The carrier *Kirov* and her escort are under way to Iceland, with orders to neutralize with aircraft and special forces an Icelandic government area. This is the base of the hypersonic . . . but not only that. The orders state by any and all means.'

'Can't you recall in any way?'

'No.'

'Oh my God . . .'

'Richard, you must believe me when I tell you I knew nothing of this madness.'

'Thank you for calling, Mikhail. I must obviously confer with my people.'

'Richard, I have a favour to ask, on behalf of the people of Iceland and the people of the Federation, who sorely regret this dreadful mistake.'

'I am listening,' Sheridan said.

'You have a naval ship near there. The *Bunker Hill*. Could she perhaps . . . she is the only vessel near enough to have any chance of intercepting the *Kirov*.'

'You are asking me to engage a Russian Navy battle

group with a single American ship?' Sheridan's mind reeled at the idea.

'Yes, my friend, I am. I need help. I would order my own aircraft to stop her, but I am told the weather won't permit that.'

'But one ship, Mikhail, she won't stand a chance against a group of . . . what? . . . four or five of yours. I will be asking the crew of that ship to lay down their lives.'

'All they need do is get the *Kirov*. Without her the group will break off and await orders, the G-RT-3 will become invalid at that time.'

'I have fighter bombers based in Iceland: they can . . .'

'A storm is building. Your Iceland-based fighters are no good. The same that will prevent my own air forces. But it means the *Kirov* will be unable to launch her planes. She will have to come right in with her group.'

'I will have to discuss it with my people.'

'Beware, Richard, others are not as honest as you and I. This will appear like the beginning of the end.'

'I hope not, Mikhail,' Sheridan answered, thinking, *it just might be.* 'I will call you back in a few minutes.'

Two minutes later the Secretary of State and the head of the Joint Chiefs of Staff joined President Sheridan from their respective meeting rooms on the first floor.

'With due respect, Mr President,' the head of the Joint Chiefs said, 'the order has gone out to *Bunker Hill*, but we don't know enough.'

'What are you saying?' Sheridan asked.

'Well, they have a man in a position to give that kind of order. What other orders has he given that haven't surfaced yet?'

'Are you suggesting . . . ?'

'Yes, Mr President, I am.'

Jesus Christ, this is unbelievable, Sheridan thought. He is right. Chekhov may have only part of the picture.

'What is your suggestion?' he asked.

'DEFCON 2, sir, with immediate effect.'

Sheridan looked at his Secretary of State who nodded quickly in agreement. An attack imminent. Full defensive footing.

'We go to DEFCON 2,' Sheridan said formally.

'Something else, sir,' the admiral added. Sheridan looked at him. 'A way out, maybe.'

'How?' the President asked quickly.

'I know the people on the *Bunker Hill*, sir. Good ship, good captain, good outfit, but they don't stand a dog's chance in a surface engagement with a whole group. This Oslo outfit. That hypersonic they have . . . will they help?'

USS Bunker Hill

The storm was now a vast swirling giant that had one foot still over the Jan Mayen Islands while the other reached out with hundred-mile-an-hour winds and seventy-foot breaking rollers for Iceland. The *Bunker Hill* ploughed as fast as she dared north-east, burying her sharp bows into the face of each wave before shaking clear the tons of water, her turbines screaming to place her in the path of her quarry. Outnumbered and outgunned for the coming fight, her captain sat in the battle chair on the bridge and wondered what he could do to get his missiles in through *Kirov*'s escort. A few years ago the inclement weather would have given cover but now, with marine electronics and see-all radar, even this monstrous bitch of a storm couldn't help.

'Commanders to the bridge,' he said to the officer at his side.

The old buildings alongside the runway cowered beneath the shrieking wind. No longer was it simply gusts pushing the old panels and rattling doors, now it was the full measure that lifted roofing sheets and turned debris into missiles. Above the huts on the ridge the grass was blown flat against the hard ground and the ventilator shaft grille that the CIA men had loosened flapped and bent against the last of the bolts securing it to the frame. Finally the wind with almost malevolent intent ripped it from the frame and carried it, spinning like a metre-square frisbee, the two hundred metres into the fenced area that secured the transmission towers and high aerials that were the basis of Omega's communications ability. The grille spun high over the fence and in the next three seconds it sliced through the two main wire stays supporting the transmission tower. The tower, its flimsy surface area already providing critical resistance to the wind speeds, was blown flat to the ground, pulling other gear down in its fall. Omega Base now had no capability to transmit their radio communications.

Kirov

'We are in range, captain, unless I am mistaken. How long till we can launch aircraft?' the admiral asked. Beneath his feet the leviathan moved on the waves, and from the windscreens on the bridge he watched the spume and salt whipped across the vast heaving flight-deck now cleared of all personnel.

'Maybe six hours, maybe more. It's difficult to say,' the captain replied.

'Then we push in closer,' the admiral said quickly.

'Admiral, I must protest. I need sea room for this ship. I refuse to risk her on a lee shore.'

'Don't disobey me. We have worked together too long. Move in closer. I want the cruisers in range as soon as possible. Maybe we can even land the Spetznatz under the cover of this.'

The admiral looked at the group operations officer. 'Signal the *Sophia*. Have her move back, and get the oiler the hell out of here. Tell them to drop back twenty miles. I don't want any collisions. Then get the two cruisers out front. I want an inverted arrowhead.'

The officer nodded and he and the *Kirov*'s captain watched the admiral walk away down the bridge, the captain with mounting concern.

'Sir?' the operations officer asked.

'What?'

'Sir, excuse me, sir, but I thought this was a limited strike against a base in Iceland. Three aircraft, possibly a Spetznatz unit.'

The captain looked at him. 'It is ... but do you really think it will remain so? Get the intelligence officer up here. I want to know the disposition of all warships within a thousand miles of us.'

'Captain ... what is going on ... really?'

'I don't know,' the captain answered honestly. 'I just don't know.'

USS Bunker Hill

Captain Hendricks was also on his bridge pacing the centre area like a caged tiger. Around him and making way as he passed were his senior officers, most looking occasionally out the bridge windows to the north expecting somehow through the huge seas and driving sleet and rain to see the Soviet battle group any second.

'So we know the *Kirov* has one of the new cruisers with her. We know that one of the new ships has the ECM gear they are trailing. What do we know about it?'

'Not much, skipper,' his EWO replied, 'but we believe they are pleased with a new type of passive sonar. It's like a sub's gear except they can mask their own engine and screw noise and listen in on others. Good range on it. It's designed for shitty weather like this. No visibility, no radio comms and they reckon they can identify another vessel under way. The last we heard was that they were having problems with it.'

'We have to assume it's working,' Hendricks said, turning to the engineering officer. 'Ed, can you shut down one side? Give us a single screw signature? A rough one?'

'Yes, sir. I can make us sound like a Yangtze River scow, but it won't do much for the gear,' he replied, thinking aloud.

'Gear we can replace. Do it and be ready to go in twenty minutes,' Hendricks said. 'Gentlemen, we are going to use the weather, slip in across their track and sow some acoustic mines. Then we creep away. Prepare an "in difficulties" signal we can let go when they get our radar trace, and when they get close enough . . .' he looked at his watch '. . . we have about half an hour to get those mines in the water. Let's move it.'

Within their silos sleek batteries of Harpoon anti-ship missiles were ready to track the Soviet group as soon as they were illuminated by radar, but for now the systems remained passive.

As she moved across the Russians' track she began to sow her mines. They were new, but reliant on very simple technology. A series of ten plastic-skinned mines were linked together with a cable. Any ship's bow hitting the cable that was suspended four feet below the surface would drag the mines alongside the hull. Spaced every sixty feet along the waterline the small but powerful charges would be activated by sensors and explode. One was enough to disable a small ship, but a warship caught in the middle of the line could detonate three or four mines along each side of her hull, in theory blowing that many holes in her side each about a square metre across.

The designers called the mine-line 'sequentially spaced ordnance', but the sailors just called it the 'linebacker'.

Dublin

'President Sheridan, I understand you want to talk to Angel Seven, but as I said we have lost a transmission tower. We are unable to contact them for the moment. We expect some positive news in the next few minutes,' Haidermann said. 'You have another two hours to agree our terms.'

'It's not your terms I want to discuss,' Sheridan replied. 'We have a problem and I think you can help.'

He explained as quickly and concisely as he could the G-RT-3 instruction to the *Kirov*.

'We knew she was heading that way. How do you interpret those orders?' Haidermann asked.

'"By any means"? Just that. Anyone gets in the way, they get neutralized. Chekhov also isn't really sure if they have an exact location . . .'

'They don't,' Haidermann answered. 'We know that.'

'. . . which means they could just attack Husavik. So the *Bunker Hill* is going to try and stop them, but in reality they stand little chance. I am risking a ship with several hundred men on board. I want you to ask Angel Seven to assist. Save some lives, and save this thing blowing out of proportion. For your information the *Kirov*'s escort carries cruise missiles.'

'We will try and contact Angel Seven now. But with the problem we have we may well be too late,' Haidermann said.

'Where is she now?' Sheridan asked.

He felt Haidermann's reluctance to answer before it became a measurable pause.

'Oh for Christ sakes! I can have my people tell me in a couple of minutes!'

'She will be over Canada somewhere . . . hold on, I'll find out.' He was back a minute later, his direct line to Omega Base open and operating. 'Over Hudson Bay.'

'Thank you. I will try and contact him direct.'

Four minutes later Sheridan was in the basement comms room with Kramer and two specialist technicians.

'How do I contact an aircraft?' The President asked.

'Easy, sir. Give me his frequency and we can call him up,' one of the men replied.

481

'I don't know his frequency, but he is over Hudson Bay in Canada.'

The technician looked at him for a second before saying, 'Ah.'

'Well?'

'Mr President, that will need a frequency scan by someone very close, and permission from the Canadians, of course.'

'Can you do it from here?'

'Try, sir, but . . .'

'Just do it! Call sign Angel Seven,' Sheridan snapped.

'This may take some time, sir. There are dozens of frequencies he could be on.'

'Can't you do all at once?' Kramer asked

'If we boost our signal, yes, but we will need to clear all the aviation channels and go right over the top. A multifrequency broadcast will also be listened into by every guy with a radio in America.'

'Do it!'

A minute later, patched through the CIA high power transmitters at Langley, the technician began, his call crossing every band frequency and wavelength used by aviators and heard by people from the Gulf of Mexico to Fairbanks in Alaska.

'Angel Seven this is Eagle . . . Angel Seven this is Eagle . . .'

For the next four minutes aircraft were held in patterns all over the country, while pilots held headphones away from their ears as the call boomed out over the airwaves. Finally through a mishmash of angry replies and abuse a familiar call reached the White House.

'Eagle, this is Angel, go . . .'

The technician grinned broadly and held up a thumb.

'Angel, cross to one one five decimal one for Eagle.'

Carson leaned forward in the seat rubbing the sleep from his grainy eyes and switched frequencies on the radio.

482

Miller had been flying while he was asleep and when the message came through on their frequency he had woken Carson.

'Who's Eagle?' Miller asked.

'The American President,' Carson replied groggily.

'Something's up.'

'Yeah. Let's see what. Half of the world will be listening to this. Eagle, this is Angel.'

'Angel, this is Eagle. Please listen carefully. My name is Kramer. I am Omega down here in the eyrie. When you left home tonight you left behind from Russia with love, do you copy?'

'Roger, Eagle,' Carson replied, his face intent.

'Things are about to get very nasty. Bravo Hotel is going to try to stop them because they won't go home, even after their dad called. Mommy wants you to stop the kids fighting. Do you understand this, Angel?'

'Roger, Eagle, but mommy can call me anytime she needs me. Nice try anyway.'

'Negative, Angel, mommy's phone is out of order. The storm has knocked the lines down. She has been trying to get you, I repeat she has been trying to raise you.'

'Eagle . . . get stuffed. One hour fifty.'

Then Kramer had an idea. 'Angel, stand by please.'

He turned to the telephone and lifting the receiver spoke quickly.

'Operator get me this number in Iceland, please.' A few seconds later and he was talking to Sagan and in under a minute Gail Samuels, feeling a little foolish, told him what he wanted to know.

'Angel seven, I have a message from mommy.'

'Go, Eagle, it better be genuine,' Carson said sceptically.

'Angel, mommy says . . . Badger wants you back at Toad Hall.'

'Eagle, Angel Seven. I'm on my way.' He managed to brush away the exhaustion and chemical withdrawal for a few seconds and 110,000 feet over Canada he pulled the

483

Tarbaby into a gut-wrenching nine G turn. As they pulled out straight and level he lit up the scram jets.

USS Bunker Hill

The ship was barely under way, her starboard turbine and screw at full stop and an ingenious jury-rigged noisemaker fixed to the port hull below the waterline. The engineering team had manhandled one of the two huge tumble dryers out of the ship's laundry and, loaded with oil and a padded weight and turning at its slowest setting, it sounded comfortingly like an old-style diesel thumping away. Amplified through the mess room's big stereo speakers against the hull it would do the trick. On the bridge Hendricks stood beside the watch keeper as he studied the radar's normally sharp images turned ghostly by the storm. All her space age electronics were useless while an ECM vessel was nearby, because even with her reduced stealth radar profile, as soon as she powered up her active systems she would be identified as a warship in seconds.

Right now her only operating systems were her standard radar that any vessel might have. Even the sneak scanners that supplied battle data to the Harpoons were shut down. They could be turned on and active inside five seconds, but even so he felt vulnerable.

This is it, he thought. The ship had a feel about her tonight. Her crew were eager for the fight.

'Where away?' Hendricks asked.

'Six miles, skipper, hard off the port quarter.'

'Disposition?'

'Unaltered, sir. The cruisers out front, the *Kirov* behind in the middle, with smaller contacts astern of her.'

Any minute now, he thought, any minute now they will be in the middle of my linebackers. Staggered as they were the four linebackers had a 2,000-yard defensive footprint. Down in ops the acoustic men had removed their headphones. When the mines went off the VU meters would peak so they didn't need them. They were also monitoring tiny transmitters, one on each mine. The transmitters worked on the same frequency as those tagged on wild animals and only had a range of ten miles. They would know when their minefield had worked. Come and get it, you big bitch.

'Send that "in danger" signal, let's suck one of the escorts a bit nearer,' Hendricks said to his executive officer.

My God, he thought, this is going to be our first true surface ship naval engagement since the Battle of the Coral Sea.

Kirov

'Captain, signal from the *Bolshoi*. She has a radar contact. Small. Fishing boat maybe. Noise emissions indicate a small merchant, but they are not sure.'

The captain turned to the speaker, his jowly cheeks pink in the soft night lighting. 'Of what? Be precise.'

'Electronic emissions, captain. They have some conflicting data coming in. Usual noise for a merchant, but some other signals they can't identify. They want to break formation and investigate.'

The admiral broke in. '*Nyet*,' he replied. 'That equipment is still under trial. I'm not risking my group on some wild-goose chase. Reply *nyet*. Remain in position.'

Suddenly the captain felt a tingle up his spine and the hair on his neck rose. He was not a superstitious man, but he felt a sense of foreboding.

'Admiral, please indulge me?' he said.

'Oh, all right. Wait . . . Signal *Vostok*. Investigate. Ask the *Volga* to join her.'

Thirty seconds later the rocket cruiser *Vostok* edged up her power and peeled away from her course, her systems sweeping the dark stormy seas ahead as the destroyer *Volga*, every wave breaking over her bows, raced to catch up.

'A "need assistance" signal, sir.'

The captain knew who it would be from, but wondered why he wasn't feeling any easier.

USS Bunker Hill

Hendricks watched two technicians as they stood to their posts in the ops room. Not even the flash hoods and helmets could make either of them look over nineteen years of age, and beneath the surface nerves and fear their excitement was obvious. Nothing changes, he thought. These kids are from the same blood as the men who fought the Armada, at the Chesapeake and Jutland. Navy men. But this was an old kind of action in a new age. Not the missiles fired over sixty miles of sea, supersonic fighter cover and chaff canisters. This was getting so close you could see them and smell the action. Point-blank range with Harpoons and then close enough to see 'em.

'Three miles, captain, one cruiser and a destroyer by her indicators.'

'Which cruiser?'

'Sounds like the *Vostok*, sir, Northern Fleet rocket cruiser, gear includes . . .'

'Status?' he interrupted.

'We have target integrity, sir, both ships.'

'She won't be visible in this till she is right on top of us. I want to hit her as soon as she is in sight, but before she gets a chance to recognize us.' Around him stood his officers awaiting final instructions. 'We ready for full ahead both?'

'Yes, sir.'

'Right, prepare to simultaneously select both targets. Salvo fire. Four Harpoons each. Then full ahead both, and max comms jamming. Then I want to be through the screen and ready to engage the *Kirov* before she knows what is happening. I want the forward missile battery locked on carrier as soon as we can uncover systems radar.'

Around him the men nodded.

Two minutes and fifty seconds later in a night frighteningly dark the *Vostok*'s riding and navigation lights appeared through the spume and surf atop a gigantic swell, falling into the trough almost as the lookout sighted her.

Hendricks waited the terrible seconds before the intelligence section confirmed her identity, his own ship in darkness without riding lights for concealment, his heart saddened at the thought of firing on a ship that was answering a call for assistance, but knowing it had to be done. Outnumbered as they were, only guile would ever allow him to halt the Russians and get his people safely home.

'She's in the minefield.'

It was fifteen seconds later that the *Vostok*'s sharp stern picked up the plastic-coated wire rope and as she fell down the side of a wave the mines were pulled alongside, three breaking the surface and the tension caught on the line.

On *Bunker Hill* the two acoustic men watched as the VU meters swung over and hit the needles.

'Linebacker strike!' he called. 'Confirm linebacker strike. I have five lights out.'

Five lights out! Yes! Hendricks felt the tension run out of him. They had her. Five mines. One cruiser out of action.

'Linebacker strike. Confirm another strike. Far end of the array! Five again, no four lights out!'

That's the destroyer. Fight-float-move. Every warship captain's command priorities. No fight in these two. Their command priorities were now just to stay afloat.

'Illuminate *Kirov* with weapons radar and fire the moment you have target integrity. Full ahead both,' he barked.

'We have radar lock on the carrier!'

'ENGAGE!'

Behind him at the after battery four of the long Harpoon anti-ship missiles launched into the night with a flashing roar of white exhaust smoke and the sea churned under her counter as the ship lurched forward, the twin General Electric turbines driving her forward into the waves and the battle.

'We have four outbound! Systems are active and we have radar lock on the carrier.'

This was the critical time. Harpoon was fire and forget, but if the remainder of the escort was awake then they would intercept with defensive anti-missile missiles and the carrier would have her own defence systems.

'Second salvo! ENGAGE!'

They had eight missiles running, but the *Kirov* was big, very big. If all eight hit she would be crippled, but any fewer than five strikes and she might be able to get aircraft away.

Kirov

'Captain,' the communications watch officer's voice crashed through the intercom. '*Vostok* has mines. She is holed and taking water. Bulkheads are holding at present. She advises the *Volga* is burning a mile off her beam, unable to raise her.'

'Sound action stations! Have the *Bolshoi* move to our port side.'

Shit, the bastards! The bloody bastard *Bunker Hill*! 'Come round to the west.'

'Wait!' The admiral moved forward from the plotting table. 'We have our orders!'

'Bugger the orders, Nicolai. That's the *Bunker Hill* out there! A brand new Aegis class guided missile cruiser! Half my escort is on fire or sinking. I will not risk the *Kirov* on whatever half-baked scheme this is!'

'You will, or I shall relieve you of your command and place you in irons! You will be tried for disobeying an order in time of battle!'

'I want my protest logged.'

'We are at war! I have waited years for this moment! Now at last . . .'

The captain looked closely, horrified at what he was hearing, and saw the fervour in the admiral's eyes.

'My God! You are insane!' he shouted.

'You are relieved. You do not deserve a ship like this. You are confined to your cabin. I am assuming command!'

The captain walked stiffly from his bridge, his anger boiling in his heart and real fear in his guts. Fear of a madman with an aircraft carrier, and the US Navy's newest battle cruiser out to stop her. Thirty seconds later the communications officer stood beside the admiral, whose brain was churning with thoughts of war and first strike advantage. Less than a minute later he had opened the safe and referred to the latest tactical cruise missile target codes book for the North Atlantic area.

'Signal *Bolshoi* this.' He handed the officer a sheet of the watch pad. The officer read the words:

OCTOBER   OCTOBER-FLEETOPS   MURMANSK-G65-TYOPNBZ-33-GORKY 651.

He looked up, his face a mask of shock.

'With respect, admiral. We haven't heard anything other than "abort mission, abort mission" from Murmansk for some hours now . . .' The communications officer had a good idea what the message said.

'Send it!' the admiral snapped back. Suddenly at his side a rating from the communications room appeared. 'You have a message coming in, admiral. Open channels.'

'I am busy,' he snapped.

'Missiles inbound! Missiles inbound!'

The captain was running for the control room.

'Admiral, excuse me, sir, but he says "talk or die",' the rating stammered uncomfortably. He had taken the signal from the burning *Vostok*. Somewhere out there in the storm was something that meant them no good and now there were missiles reported inbound. He wanted to run. To hide.

'WHAT? Give me that,' he snatched the headset from

489

the man and pulling his cap clear tugged the apparatus on to his head.

'*Da.*'

'Listen carefully. This is Angel Seven. You will turn your group ninety degrees to the west and stop engines to receive instructions from your navy. Do you copy, *Kirov*?'

'Who are you?' the admiral blustered.

'Never mind. Just do it, or I'll do it for you.' The voice sounded tired, the words slurred.

'*Nyet.*'

'Man your boats, pal,' and the transmission ceased.

While the admiral ranted insanely into the mike the communications officer quietly scooped up the codes book and looked up GORKY 651. It was an instruction to hit the American Air Force base outside Reykjavik with one of the three tactical nuclear cruise missiles that *Bolshoi* carried below her afterdeck helicopter pad. Oh my God, he thought. This is it. He had a wife and three small boys living in Kiev and he wondered if he would ever see them again.

'*Missiles inbound. Brace! brace! brace!*'

Below her flight deck her defensive anti-missile missiles seared out into the dark and across half a mile of water, while the *Bolshoi* raced round to get herself into a position where she could activate her defence systems, the *Kirov*'s vast bulk screening her target illumination radars completely.

'Captain Hendricks, signal, sir, CINCFLEET.' Hendricks looked across the red gloom of the control room where the technicians plotted the courses and dispositions of the Russian group as the cruiser ploughed her way nearer by the second.

'Read it, son,' he snapped from his position at the battle overlay table.

'Cease engagement repeat cease engagement and clear

area with all speed. Stand by to offer assistance to survivors.'

'What the hell goes on here?' he snarled, reaching for the message hard copy in the sailor's hand.

Carson pressed his mike off, edging the hypersonic ever slower and lower into the storm.

'Do we have to go this low?' Miller asked. This storm was powerful enough to rip the wings off a jumbo jet and he knew it.

'Laser is dissipated by atmosphere. We want to get real low for this one. We also want to confirm our target. The bloody *Bunker Hill* is still down there somewhere, if she's still afloat, that is.'

He eased back the throttles until the Tarbaby was dawdling on seven hundred knots, and there on the radar screen he saw a group of solid images through the noise and clutter of the storm. He flicked on the head-up display, and watched the radar image transposed over his gunsights. The chemical wind-down was all his system could cope with and the waves of fatigue washed over him, clouding his senses, his thinking process an opaque milky blur. He could not line up the target.

'Christ, I'm ... so ... tired. Can't think,' he slurred. 'Take ... control. We are going ... in slow, they won't ... be throwing anything at us on the way out ... but we will ... get out quick anyway. Take control.'

One of the solid contacts, larger than most of the others, suddenly changed direction. 'That will be ... *Bunker* breaking off. That ... means ... the real big ... sucker is ours.'

He tried again to lock his systems on the target, but with his co-ordination gone it was impossible. He waited for the aircraft to settle after a particularly turbulent few seconds and tried again only to fail.

'You ... do ... it,' he mumbled, fighting the waves. 'Line up the red prism ... on the green target and finish it.'

'Christ, Peter, I can't. There must be a thousand men on that ship!' Miller protested

'YOU . . . HAVE . . . TO! . . . Starting . . . a war . . . down there.'

'I don't. I said I'll fly. Not sink a ship, for fuck sakes.'

'Jesus, spare me . . . this shit. Line . . . her up. HURRY!' he rubbed a hand over his eyes, the aircraft bucking beneath them in the storm turbulence. 'I'll . . . do . . . it.' His hand reached unsteadily for the control column and the red trigger as Miller nodded at the compromise, and working the laser guidance control like the joystick of a child's video game he overlaid the laser prism on the green contact, now strong at only three miles' range.

Carson pressed the triggers for a full two-second burst and as the prism flashed his success back at him his head dropped forward on to his chest. The flash lit the sky blue-white like a bolt of lightning and the laser hit the *Kirov*, slicing into her, the entire rear sixty feet of the aircraft carrier shearing away as if someone had run a cheese wire through a jelly. Already wounded with three Harpoon strikes, this blow was final. The superheated steel boiling the sea on contact, the steam whipped away by the wind, the freezing greeny black sea thundering into her aft spaces. She was now a barely floating hulk, smoke rising from the two remaining fires that raged in the spaces where the missiles had hit.

Above the stricken ship Miller hit the throttles and pulled the nose up to clear the storm as fast as possible. The *Bolshoi*'s captain, as unhappy as the *Kirov*'s had been about the whole situation, contacted Northern Fleet Headquarters for instructions.

On board the *Bunker Hill* Hendricks gave an order. 'Stand by to pick up survivors,' he said.

Chekhov re-entered the council meeting, his face a mask of stone betraying nothing of the four and a half hours he had been out. We came so close, he thought, so close to war. If it had not been for Sheridan and the pacifists. All those dead men. On their souls I make my choice, and on their souls I must live with it. He walked straight through to his office, picked up the ballot box and carried it back through to the big old table around which everyone sat, tired and dishevelled.

He opened the lid, breaking the seal, and lifted out the small pile of folded slips, looked at the first, put it to one side, then at the second, putting it down on the other.

Oh boy! Ustinoff thought, sitting up, something's on here. The last time I saw the old man like this was over the Chechens.

'Kraskin,' Chekhov began conversationally, lifting another slip, 'you look a little worried. Something you forgot to tell me, perhaps?'

Kraskin said nothing but watched the pile of slips growing either side of the box and moved uncomfortably in his seat.

'Well, well, you were quite the gifted orator a few hours ago. Nothing you want to add? No?'

Chekhov looked down at the next slip and added it to a pile.

'Come, come, surely you want to tell the Council of Ministers about the changes in the command structure. How you no longer believe you have to report to me . . . or this group.' Chekhov's voice had slowed to a rasping whisper edged with ice.

Kraskin sat up in his chair. 'I am the Minister of Defence and I . . .'

'YOU WHAT?' Chekhov's voice lashed across the table like a whip.

'I felt honour bound to . . .'

'. . . put us at risk of war with another country without my direct order! Who the hell do you think you are? Speak!'

Kraskin stood up and came to attention. 'In the interests of the safety of the Rordina . . .'

'Don't bullshit me, Kraskin,' Chekhov snarled. 'I was dealing with that while you were still playing soldiers as a sweaty little two-pip section commander. You have allowed your ambitions to endanger everything we have worked for.'

He looked down at another slip and added it to the larger pile on his right.

'You saw fit to deploy military forces and issued orders to engage without authority.'

'There's more, Mikhail,' Ustinoff said. 'More you don't yet know. We believe and we can now provide proof that Defence Minister Kraskin was involved in the theft of two nuclear warheads and their subsequent sale to Iran. The same two warheads that started this whole crisis. His clan, his military and defence clan are cashing in.'

There were one or two gasps around the table. This was some claim and if true then not only Kraskin but his entire clan were truly finished.

'You have proof?' Chekhov asked.

'We do.'

Chekhov looked down again and added the last slip to the pile on his right.

'You are everything most people fear in a position of power and that cannot be . . . you have cost us much.' It was a whisper again. He looked down.

'Seven yes, four no. It is carried. We offer nuclear disarmament.'

Ustinoff jumped to his feet with a triumphant shout. Even Smetlov smiled.

'NO,' Kraskin shouted. 'THAT CAN'T BE!'

'You are relieved of your portfolio and will remain under

arrest in the Lubyanka until I decide what is to be done with you.'

'But what about the Zone?' Kraskin argued.

'Let them make boots!' Chekhov retorted. 'Now get out of my sight.' Kraskin, ashen-faced and stunned, turned to see the guard waiting for him at the door.

As the other members of the council filed from the room Ustinoff went to Mikhail Chekhov, watching the older man as an aide took the ballot box. As he reached for the fistful of slips Chekhov held up his hand.

'Leave those,' he said, and he gathered them up himself and took them to the shredding machine in the corner. Ustinoff watched him shred the slips on by one, an odd half-smile on his lips, and suddenly it dawned on him, and he threw back his head and began to laugh.